bruiser

bruiser

Ian Chorão

ATRIA BOOKS

New York   London   Toronto   Sydney   Singapore

ATRIA BOOKS

1230 Avenue of the Americas
New York, NY 10020

ISBN: 0-7434-3775-6

First Atria Books hardcover printing March 2003

10 9 8 7 6 5 4 3 2 1

ATRIA BOOKS is a trademark of Simon & Schuster, Inc.

For information regarding special discounts for bulk purchases,
please contact Simon & Schuster Special Sales at 1-800-456-6798
or business@simonandschuster.com

Printed in the U.S.A.

for Sylvia, of course

acknowledgments

To Sylvia Sichel, who has sustained and influenced me and my writing to such ludicrous proportions that putting it in these few words is as hopeless as fitting the ocean into a teacup;

To Kim Meisner, my editor, who pounced upon this book with an affection and intelligence that allowed it to fully emerge;

To Mitchell Waters, my agent, whose thoughts on, and confidence in, my work I could not do without;

To the following readers and problem-solvers, to whose help on this book I am particularly indebted: my parents, siblings, and uncles; the Sichel family; Brett Berk; Colin Dickerman; Marie Edesess; Jeremy Engle; Susan Kaufman; Marie McNicholas; Tal McThenia; Annie Piper; Emily Stone; Stefan Zicht;

To all you others, too numerous to list individually, who've offered me your generous insights, support and friendship:

Thank you.

Every blade of grass has its angel that bends over it and whispers, "Grow, grow."
　　　　　　　　　　　—The Talmud

home

Max is running toward us, across the overgrown grass, swinging a long rope round over his head. On the end is a black cat tied at the neck.

"Hee-haw!"

Behind, the line of buildings where we live face us sitting in the park. On the roof of one, a Big Kid leans out. With spray paint he finishes writing on the building's side: WEED ➔ NATURES WAY OF SAYING HIGH.

Max releases the rope. It goes through the air. The black cat's flopping legs rise up as it falls down toward the grass.

"Damn, Max!" Reid says. "That's nasty!"

"Yeah, Max: nasty!" Jimmy says.

Max's eyes are wild. "I told you I found a dead cat," he says. "Some voodoo shit, I guess."

Sometimes we find dead animals around Riverside Park. Regular dead kind: run-over pigeons, drowned bloated rats, and the voodoo kind: headless chickens, once a goat head.

We stand in a circle around the cat. I crouch for a closer look. Its mouth is open and a rough pink tongue sticks out. Its eyes are dry and sunken. I touch its stomach. They look away, tell me to stop.

"But, it's dead," I say.

"You're a diseased mother, now."

"I'm not."

"Ew, get away from him."

"That shit's bad luck," they say, which is true.

I pick up the rope and walk, the cat drags like a doll.

I swing the cat in a circle. The park blurs. I look into the cat's eyes. Everyone knows that black cats have powers, so I ask it telepathically to tell me what it knows. Where is its ghost? Where are its special powers? I spin too fast and my feet tangle. I tumble hard. On the ground I feel like I still spin. I dig my fingers into the earth to make it stop. Reid and Jimmy kneel on either side of me, take my arms, pin me down. Max dangles the dead cat overhead, right close to my face. Its tail brushes my cheek.

"Stop!"

Max lowers it more, dragging it over my face. Its claws scrape across my nose, my mouth, its head bouncing on a broken neck.

"Le'me go, le'me go, le'me go!"

Behind clouds curl like wings. Then I know: the cat made me fall.

I wrestle free, swinging my arms, stumbling up then back over on the slope. They laugh.

Max flings the dead cat over his shoulder into a bush. I sit with my back to them, plucking blades of grass. I stare into the sky.

This morning I overheard Mom talking to Dad. They talked in the hallway outside of the bathroom, standing next to the big clothes hamper, which I was lying inside of, before they came. Dad built it out of wood. It's good. Three feet high, longer than me, and just a bit wider than me. They talked about Granpa who's been sick forever with the cancer. Mom was in the bathroom all morning, and had just come out. Mom's been doing that a lot recently. I'll walk around, looking for her because I want waffles or grilled cheese, or to play Ouija, and I can't find her, and then I'll stand in front of the bathroom or her bedroom, and I'll hear her inside, making soft sounds. And I'll lie on my belly and watch the shadows she makes, and sometimes I'll see her feet, crouching in front of the toilet, and then violent splashing sounds, or feet across the floor into bed. Later when she's left, I'll lie in the bed and feel a wet spot on the pillow.

Mom said, *He seems quite bad.* And Dad said, *Yes.* Then Mom made bird sounds.

I had been lying in the clothes hamper for a long time and my legs had fallen asleep.

So you'll go down then? Dad asked. But Mom stayed quiet.

And my arms were also asleep, and my middle and my head were asleep, so when they came, my body had vanished, and deep below the clothes it was dark and the sounds soft. I stayed very still, knowing that the moment I moved I'd feel myself again.

I'm sorry, Dad said. *Yes,* Mom said.

Mom goes to Florida a lot. Until three years ago, when I turned six and started elementary school, I would go too. Now Mom leaves me alone with Dad and the brothers, Jordan and Daniel. I know I shouldn't, but sometimes I wish Granpa would die.

Then Mom said, *Can't you . . . hold—?* I heard the floor whine, Dad stepping forward. I heard clothes shuffle, two quick pats, then Dad's heavy footsteps walking away. Mom breathed a lot, then sat on top of the hamper.

That made me jerk and I felt my body again, the heavy smelly clothing on top of me warm from my breath. And suddenly I felt trapped, buried alive. I wanted to jump, to escape. I wanted to smell fresh air. I wanted to make a racket, to run.

But, I stayed very, very still.

Mom laughed. A tiny, funny laugh like she was laughing underwater.

⁓

"Ahh, yes," Jordan says. He lays his disco pants out on his bed below a polyester shirt with a photo print of a surfer. It's Saturday night and he's going to a party. I sit on the floor of the brothers' room and watch them.

"What's your curfew?" I ask.

"Scrub, I'm in the ninth grade. I'm not some little pea-head like you: what are you? in nursery school?"

"I'm not!"

"A-ha ha ha!"

Jordan, bored of me, turns away. Daniel hasn't looked over even once. Jordan runs his hands over the legs of the pants, smoothing them out. Daniel sits at his desk drawing. Music plays. Jordan, a towel around his waist from a shower, does a dance, pointing at his reflection, singing along.

"Shining Star for you to see, what your life can truly be."

I sing too.

"Shut up."

"What?"

"You wanna stay in here?"

I'm quiet. I walk to Daniel's desk. Dad gives Daniel drawing lessons. Dad has given him a little wooden man to practice with. His parts are different shapes: egg shape for the head, cylinders for the legs and arms, all flat and smooth, no eyes, no fingers. The man can be moved into different poses. Daniel has it running. I watch how he squints, looking from the man to his paper, quickly and lightly making the lines. I watch Daniel to see what it is that happens in the space between the little man and Daniel's eyes, that then runs down his arm to his hand that makes him draw so good. I get closer.

Daniel pushes at my face, but I don't move.

That is talent. Mom and Dad say so: *Daniel has a natural talent for drawing.* They say, Jordan has a talent for work, like how well he does in school.

Daniel pushes my face harder, mumbles, "Get away."

Then I feel Jordan from behind. He grabs my hair and drags me cross the room. He pushes me into the hallway, closes the door.

I go to my room. My window faces the courtyard. The left side is open air, far down the roofs of brownstones covered with white plastic chairs, trash: bottles, cigarette butts, pizza boxes. To the right are the windows into our dining room and kitchen. Mom and Dad are doing the dinner dishes. Dad washes and Mom dries and puts them away. I open the window. And right across the way are the apartments on the other side of the building. The one directly across is dark and has been empty for months. There are dried toilet paper bombs on the windows. I threw them. I was grounded because Dad caught me stealing two dollars from Mom's purse, because they were showing *Tommy* at the Thalia, and everyone but me saw it, and they were always singing, *"Tommy, oo-oo-oo, Tommy can you hear me?"* And Dad got extra mad when I told him why I stole the money because Dad had already told me that I couldn't see that sort of movie, that I was too young, and he didn't want to have to be coming into my bedroom at all hours of the night because of bad dreams. So he grounded me in my room for the day. No TV, no coming out except for meals, no dessert. He told me that I had to learn to make fun up for myself. So, I did. I used a whole roll, making the wads heavy with water.

two

suddenly a thousand butterflies a cloud of woolly wings rise up around me making soft sound woopa woopa i laugh and spin the blue sky and orangegold sun flicker between the gentle wings then their wings beat hard and scared wurpa wurpa and suddenly they are gone but there is still sound rrrr rrrr a pack of wild wolfdogs running toward me fighting and snarling and ripping at one another's coats around me now rrrrrrrr rrrrrrrr they scratch the ground they bare their fangs they growl very low then louder hundreds of horrible wolfdogs i lay down and close my eyes i wait to be torn to bits i listen to the roar so loud that it makes my body feel light like a leaf in the wind

rrrrrrrrrrrrrrrrrrrrrrrrrrrrrrrrrrrrrrrrrrrrrrrrrrrrrrrrrrrrrrrrrrrrr

I wake, sitting up quickly. The morning sun across my floor. The vacuum cleaner revs somewhere down the apartment. *Rrrr, rrrr.* I frown and look around. Light, window, bed, hand, messy floor, clock: after nine . . .

Sunday, cleaning day. Sundays, Dad moves from room to room cleaning each floor, stopping only to move something aside. Sundays, Mom's in the bathroom on her knees scrubbing the tub and toilet with Ajax.

The vacuum dies. I freeze. Dad's talking. Now he's yelling. He's saying, *Who's been messing around in my*— No one answers.

Boys, just stay out of his way, I hear Mom say, soft. She is outside my room talking to the brothers.

I listen as they walk away. I hear the squeaking wheels of the vacuum cleaner rolling down the wooden hallway floor. I quickly turn over, pretend I am asleep. I hear the vacuum again, loud, across the hall in the brothers' room.

I get out of bed and sit by my window on the radiator that's covered with a boxy metal chest, rows of holes across its front, coated in so many layers of paint that it's good and thick, which I've dug at with a knife, down to the black metal below. Mom's in the kitchen pouring the thick mix into the waffle iron. In the dining room the brothers eat waffles. The TV's on. They stare at it, cutting waffle bites without looking down. There are moving men in the empty apartment across the way. They carry in boxes. I pull on my jeans, put on one of my Pro Keds, hunt through the floor clutter for the second. I find a tube of glue.

I stop. I remember. I've forgotten all about it: my assignment due tomorrow. *My Family's Religion.* I got everything for it, then I forgot all about doing it.

I got the shoe box for the diorama, and paper and scissors, and I stole glue off Dad's desk, but I forgot to ask Mom and Dad what religion they've got, because when I stole the glue I opened it up and it made me dizzy like after I spin and spin, and I started gluing things, the pages of my math book, a Hot Wheels car to my bed, and I forgot all about the religion.

And tomorrow I won't have anything, unless I do it today.

Mrs. Lumis will have us line our dioramas up in the back of class, then over the next couple of weeks she'll choose us to go up front and talk about it. I'll just look forward, but not too forward, and maybe then she won't call on me. But, what if she does? I'm already doing bad in school. Last reading test I got a 3.5, which is below grade level, since I should've gotten a 4, and worse than that, Jordan and Daniel were getting 6s by the time they were in my grade. And Mom and Dad always look at me kind of sad, kind of angry whenever I bring report cards home. And they ask, *Why can't you do better?* They save all of our report cards, and sometimes I take them all out and line them up. Every time I hope they'll look different than I remembered them looking like. But they always look the same.

The vacuum cleaner goes dead. I run back to bed and pull the covers over my head.

The door swings open, bounces off the wall. I can smell the lint and burnt electric smell of the vacuum. I lie very still under the sheets. I close my eyes. I know just how they look. Dad's standing behind the vacuum, looking at my room. And I hate how *it* looks, mean and rounded like a single frowning brow, and the hot orange light in front that glows when Dad makes it come alive.

I hear Dad clear his throat, annoyed. I hear Dad plug it in. Then silence. I imagine his face, a little red. The clicking sound of the lever that releases the vacuum cleaner's arm, and at once, it roars.

I wait, counting how long it should take for the sound to wake me up. If I wait too long, Dad might fly into a rage. I turn over, I act groggy. I look at him. He turns the vacuum off.

"So, we've decided to finally get up?" he asks.

I look at him. I rub my eyes.

"This room's a disaster," he says. "I want it straightened

up before breakfast, and certainly before you go out to play."

I look at him.

"Do you hear me?"

I nod. I look at his head. Now is not a good time to bother him with questions about what religion he's got. His lips pull back and the ends twitch, and the angry vein that creeps along his temple rises. Today he is in a very foul mood, I can tell. He is in a foul mood every Sunday. He clicks the vacuum on. He pushes it in jerks, the vacuum's head knocks my things around. Something gets caught. It makes a loud clanging noise. He turns the vacuum off, crouches down, pulls an Evel Knievel doll out. He stands back up. He tells me that he spends his time picking up after me, and do I think he doesn't have things he'd rather be doing? I just take. Take, take, take. He tells me to look around the room. He asks me why he should spend his time picking up after me?

His angry vein starts to pulse like liquid through a hose. I wonder if that's how it works like gas into a car: pumping foul mood into his head. Sometimes I pretend his face is huge. The nose, lips: tall as trees. I run across it, away from the scary parts: the vein, the lips, the eyes dark and squinting like deep lakes of boiling tar. I run to the good parts. The funny square of white hair on his black mustache, and I lie beneath the hairs like overgrown willow. The puffy bags under his eyes, giant fleshy mounds, that make me tired when I lean against them, watching the mouth moving, blowing out wind across the field of his face.

Yelling now. I wish he would just go away. I imagine it: *Poof,* a cloud of smoke. I don't hear him because I have my jeans and one sneaker on, and I'm trying to slip them off under the covers as he yells because if he sees them he'll know I was up, and that instead of cleaning, I was just lollygagging because I am lazy and I'd rather live in a pigsty because it's no skin off my nose because Mom spoils me and Dad picks up after me, and he has a lot of work to do.

Dad's done yelling and he's vacuuming again. I watch him. Wishing never works. I'm always wishing. For money, for school to end, for a drum kit, for the brothers to go to hell, for Mom to stop going into rooms for hours, for Granpa to stop being sick, for Dad to go away. Then I remember about the dead black cat. I think about it. It's true: everyone knows about black cats. They've got special powers. Maybe I could do something with that. I think, I could probably do something with it. I'm suddenly afraid, because I think, what if it is gone? I think, I have to get downstairs.

Quick.

Dad yanks the cord from the wall. It whips backward. He rolls the vacuum cleaner away.

Mom walks in. She pushes my hair aside. I look at her.

"Honey," she says, "your father is in a foul mood." She smiles and looks around the room. "Couldn't you straighten up a little? That's all he wants."

I nod.

Mom looks at me like she's watching out a window. "Are you hungry?" she asks.

"Yes."

"Clean your room and I'll have some nice waffles for you."

I start cleaning. It's all in tangles. I pull out socks and underpants, and put them aside. Toy cars; dolls: G.I. Joe, Big Jim, Raggedy Andy, Evel Knievel; crayons; Lincoln Logs; books; colored paper; sea glass; loose sneaker laces tied into nooses; sneakers; shirts; pants; candles; clay; a fork; half an apple; balls; cards; 45s; books; pens; pencils; pins; notebooks; magazines: *Dynamite*, *The Spicy Meatball*, *Ranger Rick*, *E Z Reader*, *Spiderman*. I make piles. Now what? I open my toy chest. It's already full with dirty clothes. I shove some piles onto a shelf. They fall. I grit my teeth. I curse. I kick everything. There's too much. I pick things up and throw them. Everything is in tangles again. I push everything under my bed. Dad will see that. I pull it all back out. I look at the clock: 10:40. *Someone else will get the dead black cat.* I curse and punch at the air.

I pick up a doll and smash it against the radiator until its face caves in.

I find a crayon. I pull up the mattress. I write on the bed frame, *I hate you all. Fuk you fuk you.*

Then I have an idea.

I pull the sheet off my bed and lay it on the floor. I pile all the things on the floor onto the sheet, and gather the sheet up like a sack and hang it out the window, carefully closing the window over a bit of the sheet. I stand on the radiator and look down. It seems safe.

All the trash flies out of the bent garbage can from my flying karate kick. Enter the Dragon. I watch as the garbage can rolls down the tar walkway that cuts through the park, until it rolls off the side where the walkway breaks into chunks from the dirt and grass that push up from the bottom. I find an old paper bag. The cat is caught in the bush branches like an old shirt. A line of ants crawls into its mouth. I untangle it. I climb high up a ginkgo tree. I rest. I pull the cat out of the bag.

How do these things work: ghosts, special powers? I hold the cat by the neck and look into its mouth. There's dirt on the dry tongue. Its eyes are dry, its hair dusty and matted. I squeeze its stomach and the front paws open like a baby. I laugh. *"Maa-ma, maa-ma."*

Maybe its ghost is still stuck inside somewhere, who knows? I break off a little branch and stick it down the cat's throat. I push it around, and it presses into mushy things. I pull the stick out. It's a little wet. I think about it. The outside things, the eyes, the tongue, are dry. The inside things, are wet. Maybe ghosts escape the body like steam from water, slowly flying out as the body dries up. That means the cat's eyes and tongue are ghosts now, waiting for the rest of it.

Shoving the cat back into the bag I twist the top tight. I will trap the rest of the ghost. If I trap it I will get its special powers. Then I will do things, special things.

The guys from The Block are gathering. Right below, Poco and Jose roll an old car tire from the top of the hill, aiming it at the cars passing on the lower drive. The little kids are scattered around. Over there, playing stickball with a broken mop handle. Over there, playing Chinese handball. Over there, throwing rocks at the old pair of Keds hanging from the streetlight. A rock shatters Mr. Gordie's window. Our stuff is always going into his window. He lives on the second floor and he never gives anything back. Now he's at the window hollering. A line of the Big Kids lean in the blue shadow of the Firemen's Monument. They listen to music. Jermaine's got his turntable. The base of the streetlight is bent, a hole blown open from when Alex shoved an M-80 in there. Jermaine's dad is an electrician and that's how he knows how to hook up his turntable, using the wires in the streetlight like a socket. Ron, a little kid, walks past the Big Kids.

"Yo, it's Kike-boy," Jordan says.

Fly, a Big Kid, laughs. "Yo, Kike-boy, heard how the Grand Canyon was made? A Jew dropped a penny down an ant hole."

Jordan and Fly laugh and laugh and slap five.

One day the Big Kids decided that the little kids needed nicknames. They lined us up. "From henceforth you shall be known as . . ." moving the line along, kicking us in the butt once we were named.

Ron became Kike-boy, Reid got Bees-in-his-hair because he's got crazy curly hair that's always got twigs and leaves and things caught in it. Max got Oreo, because his dad's black and his mom's white. Jimmy got Growler, because he is so small for his age and they thought that was funny.

Fly is a nickname too, but he gave it to himself. *I so fly, ladies pass by, say my my my.*

I got Bruiser, because I'm always bruised. And I bother the Big Kids until they give me the car treatment, and I laugh as they take me overhead and slam me onto the hood of a car, and I say, *I don't feel nuthin', faggot,* as they take my head and drum it hard on the windshield. It hurts a whole lot, but I don't want it to ever stop. I laugh and call them more names and they pick me up and slam me harder and harder. Then I'll see Reid or Jimmy watching, and they'll look all scared, like they can't believe it. And it becomes the best, when finally the Big Kid says, "Damn, haven't you had enough?" Then I just want more and more, because everyone, all of them, are staring at me. And right when it starts to hurt like I can't stand it, like I'm going to start bawling, I go real still. But inside. The part of me getting pummeled is like a rag doll, swinging all around, twisting, slamming down, but inside I'm real still. And inside, hurt feels different than on the outside. Inside it doesn't feel good or bad, it just feels big, like that *pow* the first second of jumping into a freezing ocean. Like that, it's everything: freezing and burning, opening and closing, bright and dark, all at once so that it's one huge, roaring thing. Then my still insides go crazy and excited and awake, like I'm racing down a steep hill with my eyes closed. Rushing: *fast, fast, fast.* Perfect. The most perfect thing ever, so perfect I can barely stand it.

The moving men leave my building. They get into a truck. It says MOISHE'S MOVING on the side. They drive off.

Fly puts Jimmy in a garbage can and is telling him to growl

like a dog. It's funny and I laugh. I climb down the tree. At the bottom, I stop. I don't know why. I turn the other way and run quickly through the park. I can feel my heart beating hard like I'm scared. I don't know why.

I reach the stone wall and scale it, down to the lower level that has two walkways, basketball courts and baseball fields, and then finally the path that runs along the Hudson River.

I walk quietly by the river. I stop and look around, sure that someone is there. The sun is bright and it reflects off the green river. Rusted ships the size of fallen buildings pass, a cloud of seagulls squawking like crazy overhead. Garbage floats by, wooden beams, cans, tennis balls, plastic bags, Styrofoam.

I walk until I'm out of The Block's territory. I relax. I sing to myself, *"Groove me baby, ugh!, all right . . ."* I laugh. I run and stop like I'm stealing base. I fill out my chest and jive-walk, dipping and swaying.

I whisper, "I'm bad, I'm bad."

I cross my arms like Dad. "Is that *good* bad, or *bad* bad?"

I jive-walk again. "Pst, Pops, later for you . . ."

I cut up, away from the river and walk slow because the park's mine now. I've walked far: I see Grant's Tomb. Older kids hang out cool and lazy, smoking. They tag on the tomb's walls with cans of spray paint. They laugh and say Shit and Motherfucker a lot. "Motherfucker," I whisper. "Shit, mother-fucker." I climb a cherry blossom and hide in the thick smelling flowers, watching the tops of peoples' heads, letting spit dangle from my mouth.

I climb down. I kneel on the air grate over the abandoned freight train tracks that run beneath Riverside Park. A cool, dusty gravely air rises up. As I watch, a bum passes. "Mole!" I call at him. "Rat!" I continue on. I wonder if any other little kid has ever been this far before. I'm sure they haven't. I pre-tend that everyone is dead and that I'm alone. I watch two teenagers make out on a green bench. Her breasts are big and smushy. He pushes his face into hers, he grabs at her behind. He wears a blue T-shirt with faded white letters, COLUMBIA.

Dad teaches art history at Columbia. I turn, annoyed, and walk quickly until I feel better. I pick up a stick. I smack at broken brown and green glass. I drag it along the ground, bored. I kind of wish *someone* was with me, just one person, Reid or Jimmy. I see two squirrels. I grit my teeth, I chase them, swinging my stick at their backs, missing. They circle up a tree. I collect some pebbles and toss them at a group of pigeons like food. They scutter over, greedy gross coo-cooing, and I chase them. *Stupids.* I laugh. They fly into the air, and I pry a piece of cement from the walkway for when they return to the ground.

As I wait, I see a girl walking on the twisting path on top of the slope. She carries dandelions. I follow her. She looks around, I hide. She walks up some stairs. I run up the slope. I wait, then I run up the stairs, reach the walkway. The girl has vanished.

"Why you following?"

I turn. The girl is crouching next to the wall. She stands, she walks up to me.

"I'm not following."

"Sure you were, stupid."

I look at her face. It's the way she says stupid that makes me remember. "I know you," I say.

"Yeah?" she asks, then smiling. *"Stupid little kid."*

"Shut up."

She pushes me hard. "I won't shut up."

Her name is Darla. She used to live in my building, a floor below us. I used to see her in the elevator and I'd say, "Hi, ugly," and she'd say, "Hi, stupid." Then she would add, "Stupid little kid," because our birthdays are a month and a half apart, only she's a year older, except for during that

month and a half. And I'd say, "You're the stupid: we're in
the same grade. You get left back?" Then she would get all
snotty and say, "If you're born at the end of the year, your
mom can put you in school early or late. My mom couldn't
stand letting me go. That's why. Your mom couldn't *wait* to
get rid of you is all." Which seemed true. So, I'd go to my
room and jump up and down to make her mad below. Her
parents got divorced and her father left, and Mom and Dad
said how he went crazy with *'60s flashbacks,* which I figure
has something to do with flashcubes, like the kind Mom puts
on her camera when Granma and Granpa come to visit,
because those things hurt and you can't see after, and I can
only imagine what *sixty* of them must feel like. Then Darla
and her mother moved.

"What're you doing here?" I ask.

"None of your beeswax."

"I don't care anyway."

"We moved back."

"Back where?

"Back."

I look at her. "Nuh-uh," I say.

"Yuh-huh."

"Someone else got your apartment."

"So? I don't care."

We're quiet.

"Where you going to school?" I ask.

"P.S. Seventy-five."

"I go there."

"I know. I used to too." She makes a squinty face like I'm
dumb. "Remember?"

"Who you got?"

"Mrs. . . . Lumis?"

"Nuh-uh."

Darla looks at me. "Oh, brother . . . ," she says, rolling her eyes, putting her hands on her pink cheeks. "I knew we shouldn'ta come back. Queens was much better than this."

"We got a big assignment due tomorrow—"

"I know. Mom called the school. I've already done it."

"Really? The diorama?"

"Well, if I said I did the assignment, and if the assignment's—"

"Shut up." A fluttering in my stomach. "I gotta go."

"So do I."

"Good."

"Fine."

The house is quiet. Dad's in the living room at his work desk. I close the front door quietly. When he's not at school he works at his desk in the living room building miniatures. I shouldn't bother him. Dad looks up, I turn away.

Mom works down the hallway in the dining room where the TV is. Her desk sits below pots of hanging ivy in front of a window. It's where she sits and writes. I will ask her about what religion she's got, then I will do a good diorama, better than anything ugly Darla could ever do. She's on the phone. Her forehead is on her palm. She hangs up.

"I want lunch," I say.

Sun comes through the window. It shines through Mom's pale blue eyes, making them go invisible. They sparkle.

Dad walks in. He asks me what I'm doing in on this lovely spring afternoon. I say, food.

Dad turns to Mom. "Who were you on with?"

"Father."

They're quiet.

"He's well enough to talk?"

"No. He's not."

They're quiet again.

"I have a meeting at my office," Dad says.

"On Sunday?"

"Some papers," Dad says, "that I need. I don't know why I said meeting. I didn't mean to say meeting."

Mom's quiet, she looks at me. She asks if I would like a nice grilled cheese sandwich. I say, yeah.

Dad leaves, Mom goes into the kitchen. I walk to her desk. I look at her notebooks filled with words and cross-outs and notes up the margins with arrows. I smell the melting butter. Mom writes poetry. I read a crossed-out line.

~~Baby, it's your face the size of my fist~~
~~so perfect that I want to smash it in~~
~~it's so perfect~~

I pick up her pen and look at it. The window by her desk is cracked open. I let the pen fall.

The back door buzzer rings. I move toward the kitchen and crouch against the wall next to the kitchen doorway. Mom talks to our next-door neighbor, Mrs. Babcock. Mom talks about Granpa, calling him a *conservative bastard*. She says, *Oh, Evelyn, I turn right back into a little girl.* She talks about how sick he is, and, yes, he's helping out with money each month, but— She doesn't finish. She talks about Dad. How he just left for his office. *On a Sunday?* Mom says. She asks Mrs. Babcock if she's acting crazy. Maybe it's just her worries about Granpa, she says. She writes all day, she goes on, *swirling in all that shit*— I don't want to hear anymore. I've never heard Mom curse. *Maybe I need a head shrinker*, she says. Then, she yells, *I know that bastard's fucking some*—

I close my eyes and put my fingers in my ears. I hum soft and I feel nice again. I move, run to my room. I reach beneath my bed until I feel Mona. Mona's a photo of a girl in a gold frame. I hold Mona on my lap.

"*Mona,*" I whisper.

I quickly go down the hallway that leads to the bathroom. I climb into the clothes hamper. I burrow down into the clothing. I hear Mom and Mrs. Babcock stomping, calling for me. The clothes are soft. I feel better. I don't talk to Mona, but it's nice having her here. I breathe in, smell everyone's body near. Fall asleep.

Mom asks me over and over where I hid. I don't tell her. She asks me why I hid. I shake my head. She gets mad. She says she made me a grilled cheese. But it got cold. She threw it out.

I sit in Mom's lap. She rocks me. I'm too big for her lap, and I have to help her rock. I lean back against her.

"Your grandfather is very sick," she says, resting her chin on my shoulder.

"Is he going to die?"

Mom stops rocking me. "Maybe."

I slide off her lap. "You're going to Florida again?"

"Yes," she says. "Won't you tell me where you hid?"

I shake my head.

"Dad doesn't believe in ghosts?" I ask.

"No. Why?"

"We do. We play Ouija."

Mom smiles.

"What about Jordan and Daniel?"

"I don't know."

"So, it's just me, right?"

Mom smiles. She pulls me back onto her lap.

Dad walks in. I try to slide off. Mom holds me tight. Dad looks at us. He doesn't say anything. He walks into another room. I squiggle hard and Mom lets me slide away.

It's night. I look across the courtyard and see Darla in a bedroom, her mother in the living/dining room. They unpack
boxes. Her mother unloads a box of nothing but candlehold-
ers, tons of them. She puts a candle in one, and calls Darla. I
see Darla look up, then run to the living/dining room. Her
mother lights the candle and they both bow their heads, and
her mother's saying something, then they both look up. They
laugh and dance around a table.

Darla returns to her room. I throw pennies until one hits.
She looks at the window. She squints across the dark courtyard
to my window. I know she can't see me sitting in my dark
room. I smile.

"*Got you,*" I whisper. I turn from the window and open my
bedroom door a crack. A wedge of light falls across the floor.

I pull Mona out from under my bed. Mona is a picture of
Mom from when she was a little girl that I stole from Granpa
and Granma's house in Florida.

I prop Mona up, so that she's looking at me. Her hair is
messy but it looks like someone tried to comb it with their fingers for the photo. They probably said, Oh Honey your hair's
a rat's nest. Then they quickly combed it, and I know how
that feels, because they just pull hard and the hair rips and that
really hurts. She looks straight out. At first I thought she
looked worried, but the more I looked at the way she bunches
up her mouth on the sides, it's more like she's mad. She has
one hand shoved down the back of her pants. I have a pencil. I
pull my mattress back and read things I have written,
*Grounded 2 weeks. Thru Jordans homwerk out window. Stole 2 $
from moms perse. Stol Daniels kulerd drawing pensils. I hate you
all. Fuk you fuk you.* I run my hand over them. Then I write,
Uglee darla moved bak, April 77.

three

I open my eyes. 7:52. Why hasn't Dad woken me yet? Every morning it's: *Shake, shake, shake, shake, shake* until my eyes open. *What? What? . . . School.* I nod. *You're up? Yes . . .* My eyes droop. *YOU'RE UP?* I sit up. *Uh-huh . . .* His eyes, sharp, watching. *Yes,* I say. *I'm up, I'm up.*

I find my Tonka Jeep. I race it. *Uuuuuuu-Uh-uuuuu.* I make it crash and I make crashing sounds and sounds of people howling. I find a doll, a dentist doll, with a gross baby face and big blue eyes that close when you lay him down. It came with a little dentist office. Granpa gave it to me. I don't know what I'm supposed to do with a dentist. When I opened it last Christmas, Granpa said, "My, now, you see?" I looked at him, then Granma, then Mom. Mom said, "How nice, honey. A dentist. With his own office."

I stand the dentist up.

I hear the front door open, close. I go still. Dad's voice, something about Manuel, the super.

I push the Jeep at him, to run him over. It races past him, under my bed.

"*Shoot.*"

I pull myself under the bed. It's dark and I feel around for the Jeep. There are lots of dust balls, like clouds.

I find the empty box.

My diorama! I think quick. Maybe I can use some of my action figures, color with some crayons. But what'll I do it about? I think hard and try to remember what happens on *The Davey and Goliath Show*. They're always talking about God.

I push myself out. Dad's standing there.

I can see that he is in a foul mood. But it's not Sunday, when I always know what he's in a foul mood about. It's Monday. His foul mood could be about anything.

His face has changed color like it does only after he's been yelling for a while, but I haven't heard him yelling, which means that all that yelling is trapped inside him. I don't want it to come out, so I stay quiet.

Dad picks me up by the collar and drags me to the window. He opens it and pushes my head out. The sheet is draped over an air conditioner a few floors down. Scattered across the courtyard floor are my clothes, my toys, my books.

He pulls me back in. He begins yelling.

I look at him.

He pulls me over his leg and begins hitting my behind. Hard. Then harder. Over and over. I close my eyes every time his hand comes down. *I'm Bruiser. I'm Bruiser. I'm Bruiser.* Tears press against my eyes. I won't cry. I make my face tight. I stare at the dentist. He is still standing, looking at me, watching me. When Dad leaves, I will rip his head off and poke out his gross baby eyes. I scrunch my face tighter. *I'm Bruiser. I'm Bruiser.*

Dad lets go. He tells me that my things will stay down

there until I find the time to get them. He's instructed Manuel to leave them. I can't get them now because I'll be late for school, therefore, he says, if some things are ruined in the meantime, since rain is predicted, or if things are taken, or shat or pissed on by pigeons or stray cats, well, so be it, he says. Maybe it will teach me a little something.

He leaves. I say, "I'm sorry."

I close the window. Across the way I see Darla watching. When I see her, she turns away.

High up in the ginkgo tree, I open the bag. I inhale. It doesn't smell like much: dirt and brown paper bag. I figure that means there's probably not much ghost trapped yet. But, maybe there's a little. I wish for it not to rain, for none of my things to be stolen or shat or pissed on. I close up the bag. I remember about my assignment. I open the bag and inhale again. I wish for Mrs. Lumis to not call on me. Or just make her die, I wish.

Mrs. Lumis stands under the sign, still up from our class last year. HAPPY BICENTENNIAL AMERICA! Most of the glitter is gone; a couple of the people cutouts have fallen off, leaving brown glue shadows. Mrs. Lumis reads a newspaper article like she does every morning.

I stare out the window, which faces the street between West End and Riverside. At the beginning of the block is Shorty's Candy. Shorty is an old black man, who sells Now & Laters and red hots only, but who sells, the Big Kids claim, "other sorts of candy at night." Then there's a line of short orange SRO buildings, where the shell-shocked vets live, where sometimes we go and set off firecrackers. Then, a gas station with a blinking ENTER sign, and in front the sidewalk is black with oil and gas, and it's so slick you can take a running start and slide.

Mrs. Lumis suddenly starts yelling, and I jerk my head back forward. She's still on her article, banging on the board with her fist after every word, making the colored pipe cleaners we used for the sign's lettering jiggle. *Jamaican Cultists they call them! They're called Rastafarians! Damned racist—! So, they found eleven pounds of marijuana! Well, that's their religion!*

She tells Ronald to come and present his diorama, since his religion, like Rastafaria, is a mixture of Christianity and African religion.

Every month since January we've had a new project. First we had to draw the flags of the countries we came from in the olden days. Mom showed me an English flag. Dad showed me a French flag and an Algerian flag. I asked why he had two flags, and he said, because he grew up in French North Africa, that his father was French and his mother was Algerian, an Arab. "Arab?" I asked. Dad frowned, kind of mad. "Yes," he said. "I'm Arab?" I asked. "A quarter," he said. I told this to Jordan. I made fun of Arab: *"Ooo-woo-woo-woo,"* I sang. "That's the Indians, you idiot," Daniel mumbled, without looking up from his desk. "Arabs have the sheets wrapped around their heads and carry swords the size of elephant tusks, and big beards like those Jewish guys always walking around," Jordan added. Then he said, "Beside, we're not really Arab, a little, but not *really.*" So, I just drew the English flag and the French flag. Next we had an assignment on foods of our countries, then clothing, and this month a diorama showing a scene from our religions.

Ronald carries his diorama up from the back of class. It has a paper fire pit in the middle, with people dancing around it with wide eyes. His religion is called *Santería.* His family comes from Haiti. His diorama is of people who are possessed by spirits.

"Butchers!" Cormac laughs. "You the mothers that leave them hacked-up chickens all around the park."

Everyone laughs.

"That's them?" I ask, turning to Cormac.

Mrs. Lumis tells us to pipe down.

"Sure," Cormac says. "My father told me. You seen them chickens, right?"

Mrs. Lumis pulls Cormac out of his chair for the principal. He says, "Right? Right?" as she drags him past.

Ronald is saying, "Nah, nah, that's not us, that's not us."

I write it down: *Santa Reea. Kill animols, get poezest with theyr spearits.* I think about my dead black cat and smile.

"When you get possessed," I ask Ronald, who's standing silently up front, waiting for Mrs. Lumis to return, "what does that do?"

"Ooh, " he says. "It gives you special powers."

"So, you kill the chicken, then—"

"—We don't kill no chicken."

Everyone's laughing. People are singing, *"I'm a chicken hawk, chicken hawk, chicken hawk . . ."* I bang on my desk, making ghost sounds. Other people bang their desks, make ghost sounds. We're real loud now, and I feel crazy and I start screaming. Mrs. Lumis runs in. She yells, *Shut up!* We go quiet. Ronald's crying so hard that he can't continue. Mrs. Lumis looks around for who can go next. A few hands go up. I look down, turn my head a little, frown like I'm thinking. She calls on me. I tell her I didn't have my hand raised. She asks me to please come up. I lift the top of my desk. *What am I going to do?!* Inside are papers and lots of rotting apples that I always take out of the lunches Mom packs me. I can just hear Mom if she was to see these apples. "Oh, honey. Honestly. All those good apples." Shut up, I think. I touch the apples. They're shriveled and brown and soft. I look up front. Mrs.

Lumis stares at me, her eyes extra big in her owl glasses. She's always in a foul mood, just like Dad. My brain races. It goes blank and fast. Foul Mood: Dad's. Mom's sad. Sad about what? I hold the apples. Sad about the foul mood? Yes, right. Foul mood makes her swirl in all that shit. That's what she said. Then after, she said, Oh, Evelyn, maybe I just need a head shrinker. I look ahead. I'm up, walking. I carry the apples. I stand up front. Everyone looks at me. I hear a few giggles. I look at Mrs. Lumis. My body tingles. My mouth opens. Words come out. I just listen. I tell the class that my family's religion is from a long line of Head Shrinkers. The giggling gets louder. Darla looks at me and shakes her head. I say, In my hands I hold some shrunken heads. I open my eyes wide, holding the rotten apples out. Mrs. Lumis is yelling, pounding on the blackboard again. An orange pipe cleaner comes loose from the sign. It lands sticking straight up in the stiff curls of her hair. I can't help it. I laugh. My hands going tight, soft rotting apple bits fall to the floor.

I sort through my things from the courtyard. It did rain. I lay wet books and wet clothes in front of my open window so they will dry. From between pages and inside pockets, I pick off and crush tiny green hopping bugs that come from the bright sprigs of moss that sprout between the cracks of the courtyard floor.

Across the courtyard I can see that Darla's apartment is done. Her mother sits in a chair. Her head in hand. She looks up. She shakes her head, no, no, no. She stands quickly. She rushes to the window and opens it. She holds a small brown bottle. She turns it upside down. Little white pills fall down the courtyard. She throws the empty pill bottle after them. She closes the window. She lights a candle. She bobs over it. She looks up. Darla walks into the room, book bag on her back.

She hugs Darla. She kisses Darla on the cheeks and face. Her mother talks. Darla looks at her, trying to push away like a cat hugged too tight. Her mother's face goes tight, angry. Darla suddenly starts nodding quickly, nervously. She smiles, yes, yes, yes. Her mother smiles and hugs Darla hard.

Mom's in the living room, reading. She smiles when she sees me. I don't say anything. I sit next to her, look at her book. In the corner of the room is Dad's work area where he works on his miniature houses. I look at Mom.

"Did you want to play with Dad's miniature?" Mom asks. She closes the book on her lap.

"It's not allowed," I say.

Dad ropes his corner off when he isn't there. When he finishes a miniature he displays it in the front hallway on a stand he's built just for them. The miniatures stay in the dark hallway until the next one is completed. The replaced miniature goes into Dad's closet. Dad's closet has deep shelving filled with all the past little worlds he has made. When Mom and Dad go out together, I sneak into Dad's closet with a flashlight. I close the door and lie on the floor. I flash the light on the still miniatures, and after a while I can hear them making small sounds, all at once, like lots of little voices whispering to themselves.

"We won't tell," says Mom.

We walk to the roped-off corner. It is an old, old-looking house. Inside are little people dressed like the people on boring *Masterpiece Theater* shows that Mom watches on PBS, where the people just talk and talk.

Mom picks up a lady.

"Oh dear, oh dear," Mom says for the lady. "Such muddle."

Mom walks the lady up some stairs to a little room where a boy sits alone.

"How are you, little one?" says the lady.

Mom looks at me.

"Has the cat caught your tongue?" says the lady.

Mom nudges her head for me to pick up the boy figure.

I pick him up.

"Why are you all alone?" asks the lady.

"I'm hiding," I say for the little boy.

"From what are you hiding?" asks the lady.

I frown. I don't know. I say nothing.

"Have you been bad?"

Quiet.

"Are you scared by something?"

I let go of the little boy.

"They look dead," I say.

Mom blinks and places the lady back in her room.

I go to the couch. A storm is beginning again outside. Thunder rumbles over the Hudson River, over the gray factories of New Jersey.

Mom makes her eyes wide. "I know what we could do."

I begin nodding. "What?" I ask.

"Our game," she says leaning forward, then whispering, "should I get it?"

Mom returns and puts the Ouija board on the couch.

"It's a good day for ghosts, huh?" I say.

"Doesn't it seem that way?"

"You think the old man is up?" I ask. An old man died in the apartment before it was ours. Whenever there is a creak down the hallway, or a clock suddenly stops, or a sound like wind shushes in a room with closed windows, me and Mom know that it's the old man.

We ask the Ouija board silly questions to start: easy yes or no questions.

"What religion do you have?" I ask Mom.

"Religion? Why do you ask?"

I shrug.

She tells me she was raised Episcopalian. I ask about Dad. Catholic. I ask, Do I have a religion? Not really, Mom says. But, I think to myself, I have a dead black cat. She looks off and says she believes in God, but she doesn't bother much with religion anymore. Mom says that Dad thinks religion and anyone who believes in God is foolish. So, he thinks you're foolish? I ask. Mom looks at me a second, then nods a little and frowns.

We continue with the Ouija board.

We call the dead. The medium piece slides from letter to letter forming words. *Yes. Murder. Flower.*

Whenever I get scared I look up at Mom and she calms me with her eyes.

"Let's call Granpa," she says.

The green light of the storm passes through her blue eyes and turns them ghostly.

"But, he's alive," I say.

"Shh . . . ," she says, closing her eyes.

"It's bad luck!" I say. *"You can't call the living."*

The medium piece begins to slowly glide across the board.

I imagine the Ouija board sending its mystical waves from New York down to Florida and finding Granpa. I can see Granpa looking surprised as the Ouija board pulls on his ghost that isn't supposed to leave his body yet, and I can see Granpa's eyes go wide with fear.

I knock the piece from the board.

"Quit it!" I scream.

Mom jerks and looks up. She looks around, confused. Then, her eyes settle on me. They look sleepy and far away, but they also look wild, like somebody else's eyes.

"I'm tired," I say. "I wanna take a nap." I slide the board to

the floor and lie down, putting my head on Mom's lap. I close
my eyes and wait for her to stroke my head gently. She does
not. I open my eyes. Mom stares out the window at the thick
battling clouds, the black dot at the center of her eye huge, a
thin thread of blue around it.

⟶

I look at Darla's apartment. She's in her room, looking at herself in the mirror. She has on a long blue dress. I break a
crayon into pieces and throw them at her window. She turns. I
sign for her to open her window.

"Hey," I call.

Darla frowns and puts a shushing finger to her mouth.

"What?" I call.

In the living/dining room, I see her mother, dressed up. A
man is there, sitting in a chair. Lots of candles are lit. The
room flickers, beautiful.

Darla moves away, then returns with two cans connected
by a string. She throws one can out the window, and after four
tries, I catch it. She signs for me to put it to my ear.

"Can you hear?" Her voice comes weakly through the can.
I open my mouth.

Darla smiles.

"Wow," I say. "Wha'cha doing with all those candles?"

"Shabbos."

"What's that?"

"Dinner. Friday dinner."

"We don't do that."

"Duh. You're not Jewish."

Once, when we were small, Mom and Darla's mother took
us skating on Christmas Eve. After we met Dad and Darla's
father and we drove and picked out Christmas trees. I know
Jews don't get to have Christmas.

"You're not Jewish neither," I say.

"Shut up. We are now."

"Your dad came back?"

Darla frowns, confused, then getting it, nods. "That's Dr. Dan. Mom's boyfriend."

I see Darla's mother call.

"I gotta go," she says. "I need my can back."

"Let me keep it."

"Why should I?"

"Just let me," I say. "We can talk sometimes."

"Okay, you," she says. She ties her can to a plant on her windowsill.

Mom serves meat loaf and salad for dinner.

"Anyone for cake?" Mom asks.

Her eyes are swollen and shiny and smooth like two pink pebbles. I look at everyone. They hunch over, eating their cake. It's like the silent treatment. Maybe we're doing it to make Mom stop going into rooms for hours. I look down and eat my cake.

I take out Mona.

"Why don't you smile, Mona?"

Mona looks at me.

"I wish you were really alive."

I put her under my pillow and fall asleep.

↶↷

I watch Daniel lift his piece of bread where he took one bite, lowering his head, looking inside. I can see that the peanut butter is spread too thin, the jelly is clumped too thick. Usually Mom makes Saturday lunch, but today Dad did. I hold my sandwich up, proud. It's ham and Brie, like Dad's got. I like cheese. Dad does too. We both do. We like cheese better than anyone else does. Only I eat Brie. The brothers call it frozen snot. Mom got another call from Florida. She's in the bathroom again. She's been there for hours. No one says anything. We all just use the little bathroom in Mom and Dad's room when we have to go.

Jordan talks and talks.

Jordan raises his arms and wiggles as he did when he made the touchdown he's telling us about. "Ah-ha ha!" he says.

Me and Daniel smile. Dad clears his throat and takes a moment for another bite. Jordan's arms come down and he looks at his sandwich.

"Yes, I saw from the window, you boys playing," Dad says.

"You saw?" asks Jordan, looking up.

"I didn't see your touchdown, no. But I did see that Glendale boy, the older one, Saul, quarterbacking." Dad smiles. "I was amazed: such a scrawny kid, but what an arm. Just incredible."

"He throws good," Jordan mumbles, nodding.

Dad finishes his sandwich. "Your grandfather is very ill. He's in the hospital and it doesn't look good." Dad waits, looking at us. "Your mother will be flying down to Florida tomorrow," he says.

We finish our lunch in silence.

"We're gonna be playing later," Jordan says. "You'll be able to see from the window if you want. We'll be right downstairs."

"Yes," Dad says.

The phone rings.

"You'll watch?"

Dad stands. "I'm very busy," he says. "We'll see." He goes to answer the phone.

Jordan looks at me and Daniel. "I'm gonna kick some ass today, boy." He nods. "Jordan Bad-Ass is gonna kick some sad-ass. A-ha ha ha."

I collect the lunch plates.

"Mrs. Lumis?" I hear Dad down the hallway.

I freeze. Dad looks at me.

"Why are you calling on a Saturday?"

I quickly go to the kitchen sink. I run the water. I hear Dad's footsteps. I look at my hands under the water. It makes them look far away, like how buildings look on foggy days, like air. *Run, hands, run.*

Dad's large, veiny arm reaches over my shoulder and turns the water faucet off. He turns me around. I hold a plate in front of me. He suddenly smiles. "Your family's religion is a long line of Head Shrinkers?" he asks.

"I'm sorry . . ."

Dad shakes his head. "You made that woman, that self-righteous— Your teacher, *Mrs. Lumis* . . . she feels—" Dad makes his lips tight, he begins laughing.

"Dad?" I don't like him laughing. I don't want him to go off into a room like Mom, like a crazy person.

"Oh," Dad says. "At least I can rest assured that *one* of my boys won't be lost on me. At least *one* isn't fool enough to believe in God."

"I'm not in trouble?"

"Not at all."

"I can go?"

"Sure."

I walk away.

"Of course you'll have to do the project again."

I open my mouth, but I don't say anything.

Around the corner, out of sight, we hear the bathroom door open. We hear Mom coughing. There are footsteps in the hallway. They stop, then turn back. The bathroom door closes again.

*   *   *

I sit on top of the clothes hamper in the hallway in front of the bathroom door. Mom inhales and I hear a snotty sound. There are other sounds, like the kind you make after being punched in the stomach, the *oufing* sound. I hear her breathe out and spit twice. The toilet flushes, the sink runs, the door opens.

"Honey, why are you always lurking about?"

"I'm bored."

"Well, I'm not a clown." Mom walks away.

I sit for a while on the clothes hamper. The bathroom smells of insides, not b.m., but warm and sour like rotted food.

The roof has two halves with two different entrances. One side looks over the park and river. No one's out yet. The other half has the water tower. There's a ladder up its side and a little walkway around it, where I suddenly see Darla sitting swinging her legs, watching me.

I run to the other half of the roof. I rip up pieces of tar and throw them at her. The pieces blow away in the wind. I shake a piece of cement off the ledge and throw it at her. It hits her foot.

"Stop!" she screams, "I'm gonna fall."

I look at her. "Is it cool up there?"

I climb the ladder quick. The wind blows hard. I walk around the water tower to where Darla sits, where the wind is blocked. The wooden shingles of the tower are rotted, and I pick pieces off and throw them into the wind. The wind shoots them out like bullets.

"What are you doing up here? Aren't all those boys around?" Darla asks.

"Why you all dressed up again for?" I ask.

"It's Saturday. We go to temple." Darla looks at me. "I told you I was Jewish, stupid."

"Shut up, ugly."

We're quiet.

"Why'd you get a Christmas tree that time if you're Jewish? Do you remember that time?"

Darla smiles. "I was just remembering that," she says, excited. "Isn't that weird?" she adds, slapping my shoulder. "We weren't Jewish then. It wasn't until Daddy went away." Darla frowns. She tries to smile. "They're probably going crazy wondering where I am. Stupid Mom promised when we left Queens she'd stop taking all those—" Darla suddenly goes quiet, snapping her mouth shut.

"Stop taking what?"

Darla looks out over the blocks and blocks of rooftops. A whole bunch of water towers like neat, fat trees growing out from the tar like black dirt. All the yellow and red and orange brick ledges like clipped shrubs.

I look at the Hudson. There are rough waves, whitecaps. If I look the right way, I don't see the roof or the park, and I can pretend that Darla and me are out at sea riding on the rough waves.

"It was funny how Mrs. Lumis had that thing in her hair when she was yelling at you," Darla says, smiling.

"I know," I laugh. I hold a finger over my head and imitate the pipe cleaner.

We laugh and laugh.

I open my eyes and Darla's looking at me.

"You don't make any sound when you laugh," she says.

"Yes I do."

Darla shakes her head. Her brow bunches up. "Really, you don't."

"Shut Up. I'm going."

We climb down the ladder, and we clomp loudly, making a racket, all the way down the fifteen flights of stairs, that smell like smoking teenagers. *"Aaayyy." "Owowow."* We go through the lobby to the street.

"Bye, you," Darla says.

"Where you going?"

"Temple."

"Why?"

Darla looks at me. "Because."

"Baby," Reid says. "Babybabybabybaby. Oooo scarybaby-baby . . ."

I spit in his face. He chases me. I'm in the middle of the field. Big Kids charge, running with a football. They slam me. I fall hard.

"What's the little chump doing?"

"Get off the field, scrub."

"Nah, man, leave Bruiser. His little ass plays better'n Dicky."

Laughter.

"Yo, Dicky get your fat ass off the field."

More laughing. The Big Kids turn and snap on Dicky for a while.

I'm on my stomach. Reid gets on top of me, pinning my shoulder with his knees, pushing my face into the dirt.

I try to talk but I can't catch my breath.

Jimmy runs over, digs up dirt, smushes it in my hair. Max grabs my legs, pulls down my jeans. Reid's laughing, saying something about my underwear. Everyone's laughing, hooting, snapping. I try to move, but now someone's on my legs, someone's on my middle. I can't breathe. Three people on me. They rock, so I'm crushed more. More hands: dirt. On my face, down my underwear, up my shirt. Everyone's laughing like crazy. Reid, Jimmy, and Max get off me. I roll onto my back. I look from laughing face to laughing face. They each make a sound. Reid's is like he's swallowing air that tickles him from inside, Jimmy's is a small, mean rodent *heeheehee*.

Fly's is a big laugh like he's got a sound box inside him. Each laugh is different, but each laugh makes a sound.

I go:
  "Hah ha ha."
  "Ho ho ho."
  "A-tee hee hee."
I stop. I stare at myself in the circle I've rubbed out in the steamed bathroom mirror. I stayed in the bathwater for a long time, and it went dark so I couldn't see through it from all the dirt, and now my skin feels sleepy and spongy. I make dumb faces to get a laugh. Nothing. I try to tickle myself. Nothing.

"So'd you hear the one about how the Grand Canyon was made?"

"No."

"A Jew dropped a penny down an ant hole!"

"Hee hee, ho ho, ha ha."

The steam on the mirror beads up to raindrops, and the mist goes away and I see myself, my shoulders, arms, stomach. I see bruises on each arm where Reid held me down, I turn, another one on my side from a knee.

I look at my face, I can't help it: I smile.

I clean up my room. It takes a long time to do it for real. I'm tired when I'm done. In my underwear and Captain America top, I go to the front hallway. It's dark. I see Daniel watching TV. I see Dad in his corner cutting up hundreds of little bits of wood. I turn, tiptoe down the other hallway, look through the keyhole at Jordan doing his homework, then I go and listen at Mom and Dad's door, which is silent. I go to my room, get into bed, close my eyes.

*   *   *

Morning. Dad comes into my bedroom. His face is red and he opens his mouth. He looks around and frowns a little. He walks over to my window and looks out it. He turns and his eyes go over my whole neat room. He stands next to the vacuum. He looks at me. I look at his hand. The muscles rise and fall. He breathes out, then turns and rolls the vacuum away.

I sit in the ginkgo tree holding the bag. It's been a week. The cat's insides must have dried a bit. Some black cat special power ghost must be trapped by now.

"I want to make sound when I laugh and I want Mom back the way she was. But, punish her first."

I hold the bag to my mouth and untwist it. It smells a little, and I quickly inhale the trapped ghost. I twist the bag back up and climb down the tree.

It's windy and I lie back in the grass and watch the clouds move quickly by. I close my eyes. I can feel the ghost inside of me. I relax. I will try to float. I hold my breath. *What was that? Did I float?* I open my eyes. It felt like I floated, just a little. I go upstairs.

A filled laundry bag by the front door. Mom's in the bathroom scrubbing the tub with Ajax. I climb into the empty hamper. I hear Dad's footsteps.

"You don't have to clean the bathroom today," he says. "Let me."

"I don't mind," Mom says. "I kind of . . . I want to."

"You'll be ready to leave in an hour for your plane?"

"I'm packed," Mom says.

"I'm going down to do the laundry," he says.

"Wait," Mom says. I hear her stand. "I'm late," she says.

Dad's quiet.

"It's probably nothing: all that's going on with Father. It's probably just that," Mom says.

Dad says, *How late?* Mom, quietly, like me when I'm forced to say what I did wrong, says, *Two weeks.* Dad exhales hot. *Christ.* Mom says, *So—I guess that's how you feel.* Feel about what? I wonder. Dad says that they can't go through it again. He asks if she wants to go through it again. He knows that she's always wanted a . . . but— Mom says, *You can't even say it.* What? I think, say what? *Little girl,* Mom says, in a voice that isn't like hers: a faraway voice, scratchy, like the words are covered in snot and twigs. The voice sings. *Little Isabella, pret-ty lit-tle Is-a-bell-a.* I don't want to know, go away, go away, I think. *You've named it already?* Dad asks, soft. The voice doesn't answer. It continues to sing. *Pret-ty lit-tle, love-ly lit-tle, Is-a-bell-a lit-tle bell-a mine . . .*

I breathe in deeply, then let it out: special breath, magic breath. Make her stop, I think.

"I'm sorry," Dad says softly.

I hold my breath.

Quiet.

Mom starts to cry.

four

Mom leaves for two weeks. In the middle of the second week she calls to say that Granpa's gone, and that she'll be in Florida for a third week.

I sit on my bedroom floor. I'm telling Mona about how I breathed in the cat ghost, how I made Mom cry. The can next to my window makes a sound. I crawl over. I put my ear to it.

The sound is soft and garbled.

I look out the window. Darla's screaming at her mother. Her mother sits heavy in a chair. Darla shakes her mother. Her mother looks like a huge doll. Darla pulls on her arm, slaps her face. Her mother's eyes finally open. Darla helps her stand. Her mother looks very tired. She leans on Darla, her feet drag. They stop. Her mother hangs over. She vomits. Darla holds her mother's hair up, rubs her back. Her mother's body jerks a few more times, then she rises up. They walk to a different room.

*   *   *

The room stays empty. Half an hour passes.

Darla returns. She sweeps the living room moving around the vomit. She gets on her knees and wipes up the vomit. She holds her nose. She notices she has a little vomit on her hand. She sprays cleaner on her hand and rubs it with a sponge. She rubs and rubs. She rubs hard, her face a stiff frown. She throws the sponge across the room suddenly. She leans over, her head in her knees. I see her back rising and falling. I put my ear to the can, but I can't hear the crying.

Dad calls from work. It's dark out. He'll be late, but he's going to bring a pizza. To celebrate pizza, I put on my K-Tel record and dance. I'm tired and I sit on the radiator to rest. I see them across. It's evening and Darla and her mother are both dressed up. They walk around quickly. The apartment is clean. Jewish dinner.

The candles flicker, the air is gold. Darla and Dr. Dan sit at the table. In the center is a big candleholder with many candles. Darla's mother lights a couple. She talks. They all look sleepy, the flickering light makes it look like a dream. Dr. Dan stands up. He closes his eyes. He sings. I put my ear to the can. I can hear it faint. It sounds like a sad animal. Darla and her mother sing. Dr. Dan takes a bottle and pours into three cups. They sip. They put their hands in a bowl. Their hands come out wet. Darla smiles, devilish. She spritzes her mother. Her mother opens her mouth wide. She chases Darla around the table. She catches her, she tickles her. Darla laughs and laughs. They sit. Dr. Dan holds a loaf of bread. He breaks pieces, he hands them out. They eat it. Darla's mother takes covers off platters and she piles three plates high. They eat and talk and laugh.

I lower my blinds, turn the music loud, spin until everything disappears.

*   *   *

For dinner Dad makes fries to go with our pizza, something Mom would never let happen. There's a bowl of yellow, homemade mayonnaise which he dips his fries in. It's nasty, and it makes me sick to see him do it. I don't know how someone could waste fries like that. But the cool thing is that he makes the fries himself, real crunchy and salty.

"Could we have Jewish dinner?" I ask.

"Jewish food isn't very good," he says.

Jordan looks at me and shakes his head like I'm an idiot. He'll probably tell everyone and they'll start calling me Kikeboy like Ron, then they'll all start singing that me and Ron are in love, how we're kissing in a tree and all.

"I meant like they do on Friday."

"The Sabbath?" Dad looks confused. "We're not Jewish."

"Why not?"

Dad looks at me, sort of funny. "Just because: we're not."

I shrug. "I know."

Dad still looks at me for a bit. He sort of shakes his head like something's funny, messes my hair, then dips a fry into his nasty mayo.

It's real quiet as Reid, Jimmy, and me lie on the grass looking up at the sky. It's early morning, May, chilly. Clouds pass fast overhead, winds stirring the big puffs, making them shift and pull into different shapes, eyes and moving mouths, wings and arms opening wide.

God, I think.

I feel Reid's arm near mine. I feel the cold grass beneath my hands. I feel the curve and tilt of the earth.

"Look at that one," says Reid.

"Which?"

Reid's hand comes into view, pointing against the blue.

"The fish."

"Fish?"

"Yeah, there."

"Nah. That's a little chick waiting to be fed."

"Shut up."

We're quiet.

"Whose got a Spalding? I'm bored. Let's play handball."

"Mine went through Mr. Gordie's window yesterday. You?"

"Nah. The sewer. You?"

"Yeah. Upstairs," I say.

We all look back up at the sky.

Jimmy and Reid begin arguing over what one cloud looks like. Reid always wins, being the oldest. I look at the cloud. Because I don't care, I can watch it flip-flop back and forth. They argue for a while, and then they stop.

Reid sits up. "Come on, retard, get the ball."

I look over. "What? Oh. Right."

The regular elevator's out, so Manuel takes me up on the freight elevator. I open the back door by the kitchen. I hear whispering and giggling. I close the door quietly. I walk through the kitchen to its doorway. I look down the hallway. She's a pretty lady, and Dad's on the couch with her. Dad holds the pretty lady. They kiss. They pull away. The pretty lady is kind of slumped, and Dad combs away the hair from her forehead like Mom does to me. I return to the back door, open it, let it slam closed. I wait. The whispering and giggling suddenly stop.

"Son," says Dad.

"I'm just getting something. I'll be back for dinner."

"This is Megan."

The woman waves.

"She's a student of mine." Dad says. "A grad student doing her thesis. *Oh—*" he says, "it's all meaningless to you yet."

I nod, get the ball, and go back outside.

Mom returns. She spends a week in her room. She won't let me in. She'll talk through the closed door if I bother her long enough.

"Who is it?" she asks.

"Me."

"Who?"

"Me, Mom, *it's me.*"

Silence.

"Mom?"

Silence.

I stand there and wait and then leave.

The bag is filled with ants. It stinks worse than a fart, worse than the dirty Hudson River, so I figure there's a whole lot of trapped black cat ghost. I put the bag over my nose and mouth. I can barely stand it. I inhale quickly. It smells so bad that I taste it. I cough, I choke, I gag, I want to vomit.

"Make Mom happy again."

I climb down the tree. On the ground, I look at the bag high up.

"And I still don't make a sound when I laugh."

I go upstairs quickly. In the elevator I run in place, imagining Mom dressed and awake. I will say I want a grilled cheese.

Jordan and Daniel sit in the living room. They look at me, but don't say anything. Dad and Mrs. Babcock are in the dining room. Mrs. Babcock rubs Dad's back.

I walk in.

"Where's Mom?"

Mrs. Babcock puts her hands on my shoulders. "It'll be all right, hot stuff."

I look at Dad, then back to Mrs. Babcock. "I want a grilled cheese."

Mrs. Babcock smiles at me then turns to Dad. "It means it wasn't healthy," she says to him.

I walk into the living room.

"Where's Mom?"

"They took her," Jordan says.

"Who?"

"The paramedics," he says.

"Will she be back soon?"

Jordan looks at me. But he doesn't say, *Shut Up,* or *Get outta here, scrub.* He says, real soft. "I don't know."

I walk into Mom and Dad's room. It's quiet, it smells of cloth and breath. I crawl into their bed. I put my face in a pillow. It's warm still from Mom. I breathe in and smell her. I curl up in the middle of the bed. I feel the cold of it first, then I see it. A circle of blood. I scream. Dad runs in. He sees me. I sit up quickly. His face gets hard. Angry vein. He puts his hand out. I flinch. He grabs me. He hugs me. Hard.

"Shh-shh," he says.

"Is Mom dead?"

"No," he says. He's shaking. "Sick. It must have been sick," he says.

I climb the gingko tree. It is very bright out, but cold. Wind blows, making the heavy branches sway, the new spring leaves rasp like metal. I open the bag. The mouth is open, the tongue swollen. Its black face is rotted away, dry red flesh.

"Stop it!" I scream.

I put the cat in the bag and shake it.

"I say what happens! I say what happens!"

The wind blows hard and the limbs sway, trying to shake me off.

I am asleep. I hear Mom come home. Dad talks, Jordan talks. Soft. Mom doesn't talk. I hear her walking. Footsteps like whispers. Daniel mumbles something, Dad tells him to hush. A bedroom door closes.

In the morning Mom isn't up. Dad makes me Pop-Tarts. He kisses me on the top of the head. I freeze. Then I look, and Dad's down the hallway. And I wonder if I just made the kissing up in my head.

I hear the brothers laughing. I go to their room. Jordan makes fun of Mom.

"Did you see that fruitcake last night?" he laughs. He walks in circles, dragging his feet. "Woe-is-me, *Woooe-is-me!*" He laughs hard.

Daniel throws his hands in the air and howls, following Jordan as he circles.

I laugh.

Dad walks by the door. We go quiet. We wait. We can't hold it. We bust open and laugh and laugh.

Mrs. Lumis leads us outside to the playground.

We play Kill the Carrier. Mark, who we call Fairy because he's always laughing with the girls, picks up the Kill the Carrier ball that's rolled over to him and the group of girls, including Darla, he sits with. He stands to give it back. I charge.

"I'm not playing, I'm not playing," he screams.

I dive. We fall to the cement ground. I feel my elbow skin scrapping away against the cement. I punch him on the shoul-

ders and side. *"Kill the Carrier. Fairy, Fairy."* He clings to the
ball. I rip it away. He's curled on his side. He's crying and
crying. The other boys circle him. *"Fairy, Fairy, Fairy."* I
move away, still holding the ball. I run through the playground and down the stairs, onto the street, and I run until I
reach the shadows under the overpass, where the street runs
onto the Henry Hudson Parkway. It's dark and the ground is
soft from the garbage that gets caught here, turned to black
mush from the car soot and the water that puddles here, and it
smells of piss and b.o. from the bums and shell-shockers who
drink Thunderbird here, who sleep here in cardboard boxes.

Darla walks down the staircase and onto the sidewalk. She
squints into the overpass until she finds me. She stares at me,
then she turns and runs back up the stairs to the playground,
which I can hear loud in the distance.

I get home before anyone else. The apartment is perfectly
quiet. I have a note from the principal to be signed for hitting
Mark. I stand outside the bedroom door. I'll get Mom to sign
it. She's a fruitcake. I open the door. She's lying in bed. She
doesn't look over.

"Sign this." I shove the paper and pen at her.

She takes the pen and signs the paper without looking.

I turn away.

"Honey . . ." Her voice, dry and far away, deep inside her.

I turn back.

She blinks, her eyes sparkle.

I crawl into her bed. She wraps me in her arms. She cries,
hot tears, hot breath on my head.

"She would have been an angel."

"Who?"

"But, here you are already. My angel . . ."

I sit up.

Mom pulls out a scarf from under the covers. "I found this," she says. "Smell." She puts it to my nose.

It smells pretty, like flowers, like the cherry blossoms blooming in the park. I close my eyes and breathe deep.

"You like it, honey?"

I open my eyes and nod.

"Is she pretty? Pretty as this pretty smelling scarf?"

I move away, stand.

"Prettier than your own mother?" Mom's eyes are loose, like two rocks falling through dark water. She smiles, crazy-woman fruitcake smile on the side of her face. And then laughing as she shoves the scarf at me. "Smell again, smell again."

I run out of the room, I crawl deep into the clothes hamper. I hear Mom, her feet scraping along the floor. *Honey, Honey.* The front door opens. I remember. Tuesday. The day Dad gets home early. He says, *What the . . . ?* Then, *Okay, okay.* He walks her back to bed. It's quiet again. I get out of the clothes hamper. On the hallway wall opposite the living room is a mirror. I watch Dad in it, sitting at his work area, his jaw tight, working on his miniature, blinking, blinking, blinking.

Mom is gone again. She leaves for a few weeks. Dad says, To rest.

"Where?" I ask.

"A nice place."

"Yes, but where?"

"I told you."

"Why?"

"For a rest," he says. "To rest."

Everyone's out. It's warm like summer, almost. Me and Reid lean against a building, the sidewalk warm from the sun, eating Mariano's Italian Ices, mixing in 7UP so they fizz. Down the block, Jordan's hanging out with the Big Kids telling them a story. Jimmy's listening, laughing at what Jordan's doing. Jordan pretends to cry, then he puts a finger to each temple, and begins to shake like he's being electrocuted. He takes his fingers away and rolls his eyes up and walks like Frankenstein. He laughs, *A-ha ha ha*. The other kids hoot, then settle down.

"What's your brother going on about?" asks Reid.

I shrug. I fling some cherry ice, watching it melt and stain the sidewalk.

Jimmy runs over, laughing rodent *hee-hee-hee*s. He points at me. "Your mother's got scrambled eggs for brains," he says. He pretends to be electrocuted like Jordan did. "They shocked her 'cause she was crazy."

I stand up.

"Take that back, Growler."

Jimmy starts jumping up and down. *"Scrambled eggs brain, scrambled eggs brain, your brother says your mother got scrambled eggs brain!"*

I push Jimmy.

"Quit it, faggot," he says.

I push him harder, so he falls.

"What?" he says. "Your brother said." Jimmy's top lip starts to tremble like it does whenever he's about to cry.

I sit back down and eat my Italian ice. Reid flings a piece of his grape ice, which melts purple next to my red. I look at him. He smiles.

⌒

Mom comes home. She smiles a lot and makes our meals like before. She is dressed by 8 A.M. I won't talk to her.

"You're scared of me," she says.

We're in the living room. Mom sits on the couch running her finger back and forth over the brown corduroy cushion.

Dad's miniature is done and on the stand in the hallway. Around his work desk are drawings for the next one. I stand in front of Mom. She takes hold of my hands, pulls. I won't budge. She lets go.

I turn my back to Mom and stare at Dad's work area.

"Dad always did miniatures?"

"Yes," she says. "Well, no."

I turn back, facing her.

"He was trained as an architect. Was training, actually. Almost trained."

I don't know what that is, or understand what she's saying.

"But, Jordan came along. Then two years later, Daniel. So—"

Mom shakes her head. I look at her pale eyes. No one else has pale eyes. We have eyes like Dad, dark brown, almost black. Her skin, pale. Our skin, like Dad's, a little tanned. I've never noticed that before.

"Do you know where I was?" she asks.

"Are you going back away?"

"No."

I shrug.

"My special little lamb."

"Tell me a story."

Mom smiles. "A ghost story . . . ?" She begins. A big house, a sad family. A daughter, the youngest, a mere child, has died. A family in heavy grieving. Sounds: creaking floorboards. Then lights switching mysteriously on, breathing, pockets of cold air.

I sit down. I stare at Mom. I see the story in my head like watching TV, but also I just see Mom, sitting there, telling me a story.

It's June. School's over, and tomorrow we're flying to see
Granpa's headstone. Then we're going away for the summer
to Massachusetts. I go out for a final night with The Block.
The sun is setting pink and orange over the Hudson. The sidewalk is colorful with chalk drawings, hopscotch squares from
the day, pale now and dusty, rubbing away. A fire hydrant is
open. Ice cream wrappers and bottles and bags rush on the
stream down the gutter, clogging the drain at the corner. A
turning pool grows across the Drive. Darla wears clear green
plastic sandals and she splashes in the puddles.

"Hey, you," she calls. "Where you going?"

I shrug and walk into the park. I hear her soggy steps. I
stop.

"Why you following?"

She looks away, leaning against the blue chain-link fence
along the park, her back to me.

I walk to the ginkgo tree. I climb it. She jumps below, trying to reach the branch.

"Quit following!"

"I'm not following. So I wanna climb. Is it your tree?"

I turn and climb farther up. Darla can't reach the bottom
branch.

I climb down and put my arm out. Darla looks at my hand.

"Okay, but I could've done it."

We climb the tree in silence.

The bag's still there. It's bleached and torn. I open it up.
Patches of flesh and hair sprout from the skeleton. The bones
are colorless.

"A cat," I say, holding it up for her.

"Is it yours? Why do you have it for, you?"

"Why do you call me *you*?"

Darla smiles. "Ewe," she says.

"Yes: *you*, "I say.

"No. Ewe: *e-w-e*. It's a sheep. It's got curly hair like you. And sometimes it's crabby. A girl sheep, actually." Darla shrugs and smiles.

We look at each other. I hold the cat by the rope.

I look at the skinny bones. It's only a dead cat now. Rotted. And these are just bones.

"It did magic. I think it did, anyway. For a while. I don't know that it can do magic anymore. Maybe it can," I say.

Darla's looking off, not listening anymore.

The sun falls behind the river and the red sky turns to a purple sky, night coming. The tree, full of leaves, rustles over-head. Little lights glow in the soft dark air.

"Oh," says Darla, "fireflies."

Little lights pulse without a sound around us, like a sky of fallen stars. It makes me dizzy, I lean into Darla. Our faces are close. I right myself and we don't touch. We sit quietly. Far below, kids fill the streets and the park, making a buzzing. Jermaine hooks his turntable up to the streetlight and there's music. Darla moves her hand over mine. I look at her. We both look up and away, and she squeezes my hand tight as the stars appear, one by one, in the night sky.

five

Son of Sam has hunted again. In Queens. Darla lived in Queens before she came back home. Now it's ten shot, five killed.

I scream, *"Quit it, quit it!"* I thrash, then I go still. Blood rushes to my head, white sparks flash in my eyes.

Matthew McCourt holds me upside down over the edge of the McCourts' deck, which hangs over the lake.

I wonder what lives inside Son of Sam. It must be something horrible, some sort of horrible animal that lives inside him, driving him to hunt, to kill.

The other teenagers gather and watch. The McCourts: Matthew, Peter, John, Luke. The brothers. The others from town. They drink cocktails from mason jars, smoke Mary Jane out of bongs, bop to "Smoke on the Water" and "Free Bird." Their faces are dazed, eyes shiny and red like marble doll eyes. Wasted, they say. *I'm fuckin' wasted, man. Hu-hu.*

"Le'me go!"

"Hu-hu," they laugh. Matthew McCourt looks at the others. "Should I?"

Sometimes I want to hurt, to break things. Sometimes I get so mad I can't feel myself. And *the mad* feels like a thing inside me that won't go away until I scream, stomp, break something.

The water under the deck is in shadow. Then, there's the lawn that leads to sliding glass doors of the first floor. And I see her. The youngest McCourt, Robin, fourteen years old. She sits on the grass by the water. She watches me. I try to smile. She shrugs, stands, goes inside.

I am falling. I look back up. The teenagers hang over the railing, watching, laughing. Then suddenly, water. Cold. Quiet. I float below. I don't want to come back up. They will laugh more. I'm out of breath. I come up. I look. No one is there.

I swim to shore, sit on the lawn.

I hate Massachusetts. We've been here two weeks and I don't have any friends. Every morning the brothers run out of the house and down the street to the McCourts'. I sit alone all day. I sit in the yard, I sit in the garage, moving whenever Mom or Dad come near. They touch all the time now, always touching and smiling and giggling.

I walk inside. The first floor is bright and neat with furniture and short glass tables, a bar with cream padding and high swivel stools. I smell cigarette. I follow. I walk through another door and down a dark hallway to the basement. In the corner I see a bobbing orange cinder.

The cinder glows. Robin's face, then darkness.

In the daylight I watch her standing on a dock, hair pulled back from a dive, her hip to the side, sticking her chin out.

The room suddenly lights up and the pack of teenagers walk in. Robin drops her cigarette into an empty soda can. It makes a small hiss, sends out a wisp of smoke.

"On the mat," someone says. In the center of the room is a large blue gymnastic mat.

The teenagers crawl around the mat and I follow Robin through the moving bodies.

The lights go out. The bodies start shoving. Little moans rise up. The shoving gets rougher: pushing and pulling, rubbing and grabbing. I don't know what I'm supposed to be doing so I stay still. I feel a hand grab at my privates, then move away. I ball up. I look at the teenagers, a shadow body with many arms and legs, grabbing and kneading.

The lights go on. Bodies are twisted with other bodies. The light catches people: their hands up a shirt, cupped between legs, face pressed into a behind. Those people are ordered off the mat. They make a circle around the mat, and in the dark they chant. *"Feel it, steal it, too dark t' reveal it . . ."*

The lights go on and off, on and off until the only people left are me, Jordan, Robin McCourt, and Matthew McCourt. When the lights come on next, Matthew's tanned hands press down on Robin's little boobies, and the knuckles of Jordan's hand beneath Robin's bikini bottom looks like an oyster shell.

Invisible in the dark, I lie very still beside Robin.

Feel it, steal it, too dark t' reveal it.
Feel it, steal it, too dark t' reveal it.
Feel it, steal it, too dark t' reveal it.

Robin's leg moves over my front. She fingers my hair and presses her body against me. I jerk, lay my hand on her leg. I feel the round of her behind and the smooth fabric of her bikini. I close my eyes. I listen to the chanting. I feel dizzy, like I'm spinning, rising up. I move my hand, slow then fast until it makes heat. My fingers slip below the elastic of her bikini. I breathe out. I grab. I grab with both hands. I grab hard and squeeze. I grit my teeth.

I see a flash behind my eyes, a blow to my face. I fall backward. The light comes on. Robin stands over me, hand still balled in a fist.

The circle freezes, open mouths.

Robin leans over and whispers, "How could you be so rough? You're a kid."

I sit up and run through the crowd, up the stairs and out the door, and on the street, and I run until I reach home.

The front lawn of our rented cottage presses up against the lake, and out on the lake, a wooden dock.

I hold Mona on my lap, swinging my legs, toes skimming the water.

Me and her talk about things. We talk about the blood on Mom's bed before she got scrambled eggs brain. Mona thinks that one has to do with the other. I tell her I don't think so.

We're quiet.

Then Mona says, *She did ask if you wanted to know. Remember?*

"She asked 'cause she knew I was gonna say no."

You don't wanna know?

"I do."

You think it was 'cause of the black cat, huh?

I shrug.

You should just ask her.

I don't say anything.

I think you like not knowing.

I hold the photo very close, until she doesn't have a face anymore. All dots, gray and white and black.

The sun is very bright, the lake blazes like a mirror.

Mom walks out of the house. I turn. Her eyes squint

against the sudden blinding brightness. Blood rises pink on her pale skin. She tilts her head, smiles. Wind off the lake makes her nightgown flutter, opening and closing below the belt, showing her thighs spotted with pale red. She fingers her messy hair, until the bed-head tangles are flat and long.

I lower myself carefully into the water, then under the dock.

Dad walks out behind her. She turns her head. Dad wears swimming shorts. His chest and stomach hair is moist flat ringlets. His skin, from the sun, is dark as a bitten apple left out too long.

Mom turns her head back out toward the lake. From behind, Dad wraps his hands around her waist, and she rolls her head onto his shoulder. They sway back and forth, their faces side by side. Dad's eyes are smaller, and in the sun they crinkle up, sweet like an animal's. Dad lets go and walks to the edge of the lawn and dives in. I watch as he swims past, a blue wake.

I turn and watch Mom. Her mouth moves. She laughs, like someone just told her a joke over her shoulder. She squints into the water.

I walk through the house.

I left Mona on the dock, but I still hear her stupid voice, *I think you like not knowing* . . . But, that's not true. I do want to know.

I sit at the little desk that looks out to the trees by the side of the house. On top is a neat stack of notebooks and a box of pens. Mom's writing desk. But, after Granpa died, and after Mom left blood on her bed and got scrambled eggs brain, I haven't seen her write even once.

How will I ask? *Mom? Did you get scrambled eggs brain 'cause you made all that blood?* . . . No. *Mom? Jordan says you went to the funny farm 'cause—* I think hard. I know what Mona would say. She'd say, *Just ask her.* Okay. I'll say, "Mom, where did you go? Why was there blood on your bed?" I close my eyes, and rehearse the lines a few times. I see myself, and Mom. Her eyes get sparkly and she says—

"Honey, I thought you were with the older boys."

I open my eyes, and turn and look at her standing over me. "I was," I say. *Ask,* I think, *ask.* We look at each other.

I run my finger over the spiral binding of a notebook, making the coils plink.

Mom looks at the notebooks. "You shouldn't hang around inside." She puts her hand on the back of my head and gently pushes, making me stand. "You're wet. You shouldn't sit on the furniture wet."

"Are you going to do some writing now?"

Mom's eyebrows go up like she's surprised, then pushes me to the door.

I sit on the dock. I watch Dad do laps. The windows of the house are white from the sun. I listen to the water slap against the land, the trees shush in the lazy, hot wind. I watch the shirts and socks and shorts on the clothesline flap. I wish I had a clothes hamper like the one at home. I pick up Mona. Her gold frame is hot from the sun. I take my wet shirt off and press her against my chest, and it burns.

six

I walk for a long time around the whole lake. Past all the houses and the people. I walk along it where it's foresty and nothing else.

I run quickly. Into the forest, hopping a small stream, over branches, a log ahead. In the air, a thin branch snags my sneaker lace, sending me forward. I see a boy sitting on the other side, holding a magnifying glass. His eyes open wide. I fall on top of him.

We lie sprawled. He looks at me, then turns away, picks up the magnifying glass. He inspects fallen leaves, rotting bark of the fallen log. From a distance I watch the warped, magnified bits. He sees me watching. He hands me the magnifying glass. I crouch close to the ground and crawl. The forest floor squirms alive. Colors like islands on fallen leaves. Ants, green caterpillars with red and black diamond backs.

I hand the glass back to the boy. We begin walking, picking

up walking sticks that we swat at the ground, at the air and trees. We sprint through a clearing, jumping high, falling into the deep cold blue water. I am again alone. Silent. Rising back up, I breathe out hard into the afternoon sun.

"I won," he says.

"No way," I say, slapping the water.

"Sure I did."

"Aw, crap."

I push his face and he pushes mine.

"Fine," I say. I pull myself up the mossy side. I walk away.

"Hey," he calls from the water.

"What?"

"Where you live?"

"The white house with the wooden dock. Know it?"

He nods. "I'm on the other side of the woods. The one with the big bubble window."

I sit in the kitchen alone. Jordan and Robin are lying on the floating dock in the middle of the lake. They're going out now. Daniel left a little while ago, eyes red, smelling like sweet smoke, a pad and watercolors in Mom's PBS tote bag over his shoulder. I followed him down the walkway and asked, "Where you going? Can I come?" He got on his bike, without a word, and rode off. Mom and Dad took the station wagon to the supermarket.

I've played three games of paper towel basketball with the trash can hoop. I've made two iced teas. I've looked at the top shelves. I found a box of wooden matches, baker's chocolate (which wasn't going to fool me again), a bag of cookies. I ate five.

Other teenagers sit on the floating dock with Jordan and Robin now. I eat an apple, a fistful of raisins, a slice of bread with butter, two more cookies.

I get the phone book. I giggle. We do this in New York. Me and Daniel. Daniel, mainly. I just listen on the other phone and laugh.

He calls and says in a loopy voice, "Hi. This is Oliver. Charlie told me to call, says your radiator is kaplooie."

The person gets confused, saying, "I don't know any Charlie, my radiator's—"

But, we hang up. We laugh like crazy. We wait a minute, then call back.

This time his voice is thick and choppy. "Ay, hi-ya, this's Charlie. Right, right: Charlie. I just got off with Oliver. Tolds me you don't want your radiator fixed. Din'ya tell me it's gone kaplooie on ya, mac?"

The person goes haywire, hollering and screaming.

That's the best.

I dial a number. I shake. Ringing.

A man. "Hello?"

I open my mouth. *What's it again? I'm Oliver, and* . . .

"Hello? Who is this?"

"Shit on you!" I hang up. My heart beats. I look around. It's quiet. I get another cookie.

I open the book, flip for a new number. I put my hand on the receiver. The phone rings. I jerk back. It rings again. I answer.

"Hello?"

It's a woman. She wants Dad. He's out, I tell her, with Mom, shopping. She says, Oh. I ask if she wants Dad to call back. The woman laughs, Yeah right. What? I ask. She says, nasty, Oh, no. Please. Let me. Then she hangs up.

I sit at Mom's desk and open one of her writing pads. Each page is blank. I take out another and another until I've flipped through and found each book blank.

I put the books back. I leave.

*   *   *

I walk slowly up to the house. It's quiet, then there's a man's voice.

"This place is a fucking sty."

The boy from the woods walks out of the house holding a box filled with unbagged trash: chip bags, soup cans, beer cans. He sees me and smiles. He walks to the side of the house and tosses the box next to some garbage cans.

"The old man's in a flare," he says, pointing with his thumb.

He speaks like an older boy. He has pale smooth skin, tiny faint freckles on his nose, and he must have just finished a Popsicle because his lips are stained bright red and I want to touch them.

"Wanna do something?" I ask.

"Le'me get my stuff."

He returns with a small canvas bag over his shoulder.

His name is Joey and he's ten. His parents are divorced, or "split," as Joey puts it. Joey and his brother and father have been living in Pittsfield for nine months.

"But that's a while, man," he says. He smiles. "My old man's always singing that song. You know."

I nod as he sings, even though I don't.

"Lord I was born a Ramblin' Man.
Tryin'a make a livin' an' doin' the best I can."

"We've never stayed anywhere, that I can remember, for more than a year," Joey says.

We reach the end of the driveway, and begin along the road, taking turns kicking a beer can bleached on one side from the sun.

"So, you've been allota places?"

"Seems damn near every place."

"Ever been to New York?"

"Buffalo once, for the summer and fall."

He kicks the can into a bramble of honeysuckle.

I have never moved.

We each pluck a white honeysuckle flower and suck out the goo.

We walk to town. The main strip is filled with bathing suit stores, bars, an arcade, an ice cream shop, and a burger joint. The street is crowded with teenagers in bathing suits, cars driving by playing Marshall Tucker and Steve Miller and Fleetwood Mac.

"It's a hot one today," Joey says. "Must be damn near ninety degrees."

"Damn near a hundred," I say, looking at Joey, then away.

"You got any money?" he asks, wiping the sweat from his face. "Don't you wish you had a soda?"

I nod.

The strip ends where the lake gets fat and there's sand. Along the beach are more shops and restaurants. Joey puts his fingers into the coin-return slot of a pay phone. We walk into a shop and stand in front of a cooler of soda. I can see Joey's thinking, but the man behind the counter watches us. We leave. We pass a restaurant with outside seating. Joey stops, eyeing a couple as they get up to leave. The man leaves some money in a tray.

"It's like your mouth's a desert, right?" he asks.

"Yeah." I reach into my pocket, hoping magically there might be a few quarters.

The couple walks off along the footpath. Joey looks this way and that way. He goes to the table, takes the money off the table.

"What're you doing?" I whisper, standing back.

Joey glances at me, smirking. He counts it.

"The waiter's coming," I say. I step forward, pull on his shirt.

The waiter runs toward us. Joey puts the money in his bag. He looks at the waiter, then right as the waiter reaches us, Joey pulls out a chair. The waiter smashes into it, stumbling.

Joey grabs me. We run. We run fast and we laugh, and I look at Joey, his head bobbing, laughing, dark blue eyes like the deep lake: secretive and thrilling and breath-holding and terrifying and alive.

～

Mom and Dad are out front. Mom is husking corn and Dad is lighting the barbecue. The sun sets over the lake behind the trees and the air cools. Mourning doves coo. I go inside, check Mom's pads. Blank. The back door opens. Mom walks in with a plate of cleaned corn.

"Hi, honey."

The phone rings in the kitchen. She jogs in, puts the corn down.

"Hello?" she says, smiling. She waits, then again, "Hello?" She hangs up the receiver. She blinks, then looks at me and smiles.

I walk out of the house. Dad's standing on the end of the dock. I walk out. The water is dark, rolling, catching the pink evening sky. The brothers are far down on the rim of the lake walking toward home. Dad's face is relaxed. He holds wine. He smiles at me. I walk to the edge of the dock and feel the water. I stand up in front of Dad. I turn my head.

"We're having burgers tonight?"

"Yes," he says. He looks back out to the water, and so do I. I feel his hand touch my shoulder. I stand still for a moment, then I lean back into his large body. He moves his hand over my chest and pulls me closer, holding me tight against his breathing stomach.

✑

It's a big house, red and faded like a barn. Joey knows it because it belongs to *the sour old fart* that rents the house to his family. He's old, wife dead, children grown. The house is down a long dirt road through the forest, then up a hill, a long staircase. Because the man is so old, he doesn't use the house anymore.

Joey takes a screwdriver out of his bag, and unscrews the doorknob. As he fidgets, he says, "I'm so sick of moving all the time. I sometimes think I should just split." The doorknob falls off, leaving a hole. Joey looks over at me.

"Yeah," I say.

He pokes around inside the hole. "If my old man moves us again, I'm gonna run off. I swear. I'll stay here." There's a click, and the door opens. Joey stands and smiles. "You can come visit anytime."

The ceiling is high, and we run around and hoot, echoing. We go to the second floor, which overlooks the first floor. We throw things over, listening to the ways different things sound as they break. We climb on rafters and swing. It would be just like this, I think, if Joey ran off and stayed here and I visited. We run into a bedroom, and jump on the bed, flopping down then, laughing and panting. Joey stands up.

"Who am I?" He smokes an invisible joint, like one of the teenagers, making his face heavy and stupid. *"Yea . . . hea . . . hea . . . ,"* he imitates, exhaling the invisible smoke.

Laughing, I stand. I pull my shirt up to my chest and take off my shorts so I'm in my underwear. I smoke an invisible cigarette and stick out my butt and chest. *"Oh, baby I love you . . ."*

Joey walks like an ape. "You're so cool," I say. I hug Joey.

He says, "Babe, I wanna score on ya." He pushes me onto my back. He presses between my legs. We rub rub rub. *"Boo-hoo, boo-hoo,"* I say. "What's it, babe? Big daddy too large?" he asks. I smile. *"I'm being my mom,"* I explain. I close my eyes again. *"Boo-hoo."* Joey stops moving. I'm laughing and laughing. I wrap my legs tight around him, pushing my middle against him. It feels good. I open my eyes.

"You've seen your parents do it?" he asks.

I unclasp my legs. "No. Get off." I push him.

He rolls off me. "I don't care, man. I was just asking."

"Good for you." I roll onto my side, back to Joey. I look out the window. There's sky and a long field of high grass that whistles in the wind. I close my eyes and listen, pretending everything except for me and the sound has vanished.

I feel Joey's hand touch my shoulder.

I scoot forward. "Quit it."

We lie still for a long time.

His hand touches me again, his front presses against my back, his arms around me. We don't say anything.

I shake hard. *"It's hot."*

Joey sits up. He smushes my face. I feel his weight leave the bed. I listen to his footsteps down the hallway, down the stairs.

And then it's perfectly quiet except for my breathing and wind through the grass.

∽◌

Every day I check Mom's notebooks and every day I find all the pages still blank.

I sit on the couch with Mom and Dad. The news is on. They caught Son of Sam. His name is David Berkowitz, and he's a postal worker. It's hard to believe he's just a man. All he says is, "Well, you got me," just normal like that.

Robin stands off to the side waiting for Jordan. She comes and sits next to me.

"Haven't seen you in a while, squirt."

"Don't call me that."

We're quiet.

"Why'd you grab me so rough that day?" she whispers.

I look at Mom and Dad, but they're not paying attention. I look around. No Jordan. "That's what the others were doing," I whisper.

"I know they were." Robin stares at the TV.

I look at her profile. "I didn't mean to do it so rough. I'm sorry I did it so rough," I say.

Robin turns. She smiles, touches my arm. Jordan walks in, Robin stands. He wraps his arm around her neck, turns her to the door, and they're gone. A moment later, Daniel walks through the room and out the door.

I stay on the couch with Mom and Dad. The phone rings.

"Goodness," Mom says.

Dad smiles. He puts his hand on her thigh. "I'll get it."

The phone is on the other side of the house.

"Bedtime," Mom says.

I get up and walk through the dark house. I stand in front of my bedroom door. I can't see Dad in the shadows. I listen. Dad's voice is dark and hushed.

"I told you not to call. I'm trying here. Really trying." Then, silence. "In three weeks. *No.* We will talk then. Yes, okay, yes."

I look down the hallway at the back of Mom's head. Dad talks quiet, but if she wanted, Mom would be able to hear. I squint at her. *Listen* . . . I think. *Look up! Look up! I hate you. Look up!* I think. Mom shakes her head to something on TV. "Isn't that terrible," she says to herself. My heart beats fast, my feet move forward, toward Dad. Dad goes silent. He's a shadow. His head rises up, a hand over the mouthpiece. *Bedtime,* he says. My feet stop moving. His face, in the dark, looks like it's made of black sand. *Do you need water? The bathroom?* he asks. In the dark I can't see the angry vein, in the dark his face is soft, like it's not there, just dark air. *It's the pretty lady,* I hear myself say, *the pretty lady.* His voice louder, *Go to bed.* I turn and look at Mom. She turns and looks toward us in the dark shadows, then back to the TV. *Mom will hear,* I say. Dad whispers into the phone. He hangs up. *I'm your father,* he says, very low like his voice comes up from the floor. I can't move. I have to pee. *Don't you ever—* A finger comes at me. I back step, I turn, run. Bedroom door. Open. Close. Fall onto bed. Close eyes. *Shh, shh.* I hold my breath. The door opens. I'm in the air, lifted. A hand, hard across my face. Pop in my head, sparks in my eyes. I fall back onto the bed. *Challenge me, will you?* I hear. I'm spun, over bent legs. His hand comes down on my behind, very hard, harder than usual, like I'm wood, cracking. The hits feel like burning, then freezing, then they feel like nothing, like sound, and I'm deep inside my body. A little person, and my body is a big house. Outside is a foul, violent storm. It's raining against the house, *bam bam bam,* and there's a horrible wind: *challenge me, will you? cha-chu wee, ooo-ooo, shaa-shooo-wooo-ooo.* I lay on a soft shag rug. I'm very tired. It's nice to sleep to the sound of rain. Mmm, very sleepy. Is that Mom's voice? *What's going on?! What's going on?! Jesus, let him—!* Oh, Mom, it's just a storm. It's nice to sleep to. Dad was right, you're too . . . what did he call it? . . . *Emotional.* You're too emotional.

Mmm, sleepy. Very sleepy. Nice to sleep to rain.

Good night.

The birds wake me early. I sit up. My butt hurts. I frown. I stand and pull down my underwear and look at my behind in the mirror. It is very pale compared to my back and my legs dark with tan. There are little *purples* all over, like purple beetles. I get closer to the mirror. Like lines of marching beetles, three to a line, five lines, and they walk away from a big purple leaf, like a lily pad leaf. There are bunches of these. Beetles and lily pads, overlapping beetles and lily pads.

I lay on top of my covers. I hold Mona up.

"Isn't that weird?" I ask.

Mona just looks at me.

"I must have fallen last night. Maybe I fell when I was at that old man's house, running around crazy, smashing stuff up."

You never fell, Mona says.

"Sure I did. You weren't even there."

Quiet.

"What?" I ask.

I turn over, pulling the covers. I close my eyes. They open back up. Tears suddenly. And sound: *Ooo-hoo.* I fall back to sleep.

seven

Joey passes me the lighter after he lights one of the two cigarettes we've stolen from his brother. I watch Joey and copy
him, filling my cheeks with smoke, holding it, then blowing it
out slow in a long line. It's nasty and burns my mouth and
makes me dizzy and sick after a while, but it's cool.

I watch the smoke, swimming snakes, rising up into the
shafts of forest light. Around us are leaves with black burn
holes, from the sun directed through the magnifying glass.

Joey looks away.

"What?" I ask.

"My old man told me we were leaving at the end of the
week." Joey glances at me, then quickly away. He takes a deep
puff on his cigarette, leaving the tip dark with spit.

"Where you going?"

Joey taps the ash off his cigarette. "North Carolina."

"Where's that?"

Joey shakes his head.

"I wish my parents were split," I say.

Joey nods slowly. "Nah, you don't."

We puff in silence, until our filters turn from white to tan. Joey stands. We walk silently.

We walk beside the abandoned house on the edge of the lake. It's pale green. We hear music. *Sgt. Pepper's.* We look in the window. I see Daniel lying on the floor with some other teenagers. They stare at the ceiling. They don't talk, but sometimes they laugh, or nod and say, *Yea . . .* like they're watching a meteor shower. I look up at the ceiling but see only curls of peeling paint. The teenagers lie so they look like petals of a flower, and in the middle a tall purple bong. An older person walks through the room. He's a McCourt. Jude. He's super old. Twenty-six. He just got back. He was out-backing across the country for a few years. Before that, he was in the war, they say. He killed a lot of gooks, whoever they are. His hair is long and he has a beard and he wears a dirty army jacket with McCourt written over the right pocket. He walks into a different room. Me and Joey follow, look through a different window. He rolls up his sleeve. Above his elbow, he loops a leather belt tight across his arm. His forearm goes bright pink, bumpy veins rise. There are scabs there. In his mouth he holds a doctor's needle. He places the needle against his vein and slides it through the skin. In the plastic tube a small rose cloud puffs in the clear liquid. He pushes the lever, and the liquid disappears inside. He pulls the needle from his arm. A little blood dribbles out. He loosens the belt. He freezes for a moment, then his eyes close, his head sags, and his hand, before a tight fist, opens slowly.

Watching, it makes me think of Darla. I remember her mother, asleep in a chair. Asleep like Jude McCourt. A dead sleep, like she weighed a thousand pounds. I hold up the magnifying glass, directing the sun through the window, onto his arm. After a few moments, he jumps.

We crouch. I smile at Joey. We stand back up. Jude McCourt is asleep again.

We walk to the water. Joey places his bag on his lap and takes out a notebook. He looks out into the water.

Joey opens his notebook and begins writing.

"What are you doing?"

"What does it look like?"

I watch for a while.

"What do you write about?"

"Whatever. What I see or think. What I want, what I don't got. Sometimes I wonder about people, and I try to figure what they're like. Like you. You're real quiet some of the time, but you're always looking around. I wonder a lot what you're thinking, and sometimes I write what I think you're thinking." Joey's eyes go up and down over my face, like he's waiting to see if I'm going to make fun. Then, he kind of smiles.

I lie back.

He goes back to writing.

I think some more about Darla. I will see her soon. Does she look at my window? I think of The Block. I smile. I wonder what stupid thing they're arguing about now. I look at Joey. His face is bunched up as he writes. I stare at it hard. His face is right there. I think, He's right there and I can touch him. But soon he won't be. Soon he will be gone. And all the sudden it feels like I'm lying alone in the forest, remembering the day me and Joey were sitting here.

Joey looks over. "Wanna go for a swim?"

"We don't have our trunks, though."

"Neither does a dog, but he swims."

We strip naked and jump into the water. We don't play any

water games, and we don't dive below to search for turtles to bother. We swim out of the shadows of the trees into the sun that falls on our faces. I dive beneath the water and in the distance see the pink tentacles of Joey's body, skinny in the deep blue.

We swim back to the shadowed edge. A small cliff of earth rises a few feet up out of the water. We lie bobbing, breaking the water's surface with our knees, our bellies, holding on to roots that stick out of the dirt. Light falls through the trees onto the darkened water. Water laps in, making our floating bodies sway, our rubbery thighs knock.

"Summer's been a hoot."

"Damn near perfect."

I pull my legs up, and sit on the mossy lake floor.

"I once had this dead black cat. I put it in a bag to trap its ghost. I figured if I breathed it in, I'd be able to do stuff. And, I did, and I asked for stuff and stuff happened." I look at Joey. "You think that could be true?"

Joey shrugs. "You just said so."

I look out at the lake.

"I made Mom go crazy. They sent her away."

"She seems all right."

A leaf floats by. I blow on it, it spins.

"I asked to make sound when I laugh, but that didn't work. I don't make any sound when I laugh."

Joey nods. He picks up a pebble and tosses it. He turns. He tickles me. I squirm away, falling over. I laugh. "Stop!" He tickles. I laugh. I feel my stomach tighten, and my lungs fill, my mouth opens, and I shake. Silent. Joey's on top of me. My body is below water, my ears below water, my face above it. I see Joey laughing. I hear splashing water. The tickling hurts now. I look out. I see the trees overhead, the different greens of the leaves, some pale, some dark by how the sun hits. A group of crows sit on a branch. I see the blue sky, the shafts of light. I feel dizzy. I see Joey. His face is happy, it is wet. He loves me, he is going away.

He tickles tickles tickles tickles tickles and I can't breathe.

My body opens, from inside. Like doors, rooms inside rooms. The smallest room's door opens first, and the trapped air flows out, forcing the door of the next room to open, and the air pushes stronger, like wind, until the last door, right below my throat, opens, and the wind comes out of me. I laugh and laugh. The group of birds scatters. Ears still below the lake, I hear the shifting water. Joey lets go, and I sit up, ears in the air, and I listen to the sound of my laughter rise through the trees and over the lake and into the sky.

We sit quiet again, leaning against the wall of earth. I look up. Moss, white roots sticking out of the dirt; high up, little blades of grass lean over from the field on top.

"We'll see one another again," I say.

Joey bunches his lips, looks away, nods.

"Yeah," I say, smiling.

I push his face. He pushes mine. Soon the water's splashing up, catching the light. We lock arms and begin dunking each other, twisting each other's legs. Joey gets a strong hold and pushes me against the dirt. I fight against his grip, trying to push his leg out, to trip him. Our laughter is choppy. Our stomachs touch. Joey leans forward. I inhale the warmth of his breath and spit. His lips are dry. My hands fall, touching his side. He moves away. I put my arm out to touch him, then I let it fall. He grabs a thick root, and scales the little cliff, up to the grass. I watch from below as he dresses.

"I've got some stuff to do. I'll see you tomorrow."

"I'll come."

"No . . . I can't—"

"Can't what?"

Joey smiles. "I'll see you later?"

"Fine." I turn, sit back in the water.

Joey crouches over the earth above. He swats at my head.

"Quit it." I stand, slap his hand away.

He's quiet. He makes a smile. "Don't be mad, all right?"

"All right."

"Are you mad?"

I am mad, but I say, "I'm not mad."

Joey smiles down at me. I smile back. He stands. He runs off, bag bouncing at his back, and he is lost in the forest. I pull myself up to the grass. I stare at the empty forest for a long time, until the sun has dried my body. I think how I met him in the forest, and for some reason I can't move my eyes away. It's like I'm scared the second I do, the forest will have taken him back. For good.

❧

I go to Joey's house the next morning. Against the house is a line of garbage bags. The doors and windows are locked. On the front door is an envelope with my name on it. Inside are a letter and a gift.

We've left for N. Carolina earlier than expected. I'll write. Shit happens.

Yours, Joey

eight

We have two weeks left and I don't want to leave the house. Sometimes Mom or Dad make me go out. Then, I sit cross-legged on the dock.

The phone rings a lot and when Mom picks up, the other end goes dead.

"This crank calling is awful," she says, eyeing Dad. "This whole summer."

"Hmm?" he asks. "Yes," he says, frowning. "I know. I've called the phone company, but there isn't a thing they can do." Then he smiles. Mom smiles too. "We'll be home soon," he says.

I go to the old man's house. The door is still open. There are pine needles and leaves and dirt blown across the floor.

I walk in. "Joo-eey . . . *Joo-eey . . . !*"

My voice echoes. Then the house is quiet again, except for the wind outside in the field.

I find a broom. I sweep piles, then carry them outside. I leave, closing the door tight.

At dinner me and the brothers are told to pack our bags except for a few things. I pull the drawers out of the bureau and dump them upside down into a suitcase. I organize the things I've found over the summer: water-smoothed glass, a dried-out beetle, a bullet, sunglasses. I pack them. And last, Joey's letter. I take out the parting gift: the magnifying glass. I run my hand over it, imagining how his hand once touched it. I look at my fingers large through the glass. I look at the wooden drawer knob, carved into a rose. I find a cobweb between the bureau and the mirror. I rise up and look at myself in the mirror. The clear image curves and bubbles inside out. I lower the magnifying glass, and look at my reflection. I shove the magnifying glass between some clothing, shut the suitcase, and hook the clasps locked.

The phone rings. I answer it. Mom's outside watching the sky, Dad's in the bathroom.

"Hello?"

"—Yes, hello, is your father there, please?"

"Yes."

Quiet.

"May I have a word with him?"

"Who may I say is calling, please?"

"This is Megan. Megan Dunley."

"One minute, please."

I stand in front of the bathroom door. A line of yellow light comes through the crack below. I hear the page of a magazine turn. I smell the round, sweaty, peanut-y odor escaping under the door.

I turn.

Through the glass porch door, I see the moon's rising.

Behind, the western sky still has some deep sunlight. Mom stands by the water. I open the door.

"Mom! Phone!"

I race back into the house.

"Hello?" Mom says. She waits. "Yes?" She looks at me. She says that this is his wife. Mom nods and asks with whom she's speaking. *A student? Oh.* Mom says she understands. It's very hard working on such a large project. However, Mom says, she thinks that Dad prefers that his students get in touch through his service. *What is your disser—oh, you're helping him research his book? I didn't— Have we met? No . . .* Mom makes a weird smile, and looks at me again. She says that we'll be back in a week, and says that she'll tell Dad that she called. Mom says, *Good night, dear,* and hangs up.

"I think that was for your father."

"He was in the bathroom."

"That's fine. Have you packed?"

"Yes."

"Well, that's fine."

She turns and walks through the house and leaves. I watch the glass porch door bounce, until it sucks closed. I see my reflection far down the hall, small and transparent.

I wake up. It's night. 3:46. I feel for Mona under my pillow. I hold her. I open my door. The moon is bright and comes through the windows. I climb the stairs and open the door. Dad is on his side, back to Mom. I crouch down and look closely at his face. Asleep, it is a nice face. His mouth is closed. It is soft. His eyes are closed, they are soft. His arms are wrapped around his pillow. He breathes. Soft. I touch his arm, run my fingers over it. I touch his lips. I touch where the angry vein lies. His brow frowns a little. I feel the vein move slightly, like a snake sleeping beneath warm mud. I pull my fingers away. Mom is on her back. Her fingers twitch. I put my hand in hers. Her fingers curl over my hand. Her eyes open a crack. I freeze. A small smile on her face, then her eyes close. She mumbles something, then rolls over, letting my hand go. I look out the window. The moon, the lake. Everything is still, silent. I hold Mona up to the moonlight. I place her on their bureau. I turn, I leave.

It's morning. Mom's at her desk writing. It's early. No one else is up.

Her eyes look caved in, the skin around them, light purple. I look at the notebook, it's opened to the last quarter, the used pages to the left feather up with writing.

"This has been a good summer, don't you think? Wasn't it all one could have asked for?" she asks.

I don't know what to say.

Dad comes downstairs. He stops when he sees Mom at the desk. He blinks.

"Seems fall's in the air." He looks at me.

I nod. I leave the house. I sit below the window and listen.

"So, you're writing again?"

"I'm not blocked anymore."

A long quiet.

"It feels okay?"

"Yes, it feels okay."

A short quiet.

"It's just that before, remember? That the doctor suggested—"

"—Yes, I remember what he said," Mom says.

I walk across the grass still wet with dew. I run. Do cartwheels. A bunch. I get discombobulated. I land hard on my back. *Slam*. Feels like it's cracked. Maybe I won't ever be able to move. They'll just have to leave me here. They'll pack up

the car, they'll call me, time to go. Sorry, I'll say, cracked my
back, can't move. That makes me laugh and laugh.

⁓

For our last evening in Pittsfield there's a gathering at the
McCourt house. All the teenagers suck on bongs and drink
beer. They play music and the sky is crowded with stars. They
look like tiny pinpricks showing the light of something beautiful and large on the other side. Jordan and Robin sit apart
from the group, curled into each other, whispering.

Robin kisses me on the cheek and I walk home alone. Mom
and Dad sit out front, sipping wine, looking into the black
shushing lake. I sit at their feet.

"It's pretty," I say.

"Yes, lovely," says Mom.

"It's been a good summer," says Dad.

⁓

It's a sound I think I hear that wakes me. But, as I walk though
the house, the sun not above the horizon yet, the air lit, soft
dawn, I listen and hear nothing. I open doors and turn corners
and find only the still, unmoving house. I look outside. I see
Mom sitting on the dock. She looks weirdly heavy, like a bag
of sand. I walk outside and up along the dock. She doesn't
turn. A light wind makes her nightgown ripple over her still
back.

"Mom?"

I hear a drip, a long pause, then another drip.

Over her shoulder, I see that her lap is red, drenched in red.
The red creeps up the front of her nightgown. The red clings
to her legs, and runs off her thighs into raised puddles that run
across the wooden planks, dripping slowly into the water in

drops that stay whole, like red pebbles, before opening like red stars and vanishing into the dark. I look at her hands on her lap, laying palms up. The red runs out of long crossing gashes on each wrist.

She holds Mona in her hands. The red drips on the gold frame and runs across the glass, seeping beneath, trapped there.

Mom looks up. "What have I done?" she says very soft. She holds her hands up. The red is thick.

Beside her is her pad with her writing. The pages flap lightly in the breeze.

She looks at Mona.

I touch her. She looks up, head heavy. "Please," she says like breath. She lifts her hand to touch me, but it falls. Mona slips off her lap, face down in red. I pick Mona up. Mom slumps forward.

"No," I say. I shake Mom. Her head rocks. I crouch down. "Mom, forget it," I whisper. "It's nothing, Okay? Nothing. Just forget it. Mom?"

She lifts her head. Her eyes flutter. "Call . . . them. Doctor, Daddy . . . Daddy . . . ," she says, soft, almost not there.

I turn her hands over, so I don't have to see the red coming out. I sit next to her. I look at the lake. I feel wet on my legs: red. The sun pops up, bright, gold. A gold light fan across the water, a golden road.

"We'll go there," I say pointing at the golden road. "I'll get a boat. We'll sail into it." I turn. I lift Mom's chin. Her eyes open, slits.

"Please . . . ," she says. "Get . . ."

The gold light shines on her face, and it shines on the red like slices of metal.

I look back out to the water. Behind, a soft, thick thud. I turn.

Mom has fallen onto her side. She lies in the red. Her skin is pale, bluish. Her eyes roll up, her mouth opens. She is very still.

I shake her.

"Mom?"

I shake her harder.

"Mom?"

I let go. She rolls a little forward, her nose smushed, making slow bubbles in the red.

I pick up Mona. I run.

I've gone far on my bike. I don't know where I am. I am away. I am alive. I am free.

A cop passes, then turns and drives beside me.

"Son."

I pedal harder, I look forward.

The cop drives ahead and turns his car in front of me. He lifts me off the bike. The bike falls to the ground. He holds me in the air. I look forward. I pedal the air. I see the road. He talks. I do not hear. I am pedaling. I see the open road. I don't know where I am. I am away. I am alive. I am free.

⌒⌒

We drive home with Dad. Mom's getting home somehow else. Jordan sits in the front, in Mom's seat, which means I don't have to sit on the hump in the back. Jordan switches the radio stations until Dad finally yells. It is the first sound anyone has made in the hours of driving, and is the first sound since when? Since, I got home and I went into the woods and took off my red clothes, and I walked, naked, to the dock, and the red had been hosed away, but the dock was dark there, like a giant juice stain. And Dad was gone, but Jordan and Daniel were there, and they didn't say anything, except Jordan who

said, "Yes, yes," on the phone when Dad called, and after he
hung up he asked me and Daniel if we were packed, and we
both nodded. And Dad got home late and I heard him tell Jordan that Mom was going to be transported after she— But, I
covered my ears and those were the last words anyone spoke
until Dad yelled just now, because this morning we all woke
up, and we put our bags next to the U-Haul and Dad packed it
and we got in and drove, and Dad handed out Pop-Tarts and
apples for breakfast.

Jordan turns off the radio and it's silent except for the
sound of the wheels whirling on the highway.

I open the window and let the wind whip in my ear. Some
of Mom's papers from a box in the back of the station wagon
suddenly fly in the air. They flap against the windows and fly
into the front seats. Dad swerves the car, almost hitting
another car. He yells at me. I close my window.

We drive for hours.

Daniel looks pale. "I'm gonna be sick," he says.

Dad looks at him in the rearview mirror.

Dad pulls over to the highway shoulder. Daniel gets out,
crouches over. Nothing comes out. He breathes deep, then
gets back in the car. We get back on the highway. I watch the
U-Haul sway.

"I'm gonna be sick," Daniel says.

"Enough!" Dad yells.

Daniel closes his mouth.

Jordan looks at Dad, then clicks the radio on, low. Dad
doesn't turn.

"I'm gonna be sick."

Dad reaches around and slaps Daniel hard. The car
swerves. The U-Haul snakes sideways into the car. Dad
clutches the steering wheel. We're skidding across the lanes of
the highway. Sideways, spinning. We slam to a stop. We've

run off the side of the road. Dust floats up. It's evening. The dust turns orange in the setting sun. Cars whiz past on the highway. Dad releases the steering wheel. Daniel vomits on his lap.

Me and Jordan fall out of the car. Nasty! Dad leans forward and rests his head on the steering wheel. Daniel slowly opens his door. He stands with his arms out. I look at Dad. His shoulders are shaking. His window is open a crack. *Ooo hoo hoo hoo.* Daniel takes off his shirt and pants, throwing them into the brush, and he sits on the roadside in his underwear. Me and Jordan sit beside him. The sun sinks lower and it gets colder and Dad does not lift his head for a very long time.

nine

Jordan stands in front of the mirror, naked except for his new bikini underwear. He turns from side to side, then looks at me in the reflection.

"When you're a man you've gotta dress for the ladies," he says. He leans in, dots Clearasil on the pimples across his forehead.

On his bed, I lie on my back and drape his disco pants over my legs like a blanket. I mouth, *"When you're a man you've gotta—"*

Since getting home, Jordan doesn't kick me out as quick. Daniel still gets sick of me, like before. His face will get pinched and pouty and he'll push me, mumble, "Get out." But if Jordan doesn't pay attention, I'm in the clear. Then I'll give Daniel the finger, as if suddenly I'm one of the brothers.

Down the hallway the toilet flushes. I roll over. Jordan's eyes slide. His mouth pulls into a smile. He picks up the box of kitchen safety matches next to his skull bong. He runs into the hallway.

At the bathroom, Daniel tries to pass. Jordan puts his hands up. A spoiled hot smell floats out.

The first time Jordan did this, I stayed far down the hall and sneaked a watch. The next time, he nudged his head for me to come closer. Now, I know to run with him.

I make fists and think, *Get him.* I jump up and down hard.

Jordan lowers his head like a preacher. I go quiet, and silently repeat along with him:

"Oh, Lordy-Lord!" he says, raising his head, his arms. "I say there is a deep, *deep* funk possessing this bathroom—" Jordan strikes the match. "Be-gone evil odor from whence you came."

Jordan laughs, loud. *"A-ha ha!"*

I laugh, *"A-ha ha!"*

The smell of match mixes with the smell of diarrhea. Daniel edges past, his eyes rolled down looking somewhere between the floor and wall.

The front door opens. It's eight-thirty, Tuesday night. Mom and Dad are returning from a session. Mom walks into the hallway.

"He was in there again?" she asks.

We nod.

She looks at her fingers, turns. Her bedroom door closes.

Dad's in the living room, working on his miniature. I watch him from the hallway reflected in the fish-eye mirror on the opposite wall. In the mirror he looks huge with a rounded hunchback and arms that swell over the miniature, small and far away. He turns his head when I enter. Dad's making a miniature of the cottage we stayed in over the summer. He's even included the front lawn and the dock that goes out into the water.

"Are you gonna put the bat marks?"

"What bat marks?"

"Where the paint was chipped in the front of the house, where at night the bats ran into the house 'cause they're blind."

"If they're blind what would it matter if it was night?" Dad looks at me. "Bats have sonar. The chips were just old paint that was peeling," he says.

I nod.

"You're like your mother: a romantic."

I walk across the room, dark except for the corner of Dad's work area. I sit on the couch and think, I don't want to be like Mom, I don't want to be a *romantic*. I will look up what *romantic* means. Bats are blind, and night darkness doesn't make them *extra* blind. Blind is blind. I will remember this. Bats have sonar.

Mom walks in and sits next to me. She runs her hand through my hair.

"Daniel was in the bathroom again," she says.

Dad sighs, turns around. The light behind makes his front dark. I move my head, so Mom's hand can't touch me. She looks at me, then at Dad.

"Maybe he has allergies," Dad says.

"Yes, maybe." Mom says. "Maybe Steve's right."

"Let's not discuss this now," Dad says.

"Should I leave?" I ask.

"Don't you want to know who Steve is?" Mom asks.

I look at Dad. "No."

"He's the man who is helping Mom and Dad talk," she says.

"Don't force it on him," Dad says.

"I'm not forcing it on him."

"It bores him."

Mom turns to me. "Does it bore you, honey?"

I wish I knew what they were talking about. "It bores me."
I look at Dad. I ask, "Can I go now?"

"Certainly," he says.

I walk past him. He says, "Why don't you watch some TV."

I go to the dining room and turn on the TV.

In the morning, Dad's miniature of the summer cottage is on his desk, done. I'm glad too, because I'm sick of the old-fashioned house that's been on the miniature stand since before summer. When I get home from school the old-fash-ioned house is still there. I go to Dad's work area. The summer cottage is gone. Mom walks in.

"Are you looking for the miniature of the summer cottage?" she asks. "It's gone," she answers, smiling. "Your father made it for a friend." She walks into the kitchen to begin dinner.

"What are you, stupid?" says Jordan, who walks out of the other hallway.

"*What?* I didn't *say* nothing!" I back step.

He slaps me on the head. "Stop being such a baby," he says, walking away.

I wait in my room until dinner. It's late September, there's thick fog. The bottom of the courtyard vanishes into soft gray. Buildings far off are pale like trees deep in a forest after the rain. I imagine that I'm running into the forest, becoming lost. The can next to my window murmurs.

I freeze. I've told myself that I'm not allowed to do this any-more: hiding and watching. I look at my can. Across the court-yard I see them in the dining/living room. But, I think, they're not my family, so it isn't really cheating if I watch, right?

I put my ear to the can, but the voices are too far away.

Darla's mother yells something. Her lips out tight like a fish, opening wide, then back tight again. Her tongue lashes out, caught between her teeth, then it sucks back into her mouth.

I imitate her mouth, and make sounds, but I can't figure out the words.

Darla holds records tight to her chest. Her mother grabs for them. They struggle. Darla is little and her mother pries the records easily away.

Darla yells so loud I can hear it in my can.

I hate you!

Her mother slaps Darla, then turns. Darla stands alone, then she stomps to her room.

I can't move. I don't know why. I just stand and stare even when Darla looks up and across straight at me.

She picks up her can. I put the can to my ear.

"The bitch took my Dylan records."

"Who?"

"Bob Dylan?" she says, like I'm stupid.

"Oh," I say. "Why?"

" 'Cause she read he was becoming a Christian, called him a self-hating Jew."

"What's that?"

"How'm I supposed to know?"

There are sounds in the background. Darla rolls her eyes.

"She's just mad 'cause I told her I wanted to live with Daddy."

"Are you going away?"

Darla looks at me. "I wish."

I smile.

"Gotta go," she says, and she leaves.

*   *   *

Since we've gotten home from the summer, Dad isn't home on Wednesdays and Thursdays. When Dad's home the news is on. But, on these two nights we do other things. We play board games, or Mom reads us some of her poetry, or we play Go 'Round, where we write a story together, going around adding line after line. And sometimes we'll become very quiet, and I'll watch everyone. And sometimes I can't take it, and always afterward I feel bad for having done it, but before I can't help it, and I'll yell.

"Where is he?!"

Mom puts her hands to her face. Her sleeves slip down. Tears roll off her palms and down her wrists, forking at the raised smooth skin there. Skin like caterpillars. Mom doesn't show them much, and I usually forget. But, sometimes she forgets, when she's reaching forward or pulling back her hair, and then just for a moment. I see them and they look like trapped caterpillars.

"See what you did," Jordan says to me.

"Forget it, Mom," I say quickly. "I don't care. Really. Forget it."

Daniel hums, his eyes off to the side, gone.

Jordan looks at Mom. He says. "Why don't you change the locks? Why don't you do something?"

Mom sniffles, rubs her eyes clear. Then, she pulls on her sleeves, covering up her wrists. "Boys," she says.

"Forget it," I say, trying to smile. "Right?" I look at Jordan and Daniel. "Right?"

Mom continues, "We're—*Jordan, please*—" Jordan has gotten up from his seat, then he sits back down. "We're, your father and I, as you know, have been getting help." Mom tells us about Steve, their therapist. Mom says that the road will be rough, and she won't lie, they're on one particularly nasty patch right now, but, things will work out. Therapy will sort all the problems out. I repeat it in my head: *therapy*. Therapy will make everything okay. Mom keeps on talking, but I don't listen. I think, *therapy*, sounds like: *there-I'll-pee*. Like I've been holding it forever, and finally I see a place to go: there I'll pee, and, oh!, it feels good. Therapy. Mom says that Steve wants us to come in, and how do we feel about that? We shrug. Things will change, she says, therapy will change everything.

Mom smiles and clears the table.

Daniel stops humming. He pushes himself away from the table and walks quickly to the bathroom. We listen to the bathroom door close.

Jordan stands. I follow him. He walks past the bathroom into the bedroom. I wait in the hallway. He doesn't return. I go in. He's at his desk with schoolbooks.

What's he doing? He's ruining everything. I get the matches. I stand in front of the bathroom and wait. Daniel comes out. I lifted my arms, match ready.

"Oh Lordy-Lord . . . ," I say.

Daniel looks at me.

I lower my hands. Daniel pushes past me. I stand alone as the foul air drifts by me and into the rest of the apartment.

I turn off the hallway light and it's dark. "You said you wouldn't do this neither," I whisper to myself, but my hands and feet and arms and legs are already moving. I've opened the clothes hamper and have gotten in. I cover myself and curl up.

ten

My new teacher, Mrs. Eisen, likes me. Today we got the scores back on our first statewide reading test. I got a 5.5. Mrs. Eisen smiled at me all day, and didn't say anything when I went to the bathroom for over fifteen minutes, and she said, "I've seen your record, and I'll say, you sure have done a one-eighty. I keep wondering: what happened to this young man over the summer? And I think, whatever it is, I hope it pours down on him in buckets."

I just nodded and smiled.

This year's reading test had one story in common with last year's. The story of how limestone becomes marble. I remembered reading it last year, how bored I was, and how the words came apart. *Lime. Stone.* And I followed them around. I thought how lime was my favorite flavor of candy. Lime and lemon. Which, of course, made me think of Reid, because his favorite soda is 7UP, which is lemon-lime. And as I was thinking about this, the word *stone* floated down, and I tried to think what it had to do with Reid and 7UP. Then I remembered the day when I asked for a sip of his 7UP and he said, "What'll you give me?" And I took him down to the Hudson River where along it are these big stones, and one that I know of, is a seesaw stone. I showed him and we rocked, and he gave me a sip of his soda. As I was thinking this, Mrs. Lumis started tapping on the blackboard, telling us time was running out to complete the section, which I hadn't done much of. I looked at the questions. But, there wasn't anything about 7UP or the seesaw stone, and I just started filling in circles. But, then I stopped, and erased some and started making a fun pattern, which made me laugh, because it looked like snakes.

This year I remembered doing that last year. This year words began breaking apart also. Lincoln became *Link-on,* and I saw lots of linked black and white hands, and I thought, *Stop it, stop it!* The hands faded. I read the stories, and I read the questions and I answered them good.

⌒

The radio from the kitchen is playing. Mom spins out of the living room. "Dance with me."

She takes my hands and dips us back and forth. We stop dancing.

"Why're we dancing?"

She bites her lip, smiling, letting go.

We sit on the couch. Mom holds an envelope.

"A few days ago I got a call saying that I was being considered, and today I got a contract," she says.

She shows me the letter. I look back at Mom.

"I sold a poem, honey, I sold one."

She puts her hand on my head. I turn my face and rub it against her hand and wrist.

"I'll never forgive—" she says softly, letting the sentence go away. "It was as if I weren't even awake, as if it just—"

I close my eyes and continue to rub her wrist. I pretend I'm a clam or a small rock on the ocean floor, rocking gently, by swaying water.

"Everything will be fine in therapy, huh?" I ask, opening my eyes.

Mom smiles a little. "Something special came for you too," she says. "It's in your room."

It's propped beside the window. An envelope. I see my name and address written in his handwriting in the center, and I see his name and his North Carolina address in the upper left. For a moment his face flashes in my mind, silent, when I saw him last, his hair wet and the sun around him.

HEY YOU CRAZY MOTHER!!!!!!!!!

We are here in the south. It is all right. The south smells good. Difrent then there. Here it smells like flowers there it smells like green.

Dads got a good job. Says we are going to be here a while. We drove here and we drove threw ilands called the outer banks. They have white sand and wind. It is where the Wright brothers first flew.

My brother Greg found a mini bike at a dump and hes helping me get it up.

Please write and visit?! Your best friend.

Joey

I remember one day during the summer. I was coming back from peeing, and I saw Joey over Mom's desk, copying something off an envelope into his book. I was going to bust him, but he looked real quiet as he did it, like a deer or something. So, I back stepped into the kitchen, and hid around the corner and I called out, did he want an iced tea? We made them with a ton of sugar and I felt a buzzing in my head and we started running circles round and round the house until Dad came out and told us to do something constructive with our energy. Thinking of it now, I'm glad that I let him be, copying down my address.

I read the letter seven times.

"Hey, Ewe," I hear, the voice singsong.

Darla stands by her window with the can by her mouth.

"Hi," I say.

She cocks her head.

"What's shakin'?" she asks.

"Nothing."

"Liar."

"My mom says Bob Dylan sings like an alley cat," I say.

"Sure he does."

"Says he's a good poet though."

Darla nods.

"Could I come over sometime and hear him?"

"Over here?"

"I got a letter," I say. "From my friend, Joey."

"Uh-huh."

"He asked me to visit. I wish I could. I hate it here."

"When are you coming over?"

"Tomorrow."

At dinner the news is on. At a commercial I ask Dad how his friend liked the miniature. Dad looks up and across to Mom. Jordan kicks me under the table.

"*Ow!*"

"*Ooo-hoo-hoo,*" Jordan laughs. Daniel sits next to Jordan and they both smile, swaying, and they look like they used to: like the brothers.

Dad looks at them. Daniel looks down and Jordan looks right back at Dad.

"It wasn't nothing," I say.

Dad turns to me.

"It really wasn't nothing. I was just being romantic," I say.

"Wasn't *anything,*" Dad says.

I nod. *"Anything."*

The commercial ends. Dad turns to the TV, mumbling, *Sanctimonious drivel,* to something Jimmy Carter says. Then he says, *Horse's teeth, horse's ass. . . .*

⁓

I'm going long, my legs cramped and I breathe hard, after an afternoon of play, and it is getting dark in the cold fall evening sun. But, the ball will be coming: I'm going deep for the bomb. I duck my head and run hard. Reid covers me. I cut. Reid slips, falling face forward. The football arches through the air, vanishing against the dark trees. I reach out blindly. I like it: the cold crack against my hands, the cold thud against my chest.

I run. They chase. *Aaaahhhayiyiyi.* I dodge. Hands, Jimmy's, grabbing me, pulling at my sweater, fingernails scratching across my neck, I cut and he falls away. More hands, hard from behind. Max, lunging, arms around me. I hold the football tight. We come down, me on top of the football, Max on top of me. I open my mouth to get air. It won't go in. Fish, fish, I am like a fish, fish out of water. I roll on my back. I feel like I'm dying. Orange sky turning violet.

Max stands up. "You all right?"

I open my mouth, bobbing for air. Finally it catches and the air goes in. I cough, snotty spit that sticks to my chin. I laugh, I exhale, I say, "You mother, I almost had the touchdown."

We get in formation. Handoff to Ron. I block the charging defenders. Ron fumbles, live ball wild. I jump, everyone jumps. Kicking, pushing, scratching. Football rolls. Crawl, drag, punch, heaven.

We all lie, exhausted, on the dirt path next to the field, drinking soda, picking mud and grass off our knees, elbows, scraping dog crap off our sneaker bottoms. I see Darla cutting through the park along the tar walkway. She crosses the lower drive. I stand and toss the football up to myself. Darla walks to the no. 5 bus stop. I glance at the guys. They're not paying attention. I punt the ball. It goes into the street. I run to it. It rolls to the opposite curb near Darla. She picks it up.

"Hey, ugly."

"Stupid," she says. She tosses me the football. In her other hand she holds an envelope and two twenties.

I glance over my shoulder to the field, then back.

"Like you're going on the bus yourself."

She holds the envelope up. It says CON EDISON.

I don't know what that's supposed to mean.

"Electric company," she says. "I took the money from Dr. Dan's wallet. They called. Mom forgot to send in a check, I guess. Anyway, they're gonna turn off the power if they don't get their money by five."

"Where're they?"

"Downtown."

"The number five gets you to downtown?"

"I gotta get the crosstown at"—Darla looks at some writing on the envelope—"Forty-second. Then the Second Avenue farther down."

The bus comes. Darla gets on.

I walk back up the slope to the guys. They start making

fun, asking who my girlfriend is. Max says she's cute, that I should go for it. I tell him to shut the hell up.

⁓

Saturday it rains. The wind blows. The trees shake like they're scared.

I stand in the hallway and watch the rounded mirror on the wall opposite Dad's work area. Mom and Dad are in the mirror. Dad is sitting, sometimes turning his head to look at Mom standing behind. I move, and Mom's head is in the middle of the mirror, eye like a fat fish, Dad suddenly tiny, pea-headed, in the corner. Dad says, *There are things we shouldn't discuss.* I move down, and Mom's forehead swells, and I giggle. Mom asks, *What things—* And Dad says, *Megan.* I move again, and they both go small on either side. *They already know,* Mom says.

I stand up straight. I remember. I don't hide and listen anymore.

Dad says, *They don't know,* and Mom says, *Jordan's having sex, Daniel's—*

But, I hadn't meant to listen. I was just walking to the kitchen and I saw them in the mirror.

Mom asks, *Don't you think they wonder about Wednesday and Thursday?* And Dad answers, loud, *They can wonder till the cows come home. I won't have you—*

I stopped just because they looked funny in the fish-eye mirror, and I found if I moved, they squirmed around, stretching like rubber. It was just a game. And they happened to be talking, but I hadn't stopped to listen, I stopped to play.

They're quiet. *I got accepted,* Mom says. *A poem. To a little nothing literary magazine in the Midwest.* Dad spins in his chair to face Mom. He puts his hand on her hip. *Yes, I know,* Dad says. Mom blinks. I move, her head, her eye big in the middle.

I see little red veins around the blue, which goes kind of gray-ish. *They called,* Dad says. *A few days ago to confirm our address.* Mom moves away, and the bookcase billows out like a bubble. *What?* Dad asks. Dad says that he's been busy, very busy, and *Christ,* he says, *with all that's been going on. You, this summer . . . us never going to bed anymore. A person dries up,* he says. Mom's shaking her head. She moves forward. Her hip big again. Dad wraps his arms around her, puts his face to her stomach. I move. They both go far away, small in the mirror.

I look through my toy chest until I find her. I look at Mona.

"You're not real," I say. I've been remembering her and feeling bad, so I'm telling her now, "That's why I don't talk to you anymore." I look at her. "I saw a TV show once. There was a man and everyone picked on him. His wife, his boss, people on the street. So, one day his best friend took him to a head doctor and the head doctor hypnotized him. He said, 'I will count to ten and you won't remember a thing, but when you hear the words *sad sack*'—because that's what everyone called him—'you'll turn from scared and wimpy to strong and handsome.' "

I ask Mona what she thinks about the story. I ask Mona what she thinks my hypnotized word will be when we go to the head doctor.

I take Mona back to the chest. "I guess I won't talk to you anymore," I say.

I sit on my bed. There's an open map of the country I found in Dad's bookshelf. I look at the map for a long time. There are many places in the country.

A voice calls. I walk to the window and pick up the can. Darla stands in her room all dressed up in her Saturday Jewish clothes.

"I'm looking at a map," I tell her. I ask what she's doing home so early on a Saturday afternoon.

"I left," she says. "Mom's gonna have a spasm."

I nod.

"Wanna come over?" she asks.

"Sure."

"Bring your map."

Darla's apartment smells funny, like pea soup. She's changed and looks like Darla again.

"We gotta find my Dylan records," she says. "She always says she's gonna throw them out, but she never does. She just hides them for a while."

We go to her mother's room. The blinds are down. Darla opens her closet. The floor's filled with boxes. She tells me that the Dylan records were her father's: that he left them for her. Darla pulls out the boxes and begins opening them. Some are filled with clothing: colorful, thin shorts and miniskirts. One is filled with Christmas lights.

"Why do you keep this crap?" Darla says to herself.

I sit on the bed and look around. There's a drawing on the wall of a man with a big beard and two shields.

"Who's that guy?" I ask.

Darla glances over. "Moses," she says.

"He's someone you know?"

In our living room is a painting of Granma and Granpa. And in a frame are pencil drawings Dad did of Jordan when he was a baby.

Darla drags a chair over. "Come here," she orders.

I stand up. She hands me boxes from the top shelf.

"Well?" I ask, annoyed.

Darla steps off the chair. "I thought that was supposed to be funny."

I just look at her.

"Wandering through the desert? *The Ten Command-ments?!*"

I shake my head.

"He was the son of the Egyptian king, Pharaoh, who hated Jews. And Moses found out that he was adopted and that *he* was a Jew—"

"*No,* "I say. "What happened?"

Darla nods. "Right! So, he figured out his dad was a jerk, so he ran away from home."

"Then what?"

"He wandered for forty years. Led the Jews to Mount Sinai, where he gave them leadership and laws."

"Oh."

I open a box. It's filled with wigs.

"Ew!"

Darla smiles. "Gross, huh?"

We open another box. It's filled with brown prescription bottles. I know what they are because before Granpa died, he had lots of bottles like these.

"Your mom sick?" I ask.

"Her teeth," Darla says. She looks at me, then away. "They're bad, she has pain. Her boyfriend, Dr. Dan, he's a dentist. He gives them to her. The pills for her pain."

I nod. I look at the labels. *Purr-co-set, Val-ee-um.* Some I can't sound out.

Darla lies back on the bed.

"So what were you looking at a map for?" she says, look-ing at the ceiling.

I walk over. I show her the letter from Joey, pointing out his address.

"My friend," I say. "I wanted to see where he lived now." I open the map, hand it to her.

Darla nods, then stands up. "Maybe she did throw them

out this time," she says to herself. She looks at me. "Come on."

In her room she has a seven-record collection called *Hits of the '60s!*

"There's one Dylan song on this at least."

Darla sways, singing with Bob Dylan. *". . . accept that soon you'll be drenched to the bone . . ."*

I walk to her window and see my bedroom across the courtyard. It looks small. Inside it's dark and I see the shelves on the wall filled with books and toys. I don't like how I can see it all at once, like some dumb dollhouse. The door is open, and across the hallway I see a sliver of the brothers' room, and a small light, the sun behind the clouds over the Hudson River.

"He's boring," I say.

Darla shrugs, then lays on her side, her ear next to the speaker of her pink record player. She closes her eyes and silently mouths the words.

Bob Dylan mutters on.

I leave.

eleven

I'm dancing and singing to my K-Tel record. I turn it loud and spin fast to get dumb Bob Dylan out of my head. I didn't like how he sounded at all. Slow, like a lonely old hillbilly. He's stuck in my head, going on, over and over.

There's a knock on my door.

Darla breathes hard like she's been running.

"What do you want?" I ask.

Darla tries to catch her breath. "I hid 'em. The whole box of them." Darla goes to my window. I follow.

Her mother's in Darla's room. She flips Darla's bed over, pulls the drawers from a desk, dumps them. She stops. Her hair is messy, face red, wet. She looks up, sees us.

Darla turns to me. "Where do you hide?"

Her mother opens the window. "Darling, I'm sick."

Darla pulls us away from the window. Her mother continues to yell. Then it's quiet. We stand very still. Then: her mother's voice, Mom's voice. Darla opens the door. We stand in the dark hallway.

They're in his room. Is anything the matter? Mom asks. *By the way, how are you? I've been meaning—*

Darla turns to me. "Where do you hide?" she asks.

I look at her. I don't want to tell her.

"Where do you hide?"

I look at the clothes hamper. Footsteps, in the other hallway. Darla opens her eyes wide. Begging eyes.

I don't want to go into the clothes hamper anymore. I don't want to listen to them anymore. I don't want to hear Mom talk in voices that aren't hers or sing that horrible song, *"Pretty little Isabella . . ."* I don't want her to go to her bed and leave red. I don't want her to get scrambled eggs brain, or to make the dock red again. I don't want to talk to Mona anymore, or swallow dead black cat ghost, or make wishes on them all. And, already things are better. Mom sold a poem, and I got a 5.5 on my reading test and I got a letter from Joey. And the things that are still bad, they'll all go away when we go to therapy, and—

Darla's tugging on my shirt. Footsteps, close. She taps her feet like she has to pee. She whispers, *"Please, Ewe. Please-pleaseplease."* I pull Darla, open the hamper top, and we get in, closing it. Footsteps pass.

"It's best if we go down," I whisper.

We dig through the dirty clothes. It's very tight for two people. We press against each other, our legs, bellies, faces. We go down and cover ourselves with clothes, resting on the wooden bottom.

"Have you ever been camping?" she whispers.

"No."

"So, you don't have camping stuff?"

"I said, no."

"I got alotta camping stuff. A two person tent, a—" She goes quiet, then, "My daddy and me used to go—"

Footsteps again. I can feel them through the floorboards.

"Shhh . . . ," I say.

I can't imagine where— Mom says.

Didn't you see if they went out? Dad asks, annoyed.

Didn't you? Mom asks.

I can feel Darla's heartbeat and her breath.

"I used to sometimes lie here," I whisper soft into her ear. We're quiet. I feel her arms go around me. "Now you."

I wrap my arms around her.

I hear the hallway light switch go on. The vacuum cleaner closet opens, closes. Dad's miniature closet. Open, close. More footsteps. Like Dad's, but less: Jordan, and dragging: Daniel.

Darla giggles.

"Shh-shh."

She can't stop, and it makes me giggle. Darla squirms, trying to stop. Her foot bangs against the side of the hamper. We go still. Outside, voices stop. The top of the hamper opens. Some light comes in. The weight of the clothing gets lighter. I feel the clothes covering me lift. My eyes are still closed. I open them. Darla looks right at me. We're still hugging. I look up. Faces. Mom, Dad, Darla's mother, Jordan, Daniel. Jordan smiles, then laughs, moving away. Daniel smiles, and his face goes away. Dad's face is confused, then he smiles a little. Mom glances at Dad and smiles, then she looks at Darla's mother and puts her hand over her mouth. Darla's mother does not smile. Her face shakes a little. She reaches in, pulls Darla roughly out.

"Oh, come on," Mom says to her.

"No!" Darla's mother says.

Darla tries to wiggle away. Her mother takes Darla by the

shoulders and shakes her. She shakes her very hard and very quick. Darla goes limp. Her head whips backward and forward.

Mom grabs Darla's mother's arm. "What are you doing to her?!"

Darla's mother stops shaking Darla. Dad pulls Mom's hand away.

Mom crouches to Darla. "Are you okay?"

Dad pulls Mom up, and shakes his head at her.

"You haven't gotten in touch since we moved back," Darla's mother says, face red, veiny. "So, I'd thank you very much if you didn't choose *this* moment to suddenly show concern."

Darla's mother holds Darla tight by the arm as she talks. Darla won't look at me. Darla's mother stops talking, and they move away. Footsteps, then the front door opens and closes. I sit up. Mom hugs me. Dad tells me to put the clothes away.

twelve

I'm dressed in my good corduroys and button-up shirt and black and white Buster Browns that pinch my toes. I sit on the floor, Mona on my lap.

"I shouldn't talk to you," I say.

Quiet.

"I'm going to therapy. I'm not scared."

Quiet.

Dad calls.

I reach to put Mona back into the chest, but I stop. I lay her on my bed and leave.

⌒♈

We sit in a line like an audience. Steve, the therapist, sits facing us, his legs crossed like a woman. He tells us Mom and Dad have some unhappiness, and they wondered if we also had some unhappiness.

Dad lets out a breathy laugh. Mom sits with her coat folded over her hands in her lap. Steve asks each of *the boys* how we are. We shrug and say "fine." Steve rubs his face and pinches his eyes beneath his glasses. I'm bored, but I try hard not to think about other things.

"Let's start this way," Steve says, "by telling me about what you do on a given day. Jordan?"

Jordan looks at Mom and Dad.

"Just regular days," Jordan says. "I go to school, hang out, go to parties on the weekends."

"What about the weekdays?"

"I occasionally go out."

"What do you do when you don't go out?"

"Have dinner, watch TV, do homework. Whatever."

Steve looks at my parents. Mom is smiling, Dad blinks.

"Tell me about your nights on Wednesdays and Thursdays."

"That's inappropriate," Dad says.

Mom looks at Dad, then at Steve.

Daniel stands up holding his stomach. He leaves the room.

Mom leans over, and in a secret-whisper voice says to Steve, "Daniel's been having diarrhea problems recently."

"How long?" asks Steve.

"Not long," Dad says.

"Since the summer," Jordan says.

I wonder when he might hypnotize us. I hope that he'll do it without telling us. I wonder what my secret word will be.

Steve looks at me.

"Is that how long your older brother has been having this problem?" he asks.

I swing my feet. I look at Dad. "I guess," I say.

"Why might that be?"

I shake my head.

"He's always been a nervous boy," Dad says.

"Why is he nervous?" asks Steve.

"Not nervous," Mom says. "Sensitive."

Steve breathes out.

"Let's look at the summer," Steve says.

"Summer was a gas," Jordan says. "We all had a blast."

"All of you?" Steve asks. "Do you mean your whole family had a *blast?*"

I look at Steve. He's a liar, I think, the way he uses the word *blast.*

Jordan nods, annoyed. "Yeah," he says.

"Then why might Daniel be feeling poorly these days? Was he upset that summer ended?"

"How the hell should he know?" says Dad.

Jordan slides down in his seat. I lower my head and follow the tan lines on the cream floor tiles that are supposed to look like marble. Marble comes from limestone. Lime stone is when Reid'll only give you 7UP when you show him—I look up quickly. *Pay attention,* I think. I look at them. They talk. I try to listen hard. I'm tired. *I'll just look down, but I'll still listen,* I think. I look at the tiles. I listen to them talk. . . The darker tile lines are mist and I hear an *oohing* in my head. I imagine that I am the sky and they are streams, and I hear water crinkling and birds.

I jerk up. Everyone looks at me.

Daniel returns. Mom watches him walk by. She massages her palms and wrists.

"Feeling okay?" Steve asks Daniel.

Daniel shrugs.

"How was your summer, can you tell me about it?"

I find that if I stare at the same spot for long enough the floor seems to actually move. A little at first, then more. The lines begin to waver, like thin wings flapping. I begin making a sound, softly beneath my breath, as the floor falls away, and the wings rise up, hundreds of molten, flapping wings.

Other sounds appear: *"Wur-wur, Whar-whar . . ."*

The wings freeze and fall to the floor, and I see the still, ugly tiles. I look up. Everyone looks at me.

"What?" Steve says. "What are you saying?"

My mouth still moves making the babble sounds. I look at my family, and I hear myself.

"Butterflies, butterflies," I say. Is that my word? I wonder. Was I hypnotized?

"Butterflies?" Steve asks, shaking his head, looking at my family.

"What caterpillars become," I say, catching Mom's eye. I look down her body. Her eyes followed mine until my eyes stop on her covered wrists.

"He's only nine years old," Dad says. "They just talk."

"Caterpillars, honey?" Mom says. "Oh, honey . . ."

I have a word, I think, I have a word! *Butterfly* . . .

Mom begins crying.

Steve tells us our time is up.

We leave Steve's office and wait for the elevator. When it comes, it's empty. Dad stands with his back to us watching the blinking floor numbers.

"This is ridiculous," he says.

"I think that's—" Mom begins.

Dad turns. "You started crying because he babbled some nonsense!" Dad points his finger at me.

"—It wasn't nonsense," Mom says quietly.

I made Mom cry?

"And please don't yell at me," Mom adds.

Dad opens his mouth to yell, but right then the door opens,

and his mouth closes. He leads us through the lobby and down
the street.

"We're not done talking," Mom says.

Dad says that we're in public. Mom says, So? Dad points
his finger at her. He says that therapy is only making things
worse, that some things are better left alone, and that certainly
it is no place for the children. Then Dad says, very low and
mean, *Enough.* Mom stops walking. We follow Dad. He stops a
few steps away. We stop. He turns. We turn. He waits, we wait.
Mom walks over. Mom opens her mouth, but Dad starts talking
first. He says, that if she doesn't start acting like an adult—

Therapy is making it worse? I think. I don't understand how
that could be. I remember that I have a special hypnotized word.

"Butterfly, butterfly!" I say. I'm happy, I hop. "Butterfly!"
Dad turns quickly to me. He asks if I'm trying to be funny.
I stop hopping. "No," I say quickly.

"Forget this," Jordan says. He turns and walks away.

"Jordan!" Dad calls.

Jordan doesn't turn. He runs, lost around the corner.

Dad's angry vein pulses. Dad walks. Mom walks. Me and
Daniel walk.

We reach the subway. The train is rushing into the station.
Dad quickly hands out tokens. We run and squeeze through
the train doors, except Daniel who has dropped his token and
is chasing it rolling away. We watch as the doors close. Daniel
stands up, holding the token, a small smile appears on his face.
The train leaves the station.

⌦

"I've been calling you forever," Darla says, holding the can.

"I was out," I say. I look though the courtyard into the dining room. Mom places a salad on the table. Dad walks in with
boxes of pizza.

"Why do you do that?" Darla asks.

"What?"

"I've been talking and you're looking off like an idiot," Darla says.

"I wish I could go away. Go to North Carolina to see Joey," I say.

"Mom grounded me. She also threw out the rest of my records." Darla looks at me. "I've been looking at your map. You forgot it here the other day. There are a million places, huh?"

I nod. "I gotta go," I say.

"Yeah, okay."

As I put the can down, she says, "Hey, Ewe?"

I put the can to my ear.

"Would you—like if I went away, would you come, or visit?"

I look into the dining room. Daniel and Jordan still aren't home, and I want first dibs on the best slices.

"Sure," I say.

"Really?"

"Yeah," I say. "Really."

Mom and Dad don't talk. They look at their plates and eat. Sometimes they look up when the other is looking down, and their eyes get hot, and sometimes their lips move, but they don't make a sound.

"We're not going to therapy anymore?" I ask.

"Ask your father," Mom says.

I turn to Dad. "We're not going to—" I begin.

"—Tell your mother that she and I will discuss it later."

I stare at him.

"Tell her!"

I turn to Mom. Inside is a fluttering, a wing, inside my

stomach, flapping against my throat. "He will . . . discuss it . . . later."

Mom leans over to me. "How would you like to visit your grandmother?"

"He's not going down there," Dad says.

"Tell your father I can't hear him," Mom says.

I look at her and shake my head. But Dad is telling me to leave. I look at Dad, then back to Mom. I want to leave, but I can't. I'm scared to leave. I look back at Dad. I shake my head. Dad pulls my chair out.

"Butterfly," I say.

"Go to your room."

"Butterfly!" Why won't it work?

Dad lifts me out of my chair.

"Let him go!" Mom screams.

"Butterfly! Butterfly! Butterfly!"

Dad carries me to the kitchen. He runs the hot water. Steam rises up. He grabs my hands by the wrist, he puts them under the water. It burns. I scream. I try to pull away. Dad is too strong.

". . . *Butterfly* . . . *butterfly* . . ." I can barely make a sound.

He lets go. I curl up on the floor.

Mom's screaming. She hits Dad on the chest, the face. He stands still. She calls him a *son of a bitch.* She tells him to get out, to go away, that she never wants to see him again. She says, *Just get out, go to your whore.* Dad says, *You drove me to my whore.* Mom stops hitting him. She says, soft, *Get out.* She kneels next to me. Her face is red and wet and her hair, still sun-bleached from the summer, sticks to her cheeks and fore- head. She's crying, she's calling me, *Her baby, her sweet sweet, precious baby.*

She rubs butter on my red hands. The skin's bubbled.

I pull away. "I'm taking a bath," I say. I'm a good boy. I

take my bath without being asked, I do my chores, I do good
in school, I don't ask questions. I will make everything better.

But after I fill the tub and get in, it burns so bad when I
touch the hot water with my hands that even my bones feel
like they're cracking, on fire. So, I just sit there in the water
with my arms crossed, holding on to my shoulders. And after
a while I get out.

Mom is standing at the end of the hallway when I'm done with
a bath.

"Are you going to bed, honey?"

"Yeah."

"May I tuck you in?"

I nod.

Mom smiles.

"Say good night to your father."

I look at Mom.

Mom smiles, blinks. "Go on."

Dad's in the living room working. He's begun building a
new miniature, the frame already up.

Dad looks over at me. His lips move to talk, but they don't.
His hand moves toward my head, but it jerks to a stop like a
broken wing. He pats me on the shoulder. I look at him. He
looks away. I think, He is my father. I kiss Dad on the cheek.
He is stubbly and it reminds me of being very small.

Mom wraps me in my sheets and blankets, then sits
beside me.

"Your birthday's coming soon," she says. "You should
think of something special that you would like."

I nod.

Mom puts a small narrow box on my chest. She whispers,
"I shouldn't, but I couldn't help giving you one present early."

It's a Mickey Mouse watch. His arms are the watch's hands.

"I've set it," Mom says. "And look, it even shows the date."

Mom strokes my hair. I touch the scar. It's smooth. Up close it doesn't look like a caterpillar. It looks like a scar, like the skin has been carved open and sewn back together, a little melted-looking.

Mom opens her mouth, I shake my head. I run my finger over the scar, then take her other hand, and lay them both out, palms up on my stomach.

Nothing lives beneath the scar: it's just a scar.

Mom lays her head on my pillow, touching her cheek to mine. She whispers quiet, "We could go away, hmm?" When her mouth moves I can hear the spit softly pop. "Wouldn't that be fun? Just you and me. We'd be partners, like the old west, two cowboys."

"Without Dad?" I ask.

Mom nods, our cheeks rubbing, hot. She puts her hand on my chest. I can feel my heart beating up to touch it.

"Would you like that, honey?"

"I'm tired." I roll away.

I feel Mom's weight rise up, and leave the bed.

"I'll leave the door open a crack, just like you like?"

"I don't care."

"Your father didn't mean it. He meant it for me. He feels just terrible. It won't happen again."

I don't move.

"Honey . . . ?"

I say nothing else, and neither does she.

thirteen

A voice wakes me. It's after 2 A.M. I sit up and walk to the window.

"Be at your back door in two minutes," Darla says. "And open your window."

I open my window.

"Let go of the can," Darla says, tugging on the string.

The can falls and clangs against her side of the building. Darla lets them go and they clang down the courtyard.

She stands outside the back door.

"Let's go," she says.

"Where?"

"To run away."

"We can't do that."

"Why not?"

I open my mouth, but I can't think of anything to say.

Darla walks past me into the apartment.

"You'll need clothing. Plus money, you got any?"

"A little."

"What about your parents?"

I nod.

"Good. Get all your stuff and meet me at my back door when you're done."

I pack. I steal the month's grocery money. I see Mona on the floor. I hold her, the red still stuck to the frame, now dry and dark. I walk out the back door. Darla opens her door before I can knock.

We walk through the kitchen, past her mother's room. The door is open a crack. A bedside lamp is on: a dim orange light. Her body is sprawled on the bed, but she doesn't look asleep. She looks like she's fallen from the window. There's an arm over her stomach, but the rest of the other body is out of sight.

"Help me," Darla says, handing me bags.

We take the elevator down.

"We can't really go anywhere," I say.

"I called Joey and told him we were coming."

I stop. "You did not."

"You left his letter at my house with his number."

The bags are heavy, we walk slow.

It's cold outside, a wind sent off by the black river. The street is empty. I follow Darla. She leads us into the park. We walk to the lower drive and wait for the no. 5 bus.

"This is stupid," I say.

It's quiet except for the faraway hum of the Henry Hudson Parkway. I look at our building. I count up to my apartment. The windows are dark.

The bus comes.

The bus driver looks at us. Darla puts two tokens in, the bus driver says nothing. We sit in the back. The hard plastic seats are hot from the engine. We are quiet. The bus goes along Riverside Drive, then cuts up east. We get off at Forty-second Street.

There are men and women like the kind I see on TV. Gold teeth, coats with feathers. Coochie women, men sprawled across the sidewalk, mumbling. Empty bottles in brown paper bags. Cigarette butts. Trash on the sidewalk, in the gutter. Men with accents dressed like Jordan when he goes to parties stand in bright doorways calling, "Best fuckfuck girls, man. Biggest titties, deepest fuckfuck holes, man. Good show, man, good show." We walk past theaters with rolling blinking lights and pictures of naked women. We come to a big building. Outside it smells like pee and vomit. We take the escalator. The light is yellow. There are ticket windows. There's a waiting area with a few people. They look at us bored, then away. We drop our bags, and sit.

"I'll get the tickets," Darla says.

The room is big. A man looks at me. His nostrils move, big-small, big-small. He smiles. I look down. Darla returns.

"Darla, let's go."

"We are." She shows me two bus tickets.

"Home."

She looks at me. "I know," she says, thinking of something.

She leaves. My stomach feels empty and cold, and my feet tingle with sleep. Darla returns with two hot chocolates. They're good. We slurp. We don't say anything. We look at each other and smile a little. Darla has a creamy hot chocolate mustache that dries dark brown like two little wings. An announcement. Darla stands. I follow.

We go down some stairs into a dark tunnel, the ground black, oily, slick. People stand in line. There's a woman in front of us. Darla says to get close to her, to pretend she belongs to us. My heart beats hard when we get close to the ticket-taker man. He takes the lady's ticket and puts her bags in a compartment below the bus.

"Don't wait for us," Darla says to the lady who moves to the bus door.

The lady looks at Darla, frowns, then climbs onto the bus.

Darla looks at the ticket-taker man, and whispers, "Dad died a few years back, so Mom's really got her hands full with me and my brother." Darla touches my shoulder.

I look at the ticket-taker man. "Right!" I say too loud.

The ticket-taker man looks at us bored. He takes our tickets and bags. We climb into the bus. It is very dark. The seats are soft. I sit next to the window. Darla puts her head on my shoulder. The engine starts, the bus trembles. A few people cough, the bus moves. Through a tunnel, then through the city. It is shiny and dark. People walk, stand, shadowy, and I like looking at them through the window, and I like sitting in the cushy seat. We go through another tunnel.

On the other side, I see Manhattan across the river, lit up, and for a while we drive beside it. It looks like something breaking apart, the way the light comes out from the insides of the buildings. Darla looks at me and smiles sleepy. She puts her head back on my shoulder and falls to sleep.

"I'm awake," I whisper. *"I'm awake."*

I think, I'm on a bus. I could be, should be, in bed, at home.

Am I on a bus?

I pinch my cheek.

I'm on a bus.

I look out the window, and Manhattan is gone except for the tips of the twin towers, which slip away as I watch. New Jersey is dark and low. The moon is out ahead of us. It is three-quarters full, and it looks like a face standing behind a doorway, waiting for us to come through. I look toward home once more. Dark. The city is gone. I look ahead. The bus is dark, it rocks. People make sleeping sounds, and I listen to the wheels whirl quickly across the road. I slide down in the seat. Darla's head rolls off my shoulder and I put it back. I rest my cheek on her head.

I smile at the empty sky. I close my eyes.

away

one

My eyes jerk open. I inhale, jumping up, awake. Darla's seat is empty. I look both ways, up, down the aisle. Then the breathing starts, like it has all night: quick and fast. I bite my lip to make myself go quiet. People's heads sway lazy with the bus, asleep. I look out the window.

The sun is just coming up. We're on the highway. The air is soft and pale and people drive with their headlights. The traffic is thick. People with cigarettes, cups of coffee, fat faces, rubbing their eyes.

I'm tired. I didn't sleep well all night, waking up many times with fists. Waking up and breathing fast like I had been running. And every time, the sound of my breathing made me more scared, because in the dark it sounded like a separate thing, like it wasn't coming from inside me, like it was something in the dark watching me. And the more scared I became, the harder I breathed. And I would close my eyes and hum, and I would crouch over and put my face real close to Darla's. And I would watch her, and feel the knobby fabric of the seat against my cheek, and I would listen hard to my humming, and slowly the dark would become good. It would become a small space, like under the living room couch, and the bus wheels whirling outside would become the wind, whistling off the Hudson through Riverside Park, and the few voices of the adults on the bus who weren't asleep, would be just that: adults talking, like company was over, company sitting on the couch talking, with me under it in the shadows listening, the wind in the background blowing outside, and I would close my eyes and the breathing would fade and I'd fall back asleep.

But it's light now. I pull out the map. I've marked our stops. Trenton, N.J., Philadelphia, Pa.

The bus driver gets on the loudspeaker. "Wilmington, Delaware, next."

I mark it.

I connect the red dots on the map, and there's a red line. A red line the length of my pinkie. The first red dot is home. Home isn't far. It's only a pinkie finger away. I lay my pinkie flat and with my other hand I make two fingers into legs. Let your fingers do the walking. I stand them on the first knuckle of my pinkie. They take one step, and they're on the nail of the pinkie. Home. I step them back. Here.

A man passes, glancing at me. He rattles the locked bath-room door, then stands beside it a moment. He takes Darla's seat, waits. He looks at the map and smiles.

"You've come quite a-ways."

I look at him. I don't know what to do, then I remember there's a rule: don't talk to strangers. I feel better and continue to look at him silently.

"Cat's got your tongue?"

His breath smells bad, but in a way that I like. It's how
Mom smells in the morning. He holds the cup-shaped top of a
thermos, filled with coffee.

"You come all this way alone?"

Our seats are behind the lady we pretended belonged to us
when we first got on the bus last night. She stands. She opens
the overhead bin, and takes down a large purse.

I shake my head.

The man sips his coffee and leans heavy back into the seat.

I wonder where Darla went. I start to imagine that maybe
she got off somewhere while I was asleep. But, as far as I
knew, I always woke up when the bus stopped. Usually Darla
was asleep, her bottom lip out like a baby, her head in her
chest, or sideways with her mouth open. I wonder how she
slept so easy. Once I put my finger on her tongue and her head
shook, but she didn't wake.

The man has his eyes closed even when he raises the coffee
for a sip. He says, "I got a boy about your age." He opens one
eye and peers it down at me. "You 'bout nine?"

I nod. "Almost ten," I say, proud.

The man closes the one eye and smiles.

"Well, happy birthday if I don't see you."

The coffee in his mug sways with the bus. I look at the
man, watching his closed eyes. I reach out and dip my finger
into his coffee and I quickly bring it to my mouth. I close my
eyes, Mom's morning breath in my mouth like a kiss.

"Where you heading?" he asks.

"That's none of your business, Mister," says Darla, standing in the aisle. "And that's my seat," she says.

Darla is dressed in one of her mother's brown blouses, that
hangs to her knees like a dress. And she has on a wig, and four
slashes on her face: two heavy red slashes on her lips, two
softer pink slashes, like clouds on each cheek.

The man smiles at first, then he frowns, serious. "Where
are your parents?" he asks. "You better sit, young lady."

I glance at Darla and nod toward the lady in front of us, so
that Darla knows the lady's getting off and that she's not good
to pretend with anymore. Darla sees. Her eyes freeze. Then
she looks up at the man. She's still standing.

"Mom's back in New York," Darla says. "Daddy's in—"
Darla glances at me. "We're going to Daddy's." Darla smiles.
"It's safe. Mom told us to just stay on the bus, and if we get off
to inform the bus driver of our whereabouts."

Sometimes Darla talks neat. Not cool neat, but neat neat.
Straightened up. Tidy. Like a lawyer on TV. And she can just
do it, like now, with the man. I wonder how she knows how to
do it, how she makes it work, the words, how she can make
them come out neat like that. And how she just looks at the
man without biting her lip or looking down or pulling on her
sleeve.

But the man is still staring at Darla suspiciously because of
her makeup and wig.

I'm still wondering about the calm way Darla can talk
when she knows she's caught, and I want to try.

"Mom's bag," I mumble. I look at the man. It's like a flash:
I think of how I sometimes try on the lipstick Mom keeps in
the bathroom cabinet. "We got a bag for Mom—she's coming
later." I nudge my head toward Darla. My mouth is dry and
the words stick to my tongue before coming out. "She was just
messing around with her stuff."

"You're brother and sister?" The man looks at me. "You *do*
look alike," the man says, smiling.

"We do?" I ask.

The man laughs. "I used to hate that too, when anyone said
I looked like my brother."

The bus comes to a stop.

The man looks up. "That's me." He turns and leaves, behind the woman in front of us.

Darla flops onto the seat. Orange sunlight falls across the fake brown curls of her wig. "That was close, huh?" She laughs, looking at the man through the window, waving to him. She looks at me and smiles. "A disguise," she says. "They'll be looking for us." She puts on a pair of her mother's sunglasses that cover half her cheeks.

I lean back into my seat, and turn to the window as the sun rises above the horizon opening up another day.

We're quiet for a long time, and I don't feel like anything. Not scared. Not excited. I watch miles of highway pass until it looks like nothing, like a field of grass, like the sky without clouds, like lying on the bottom of the clothes hamper, and how dark and how quiet it is in the early morning before anyone is awake, feeling my different body parts one by one fade away, until I can't feel myself, and I feel perfect. And then the first noise, Dad's footsteps, heavy on the hallway, like the only sound in the world, hard and loud. Suddenly I feel the clothing on top of me again, like I'm suffocating. But, then there are more sounds, Mom's footsteps, the brothers, the bathroom door opens and closes, running faucets and flushing toilets, and voices, the TV, until sounds aren't scary anymore, and I giggle at them, because they are stupid, those sounds. They're big and stupid because they don't know the silence that was there before, the silence and the dark that made me perfect on the bottom of the clothes hamper. And Mom and Dad should just now be noticing that I'm not in bed. I listen to them going to all my usual hiding spots. They ask the brothers if they've seen me. Dad's annoyed, he says, "Where's that damn kid?" But, Mom remembers suddenly, the day they found me and Darla hiding at the bottom of the clothes hamper. I can hear

her above, and I'm excited. I can jump up and scare her, I can
wait, her sweet lamb at the bottom, like a present. And light
comes in, and she digs through the clothes. She's getting
closer. She takes out the last layer of dirty pants and shirts and
underwear, and her shoulders sag, and she runs her fingers
along the empty wooden bottom. "I'm here! I'm here!" I say.
Mom looks up, Mom looks lost. She puts her hand over her
mouth. She's beginning to wonder, she's scared. I want to
touch her, but I'm air. I'm nothing, I'm not there. Mom knows
something, she can feel it in her stomach, I can feel it in her
stomach, it's like a pinch, like heat. Dad is stomping about
somewhere down the apartment. He is not thinking of Mom.
Mom is alone and she opens her mouth, but thinks that if she
makes a sound the worst will be true. I call her again. She
looks straight at me, but she does not see me. Mom blinks and
she begins to fade away. And as she fades she stretches across
the windy highway. Her hair turns to the dying gray autumn
willows, her blue eyes into the sky, her nose ripples out across
a field, her mouth, thin and dry and pink turns gray and flat
and stretches out to the endless highway. And I am on the bus.

Darla leans over and touches me. "What's wrong, Ewe?" Her
wig has fallen forward over her forehead.

"Who's chasing us?" I ask.

Darla frowns. "What?"

I look back out the window, and close my eyes like I'm
sleeping.

More red dots. Baltimore, Md., Washington, D.C., Rich-
mond, Va.

It's late afternoon. I watch the signs. 64 West. I look at the
map and frown. I show it to Darla.

"Why's he going on Sixty-four West?" I ask.

Darla shrugs.

I tap on the map with my finger. I run my finger down 95 South. "That's how to get to North Carolina," I say. I follow 64 West. It cuts across Virginia, turns down another route that crosses mountains and goes into West Virginia.

"I think the driver knows what he's doing," Darla says, snotty.

"I know, but, look."

Darla stares at me with her ugly makeup face.

"All right," I say. "It seems wrong, but—so you think he—?"

"—Of course, Ewe." Darla smiles.

The driver announces that we will be making a twenty-minute rest stop.

"Food," I say.

"Foooood!" Darla says, standing.

"You can't go out like that," I say, grabbing her wrist. "You look stupid."

Darla snatches her wrist back. "It's a disguise. They'll be looking for us."

I know that they're probably not even looking for us, but if they are, they won't be looking in Virginia.

"People'll notice us more with you like that," I say.

"You think?" Darla looks hurt, falling back into her seat. "But, maybe I'll keep on the glasses just in case."

We stop in a small town. There's a post office with a faded American flag waving out front. A white church. A gun store with orange overalls and deer heads in the window. A general store with yellow signs posting sales.

The bus stops in front of a closed-down antique store. Me and Darla stay in our seats as the people file out of the bus. We go to the bathroom at the back of the bus and close the door. I sit on the toilet like a seat, watching as Darla slaps water on her face. The makeup fades, but she looks like she has sunburned cheeks and lips. She undoes the wig and bobby pins that hold up her long brown hair. She looks at me in the mirror and smiles. She opens the knapsack she brought in. All our money's there: $142 from Darla's mother, $200 from Mom and Dad, $16 of mine, $7 of Darla's. The bus tickets were $27 each, so we have $311 left. Darla pulls off the brown blouse. She shivers in her tank top and green corduroys with red, white, and yellow flowers bursting all over. She looks through her bag of clothing, pulling out a pink sweater with ladybugs crawling in circles around the arms.

I put the wig in my lap, run my fingers through it.

"Why's your mom got this?" I ask.

Darla blinks. She turns back to the mirror. From a clear plastic purse she takes out a wooden comb, carved-in flowers, painted pink, along its handle. Tilting her head from side to side, she combs out her long hair. I look at the little purse sitting now on the sink. Inside Darla also has a toothbrush, toothpaste, little seashell-shaped soaps, nail clippers, file. She combs out her hair, and talks.

"Mom used to be real pretty. She wore pretty clothes, all these beautiful colors." Darla looks at my reflection. "You should see pictures." Then she turns back to her reflection. "She and Daddy used to always have big parties. And Mom wore these clothes and makeup and jewelry, and she would wear wigs, you know, to go with the outfit. But," Darla says, returning the comb to the little purse, "when she became a Jew she stopped wearing the wigs, or wearing the clothes. Everything is all dark now." Darla shrugs, chewing the inside of her cheek.

"You don't look like a Jew," I say.

"What's that supposed to mean?"

"I don't know." I stand next to Darla; we both look in the mirror and make faces.

"You could be a Jew," she says.

"No, I couldn't," I say quickly. I open the bathroom door and walk off the bus.

The bus drives quickly. We eat Drakes coffee cakes and fruit pies, drink Dr Peppers. The road empties out to long stretches of farmland, and faded houses, slanted barns, some with words painted across: JESUS LIVES. The sky is heavy and gray. It's late October.

We use the road map as an eating tray. After we're done, we press our fingers into the map to get the crumbs, leaving little oily prints. I roll a crumb between my fingers until it's a dirty worm. Darla runs her finger over the Appalachian and Shenandoah Mountains on the boarder of Virginia and West Virginia.

Darla tells me that Virginia broke up after the Civil War, and that's why there are two of them. She says that her daddy told her that. She talks about all her camping gear, how her daddy gave it to her, how she and her daddy used to go camping all the time. And once how they saw a bear in Yellowstone. I stop her and say, Aw, now I know you're lying. You never seen a bear! She says, Swear to God, I did. In Yellowstone, like the cartoon, Yogi Bear, that's where he lives. I nod a little, trying to remember the cartoon. Well, where's Yellowstone? I ask. She says, California? She talks about things called geysers, blowholes that shoot boiling water out of the ground. Different sorts of leaves, small as a fingernail, big as a manhole cover. Silver fish that darted in streams. After a while, I get bored and I stop listening.

Overhead the window is cracked open and cool evening air blows in. Flat stretches of farmland on either side. I watch night roll across them.

It feels kind of good and safe now, because the outside is getting dark again, and inside dim yellow lights go on, making the outside fade away even more. And Darla's singing softly, some song she says her daddy made up, *I'm a-thinkin' an' a-wonderin', walkin' down that road. I once loved a woman, a child I am told.* And it feels like we're in a little room, and like the outside isn't there. I close my eyes and listen as Darla's singing ends, and she continues to go on talking.

Darla has a letter on her lap, and when I lean over to see, she puts it away in the knapsack.

The bus driver announces that we're coming onto Harrisonburg, our final stop. The road suddenly lights up with Jiffy Lubes and McDonald's. I look at the map.

"We got to North Carolina already?"

I draw a slash on the top of the map to mark our first full day away.

Darla just looks at me.

I'm excited to see how close Harrisonburg is to Joey. But, I can't find it, so I look back at Virginia. Remembering that we were driving on 64 West, I try to retrace the drive so I can locate Harrisonburg. My finger twists and follows the thin line, until I almost have to climb the mountains into West Virginia. I backtrack, and go up 81, and there's Harrisonburg, on the western border of Virginia. I look at Darla.

"We're at the wrong place!"

Darla looks at the map.

"Maybe we got on the wrong bus," she says.

"What're we gonna do?!"

"Get off."

two

We stand in the parking lot with our bags. Darla wears her mother's big straw hat. Cars race along the interstate. A man walks by. He has a mustache like Dad's. I follow behind him. The man stops. I look up at him. Darla runs over.

"Sorry, Mister, he just thought—" Darla says.

The man leaves.

"What's wrong with you?"

People from the bus walk with their heavy bags to waiting cars. Cars with men or women, children. They hug, they smile, they talk quickly and happily, they hug again. They throw their bags in trunks, they get into cars, they drive off. The bus driver pulls the bus around the side, then he walks into a nearby diner. I pick up some bags and follow him in.

The bus driver sits at the counter. He knows the waitress and they laugh. My heart is beating fast and hard like it might fly out of my mouth. I sit near the bus driver. I keep an eye on him. I think, This isn't regular lost, where I can find a cop and he'll drive me home. This is . . . this is . . . My brain goes white.

Darla walks in and drops the rest of the bags on the floor. "You could've taken more bags," she says. She notices the bus driver. She whispers, "What're you doing sitting so he can see us? You wanna get caught?"

I shake my head, but I don't move. She keeps saying that: *caught,* us getting caught. Sometimes I know what she means. But right now I don't. We just got on a bus, I think. People who get caught have done something wrong. We just got on a bus. I look outside at the few remaining people from the bus waiting, as their rides finally arrive. They drive off, to homes, to dinners, I think, to mothers, fathers, to all their stuff on shelves, under their beds. I try to think, but I'm confused. Why is it that we'd be caught like we're in trouble? Why doesn't she say found? *Maybe we'll be found.* We're lost. When you're lost you're found. We got on a bus is all. They'll find us. Then I notice our bags and that makes me remember. We meant to leave. We want to be here. We did it on purpose. We didn't get lost, we ran away. Caught. That's why she says it, I remember now. I understand. Not found: caught.

Darla drags my chair so my back faces the bus driver. Then she pulls a chair over and sits right next to me, so her back also faces him.

I turn and look at the bus driver.

"*Stop looking,*" she hisses.

My flapping heart goes still. It stops, like a stone. "You got us on the wrong bus."

"You said you wanted to get out of—"

"You said we were running to—"

"What can I get for you two balls-o'-love?"

We both go silent and look up at the waitress.

"Newlyweds?" she asks.

We don't answer.

She shakes her head. Then, seeing our bags, asks what we're up to. "You-all aren't runnin' from home now are you?" She laughs, a joke. Darla laughs, I turn and look at the bus driver. He has fried eggs and bacon and toast and fries. I think, You can do that: breakfast for dinner?

"My daddy's just late picking us up," Darla says. She points at the bus driver. "We just got off his bus."

The waitress looks at the bus driver, nods and says, "What 'cha havin'?"

I order two eggs, bacon, fries, cinnamon toast, and a Coke. Darla orders a steak, a fruit bowl, and cornflakes.

"You have Cap'n Crunch?" I ask.

"Sure do," says the waitress.

"I'd like that," I say.

"Instead of the eggs?"

"Also."

"Me too," says Darla, "instead of the fruit bowl."

The waitress looks at her. "You want a steak, cornflakes, *and* Cap'n Crunch?"

"And we'll share the fruit bowl," Darla says.

The waitress taps her pad.

"Y'all got money for this?"

Darla stares at the waitress. She dumps the knapsack on the table, unzips a front flap, and takes out a handful of bills.

"My, my," the waitress says, then walks away.

I look at Darla.

"What're we gonna do?" I ask.

Darla's straw hat darkens her face with crisscross shadows, dots of light. "Stop asking that," she says. "I gotta pee." She gets up, leaves.

Some bills have fallen on the table. I straighten them and fold them with the rest so all the presidents' heads are right-side up, and the bills are in order, ones, fives, tens, twenties. Last birthday Dad took me to the movies. He handed me his wallet and let me take the money out and pay for the tickets, popcorn, soda. It was pretty cool. Dad had told me how a person's got to learn how to handle money. That's how Dad handles his money: neat, heads and numbers in a row. I put the money neatly into the pocket of the knapsack. I see the envelope that Darla had been looking at. The postmark is from West Virginia, March 1974, three years ago. The paper inside is old and soft. It's a little map of West Virginia. There's a line drawn in red over Route 66 to Route 81, west to Route 33 across the mountains. The line ends with a red dot in a town called Brandywine. There is writing. *Follow 33 until you see Fat Boy's Pork Palace on the left, making your next left ½ mile up. I'm the white house on the end. Love, Daddy.*

Darla's hand reaches over my shoulder.

"Give it."

"No."

"Give it."

"Did you tell him we were coming?"

Darla snatches it from my hand. "I've got the map don't I?"

Looking at her, I want to crush her head, to slap her, pin her to the floor and dangle spit over her face. I look away and take off my Mickey Mouse watch. It's 7:53. Where the 3 should be is a little box with the date. 10 23. I wind the watch. I like the way it feels as the spring inside goes tight.

Our food comes. We eat quickly and silently. I won't look at Darla.

She pours half the bowl of cornflakes and half the bowl of Cap'n Crunch into a napkin that she balls up and puts into the knapsack. She mixes the remaining cereal together, draining in the syrup from the fruit bowl, spinning her spoon fast until it turns into a yellow mash, which she eats for a while.

She cuts her steak into cubes, eating them with her fingers, her chin shiny with meat juice. Full, she plays with her cubes, making a little pyramid.

"I miss my daddy," she says.

It's nice eating without the evening news on, without being told to hush. It's nice ordering what I want, eating what I want, not eating what I want. It's nice eating without having to mind my manners: my elbows on the table, licking ketchup off my knife, not putting a napkin on my lap.

I don't want to, but I do: I look straight at Darla, but I won't speak.

I take some of her cereal mash and mold it over the pyramid of steak cubes. She sprinkles pepper and salt over that. I add some sugar. We stick in straws, adding pieces of fruit on their ends.

The restaurant fills up and the waitress clears our plates, frowning at the pyramid. She asks if we want anything else, we say no. She leaves the check, and we watch people eat. Dusty tanned men, families, people alone. I watch them chew. It looks gross, the way they put food in their mouths, and chew and chew until it's mush, then swallowing, sometimes taking a sip of something as they chew. I think of them going to sleep and the food going down them overnight, turning brown and shitty, plopping out, wiping their behinds, washing their hands, flushing the toilet, going to the table, getting more food, chewing all over again.

The bus driver, done eating, sips coffee and smokes cigarettes.

"When're we going to Joey's?" I ask.

"Soon."

"He thinks we're coming."

"I told him we were coming *soon.*"

"When's your dad picking us up?"

Darla looks at me. "He should be here. Anyway, don't worry about it."

We give the waitress money, and Darla says, "Thank you very much. Daddy's out there, thank you."

We stand outside, looking at the highway.

"We'll wait over here," Darla says.

"I thought he was out here."

Darla starts walking. "He said, either wait in the restaurant or over by—"

I look at where we're walking. "By a Dumpster?!"

Darla turns. "That's what Daddy said."

We close the Dumpster's open metal lid and hop on top. Darla pulls out a pack of unopened cigarettes.

"Like you smoke," I say.

"I got them don't I?" Darla stares at me. She unwraps them. "They're Dr. Dan's." She lights one, blows smoke into the cool night air.

"We should call home," Darla mumbles.

"You wanna go back?"

"No."

There are two pay phones on the side of the restaurant.

"You first," I say.

"No, you."

"The same time then."

"No," Darla says. "You first."

I pick up the phone and dial 0. I tell the operator I want to make a collect call to New York. Jordan answers.

"Dag, boy: where are you?" he asks. "You lost?"

I am lost, I think. "Nah," I say.

"Just hiding out, huh?"

"Yup."

Jordan laughs. "They're gonna kick your scrawny ass, boy."

I hold back a smile.

I can see the hallway where the phone is. The cup carved from a branch, some of the bark still left, holding pens. The turn-of-the-century school table where the phone sits, with the round inkwell, smooth, in the right corner. Behind me, Dad's miniature.

Dad gets on.

"Where are you, are you okay?" he asks. "We're worried sick. Your mother is beside herself, you know she's not well—"

He asks lots of questions. I like his voice inside my ear. I want to be home. I want to be caught. I want to be found. I want to open my eyes, and really be in the hallway. I put my knuckles to my mouth. There's curled dead skin over the top like the skin of chocolate pudding, but thinner like tracing paper. Dead skin from hot water.

There's silence.

"You had better tell me where you are."

I don't speak.

"Are you lost? What do the street signs say? Tell me what they say."

I hold the dead skin in my teeth and pull. It pulls good and easy, like dried glue. Then it hurts. I open my eyes. I've pulled the dead skin to where there's alive skin. I jerk my mouth. It stings, and the dead skin comes off with a little piece of alive skin. I lick the skin off my teeth with my tongue. I chew it. It tastes good, like nothing. It's chewy a little. I swallow.

I see the empty parking lot, the road, the moon.

I want to say something, but when I open my mouth no sound comes out.

"Tell me where you—"

I hang up. I look at Darla. She lifts her hand like she's going to touch me, but instead her hand reaches for the phone.

"Go away," she says.

I walk back to the Dumpster and climb up. I go through a bag and find Mona. I hold her in my lap. I look over at Darla. Her back is to me. "Hi," I whisper. Mona's quiet. "Okay, you don't have to say anything. . . . This is Virginia." I hold her out, and move my arm so she can see. "We had dinner here." I face her to the restaurant. I bring her close to my face, and pick away some dry red that flakes off and twirls in the air. I put her away.

Darla has the phone to her ear. She leans against the wall with her head down. She nods. Her legs are twisted as if she has to pee. For a long time, she doesn't say anything. She lets go of the receiver and watches it dangle.

Darla sits back next to me on the Dumpster.

"How's your mom?" I ask.

Darla smiles sad, then looks straight ahead.

"I gotta pee," I say.

"Go there."

"You won't look?"

"*Ew!*"

I hop down. I stand between the wall and the Dumpster. I pee. It feels good. I like the pattering sound of it. *There-I'll-pee,* I remember. It makes me laugh. It sprinkles on the dry ground, first in dots, then making a little puddle, then a stream that goes under the Dumpster.

"*Move!*" From behind Darla pushes me farther behind the Dumpster.

"*Get out! I'm peeing!*"

"*Shut up! Shh-shh!*"

I zip up. Darla peers around the Dumpster. I look too. I see the bus driver. He leaves the diner with his arm around the waitress. They laugh, and stop once to kiss.

I knock my sneaker against the Dumpster to knock off the pee-mud.

The bus driver sees the phone receiver Darla left dangling. He picks it up. His head jerks away—Darla's mother must have screamed into the phone. We hear him say, *Calm down, calm down. Who? Your little girl?* The waitress whispers something to the bus driver. The bus driver runs into the parking lot, back and forth, calling, *Darla! Darla!* We duck far back into the shadows. The waitress calls, *Darla!*, and walks a few steps out onto the parking lot, watching the bus driver running and calling. A car pulls up. A fat man gets out. He walks toward the diner. He sees the phone dangling. He hangs it up. He goes into the diner. The bus driver walks back to the waitress and shakes his head. He walks toward the phone. He sees it's hung up. *The phone's hung up!* the bus driver says, running to it. The waitress turns. *You let someone hang up the phone?! What's wrong with you?!* the bus driver yells. The waitress starts crying. The bus driver asks, very annoyed, why she's crying, and she says, *They're just so little. And you're yelling, making me feel just awful.* She looks up. *And you drove them here,* she says crossing her arms. *They had tickets!* he yells back.

Darla points. Our bags are on the ground. Darla covers her mouth. "We're dead if they see them," she whispers.

But, they don't see them. The waitress says, *We gotta call the cops.* They go inside.

We pick up our bags and run. We run like crazy. We stop when we can't run anymore. We bend over, panting, trying to catch our breaths.

"*Where's your dad?*"

"I'll figure it out," she says, pushing me.

"They got the cops after us!"

Darla opens her mouth, but she doesn't say anything. She turns and walks to the interstate.

"The cop'll see you."

"I'm just seeing if any cabs are coming."

We're in front of a liquor store. A group of teenagers stand off to the side, smoking.

"Come on," I whisper.

Teenage girls are all right, but I don't like the boys. Teenage

boys look like lizards. Their eyes are always half shut, fooling
you that they're calm and nice. But right then their eyes snap
open wide. And they're running at you and you start running,
but they're bigger and faster and they catch you like nothing.
You squirm but they've got you tight. And that part feels good at
first, a little like being hugged, but they always do it harder until
you can't help it, and you make funny squeaks because it feels
like your insides are popping. And that makes them laugh and
call you names, and then the other older boys notice and they all
wander over with their lazy lizard eyes. And all their eyes snap
open wide, and they all start calling you names at once, tossing
you in the air in a game of catch, dropping you sometimes, holding you upside down until your head wants to burst, giving you
a wedgie until your underwear feels like a blade.

A teenage boy walks out of the liquor store. The group looks
up. The boy shakes his head. The group looks down. Darla walks
toward the teenagers. I whisper, *"No,"* but she doesn't listen.

"What're you doing?" Darla asks.

They look up. A boy says, *Who let the little lady out so past
bedtime?* A girl crouches down, says, *Shouldn't you be home,
darling?*

Darla looks at the truck the group huddles around. Darla
asks if it's their truck. Some of the group laugh, someone
says, yeah.

"I could get you your liquor," Darla says, "if you give me
and him a ride." Darla points toward me in the dark.

They laugh and laugh.

Darla waits for them to be quiet. I look at the road for
flashing police lights. Coast is clear. I look back quickly.

"You get us whiskey, I'll sing the national anthem in the
raw," a boy says.

Darla walks up to him, puts her hand out for money. "A
ride," she says, "over the mountain to West Virginia."

"I don't know," a girl says.

A boy says, "Don't worry your head, she ain't gettin' nothing."

Darla walks into the liquor store, returns with a big bottle in a paper bag.

The teenagers open their mouths.

I don't feel jealous of Darla. I know I should, but she's a little like magic, and I can't do anything but watch.

"Told him it was for my mom. I've done it a million times," Darla explains.

Driving over the Appalachians is slow. We drive in a pickup. Three boys sit up front. In the back bed are two boys who smoke quietly, and five girls, and because there's not enough room, me and Darla have to sit on the laps of two girls. They ask where we're from.

I say, "New—"

"—Hampshire," Darla cuts in.

"New Hampshire?" A girl says. "Wow."

One girl asks why we're going to West Virginia, and a second girl calls the first a busybody, and the first says, I'm not being a busybody, we're driving two itty-bitties across—but a third girl butts in and says, one of us isn't such an itty-bitty that she couldn't get a bottle of hooch, and then all five girls laugh, and the two boys pretend not to listen.

The moon's full, it's deep night. Large stretches of the mountainside are black. I look behind: dark, no cops. The boy driving hands a plastic cup of whiskey to his friend, and leans his entire body against the steering wheel. A fog, thick and rolling, stops the headlights a couple of feet ahead. Curves suddenly appear. Each time, the girl whose lap I'm sitting on, whose arms are wrapped around me, squeezes tight, and I can tell she's scared because I hear her breathe in. I lean against her. Nice. Darla's body rocks, and she leans her head against her girl's shoulder and I think how small Darla looks.

We reach a straightaway and the boy hits the gas hard. The boys in the front, *Yeehaa!* and the boys in the back, *Yeehaa!*

I look behind at the mountain, the long shadow it casts, and the shadows cast by the trees that grow on it, and I think how we just came over it, and I can't hardly believe that, it's so big.

I think about the red pinkie-size line I drew on my map, and how it grew as the bus drove: two pinkies, a hand, two hands. And looking at the mountain, I imagine the red line, and I see it zigzag over the mountain, now shooting out from behind the truck.

I think, This road, that mountain, they aren't even a pinprick on the red line on my map. How far have we come? I think how I've been kind of pretending that home isn't that far away: a pinkie away, a hand away. But it's far. Really, it's much farther away, I think. It feels good, having the girl hold me tight as a cold wind blows, and I think about it like it's something fun to think about, like it's something I'm watching, like it's a riddle. Far, far, far, far, far. I can't think of it: even if I use my imagination, where I can imagine anything if I think hard enough. Even there, in my imagination, I can't imagine how far we've come.

We pass a shack with a turned-off sign. Fat Boy's Pork Palace. Darla taps on the window to the cab and points. The boy takes the next left.

"Which house?" he asks, sliding a little window open.

"You can drop us here," Darla says.

The boy stops.

We unload our stuff.

A girl whispers to the others, "We're gonna just leave 'em?"

A boy shrugs.

"I can't just leave 'em here," the girl says to her friends. She climbs out of the truck.

I look away, pretending like I'm not here. We're going to get caught, I think. This is it. But then I think, *I am here.* My heart beats. *I am here.* I slowly lift my head. I pull out the letter from Darla's father and show the girl the map. She nods.

I stare at her, amazed. Amazed that doing something worked. But then she wants more.

"Maybe I'll take you to the door. Why didn't he come pick you up himself?"

The boy has turned the truck around. The boy honks the horn, says, "Come the fuck on." The girl stomps the ground and bugs her eyes out. The boy raises his eyebrows, shrugs. He floors the truck past. The girl yells at him. The truck skids to a stop. The boys laugh. The girl looks at us, a little worried, pats us on the head, then runs to the truck, hops back in. The truck drives off. We watch its red lights. Then, it's dark again. We can hear the truck rev back toward the mountain, then, quiet.

I pick up some bags.

"No," Darla says.

I look at her.

"I don't wanna yet. Can we just sit here a minute?"

I drag the bags to the side of the road below some dark bushes. I pull out a sleeping bag, and sit beside the bushes. Darla sits next to me and wraps herself in the sleeping bag.

We sit there for a long time, staring off into the dark road. I'm very tired. I feel my eyes begin to close. I try to keep them open. If I look there, it's pitch black, if I look there, I see a slice of moonlight cut across the road. I smile because it makes me think of bedtime, my door open a crack, sound and light cutting through the dark. Every morning the door is closed, and some-times at night I wake up when he closes it. Why does Dad have to close it? It's not hurting anyone being open. He closes it because it's wrong to sleep with a slice of light. Grow up little baby.

"Why is it bad?" I ask aloud.

I wonder, Is my door open or closed tonight? If it is open will Dad still walk by and close it? Maybe he'll remember. *Oh, he's gone. I don't have to do that anymore,* he'll think. One thing off his mind. Maybe that will make him nicer. Maybe he'll smile at Mom because he's feeling nicer. I'm sure Mom's crying. She needs Dad to be nicer to her tonight. I'm glad that I'm gone because it'll make Dad not have to worry about my door anymore, which will make him nicer tonight because Mom needs him to be, because she's crying because I'm gone.

"Good night," I whisper to her.

"You're awake still?"

I look over. Darla's eyes are open.

"Before when you said *Why is it bad?* I thought you were having a bad dream. Aren't you tired?"

"Why you still up: you scared?" I ask.

"Why: are *you?*"

We look at each other.

"I'm cold," I say, looking away. "Are you?" I look back.

Darla nods. She smiles. Her spit makes a sparkle sound. She pulls her legs to her chest, rests a cheek on a knee.

I scoot over, touching her side.

She turns her head and looks at me. I slide my hand over her shoulders. She leans, circles her arms around my middle.

The moon sets. The road turns deeper black.

I look at Darla's face in my lap. She is sound asleep, blowing out puffs of air like a little train. I close my eyes, and her puffs make the dark gentle. My hands relax and my body falls into sleep.

three

One bird starts, waking all the rest. I open my eyes. Over the mountain, night breaks. From behind: the rising sun, pale light.

"All those birds," says Darla from below, her voice thin and dry. It's still night in the shelter of the sleeping bag, Darla's head in my lap. I'm excited to show Darla the coming day. I nudge her, she sits up. Her face is puffy.

She stands. She walks a few feet toward the coming light.

"Cold," she says, turning back, wrapping her arms around herself.

She looks down the dark lane, her father's house invisible, somewhere at the end. She looks with a funny smile, then she walks, the sun now shafts through the trees, the light shining on her hair, catching stray strands, turning them golden.

There are two houses on the road separated by a long, long walk. We stand in front of the house on the end. It is small and white, with a screened porch in front. The bottom of the house is green with moss. There's no sound. The grass ticks as the heavy dew balls up and rolls into the soil. The yard opens up into a meadow, then a big hill with thin trees, and to the side, a forest. We circle the house. The windows are pink and pale blue from the dawn. I open the sleeping bag and put it over our shoulders. We stand in front of the house. I hear a chiming. It comes from beyond the meadow.

"He's probably asleep," says Darla.

We walk into the meadow.

"Thicker than the grass back home," Darla says.

"Less dog crap," I say.

The chiming gets louder when we reach the end of the meadow. Darla moves ahead. I roll up the sleeping bag. Through some brush we come to a clearing, a carpet of moss, flat rocks embedded into the ground, and a clear, brown stream, too wide to jump, twisting by, forking at rocks.

I take off my sneakers and socks, roll my pants to my calves and step out onto a rock. The water's super cold. It feels nice. I walk the rocks down the center of the stream. Darla follows.

"Watch it," I say. "Slippery."

"Shut up."

I hop quick.

I place a foot down. The moss is brown, so I can't tell it's moss. My foot shoots forward. I see the tree limbs overhead, the sky, white clouds, edges soaked pink. A shoulder whams hard on the rock and I open my mouth to cry out. But everything tightens up when I feel the deep cold. The sky turns liquid. The rocks on the bottom are smooth. The current moves me forward. It makes me sleepy, the cold. And in the cold, I feel my breathing stop. I stand quickly.

Darla's back on shore. "Spaz," she calls, laughing until she's spitting.

The water's to my waist. My legs are numb. "Shut up!"

She falls, rolls on her side, hamming it up. "Show off," she says.

Birds fly off scared.

"I'll get you some dry clothes," she says, her eyes twinkling.

I go to the sleeping bag and wait. There's a big bruise already forming on my shoulder, faint like a jellyfish rising to the surface. I smile. *Bruiser,* I think.

"*Ouch,*" Darla says, squinting at it close, handing me a shirt.

"It's cool-looking," I say.

"It's gross," Darla says.

We open the sleeping bag flat on the ground, my wet clothes in a pile on the side. We eat leftover cornflakes and Cap'n Crunch. I notice my Mickey Mouse watch then. The seconds hand isn't moving. I put it to my ear. No ticking. I wind it. I put it to my ear. Silent, broken. I can see the water under the glass. I look at Darla. She's not paying attention. I want to have a fit, a tantrum. But that won't do anything. There's no one here who would care. No Mom. No Dad. I look at Mickey. I slide the watch into my pocket. Darla takes out the pack of cigarettes. We lie on our backs and look at the sky, fill our cheeks with smoke.

"Last time I saw Joey, we were smoking. We played a game to see who could make the filter the darkest."

Darla nods, silently puffing.

"It was a lake, though: where we would sit, I mean." I look at Darla. I ask, "Why aren't you talking?"

Her eyes slide over to me, then they return to the sky. "You're not with Joey." Darla throws her cigarette butt overhand into the stream. She rolls over, flattening her hands into a pillow below her cheek.

She's mad. Good, I think. I look away, at the stream, and smoke until the cinder reaches the orange filter. Darla rolls over and looks at me for a long time. I pretend not to notice her.

"We're here," she says smiling, sleepy. "I remember looking at that map and walking my fingers over it, and how close West Virginia seemed that way. But, then I thought of it in real size. I thought how far it is to walk to Grant's Tomb from our house, and that's like nothing, *less than* nothing compared to how far West Virginia is. It's so far it doesn't seem real. Now, we're here and I can't believe that all that stuff back home is still happening, but it is, *this very second*, it's all going on so far away." Darla looks at me. "Don't you think, Ewe?"

I think how that's just what I thought. I think how I even made legs out of my fingers and walked them over the map like I was a giant, and how great that felt. But, I'm too tired to explain it all to Darla, so I just nod before falling asleep.

We stand in front of the house for a few minutes.

"Want me to knock?" I ask.

"No." Darla steps forward, takes a breath. She closes her eyes, knocks. She lets her hand fall. She opens her eyes. We wait.

"Maybe he went out while we were asleep," I say. "Maybe to breakfast. Or work— What does he do?"

Darla shakes her head.

"Let's get our bags," she says.

We're quiet as we walk our bags back along the dirt road. We pass the first house, I see a pale image of a man standing there, looking at us. Darla walks straight up to her father's house and pulls on the porch door. It opens. The air is musty like a basement. The corners of the floor and ceiling are rounded with old cobwebs like hammocks holding dust. Darla stands by another door, turning the knob.

There's the sound of a car outside. We turn and see an old truck pull into the driveway. An old man gets out and he stands beside his truck, scanning the property. Then he looks at the house and squints. The old man walks toward the house calling out for Darla's father. We kneel and peer through the screen windows. I look around. A pile of logs, a chair. Nowhere to hide.

Darla stays, frozen, staring at the old man getting closer.

The old man walks slowly through the tall grass, looking this way and that, talking to himself. "Seen two hooligans. Came this way . . ."

"Darla," I whisper, but she's like a zombie. I look up and see a latch lock on the door. I feel the floor rattle, the old man's foot on the first step. I reach and quickly lock the latch. I pull Darla down. I press us against the wall below the window. He makes his way up the stairs. The door rattles, the old man trying to open it. He presses his face against the screen door. His eyes are old and milky and wet, and his mouth quivers, and around it are long white whiskers, yellowed like pee stains. He gives the door one last rattle, then climbs back down the stairs. I wait. I let go of Darla. Without a word, she rises up onto her knees. The old man walks to his truck, looks around a last time, saying, "Hooligans musta just been shortcutting on through." He spits once, then drives off.

We stay in the house, finding the front door key on top of the doorjamb.

"What about Joey?"

"It can wait."

Darla says we should clean up for when Daddy gets home. Darla sweeps and dusts and mops, cleaning all the utensils and plates and cups. She takes the rugs outside and hangs them on the line in the sun to burn away the mold smell, and she beats them with a rake, dust flying in the air.

I find an old hand mower, and mow the front yard.

We spend the days by the stream, looking at the sky. Sometimes we climb the hill and forest beyond the stream, collecting wood for the stove, which warms the house. We get food at The Food Shack down on 33. We cut into the trees when we're passing the old man. He falls asleep for a nap every afternoon. We listen for his snoring and walk real soft through the trees and bushes because the leaves and sticks crunch like crazy. Sometimes, the snoring stops and we fall onto our bellies and freeze, and we have to bury our faces in the rotten-smelling leaves to cover up our breathing and laughing.

The lady at The Food Shack looked at us the whole time when we first went in, and we stood at the counter with all the food we wanted to buy and she didn't ring us up. She just stared and stared.

She asked, finally, "You-all got folks?"

"What?" we both asked.

"*Folks*. You-all got folks?"

Darla looked at me and shook her head, but I didn't understand either. We both looked back at the lady.

"Parents?!" she said, going red.

Darla started to nod and nod.

"Yeah, yeah," Darla said. "He lives down there, down—" she said, explaining.

The lady looked at Darla funny, then put her lips tight together. "I shoulda known," she said, very nasty. "Y'all're just his sort."

She looked over our heads at the lady standing behind us, saying that we were Darla's father's kids, and wasn't that the living end? And the lady behind us said, "Who knew britches

that big could fit in-a human bed, let alone in-a some sorrow-
ful woman, let alone make a child of it, let alone two."

We left that day and made fun of their stupid hillbilly
voices all the way home, laughing so much we forgot to hide
when we passed the old man. Luckily, he was snoring up a
storm.

I said, "Those ladies sure don't like your father."

Darla stopped. "They don't?"

Now when we go in, the lady says, "Oh, it's your prince
and her highness." And she always says under her breath, as
she's checking us out, "Makes servants outta his own tykes
even," and we just look at her and smile and nod and she rolls
her dumb hillbilly eyes.

Every morning we make our bed and we clean our dishes
and our messes for when Darla's father comes home. I don't
say anything after three days pass, which I keep count of with
slashes on the map, ///, then five, /////, when we both can
tell that it's not her father we're cleaning for anymore.

In late afternoons, if it's warm, we sit out back, watch the
sun fade away.

"Remember that night in Riverside Park, the night before
you left last summer?" Darla asks. "And then all those fireflies?"

"Yeah."

"I was just remembering it; it seems like a long time ago,"
she says, nodding.

We're quiet.

Darla turns to me.

"I never talked to Daddy before we came."

"I know."

We always eat dinner after the sun sets. Sometimes Darla
says she wants to wait, and I get mad. I say, "But, it's dinnertime." And Darla says, "But, why?" And I say, "Because it's

*dinner*time!" We cook on Darla's camping grill and eat by candlelight, since there's no electricity. When we're done we open up the black door of the woodstove, and it lights the room in a blazing flicker, and we sit beside it on a white shag rug playing cards. We take turns reading each other to sleep, using books we found in a box in the attic, and though I think it, I never say it: *Now what?*

I keep my watch on the floor next to where we sleep. I don't know why. I just like it there. Sometimes I look at it like it will tell me the right time. But it's always the same. 5:38, 10 24.

Darla falls asleep before I'm done with the first page, but I continue to read out loud. I like the feel of my voice made big by the still house. Many of the words I can't pronounce, and more I don't know. But the words feel good.

I look at Darla, a golden light across her face. I touch her cheek, run my fingers up to her temple, brush her thin hair behind her ear. I think how weird it is to be sleeping next to her. How I would never do it if everything was normal. How if everything was normal, I'd think it was gross. I think how weird it is that it doesn't feel weird at all. My eyes become heavy, and my body is already well away into sleep and I want to read some more.

". . . He waited for some minutes listening. He could hear nothing: the night was perfectly silent. He listened again: perfectly silent. He felt that he was alone."

I put the book on the floor, and lie on my side. My eyelids feel like rocks, but I want to look for a bit longer and I fight to keep them up. I look into the fire. I watch the flames and try to see where they end, but they flicker and are gone. Below, more fire rises, again and again, and it is gone, and I wonder if it's really there at all.

My eyes sting from the flames. I know that we will have to do something. This will end. Sometimes it's so boring. Sometimes I want everything back. Sometimes when things are wrong: the bed isn't made, we eat dinner too late, the sink is filled with too many dishes, I get so angry, but sometimes, I don't know why, those things make me feel like I'm drifting in space, just spinning, silently and slowly, circling nowhere. Today I counted eight slashes, ⫻⫻ ///, in my map. I look at the date on my broken watch and figure it out: today is October 30 1977. I will be home again, one day. I turn over and snuggle against Darla. I look into her sleeping face. Her cheeks are cool and smooth, her sleeping mouth smiles almost. She will not be here when this is over. She will be somewhere, but not here, because when the time comes, here will mean somewhere else. I will be alone. Maybe at home, with parents and everything. Someday I will be somewhere else. I run my hand over Darla, over the shag rug, the sleeping bag. I look at the light flickering against the wall. I am here right now, but all that I feel and see, it's like they are already gone, like a memory, because one day I will not be here.

four

I wake. It's bright, sunlight on the floor: time-for-school light.

I sit up quickly. "I'm awake!" I look around. I remember. I smile. I walk to the window. The autumn trees on the hill, in the forest, blow. Orange leaves with still-green bellies rustle free, tumble across the meadow. I open the window and yawn in the outside. The air smacks me, cold. Perfect. A perfect fall day. I remember all those mornings on the way to school, seeing the perfect fall park, left empty, wasted.

I smell butter and eggs and toast. I walk to the kitchen.

I open my mouth to tell Darla how starved I am, how glad I am to be a runaway.

Darla sits on a stool. She looks at me, then she looks back to where the portable stove is on the kitchen counter, where a man is hunched over it, cooking.

I freeze. *"Who?"* I mouth to Darla, pointing at the man.

Darla doesn't budge.

From behind, a lady's voice, "The second child's up."

I scream, looking behind. A lady with long red hair stands in the doorway. The man turns when I scream. I scream again.

I run, slipping on a little rug, slamming into the door. I grab the doorknob, open it. I run down the sloped meadow, faster than my feet can go. They tangle. I'm in the air. Belly flop. I roll. I look at the house. The man watches from the doorway. The lady peeks her head. The door closes. What should I do?! I can't leave Darla. I cut across the meadow into the forest, I run back through the trees. I need something. I look around. *Rocks.* I fill both pockets. I find a stick. I run to the house, crouching when I get close, stopping below a window. I look left, right. I haven't done my morning pee, and suddenly I really have to go. *Darla,* I think. I hold it. I rise up, peer through the window.

The man pours scrambled eggs onto four dishes on the kitchen table. The eggs look good. Even outside I can smell them. If he's going to take us away, it's very nice of him to give us breakfast first. What if I hide and he just takes away Darla and I'm left alone?

I can't hold it any longer. I unbutton, unzip. I pee.

I've got my rocks and my stick. I'll eat first, then we'll both escape.

I shake, zip, button. I walk into the house. I sit at the empty chair, leaning my stick against the table.

No one makes a sound.

"Who are you?" I ask.

Darla, who stares at the man, looks at me. The man looks at me, the lady looks at me.

Darla is the first to smile. She laughs, then the man laughs, then the lady laughs. Their faces turn red, their eyes wet. The man slaps the table, coughing because he's laughing so much.

"What?" I ask.

"It was just . . . when you ran," Darla says. "That was so funny." Her eyes sparkle. "Ewe," she says, glancing at the man, "meet Daddy."

Later her father says, "You can't imagine my surprise when we walked in this morning. It was quite a shock. Ha ha. But, yes: wonderful. A wonderful surprise. A shock. I was, well . . ." He waves his hands, and shakes his head. "Wonderful, wonderful. Look at me. I must still be in shock. I can only say one word. *Wonderful!*" His eyes go wide. "Summer, isn't it just wonderful? A real surprise."

The lady has a mouthful of eggs. I guess her name is Summer. "Hmm-hmm," she says.

"I mean we weren't even supposed to *stop* here, for Christ sake," he says. He laughs a little. A funny laugh, where his eyes continue to watch.

Darla frowns. "You're leaving, Daddy?"

He glances at Summer, then at Darla. He smiles. "Well, we *do* have plans to head out west. We only stopped off here to exchange my car for my truck."

Darla suddenly looks like a tiny cloth puppet slumped on a rock. "You're leaving?"

"Just like a present you were," her father says. "There you two were. Right there! Wouldn't have guessed it in a million years. A shock."

"We surprised you, huh, Daddy?" Darla says, smiling bright, legs swinging.

"Oh, angel, you can't begin to imagine."

After breakfast Darla's father flips some switches in the kitchen, and suddenly the lights work, the refrigerator hums. And outside he turns a valve on a big white tank and gas hisses through the oven's pipes. He shows us a ladder built onto the wall. We climb up to a loft. Our sleeping bag lies across a mattress and two pillows. We turn back.

I watch them looking at each other.

"You want us to sleep up here?" Darla asks.

Becoming excited, I think, She's annoyed. Her father thinks he can just move us: we liked it in front of the woodstove.

"An angel can't sleep on the floor," he says, smiling.

I watch him grinning. I look at Darla. She smiles back.

She hasn't looked at me barely once all morning.

They just sit there smiling at each other.

They make me sick.

Me and Darla sit on the back stairs facing the hill and the little shed that, until Darla's father arrived, had been padlocked. I'd gone up to it many times, pulling the doors as forward as the lock and latch would allow, putting my nose to the thin crack. It was dark and moist, smelly of earth and stillness, too dark to see. I imagined that it held things I couldn't even imagine. But now with the doors open, the surprise isn't much. Jars with screws, tools, a workbench.

It's late morning and the sun is warm, glints of reflected light snake back and forth across the faraway stream. We take off our sweaters. We watch Darla's father stand logs up on a chopping block, coming down on them with an ax, splitting them into halves, into quarters. I take the rocks out of my pocket and leave them on the stairs. Darla looks at them, but doesn't ask.

While he chops, Darla's father tells a story about the man who built this house. Darla's father owns over four hundred acres, he says, which includes forest and a side of mountain. He tells us how West Virginia was formed after the Civil War, and he tells us how it divided people. Neighbors from neighbors. That to this day there are families living on opposite sides of the mountain who bear a grudge. The man who built his house owned land in the valley and the hill, making it hard for him to choose sides, since the feuding was between valley people and hill people. Some folks hated him for not choosing, some thought he was saintly because of it.

I have to admit that Darla's father tells good stories. He acts out the parts using different voices. And he's been everywhere. He's swum in underwater caves in Hawaii, hunted alligators in the Everglades. He's meditated in the foothills of the Himalayas. Climbed the pyramids. Built waterways in Borneo. Banged drums on Indian reservations.

Mom tells stories good too, I think, using different voices. But, that's Mom, so it doesn't count. Dad just tells stories using his own voice. But, Dad does other stuff. Once when I cut my ankle real bad, he carried me in his arms, running sixteen blocks to St. Luke's. Once everyone was playing Guns, and I asked for a gun and Dad carved me a rifle out of wood. I thought it sucked, because everyone else had painted plastic rifles with moving hammers and triggers from Woolworth's. But when the kids saw my wooden rifle they all started begging for a turn with it, and I gave them one if they stood there and let me kill them once. And Dad grew up in Africa. And Dad builds miniatures. And Dad is strong and can do a handstand and walk up a flight of stairs that way.

I go inside. I see them through the window. Darla's father scoops Darla up and swings her.

"Angel in the sky," he says.

She squeals, giggling crazy, like an idiot.

I give them the finger. I sit at the table. I drum my fingers on it. There's a phone in the kitchen. I pick it up. I dial the number. A man answers. I ask for Dad. The man says he's not in. The man asks who's calling. I say his son.

"You must be the young one," the man says.

"Yeah," I say, waiting.

The man says, "I'm just a student, the professor's assistant."

"Oh," I say.

We're quiet. I wonder why the man isn't asking me where I am.

"This isn't Jordan," I say. "Or Daniel."

The man says he can tell, that I sound little.

We're quiet again.

"The professor should be back from his lecture in forty minutes. Do you want him to call you back?"

"No," I say.

"So, no message?"

I shake my head.

"Okay. I guess he'll see you back home then."

I nod, hang up.

When I go back outside, Darla's gone. Her father gave Summer a credit card and asked her to take his angel over to Virginia for a little spoiling. He's sweaty, and he piles chopped wood.

He looks at me and says, "There'll be no Mister business out here." His real name is Phineas, he tells me, but I must make a face because he smiles and says, "Sounds like a Latin fish, huh?" which I don't understand, so he asks me what name I'd like to call him.

Just to be kind of stupid and mean I say, "Ham."

"Ham." He tips his head from side to side. "Good: Ham." Then he squints at me. "I remember you," he says.

"You do?"

"You were smaller, of course." Ham nods. "You have an older sister?"

"Two brothers."

Ham nods again, looks off. "That's right. Your father's a teacher. Sort of a hard-ass."

I feel a rush of excitement when he curses.

"Yeah, I remember you now."

Ham smiles at me, and I curl in my lips, embarrassed by how good it feels.

I like how Ham looks. Green eyes. Wavy hair the color of pale wood, that blows out like wings in the wind. Big sideburns. The skin under his eyes pink from the sun and the cold.

"I remember once, we gave a party, Darla's mother and I. Your parents came, of course. For some reason you were there, I guess they couldn't find a sitter for you. Do you remember that?"

I shake my head.

Darla looks different. She has brown eyes and blackish brown hair like me. But, if I look harder I can see Daddy Ham in her. In the sun, I see copper in her dark hair, and I see him in her small round nose, her pointy chin.

"Your father: I remember this, because it was so funny. He was always on his high horse about our shenanigans. But this one party, I finally got him to take a hit of grass."

"Dad?!"

Everyone says me and Darla look related: just like brother and sister. So, I could be Daddy Ham's kid, I think, because I could be Darla's brother.

"The littlest hit you've ever seen." Daddy Ham is smiling, a bright smile, like a laugh is fluttering around inside his head. "The funny part was you. God, now I remember. I'm sure we must have put you off to sleep with Darla or something, but I guess you woke up. Since you were only yay high, no one noticed. You toddled over and stood in front of your father, and you started imitating the prissy way he had taken the hit of grass. I think they probably left soon after that."

⸎

Daddy Ham lights a fire. Night is coming. Outside the wind whistles fast and low. He makes us tea with lemon and honey. I lie on the floor next to Darla, staring at the ceiling that fades away in the growing darkness. Darla lies on her stomach, closer to the fire, reading from a box of old *Nature* magazines she found. In Virginia she and Summer got their nails painted red. And Darla bought a baby seal doll and a leather dress with flowers sewn in the middle. Summer gives Daddy Ham a look, a private kind. Daddy Ham puts his hand up to her, and she answers by bugging her eyes out.

Daddy Ham turns on the light. He straightens a rug that's bunched up.

He glances at Summer, then quickly away. He scoots a footrest over next to Darla and me. He sits on it.

We both look at him.

"Should we call your folks now?" he asks. "We've had a wonderful day, huh?"

We're quiet.

"No, Daddy," Darla says. "Please."

Daddy Ham looks at us for a while, his hands flat, palm to palm, finger to finger. He rubs them back and forth. He stands and goes to a desk. He opens a drawer. He returns with paper and envelopes.

"You didn't have to come to me. You could have gone any- where, but you came to me. I will respect that choice as a priv- ilege; an honor and a blessing. And I will treat it as such: who am I to tell you what to do? You're both obviously capable beyond your years . . . you're on a path," he says, nodding.

"You write them. Tell them you're safe. I'll mail them." He smiles. He glances at Summer, then quickly stands and walks into a different room.

At night we hear them. Summer says, *Phin, right there, Phin . . . Right! There! Phin!* Daddy Ham goes, *uh-uh-uh-uh-uh . . .*

Darla climbs down from the loft, walks across the room. She closes their open door, and their grunts go muffled. Darla climbs back up and we huddle below the sleeping bag because it's cold.

"*So gross,*" she whispers.

I laugh and make fun: "*Oh-oh. Ah-ah.*"

Darla hits me very hard. "Shut up," she hisses.

five

We're all in the kitchen. Me and Darla sit at the table playing Spit. Daddy Ham and Summer stand by the counter making breakfast, drinking coffee. Summer presses a silver stick-on star to her forehead.

"Third eye," she laughs to Daddy Ham, nudging his side, spinning then, the tiny mirrors sown into her dress sparkling in the morning sun.

Darla watches them.

All of us except Darla, who swatted Summer away when she came near, have silver stars stuck to us.

Daddy Ham notices Darla looking.

"How's your mother?" he asks.

"She's seeing a doctor. As a boyfriend, I mean, not that she's sick."

Summer leaves the room. Darla watches her go.

"I suppose that's all she's ever really wanted."

"How would you know?"

"That's the sort of life she wanted, angel. I was her husband."

Darla stares at her father, then she looks at me. She picks up a Spit card, and says, "Well: you ready?" like I've been making her wait forever.

"What sort of life?" I ask. "What sort of life did she want, Ham?"

Daddy Ham leans over, and he whispers in a pretend-secret voice. "Square," he says. "Very square."

I don't know what that means.

Summer returns. She glances at us, then away. She opens the oven door to check on a pan of bacon. A good sizzling, meaty smell comes out.

"I can't eat that," Darla says, nudging her chin at Summer. "It's pork."

"You love pork," Daddy Ham says.

"I'm a Jew now. I don't eat pork."

"You're half Protestant."

"I'm a Jew."

"Fine, you're a Jew. Summer'll make you something else." He looks at Summer.

Summer stares at him. She turns to the refrigerator. She takes out a box of Eggos. She mumbles as she jams the waffles into a toaster.

"What's your job?" I ask.

"He doesn't have a job," Darla says. "And, you know why?"

I shake my head.

" 'Cause when his dad died he left him a whole bunch of money." Darla looks at her father. "That's what Mom says. I was only four when you got it."

Daddy Ham nods.

Darla looks back at me. "Mom says that for a while we were living on top of the world. I don't remember anything, except I remember I got a rocking horse." Darla looks straight at her father. "Remember? It had a saddle covered in pink silk, and flowers painted on its belly. But then Daddy left and it all changed."

Summer accidentally drops a glass bowl onto the floor. It shatters. We all look over at her. She stares real hard at Daddy Ham.

Looking at her, Daddy Ham nods. He walks around the table, scoots Darla in her chair out, so she faces him. He holds both her shoulders.

"Angel."

"Darla."

Daddy Ham breathes out. "See, if I had known you were coming—"

Darla starts blinking.

"Don't cry, angel."

"Darla." Tears come. They're almost invisible, watery and quick.

"Summer and I had it planned: this place we're going to," Daddy Ham says, "for a long time. Imagine how *you'd* feel if you had your heart set on something for a long time. It's a wonderful place. We've even paid for it already." Daddy Ham tries to smile.

Dark spots appear on Darla's T-shirt, tears dripping from her chin.

"There's a nice man who runs the place called Guru." Daddy Ham talks for a while about the man named Guru.

"Take me," Darla says. She wipes her eyes.

"We can't."

"Why?"

Daddy Ham looks at her.

She says it again, louder. *"Why?"* She says it again and again until it's a loud and sharp sound, like a siren.

"Stop it!" Daddy Ham orders. He shakes her. "Stop it. Please."

Darla's face goes red, eyes popping. She screams and screams.

"I won't go! I won't go!" Daddy Ham says.

Darla goes silent. She looks at her father. "Really?"

Daddy Ham stands. "Let's go for a drive. How does that sound?"

He looks at me and he nods, like he wants me to go along with it.

"I'll pack us a lunch," he says. "A picnic."

Daddy Ham and Summer sit up in the front of the Bronco truck. The roof is down and we drive fast. Me and Darla play a game. We put our heads back. The fiery fall leaves and the sun shoot out like streamers, the wind snaps up our noses and in our ears so we can't hear and we hoot loud. It tickles and makes us laugh. I crouch forward, behind the back of the front seat for a second, to get my breath. Summer's face is tight. She's yelling at Daddy Ham. I can't really hear her. Daddy Ham says, *I'm a cinder back.*

Darla tugs on my sleeve.

I lean my head back and scream.

We pass through a town called Sugargrove. There's a big train junction. Me and Darla start bouncing in our seats, begging for Daddy Ham to stop.

"You want to have a picnic here?" he asks.

"Yeah, yeah."

"Yeah, yeah."

Summer refuses to come, instead staying in the truck smoking cigarettes.

We climb over a chain-link fence. It smells of oil and smoke. Trains slowly lumber by, moaning. Tracks run and cross as far as I can see. The trains are red and rusty and gray.

Daddy Ham takes out a bag of dried apricots and we each take a handful. He passes out sandwiches.

I notice that the trains have different states' names written on them. I ask why. He explains that the name tells you the train's home state. He says they travel to different states to give those states the things they need that they don't have. He says, for example, Maine might give Mississippi lobsters, and Georgia might give New York peaches. Then they all go back home and do it all over again, he says.

We drive back. It's colder and Daddy Ham puts the top back up. I lean my head against the window. Speckles of yellow, late-afternoon sun flit past my eyes. I close them. I don't sleep, I kind of nap. But less. I kind of float.

I'm a cinder back, I think. The car driving, rocking, feels good. The sunlight whipping by my closed eyes, making me dizzy. *I'm a cinder back . . . cinder back . . . cind-er back . . . send . . . her . . . back . . . I'm-a . . . Al-ma . . . I'll-a . . . I'll send her back.*

Darla's real quiet when we pull up to the house. She opens the truck door and walks away, along the meadow. Daddy Ham watches her. I sort of smile at him, then turn and catch up to her. She finally sits. She leans forward and takes out the crumbled pack of cigarettes from her back pocket.

It's evening, dark. Daddy Ham and Summer move inside a lit window making dinner.

Darla blows out smoke. She burns a leaf with her cinder.

I puff my cigarette quickly so the smoke comes out like a train.

"He's my daddy. I'm not saying he's not . . . ," Darla says,

like I had said something first. She stares at him through the window as she talks. "I didn't hear from him except for that letter, the one you saw with the map. I showed it to Mom. She looked at it, handed it back, slapped me in the face, and walked away." Darla looks at me. "Right after, we moved to Queens."

Darla's quiet and she burns more holes in her leaf. Leaf bits, edges black, float to the ground.

Darla bunches up her mouth. She tells me that it's when they moved to Queens that the Jewish ladies started coming around. They talked to her mom, about how she was a Jew even if she hadn't been one for a long time. They said that even though Darla's father wasn't a Jew, Darla still was. They started lighting candles on Fridays, and her mom started dressing like an old lady. The people from the temple used to give them money, before her mother got a job with Dr. Dan. Darla's mother cried a lot. Once they gave her a bag. At home her mother put the bag in her closet. While she was taking a bath, Darla went to the closet and looked in the bag. Inside were clothes. Darla pulls on the cuff of the ladybug sweater she wears, and looks at me.

"This was in there. The next day Mom came into my room with a crumbled Macy's bag full of clothing. She sat on my bed and smiled. *Did a bit of shopping today,* she said. Then she took the clothes from the Macy's bag, and they were the clothes from her closet. *Aren't they lovely,* she said, standing in front of the mirror holding a sweater in front of herself, saying, *The saleslady said I looked smart in this.*"

Darla stands and walks toward the house.

We walk through the house. Darla picks up her tent and sleeping bag and walks back outside. We walk across the meadow, walk a little into the forest.

"You tell a story now," Darla says.

From behind we hear Daddy Ham. *"Dinner! Dinn-ner!"*

The house is small in the distance. It's dark. Daddy Ham stands on the steps under the yellow porch light. He waits, then returns inside.

Dad is the one who always calls us for dinner. He calls just like Daddy Ham. First quick, then a second time, louder and longer. Always at six exactly. Every night.

I turn back, and Darla's setting up a tent.

"You wanna sleep here tonight?" I ask.

"Can we?"

It's nice breaking the rules again. It excites me. Breaking rules. I've kind of missed it. But I am hungry.

"Should I get us some food?" I ask.

"I don't want their stupid dinner."

"I'll make sandwiches."

"Oh, yeah. Sandwiches." Darla sits on the ground. "Tell me a story."

I don't know what to tell.

"I called Dad yesterday," I say.

Darla's face goes flat.

I don't want to tell any more. I want to go, get us sandwiches.

Darla says quietly, "You're going back?"

"I called him at his job. He wasn't there. I talked to his assistant."

"What'd you say?"

"Dad was in class."

Darla frowns.

"It wasn't a big deal. The assistant wasn't surprised or nothing. He didn't ask anything."

I want to leave. I want to be alone.

"He wasn't surprised?" Darla asks.

"Dad was in class. He teaches."

I stand.

"I'm gonna get sandwiches."

I turn. I walk, then I trot. I run as the tears start. It's better at home, I think. It's good I'm gone. They're going on like normal. I can't see as I run. Before I left it wasn't normal, but now it is. But, it's fun here, I think, nodding to myself. Like now, camping out. Home is normal now that I'm gone.

Daddy Ham and Summer sit Indian style in the living room, eyes closed. They both made low sounds.

Ooooommmm.

Ooooommmm.

Daddy Ham opens his eyes, says, "Hey, little man. Dinner's on the stove."

Summer continues to make the sound. I watch her.

"That's om," he whispers, standing, moving close. He tells me that om is the first sound and the last sound and that it's been going on forever and ever and it can't ever die. He says that it's bigger than us, our lives, our petty problems. It doesn't know good or bad, right or wrong. Those are just human hang-ups, he says. Om doesn't judge.

"Oh," I say.

I go to the kitchen. Daddy Ham follows. He looks out the window, for Darla, I guess.

"Tell me about the time you saw a bear," I say.

"Hmm?" he says, still searching out into the darkness.

"In California, Ham," I say. I try to remember what Darla had told me that day on the bus. "At Yellowstone."

"Yellowstone's in Wyoming," he says, turning to me.

"Must have been something," I say.

"What are you saying?" he asks. "Bear? I've never seen a bear."

"You and Darla camping at Yellowstone."

He frowns a little. "We never had a chance to camp. She was only a little thing last time I saw her." His mouth bunches up just the way Darla's sometimes does. Then he goes back to the other room where Summer has been moaning the whole time, and soon I hear Daddy Ham moaning too.

I wrap the sandwiches. I see Summer's purse on the kitchen table. I swipe it. I go outside. I stop. I return, putting the sandwiches and purse on the outside steps. I go inside. I stop. Daddy Ham's on the phone. *You haven't left yet?* He swings around when I enter. I can tell his heart's beating fast. His face goes red. He says into the phone, *Yes, yes. Okay. Bye.* He hangs the phone up.

"Whoa, scared the crap outta me."

"Sorry."

"What're you kids—"

"Camping."

"She's—?"

I wait, but he just looks at me.

He takes my hand and kisses my palm, then curls my fingers over it.

"Put that on her cheek tonight for me, will you?"

"Okay."

I walk past him. I climb up to the loft. I search through our bags. I don't know why, I just want her tonight. I find Mona. I go back outside.

Darla's built a fire. I look at it, but I don't say anything because I don't want her to know how jealous I am that she knows how to make fires.

We eat the sandwiches. We go through Summer's purse. We find cigarettes, which I take. A lipstick, which Darla takes. A Connecticut driver's license. Her real name is Rhonda Werner. I once asked what her last name was and she said, *Rain, Summer Rain. I'm part Indian like Cher,* she said. *At least, in spirit,* she said.

"Rhonda!" We both laugh.

We say it stretched out and ugly, "Rooon-duh." We say it over and over, "Rooon-duh, Rooon-duh, Rooon-duh," and we laugh like crazy.

From the DOB on the license I do the math: Summer's twenty-four.

I wonder if Dad still sees Megan. I think that he probably doesn't. Everything is normal and regular. Dad doesn't see other women when everything is regular and normal. He teaches. Mom writes. Daniel draws. Jordan does good in school and on the weekends *gets some* from girls.

I smile. I hope Megan's sad. I hope she misses Dad. So long as I am away, he won't see her. I laugh. I feel like I'm crushing her. As long as I'm away, it's all regular and normal.

The flames of the fire crackle and whip softly outside. I sit up. I look at Darla. She's asleep on her back, mouth open, soundless.

I hold Mona. I make a face at her. I smile, I stick out my tongue, pull my nose to a piggy snout. Mona just stares. She's not going to say anything. If I want to say something, then I have to say it.

I crawl out of the tent. I crouch in front of the fire until my sweater is hot. I throw in more branches. It's cold and the sky is clear, lots of stars, the air and ground black in the moonless night. I walk along the side of the forest. I come to an old, abandoned tub. I get in.

I close my eyes. I see my family out my bedroom window, through the courtyard, in the dining room. They're eating dinner. The four of them, like regular, but more than that, like that's how it's supposed to be. I think about it. It's true. Regular families are always four, never five. Four is a box. Four is good. Like families on TV. *Happy Days:* 4. *Davey and Goliath:* 4.

The tub's iron sides are cold, the bottom's covered in cold frozen leaves, and the cold feels like it's pulling on me. It makes me tired.

"*Oooommmm . . .*"

Om goes on forever, Daddy Ham said. So, when I say om, that must go on forever, my om. And if my om goes on forever, what about other sounds I make: are they all floating far away in space? Are my sounds still home, bouncing around getting smaller and smaller? Does the house remember me? Does my bed remember how I felt, the front doorknob, the forks, the TV? Am I still there? From opening the front door too quickly one day that makes a quick wind that makes the ivy plant over Mom's desk sway that makes the dust on their leaves float in the air over Mom who breathes it in making her sneeze who gets up to blow her nose using the last tissue so she writes down *tissue* on the grocery list for when Dad shops and that makes Dad take a little longer than usual looking for tissue and in that extra minute alone in A&P more thoughts go through his head and he thinks of Megan and he thinks of her as he walks on Broadway then up toward West End and because of this thought he stops at the corner pay phone and it's because he's stopped that he's there when Daniel walks by and Daniel doesn't stop or say *Hi* or ask Dad why he's there but he knows seeing Dad talk on a pay phone a block from home with the shopping cart full of groceries can't be good and thoughts start to bounce around in Daniel's head and they bounce so much that he has to walk quickly because the thoughts have gone to his stomach and turned to diarrhea and Jordan who's walking to the park with a dancing girl that he rubs against on Friday nights sees Daniel walking quickly to the lobby door with that face Daniel gets when he has to go that makes Jordan call out *Hey Shitty ha ha ha* but Daniel just runs into the building and the

dancing girl looks at Jordan and he goes *Ah ha ha ha* again
but inside he is so annoyed he could break something because
he likes it when you look hurt and as Jordan and the dancing
girl enter the park Dad reaches the building and he waits for
the elevator to come down and it makes that rumbling sound
that echoes in the shaft that always makes Dad think of a
grumbling stomach and as the elevator door opens for Dad
Daniel's in one bathroom making hot smells and Mom's in
the other making hot sounds.

I sit up quickly and grab the tub's side. I look around. I lay
back down. I hold Mona close to my face. Tiny stars shine in
the glass, and Mona looks through them.

"What are you doing?"

Darla stands beside the tub.

I'm curled on my side.

"I heard you. You were talking to yourself."

"I wasn't."

I sit up, sliding Mona under my sweater. Darla puts her feet
in the tub, sits on the rim. I sit up next to her.

"You're always leaving me," she says, "without ever saying
anything."

"Do you wanna go back to the fire? It's cold."

I step out of the tub and start walking.

"We should probably go soon," she says. "To Joey's."

"Really?"

"That's why we came," she says, nasty.

We walk silently for a while.

"I asked Ham and he said he never took you to see any
bear, and he said that forest isn't even *in* California."

Darla doesn't say anything for a long time. "He told you?"
Darla looks at me, and I wish that I hadn't said anything.
"Wyoming," she says. "You're right. I messed that one up. It's
in Wyoming, not California."

"Then why do you have all that camping stuff?" I ask. "How'd you know how to make a fire?"

"Last summer," Darla says. "I went to camp. Upstate. The Catskills. It was a camp where you actually camp."

We reach the tent.

"Who were you talking to?" she asks. "I know you were talking to yourself, but who were you talking to?"

I remember Daddy Ham's kiss that I still hold in my hand. I press my palm against Darla's fat, cold cheek. She looks at me funny, but doesn't say anything. Then she kind of smiles and we crawl into the tent.

six

Darla nudges me and I open my eyes. It's morning. I roll away. She nudges me again. I turn my head.

"*What?*"

Darla holds up Mona. "Who's this?"

I reach over, Darla moves back.

"Where'd you find that?" I sit up.

"It was right here in your clothes."

I lean over and snatch Mona back. "None of your beeswax."

Darla's brow wrinkles, lines moving up like a little roof over her face. "Ewe, who is she? Why do you have it?" She looks down. "I mean, is she a friend of yours? I've never seen her. She doesn't go to P.S. Seventy-five does she?"

"It's Mona," I say.

"Oh."

I run my hand over the glass. "That's not her real name, but that's what I call her," I say.

"What? Like a fun name, like I call you, Ewe?

"Yes."

Darla unzips the door of the tent. Light and air rush in. She looks outside as she talks. "What's wrong with her real name?" she asks. She turns around and looks at me. "Huh?" she says. "You never gave me a fun name, is that 'cause you like my real name? Why do you call *her* by a fun name?"

"It's my mom."

Darla crawls back beside me, taking the picture. "Your *mom?*"

I nod.

"That's so weird . . ." Darla smiles. "It's really . . . your *mom?* Look," Darla says, like I haven't noticed, "she's a kid, she's just . . . like us." Darla looks at me, her mouth open. She looks at Mona close up, and says, "It's kinda gross almost."

"I know," I say, smiling, nodding.

We pack the tent and the sleeping bag. We cross the meadow. The Bronco's gone.

"They musta gone out," Darla says.

The back door's locked. We go around front, the front door's locked. We look at each other. We go to the window below the kitchen and it's open. We climb through.

We eat.

"What are we gonna do?" I ask.

Darla chews. "Stay."

"But, you said—"

Darla shrugs.

"He's not my dad," I say. "You said we were going to Joey's."

"So go," Darla says.

Darla goes out the back door to get wood for the wood-stove.

I think, *Where? Where will I go?* I wash the dishes, watch-

ing the colors of the rising sun press against the belly of the
hill, the dew of the meadow. I've brought Mona to the sink to
clean the rest of the dried red off her frame. Darla walks into
the kitchen. She tugs on my sleeve, her face is pale, she drags
the duffel bag, dropping it beside the tent and sleeping bag.

"Now," she says.

She tosses her camping stove into our duffel bag with our
clothes, money.

"What?"

Below the kitchen window I see the top of Dad's head. He
looks up to the window, but the sun is in his eyes. I move back.
Through the doorways I can see Mom and Darla's mother
leaning into the porch screen door, squinting, knocking.
Beyond them, the old man from down the road stands next to
his truck, his head high, straining to see.

Darla pulls me into the cupboard below the sink. It's big
but we both have to ball up tight to fit. We close the two doors
and look through the cross-shaped holes of their mesh fronts.
I hear Dad enter, his footsteps I remember right away. I feel
my heart. I scrape my teeth along my knuckle, on the smooth
scar skin that grew in after I chewed all the dead skin away.
His legs come into view. He stops. He turns a little. He picks a
plate out of the sink, then puts it back, the water overhead
moving a little. *Christ,* he says, very low; more angry than his
yelling voice is his low voice, where the words have to squeeze
through the clamp of his closed teeth. *God, Christ,* he says,
hitting the counter. The walls of the cupboard around us
shake. My stomach, my chest, my whole body trembles. I
shove my knuckles into my mouth, running my tongue in circles around them. Darla squeezes my arm. They're here, I
think, and we're in a lot of trouble. I could open the door, and
there we would be, next to each other.

What would our punishment be? How long would we be

grounded? How long without TV, without dessert? How hard will we be hit even though they don't mean it? What will their faces look like when they do what they don't mean to do, what they'll be so-very-sorry-honey for after they've done it?

I remember what home is like when I am there: dead faces, red faces.

I know how much better it is now that I'm gone. Normal, regular.

And I saw it: what just that little bit of me still left swirling back home like om did to them.

I don't know what to do.

An idea flashes: I will let them decide. I will tell them telepathically, that I'm here, and they can choose.

I'm here! I'm here!

Dad's feet move away, through the house. The front door unlocks and Mom and Darla's mother rush in.

The mothers make lots of sounds, calling for us. Dad tells them to quiet down. It's silent. They listen for us. I look at Mona. I make her expression, her sad-angry face. I look up. Darla's smiling at me.

I thought they was hooligans at first, the old man is saying. Dad asks the old man if he's seen Daddy Ham today, but he calls him by his real name, Phineas. The old man says, *Nope.* Dad asks, *Why are you here?* The old man says, *You think you can just come here with that fancy-pants accent of yours.* The old man then asks Dad where he's from, then he says how me and Darla were always tearing up and down the road enough to wake the dead. He goes on talking, and I think it's funny and it's sad because no one's listening and I know just how it feels. There's crying. I look at Darla, and we both listen hard to try and tell which mother it is. Dad says something about how we always hide, and his voice is nice sounding when he says that, like he's remembering and it makes him smile a little. Then we hear doors open and close. Someone climbing the ladder to the loft. They call our names.

Mom walks into the kitchen. She talks to herself quietly. "Where are you?"

I lean close to the mesh door, and put my hand out. Mom sits at the kitchen table.

Mom will hear, I think.

I'm here, I'm here.

She looks at the back door. She cries soundlessly.

Darla pulls me back, she looks at me and shakes her head, no.

Mom stands, clearing her eyes. She comes toward us.

"Soap," she says. She bends down and I see her face. Her hand reaches out and takes hold of the doorknob, her eyes looking right toward mine, into mine if not for the darkness. But, her face looks up, toward the counter, and her hand falls away.

"There it is, right in front of my face," she says.

My heart hurts like a cramp, and it's a heavy thing, like a metal bucket filled with rocks sinking into cold water.

Overhead the water in the sink sloshes, plates moving to the drying rack.

Dad's feet, then. He clears his throat, like he always does before he speaks, so that you know to shut up. But, the water keeps sloshing above us. *Stop doing those,* he says. Mom says, *I need to.* Dad breathes out. The sloshing stops. Mom's feet turn toward Dad's feet. *What? You're going to start a fight?* she asks. Dad says he's not fighting, he just finds it odd that— Mom says, *Jesus Christ.* Dad's quiet. Then, he says, *Don't Jesus Christ me.* Mom says, *I'll Jesus Christ you: Jee₹-ass Ca-ryst, Jee₹-ass Ca-ryst,* she says in Dad's voice, low and quick, choppy for his French accent, I guess, which I can never hear unless someone like Reid is making fun, imitating him.

They start yelling.

Why are they fighting? I think.

I called: it was all regular, like normal.

Then, I understand.

Me: that they are near me.

I'm here! I'm here! Don't they know I am near? Don't they feel me inches from them?

In the distance, from the outside, Darla's mother calls our names, echoing across the empty meadow.

Mom and Dad move away, toward the living room door. Dad's legs go close to Mom's. I hear fabric, and hands patting. They're both saying sorry, sorry. Moving even that little bit away from me helps, I think. Mom's feet turn back to the sink. She pulls the drain plug and the water rushes between me and Darla through the twisting pipes.

Mom and Dad return to the living room. The front door opens, closes. We wait.

"Think they'll go back home now?" I whisper.

"Not till they find us," Darla whispers.

We slowly and quietly crawl out into the kitchen.

I look out the window, see our parents move around the yard.

"You're gonna stay?" I ask.

I open the arm on the back of Mona's frame and prop her on the floor of the cupboard.

"You're leaving?" she asks. "Why didn't you open the door when they were here?"

I look back out the window. They've moved to the front of the house near our brown station wagon. I pretend that something's caught in my eyes. I squint and rub my wet eyes. But, below this feeling, I feel another feeling rising up. It's hotter and more muscley. I suddenly want to break something. I like the new feeling. I let it come up quick. It feels good. Strong. I turn.

"So, you wanna go?"

Darla doesn't answer. She doesn't even shrug.

I move to the back door, my hand on the knob. "If I open this door, you'll come?" I ask.

She's slouched. She straightens her back. "Yeah," she says.

We sling the bags over our shoulders. We walk quietly to the back door, carefully opening it. They can't see us since they're on the other side of the house. We run into the forest, and through it, we run alongside the meadow, across the stream, up the hill. On top we stop. We look down. The adults circle the house. The old man moves forward, shaking his head, spitting. Mom turns to him and puts a finger in his face, and yells something. Darla's mother shakes, hands to face, crying, bobbing. Dad paces back and forth and I see, even from far away, the red rising up his neck, across his ears, the angry vein growing.

The good feeling fills me completely now. I could run forever. I'm super bad. I can feel it in my legs and arms, my head, my stomach. I want to hurt, I want to break, I want to curse. I feel like one of those smooth badasses: *Listen, baby, I'll knock you out.* It excites me like too much sugar. I watch them down there: chumps. Hahahaha! It's like when we throw water balloons from the window at the people below. The best part isn't hitting them and watching them jump and scream: that's just the funny part. The best part is before: holding the quivering balloon out, how in that moment I'm so excited that sometimes I want to just throw *myself* out the window: knowing that they have no idea that someone's watching them, knowing that there's nothing they can do, knowing that I'm about to do something to them, and they have no say.

We go down the other side of the hill that leads onto Route 33. We stand there a moment. I wait for Darla to say what we should do now. She looks at me.

"I forgot my dress," she says. "I laid it out 'cause I wanted to wear it today." Her face crumples, and her chin trembles, and her eyes begin to sparkle, and she stares off into space.

I remember. It's this way. I don't want to see Darla's face. I turn her in the right direction and push and she walks, and I follow behind, watching out for cars, pulling us into the brush whenever one passes. It's a long, long walk, and it's afternoon when we get there, and we have no food, and I know we won't for a long time, so I decide not to think about it again.

We watch trains exhale heavy as they come in from far-away places: Utah, the Dakotas, Maine. We cross the tracks until I find a train sitting there that says NORTH CAROLINA. We throw black gravel rocks at the tracks trying to make a spark. Dusk comes, and we slink to the train. We walk along-side it until we find a half-empty car with an open door. We throw in our bags, then climb on. A few sharp stars appear in the night. The train blows out some steam. It rolls east.

Night falls and the land turns black and cold, a slash of light when we rush by homes. We wrap ourselves in the sleeping bag, and let our feet dangle out of the train.

Darla lights a cigarette. She holds out the pack.

"Let's share," I say.

We rock with the train, the wooden body, the rusted metal hands that link car to car, rubbing loud. There are wooden crates. ORANGES, they say.

Darla leans over and takes two envelopes out of her back pocket. She hands them to me. They are the letters we wrote to our parents to tell them we were okay.

"He must have forgotten to mail them," Darla says. "I found them. They'd fallen behind his desk."

I hand them back, and Darla puts them in her pocket. Darla takes puffs, then passes the cigarette to me, letting her head fall against my shoulder.

I see my parents at the bottom of the hill. I remember how under the good badass feeling the wet-eye feeling returned, and how that feeling made me want to run back to them, how much I wished that they had really wanted to take me home. But, I didn't because they didn't. So I turned. I ran away.

"You're shivering," Darla says.

She puts her arm around me. "I wish it weren't so dark."

I stand up and have to walk slow because, like the old drunks on Broadway, I stumble side to side a bit because the train's rocking so hard. In the shadows, I feel for the duffel bag. I drag it back to the open door, and take out the camp stove. Because of the wind it takes eleven matches and Darla finally having to lean over like a shield, to get it going. The car lights up, a warm mud color. Darla searches the duffel bag. She takes out a little radio. It crackles until a station comes softly into tune. A song begins with a faraway strumming guitar. Darla laughs out, there are tears on her cheeks, her lashes dark triangles, her cheeks pink.

"Oh," she says, "I love this song."

She hangs the little radio on a loose wire from an orange crate.

Now a banjo and a harmonica and a swooping bass.

Darla sways, then she reaches her right hand out, letting it waver like something under the water. She turns and looks at me. She hops, off one foot then the other, bouncing her head from side to side, stumbling side to side. She smiles, her face sparkling by the drying tears. Her shadows, thin and brown, fall long on the floor and up the walls, and they spin as she dances, circling around the car like ribbons.

"Whoo-ee! Are we gonna fly,
down in the easy chair. . . ."

Darla takes my hands and spins me around. I raise my head, and watch the shadows turn and the light flicker, and we hop and spin, singing out together, *"Whoo-ee . . . !"* until we are laughing too hard.

Then we just squint through our sparkling eyes and dance. And dance.

seven

For a while the train moves slowly enough that we can hear the sounds made in the rising sun. Some birds, the quiet from the night wind dying down to a day breeze. We sit beside the open door, chewing on dried apricots that we found packed deep in our duffel bag. (We also found a block of cheese, a loaf of bread, nuts, and a dried sausage. Darla looked at me, sausage in hand. I shrugged, then she shrugged.) We pass flatland and farms. Far out, a farmer walks slowly toward a red tractor, bending down to check his crops. Pumpkins, large and orange with thick spiky green leaves, edges brown.

Darla turns the duffel bag over and shakes everything out.

"Wanna see what we still got." She holds a paper bag with our money. "We've got this, which is the most important, and the camping stuff."

We also have enough clothing. When Darla saw our parents and was shoveling stuff into the bag, she got my broken watch but forgot the map.

Darla sorts through the clothing. Then she stops and smiles. She holds up a T-shirt. She puts it on over her ladybug sweater.

"What's it say?" I ask, leaning closer.

Darla holds her arms down. In the middle is a face half in shadow with a crabby bush of hair. In a circle around the face it says: BOB BACKWARD IS BOB. GOD BACKWARD IS DOG.

Darla turns around and the back says: IN WHOM DO YOU TRUST?

"Bob Dylan?"

"Mom never let me wear it. I made it last summer at camp."

"You lie."

Darla raises her eyebrows. "I got a lot of help," she says.

We sit on the floor and fold and repack the clothing, eating oranges from a crate we've broken open. The train ambles slowly, like it's soon coming to a stop, but then it rolls on like that for hours.

I think about Mom and Dad. I see them. They're in the station wagon. Darla's mother is sitting in the back. They're driving home, because by this afternoon, they know we're gone again. Mom got real upset, acting *romantic* like she does, saying how they had to find us, how they need to keep looking for us. God, where are they? she said in a loud, crying voice. That made Darla's mother start crying and bobbing again. And Dad's face got red and annoyed, and he said, that getting upset wouldn't help anything, that we were gone, and that it's best to inform the police, and to go home and wait, which is just what they did.

We line orange peels along the floor, and flick them, one by one, out of the train.

*   *   *

"What do you think happened when Daddy got home and found Mom there and your parents; that we got scared off by them? You think he was probably just out getting breakfast stuff? There were only two eggs in the whole house. I bet he got super sore and really told them off." Darla smiles, thinking about that, then her face gets serious and she looks at me. "I hope he doesn't feel too bad about us running away, feeling like he shoulda been there."

I look at Darla, but I don't say anything.

I think of telling her that it's my birthday. But I don't. I don't know what day exactly it is today. I was keeping count on the map, but we left that. My watch tells the date, but it's broken. My birthday comes at the beginning of the month, so I figure it's around now.

I get to choose dinner. Pizza and lemon cake is what I always ask for.

We hear a man, *Halloo*. The train starts chugging. Steam hisses, burnt-smelling wisps curling into the car. A deep whistle blows.

We figure we must be in North Carolina because the train stops for a long time, and then men start to unload the large wooden crates. So, we get out.

"Why you walking so slow?" I ask.

Darla walks balanced on a track, but the duffel bag on her back makes her slip a lot. Her Bob Dylan shirt is stained with orange dribble lines. Darla hops from the track, crosses over, and walks beside me. She looks down the road, squinting.

"Why're you walking this way? Is this north?" she asks. She looks at me. "If we wait a bit longer the stars will be out and we'll be able to tell that way."

"Is that another thing your *dad* taught you?" I say, looking away.

Darla taps the side of her head, ignoring me, and laughs. She points to the setting sun. "That's west," she says, "so, that way *is* north."

I cross my arms proud.

"Do we want to go north?" she says, turning.

I start walking.

Darla jogs up to my side. "You think we should go north?"

I don't know. How would I know? I just want to walk, need to walk.

Darla shrugs and follows, which annoys me even more.

The sun falls away and the sky goes black and we hide whenever a car passes. I tell Darla I have to go b.m. She looks at me blankly. I say, *Number two.* She nods. *Me too.* We find a bush. *No looking. Ew!* We squat on either side. It feels good. We use dry leaves. They hurt.

We walk again. Not that many cars pass and mainly it's just the sound of our tired feet scraping the hard dirt beside the road, and the dark and us not talking. I try not to think.

"This road's never gonna end," Darla says. "It's not right," she mumbles.

"You said it was north!"

"So what?! What's north?!"

"Just shut up."

"I'm so tired."

"I'm so hungry."

We sit on the side of the road. We got through the bag. Half a loaf of hard bread. Some cheese that's gone warm and moist and smelly. Half a dried sausage.

"We could eat the stuff Ham put in our bag," I say.

Darla frowns. "Daddy didn't put that food there. Why would Daddy put food in our bag? Why do you think that? He didn't know we were gonna be chased off. How could he have known that? Why'd you say that, Ewe?"

I don't say anything.

Darla has a mermaid key chain. A small blade, the size of a pinkie, flips out of her tail, and we use it to cut. I break the bread in half, cut it down the middle. I cut cheese. I cut sausage.

"Don't put that on mine," Darla says, grabbing for one of the breads. "I can't eat milk and meat."

"It's cheese."

"That's milk, idiot."

I push Darla hard. She jumps at me. We fall. I'm stronger. I pin her down, slap her face. Her legs kick up, around my neck, flip me backward. I grab some sausage and cheese. I try to open her mouth, shove it in. She kicks me in the middle. I fall over. She spits.

Darla picks the bread off the ground. She wipes away the dirt.

"We don't have nothing else," I say, meaning about the food.

"*Any*thing else," she says like a grown-up. She's smiling, a joke. We laugh. She puts cheese and sausage in one, and cheese in the other. We eat. Crunchy like a picnic.

We eat silently. I know she's thinking the same things as me, but neither of us will say it. That we're scared and cold. And when the snot starts running quickly and we sneeze, we turn away and pretend like it didn't just happen. But, sometimes I look at her, and she forgets I'm there and I see her face, eyes wide and looking out, biting her bottom lip, wishing for something. Food maybe. Or Bed. Home.

I remember when I was home, how I'd take long walks by

myself. How every time I'd become scared because everything would suddenly look strange. And I never noticed as it was changing, but suddenly, I'd look up and nothing would look right. Uptown: buildings, run-down and abandoned, with cemented over windows, kicked-in walls covered with graffiti, empty lots of broken brick and concrete and trash. Downtown: groups of super-high buildings, tube-shaped and bunched together so that they all looked the same like a private city. My heart would start going, and I'd want to run and stand still all at once. Then I'd remember that all I'd have to do was look up, and there I'd find a street number. 129th Street. 67th Street. I'd subtract the street number from home's street number, and all the scared I'd be feeling, I could just turn into a number: 28, 34. Then I would pretend that the scared I was feeling was a thing: a shadowy, dirty, icy ball in my stomach. I would cut it up into the right number of pieces, and as I'd walk back the pieces would slowly be eaten away, and the scared would slowly shrink smaller and smaller, until suddenly the ball would vanish, and I'd be on The Block.

There's nothing like that here. No street signs, no people or buildings. No subways or cabs. Just open road. And I remember that we've run away twice. And the second time it was me who made us do it. *I want to be here.*

Then, I remember why we ran. It's like a flood. Mom locked in a room. Dad yelling, hitting. Mom on the dock covered in red—*blood*. Covered in blood. Dad kissing Megan in the living room. It's sort of like counting blocks, remembering these things. It makes me feel better. Then there's too much. They don't stop coming. I hold my breath and try to remember something smaller. Moments. I look real close to it, like through a magnifying glass. Dad's angry vein rising up. Mom leaning forward, tears rolling off the scars on her wrist. I feel mad. I feel worried. I feel sick. But, that feels good. It feels good to feel one little thing about one little thing. Even if they are bad things. I close my eyes tight so that it feels like I'm holding them.

"We should sleep."

"I'm real tired too," I say, smiling, glad that Darla's here, remembering that she's here, looking at her like I'm holding her.

One little thing. Bedtime. Another little thing. Sleep.

"I'm too tired to put up the tent."

We walk a little away from the road. Darla pulls the sleeping bag out from its bag, unrolls it. The red polish on her fingernails that she got that day in town with Summer has begun to chip.

We get into the bag. It feels super good to take off our sneakers and socks. First my feet burn. Then the burn turns to ache. Then they fall asleep. My socks' bottoms are smooth and stiff and they can almost stand up themselves.

I go through the bag. I find my broken Mickey Mouse watch. I put it on my wrist, even though I know it's silly. It just makes me feel good.

It's cold and the wind blows along the empty road. Darla falls right to sleep. I listen to the dead leaves on the ground shift. I close my eyes, feeling sleep shush over me. I hear a voice very far away, or nearby whispering. I sit up quickly. I look around: nothing. I listen again, but I hear only the empty road, the empty field: the leaves shifting, the wind.

I lie back down, keeping my eyes open on the night sky.

"Mom," I whisper.

Mom is in the station wagon. Her eyes are looking out, blankly at the highway. She looks up, around. She hears something.

A small thin cloud like a legless sheep drifts by, below the thin slice of moon.

"Mom," I say, "I bet you miss me, 'specially now that it's my birthday. Me and Darla are okay." I stop talking for a moment. I watch the little cloud stretch out against the black sky.

Mom frowns. She looks at the sky. She spies a cloud. Her eyes follow it.

"I was on top of that hill, Mom. I was watching you and Dad and Darla's mom. We're in North Carolina to visit Joey where he lives now. That's where I'll be, just so you know." I close my eyes tight, then I open them when it seems like enough time. The wind blows, fallen leaves scratch and circle, and high up the little cloud vanishes against the unmoving sky.

I dream. We're in the sleeping bag, sleeping by the road. I look up. I see a car idling. Its back lights shine brighter, exhaust curls up, the car rolls back.

Headlights, bright, blinding. I see the waffle glass over them.

Feet. Hands, picking up our bags. Feet walking away. Feet returning. Hands, picking up me and Darla in the sleeping bag. Being carried into the car.

Mom, Dad, Darla's mother. They've found us. They look at us smiling. Darla is asleep. My head is raised. Dad goes, *Shh,* for me to not wake Darla. I'm a good boy. I nod, sleepy. The car rocks. Sleepy, sleepy. I put my head down, closing my eyes. Sleepy, sleepy. Sleep.

eight

A slammed car door.

I shoot up, awake. I listen: there is no sound. Darkness. Pitch darkness. We are sprawled across a large car seat. Darla rolls over.

"Quit moving so much," she mumbles.

I nudge her.

"What?"

"Shh-shh."

I feel her freeze. "Ewe?"

I lie back down. I whisper, "I just woke up too."

We listen. We lift our heads. We see a shadow of a large house.

"Do you please?" A man's voice. He sticks his head in. It's only a shadow.

We both scream and squeeze hard against the opposite door.

The man clicks the door handle and the overhead light goes on. We go silent. Four triangular shadows cast down his face: an old face, white hair.

"I won't hurt you. I couldn't just leave you."

We don't move. We're squished together.

"Shall I bring you back?"

We don't answer.

"You could stay in the truck."

"Okay," I say.

The man looks at us. "Of course, I'll have to call your parents."

"No," I say.

I look at Darla. She stares at the man. Her cheek is squished against my stomach like a cat.

The man notices Darla staring. He looks at her. "Are you hungry?"

She nods.

The man pushes himself away. The door clicks closed. The light goes off. Darkness again. I can't see.

"What kind of voice do you have?" is all I can think to say, not sure if we're supposed to move.

The man's laughter rises out of the darkness. "Too many," he says.

Inside the sleeping bag, I slip my hand into Darla's. She squeezes.

"English with a Japanese accent, plus I've lived in England, and now southeastern America."

"Oh."

We hear footsteps.

"Mister?"

Footsteps in the distance.

A light in the house goes on. The man walks past a window.

We're hungry. We're cold. We screamed and no one came. What can we do? We walk to the house.

The man heats up food for us. He tells us he's been driving all day. That he picked something up in Virginia. He puts the food out for us. He lights a mountain of candles on the middle of the table. He goes to the door.

"Aren't you gonna eat with us?" Darla asks.

"Thank you for the offer, but I ate on the road," he says, flicking a switch. Outside a light goes on, and we can see the yard, and his truck, the bed built up with a little shed with a triangular roof, little windows and shingle.

We shove food quickly into our mouths. Small, squishy dumplings with something pink inside, but with a green goop that's hot and soy sauce to dip them in so all it tastes like is salty hot. And wide flat noodles with garlic, and slimy vegetables that I pick out.

From the bottom of the truck the man pulls out a metal ramp. He opens the door to the little house in the bed and a small red cow walks down the ramp. The cow waits while the man slides the ramp back up into the truck. The man pulls on the cow's collar twice, but the cow doesn't move. The man pulls again, very hard. The small cow's head jerks down. It moans. The cow ambles, and they are lost in the dark.

A few minutes later the man is standing at the door, mud on his boots and mud sprayed on his face. He smells of animal and earth. In the candlelight his face is soft. His Japanese eyes are dark beneath the hoods of his lids, but the rest of his face has no shadow. The tops of his ears are pink.

"Good?"

We both nod.

"Sleepy, I bet," he says, raising his pale eyebrows. He holds an orange and he peels the skin in one piece. He slides a section into his mouth. "You'll spend the night, children?"

I look at Darla. She's thinking like me, what can we answer?

"Do you have a bathtub, Mister?" she asks.

The man nods.

I sit with my back to the tub, watching the closed bathroom door while Darla takes a bath. Then we switch.

I've never liked a bath before. But, this bath is better than anything. After, the water is dark gray, and I am warm, and soft, and much more tired. The man waits on the other side of the door. He leads us to a bedroom. We get in. Soft, warm. I feel heavy. I snuggle next to Darla. The man tucks us in. He calls us Darlings. *Night night my darlings,* he says. We say, *G'night . . . g' . . . nigh . . .* The door closes.

Sleep.

My eyes pop open. I feel for the door. I find it above the doorknob. A bolt. I lock it. I lift the covers and slide back into bed.

Sleep.

࿔

I wake before Darla. I forget where I am. I sit up quickly. I look around the room. I remember. The bed faces a windy window, and outside is a large old tree with dying green-orangebrown leaves shaped like tulips that sway back and forth. I pull the many quilts back over my chilly body. The bed is big and soft and smells old, like all the things at Granma and Granpa's. Darla makes a sound and frowns in her sleep. I watch until her face relaxes. I step out of the bed wearing a T-shirt and underpants. I hold myself, I shiver.

I walk to the window. To the side I see a barn and next to it an empty fenced-in field. The man walks into the barn. I shiver again.

My jeans are nasty. They're muddy and smooth, oily feeling. They smell of mold. I brought two pairs of jeans. I
haven't worn the second pair yet. I brought the second pair by
mistake. I had meant to bring a different pair, a cool pair with
a *Mod Squad* patch on one knee, a yellow smiley patch on the
other, a red heart patch on the behind. The pair I brought
instead is gross. I pull on the dirty pair. They're okay, not
bad . . . Suddenly they feel like they're filled with tiny bugs
and my skin begins to itch. I rip them off. I look at the other
pair. I hate them. I pull them on. I turn to the mirror. They're
high-waters. Last time I wore them, the guys called me sissy. I
stare at them. I wonder what it is about high-waters that makes
them look so sissy-ish. I wonder, When do they become sissy
pants? I imagine them falling down to the soles of my feet,
and I imagine them rising slowly up above my ankles. When
do they change from cool to sissy? For a second, standing here
alone, I think that the whole thing is stupid. They're just
pants. But as I stare, I can't help it: they just look sissy-ish. I
put my feet together. The bell-bottom cuffs flare out to the
sides and they almost look like wings sprouting off the sides of
my ankles. That's kind of cool. I nod. Yeah, they're cool, I
think, like wings.

"Hey, Ewe."

I swing around. I flop onto the bed.

We talk in whispers.

"What do you think of this guy?" she asks.

"It was nice to sleep in a real bed," I answer.

Darla yawns, then nods.

The house is big and confusing with all the rooms and hallways and doors. We walk up some stairs to the second floor
and down a hallway. We come to a string attached to a hatch in
the ceiling. We pull it. A folding staircase slides down. We
climb up.

It's a single room that spirals up to a point, a circle of windows. In the center is a dark rug. The walls are covered. Swords in gilded cases, guns in holsters. An old, yellowed flag with a red circle in the middle. There's a dirty military uniform tacked to the wall, slumped to the floor, as if a deflated man sits there. Above it is a leather helmet, and at the bottom of the legs are boots. The right leg has a big tear. There are old photographs up of Japanese men. They stand in front of planes and have flat expressions. There's a picture of a Japanese man in an officer's suit, smoking a cigar, standing with a group of white men next to a Jeep, in the distance a waving American flag. There are medals on the wall.

We turn to the windows. The man's got a lot of land. On one side is a rolling meadow, and then a thicket of trees. There's also long rows of a harvested farm field, and farther away, the barn. The man walks out of the barn leading a big black and white cow to a fenced-in field. The cow walks into the field, then stops and gazes out. The man returns to the barn. He glances up toward us.

We both fall to the floor.

After a minute, I rise up and peer out the window. A cow stands alone in the field.

"Where's the flood?" Darla says.

I look down. Darla points at my pants.

"Nice high-waters," she says, happy. "Sissy."

"Shut up."

I think we should leave. Darla says we have to find out where we are. I say that we should just leave and find out. She says very nasty, Like we did after the train?

The air outside is clear and cool. There are three more cows in the field. We walk up to the fence and cross our arms over the rail.

"Here cow, here cow. *Moo, moo*—"

"Cow, cow, cow, cow, cow—"

Two cows look over, then look away, flicking their tails against their big behinds. Darla pulls up a clump of grass and holds it out to the cows. One cow ambles over. Then the rest follow.

"Open your hand wide, so that your fingers are back and your palm is flat," the man says from behind.

Darla does as the man says. The cow's tongue is long and thick and gray. Darla laughs, then scratches the cow behind its ear.

The man nods for me to try.

I pull up a clump of grass and hold it out. A second cow lumbers over. It leans its head out and I pull my hand back and the tongue licks the empty air. I look at the man, then put my hand back out. The tongue is heavy and rough. I look at the cow. It's slow and has long eyelashes and mulls the grass.

Darla looks over. Her cheeks are red. "They've got a whole field of grass," she says. The cow nudges her shoulder with its nose. "Why do they come over when we hold out grass?"

"Tastes better that way, perhaps," the man says.

I watch the man, waiting for his expression to change, to tell us that he saw us up in the little room. I can always tell when an adult is about to speak, especially if they're in a foul mood. Their mouths move just a little, like a cat's behind twitching before the pounce. The man looks at us. Eyes clear, mouth relaxed.

"Would you like to help with the others, children?" he asks.

Darla jumps off the fence excited, and she runs forward. I look up at the man. The man looks at me.

"Don't worry about him, Mister," says Darla.

"Shut up."

"Little sissy with your high-waters," Darla sings. She laughs and runs in a circle, like a dog after a bath.

The man smiles. "What does 'high-waters' mean?"

I look at my jeans. "When your pants are too short for you, they're high-waters. It's like if you go to the beach and walk next to the water and how you roll up your pants to keep them dry. Get it?"

"I see."

"Well, so, my pants are too short, so they're high-waters." We look at each other.

The man puts his hand out, for me to take it.

I look at the hand.

I walk past the man, into the barn.

"Hey, Mister, you sell milk or something?"

"Yes: sometimes."

Darla looks at the man. "Never seen a Japanese farmer before."

"I imagine that there are quite a few in Japan," the man says.

At the back of the barn the man brushes away some hay and cow dung and opens a trapdoor on the floor. He leads us down the stairs.

The air is heavy and moist. Along the walls are wooden shelves holding brown and black blocks. Above each row are signs: CHEDDARS, BRITISH, HARD CHEESE-COW, SOFT CHEESE-COW, BLUE, GOAT, SHEEP. And below each individual block are more tags: LANCASHIRE, STILTON, GLOUCESTER, DEVON, DUR-RAS, FETA.

"Smells like feet," Darla says.

"Worse, even," the man says.

I walk ahead and touch the blocks of cheese. Some are

wrapped in cloth that is brown with rot, and some are black with stars of furry white mold, and some float in cloudy liquid.

"You made all these?" I ask, amazed.

"Mmm, no," says the man. "Only the cheddars. The rest I order. It's a sort of club, we trade cheeses back and forth by mail. This is a collection, you might say."

"I didn't know there were so many cheeses," Darla says.

I know that there are. Dad buys lots of different cheeses. It's one thing that he likes about me. Even the real smelly ones that Mom makes a face at and says, *Ou,* to, which the brothers say, *Nasty,* to. Sometimes Dad will call me, and we'll sit on the kitchen stools, and he'll cut a pear into thin slices and crumble different cheeses over. I'll say, *"Mmm,* this one's the best," then *"Mmm,* no, *uu-mmm,* this one!"

"This is a mere scrape of the whole family," the man says.

I smile at Darla, sticking out my tongue.

The man holds a knife. He looks at us. He moves to the cheeses.

"Each cheese is like a person."

The man begins shaving pieces of cheese for us. His face is happy. He hands us shavings.

"Now maybe this is father, rather sharp and strong." The man shaves a piece of hard cheese. "Now this cheese has a rather acidy bite, like Grandfather." He goes on, his eyes wild. "This one is Grandmother, mellow, but see how the flavor lasts? This one, a salty tang like older sister, this Blue, sharp and bitter like older brother."

The slices of cheese the man gives us get larger and larger. Darla sniffs the smelly ones and hands them to me.

The man's wild face suddenly closes down. "Really one can be surrounded by family or friends-passed-on in so many ways, children." He blinks. His smile returns and he works around the cheeses, tossing pieces out to us, only stopping, on second cousin, when we tell him that we feel sick.

But, I just say I feel sick, because really, I could eat lots more cheese; it's that I feel funny: sad, sort of. All the talk about family makes me remember how sometimes it was fun with them. Waffles on the weekend. Early summer away, with the brothers, rolling up our jeans running through cold sand and water. McDonald's in the car before a long drive.

I walk outside alone. The little red cow from the night before is standing by the fence where the door has swung open. I walk up to it.

"Shoo, cow, shoo," I whisper.

"She won't run." The man says from behind.

Darla walks out behind the man. The man walks toward the house. I walk over to Darla.

"He asked if we could do some work on his farm and I said yes," Darla says, snotty like she's special. She turns and walks away.

I watch them both walking. They walk side by side. It's pretty on the farm. I like how it looks, how it smells. It's a nice place, the sort of place I always asked Mom if we could move to. The country. Watching the man and Darla, I think how nice they look, like a grandfather and granddaughter. They look happy that way. Not ha-ha happy, or spastic-running-around happy, but calm happy. I feel a bit jealous, standing alone, watching them. I feel lonely, a little. I want to walk with them, but I'm scared if I run to them, they'll be able to tell how much I want to walk with them, and that's when they really get you, when they know they've got something you really want. That's when they make all kinds of fun of you, especially when I already have on sissy pants. So, I don't move. I won't let them make fun. *Screw you,* I think. Suddenly, I feel very mad. I hate the man. I hate his property. Why are we here? He's weird and creepy. I hate Darla. And doesn't she remember yesterday morning on the train? She was already awake, sitting by the door looking out, and I woke up and she turned and said, "They always lie." She said it. Adults always lie. So, why is she being so nice to the old man? Why does she stare at him with a quiet, dreamy face? Why does she always want to hang around him, why does she walk with him like she's his granddaughter? They always lie, Darla, I tell her telepathically.

I look at the red cow.

"Shoo! Shoo!"

The cow doesn't move.

I pick up a fistful of dirt and throw it and it hits the cow's backside and I run.

⁓

The man sits on the seat of the tractor.

"Gas here," he says pressing a pedal. "And brake here. And this green lever lowers the mulcher and the red one lifts it up."

The man looks over to see that we're getting it. Darla nods. The man turns to me.

"Why you here?" I ask.

"In this field?"

"No, this country."

"Stop it, Ewe," Darla says.

"Same as everyone else," says the man.

"You're rich," I say. "You get rich here?"

The man doesn't look surprised or irritated. He was rich before, he says.

The man turns the key and the tractor starts up. The man lowers the green lever, an arm of rotating metal wheels spin. The man hits the gas, the tractor moves. The wheels in the back sink into the ground, churn the soil.

"Your guide is the front right tire, just follow the furrow between the rows," he says. "Good?" he asks.

Darla nods.

Without a word he jumps from the tractor and walks down the moist field.

Darla goes first because I just look ahead, refusing to move. She starts up the engine and drops the mulcher. The dirt behind churns, occasionally bits of soft unpicked vegetable, spotted and black, rise up in the swell of dirt.

To the side of the field is a thicket of bare trees. The man walks ahead of us. He turns and walks toward the house.

Darla watches the man walk away. She looks at me.

"When I asked him about being a Japanese farmer?" she begins, "I felt bad. He made a face. I've seen it on Mom before. It was after Daddy left, we didn't have any money, and Mom just sat in her dark bedroom. The power people would call, and I'd say, we sent a check two days ago. Eventually, they turned everything off. Then the super came up."

"I like the super. Manuel," I say. For some reason I don't want Darla to know how mad I feel. I want to keep it to myself, like a secret, so I act like I care about what she's saying.

"Yeah, he's nice. He told us we had to get out. We went to Grandma's in Queens. She would drag Mom out of bed, dress her up in her pretty clothes and makeup. Grandma would have people over. Grandma would whisper, *Husband's left her, poor thing.*"

Darla sometimes just talks and talks.

"Then the Jewish ladies started to come over. Grandma went crazy, telling them to get out. They said how she was a Jew, and Grandma said, *I left all that on the Lower East Side forty years ago.* The Jewish ladies started to call. If I answered they would tell me to get Mom. They came over when

Grandma was out. They invited Mom to their house. Grandma was happy Mom was going out. She asked, *So, who is he? Is he a nice fellow?* But, then she found out. She got super mad. But, I thought it was okay. Mom was coming out of the bedroom herself. She got a job with Dr. Dan. She bought new clothes, because she said that the pretty clothes attracted trouble. Grandma asked Mom, Why couldn't she be a normal Jew? She said, *The High Holidays are one thing . . . First she marries a lazy goyim, and of course he leaves you, and now, now! Did I raise a daughter to bob and moan like she's some cleaning lady right off the boat? Look at you!* Grandma screamed. That's when I saw Mom make that face."

"What's that? Off the boat?" I ask.

"People who come here, to America. People who weren't born here."

"Your mom's off the boat?"

"Grandma said she was like she was."

I nod. I wonder if Darla knows that, like her, I've got a parent off the boat. Dad.

The tractor goes very very slow, back and forth over the rows. It drives me crazy. I jump off and jog next to it. Stand in front of it, and back step. I get back on.

I see the man standing in the top spiral room looking at us.

"Let me drive now."

I drive, it's boring. I look at the sky, at the forest next to the farm.

"You're driving off the row," Darla says.

I jerk, straighten the wheel. Darla's a goody-goody, I think. I turn the wheel, cutting over the row.

"Quit it!" she screams.

I turn the wheel back. If the guys from The Block were here we'd have fun and laugh. We'd drive the tractor in circles. The man would run out and yell at us. We'd laugh and

say, "Shut it, Chinaman." We'd say, "Hear how the China-
woman named her kids?" "No, how?" "She threw some forks
and knives down some stairs: *Ching, Chong, Ping, Pong!*"
We'd make fun of his voice. "Let's get some *Chy-knee fo' da-
rib-er-ree.*" We'd pull our eyes slanty. *Hahahaha.* "Yo, Kike-
boy, you heard how the Grand Canyon was made?" "Hey, you
been to Bruiser's house on Sunday? His pop is a madman."
"The Enforcer?" *Hahahaha.* "Yeah, The Enforcer." They
make fun of his voice. "Kleen op thees ruem!" "He doesn't
talk like that!" "He does, the frog." "Well, your father's a
drunk, found his ass sleeping in the bush." "Wait, wait." Reid
would laugh. "Bruiser told me his pop's mom was an Ay-rab.
Hey sheik. You got any oil wells?" "At least I ain't no half-
Jew." "Haha, Frogy Ay-rab, Ay-rab, Ay-rab."

The man still stares at us through the window.

My hands wrap around the steering wheel tight. I can feel
my fingernails digging into my palms.

I turn the wheel a little and we veer off the row.

"Ewe, straighten it out."

I turn the wheel more, cutting straight across the rows.

Darla stands. She looks at me mad. She jumps off the tractor and she walks across the soft turned field, leaving footsteps
deep like empty eye sockets.

I look at the room. It's empty. I give the house the finger.

I drive in circles making soft *O*s. I laugh and drive along
the edge of the small forest. The day isn't sunny anymore. I
drive for a long time. No one comes. I am alone. I feel angry. I
want to break something, but there's nothing to break. The
farm is long and far ahead and open. I drive in crazy lines.
After a while I feel calm, and I forget how angry I feel, and my
mind goes calm, then it wanders off.

The wandering and the vibrating of the tractor make me
sleepy.

The stream near Daddy Ham's pops into my head. I liked the stream, going off alone and lying beside it, closing my eyes, listening to the moving water. I close my eyes to remember better, the sound when I put my ear close, like thousands of fingers combing through a river of glass beads. I kneel beside the stream, eyes closed, and I listen. And I open my eyes, and my ear is over a filtering jet of blue-green pool water. The sun comes down hot and quivers like snakes across the spongy white pool bottom. And it is hot and around each arm are orange water wings. I giggle and splash in the water. *Ai yi yi yi, Ai yi yee!* That makes Mommy smile. Mommy with big sunglasses and a scarf around her head. And Granpa sits next to Mommy, a blanket around his legs even though it is very hot because we're in Florida because Granpa is very sick, and Mommy has to see him, and I'm too small for school and Daddy has to teach and the brothers have school, so I come. I dive below the water. I sit on the pool bottom, spongy white bottom like skin when I rub it, cold and fat and pale, and I look to the top of the water that is beautiful, like being inside a wave, how a wave sees is how I see, sun through me, quiet, wurble water wobble. But, suddenly I'm pulled forward, I'm in the ocean, dark and very cold and salt in my nose, a riptide pulling me out like a bullet into the dark . . .

    . . . There's a roar, the mulcher caught on a fallen tree, grinding against the whining wood. I see the tractor behind me caught in the fallen tree, lurching forward like a scared ox. I see the farm and the man's house. I look ahead, and I'm flying forward through the air of the forest and I see the tree in time only to turn my head away. I close my eyes and my head cracks, deep in my ear, crack. And it's quiet and dark . . .

    . . . I open my eyes and the good sun is in the nice pool. Mommy leans over the pool edge, flattened and fanned across the surface ripples. She waves. From below in the water I wave. She waves and I am happy. And a drop falls. It falls from her hand. No. It falls from her wrist. An opening on her wrist. A red drop. Just one, into the water and it fades to pink then white then away. But, then there's another drop and another, falling quickly. Mommy waves, as they drop so fast, to her honeybaby with her big hi-honeybaby smile, *wave to Mommy, it's all right honeybaby, nothing's the matter, Mommy loves you.* The red drops form a line and the line moves like a snake, and it coils around me and it squeezes. Around my head, and it fills my mouth, it fills my eyes, it goes in my ears, through my fingers, it fills my stomach. And through all the blood I can see Mom. She's laughing and waving, and beside her is Dad. He doesn't laugh, he just looks. I close my eyes and the red goes away, and I fill with an empty cold black.

nine

I don't know how much time has gone by. My eyes open and they wobble and they're blurry and slowly they become clear. I'm on the ground and I can see trees above. Everything is very quiet. My head feels split in two. I try to sit up but it hurts too much. I see the tractor. It's cut through the fallen tree and has mulched across the forest floor up to a tree, and its fat back tires spin in place, digging two deep holes, and the mulcher digs a third.

I see the man running across the field and behind him Darla. They run funny, a hop-run in the soft sinking farm dirt. They don't make a sound. They are small. They look scared, they look beautiful.

I let my eyes fall to the ground, and I roll my head on its right side. A pain shoots across my head, like electricity running up through my right ear. I touch my ear. Red. I look at the red on my fingers and I taste. Salty: blood. I notice just now that the sounds of the earth and the trees come only through my left ear, and what comes through my right ear is thick and muffled, and below is a slow liquid sound like a dripping deep inside my head.

I roll my eyes up the tree. The moss on the brown bark is nice. On the bottom where the tree pushes out of the ground the moss is soft and grassy, and higher up the moss hardens like clover-shaped scales. I touch it with my wet hand and leave red on the pale green. Higher up I see a quick star of blood, where I hit. Then I fade away.

I wake up. I'm in bed. I'm sore. I feel vomity. I vomit. I fall asleep. I wake up. Vomit's gone. My neck hurts, my face is hot, puffy like a sponge. The man comes in. I make my eyes slits, so they look asleep, but so I can still watch. He looks at my ear. He wipes my forehead with a cold cloth. He sings to me. He cries. He tells me how scared I've made him. He touches my face, shoulder, he smiles at me like a mom. I sleep, wake up, sleep. The day passes. Maybe two. Maybe three.

My ear hurts. Usually it throbs, but sometimes the pain shoots like when I once had a rotten tooth and I chewed on ice. Mostly, it's just quiet like cotton.

I open my eyes. Darla sits on the bed looking at me. We don't say anything for a while.

"I hate you."

I don't say anything.

"You're gonna ruin it."

"Why didn't I go to the doctor?"

Darla stands. "I told him not to. He was gonna take you. I had to beg him." She moves to the door.

"I didn't mean to," I say, but Darla's already gone.

*   *   *

Out the window I see Darla sitting alone on the fence, talking to the cows.

I look in the mirror. I touch my silent ear. It is red and puffy, twice its normal size. Across my face, from my eye down my cheek to my chin, is a big bruise. I look close. There are many colors. Greens and blues and reds and purples. I press on it and it's soft like a pillow filled with jelly, and the colors move when I press hard.

I dress.

I walk around. It was nice having the man come into my room, to sing to me, take care of me. It's pretty here. The big house, all the trees and fields. It would be okay, I think. I think, that's what Darla wants. To stay. I can tell. I don't want to run anymore. It feels nice here. Safe. There's food and bed and it's warm. I wonder if the man has a TV. I miss TV.

Home has TV, I think, almost like someone else is reminding me.

Suddenly I want to cry. Really, really hard.

I can't hear out of my right ear. It scares me, but I pretend like it's not true.

I sit by the edge of the farm and follow the two trails of running footprints to the tractor hole in the forest. The forest reminds me of Joey. I feel excited, thinking of Joey, like I have to pee.

I walk to the big tree outside our bedroom window. I look at the house.

We're stupid to stay here with the man. I think that in my head. But, I hear it, like a voice that sounds like Mona. I've forgotten all about Mona. I don't like the thought. I want to stay. But, it's a voice and it talks even though I want it to shut up. It says that we're stupid to stay with the man, that he could do anything to us, kill us maybe. Who would know? One minute me and Darla could be walking and laughing and talking and the next, *poof,* quiet, we would be gone.

I stare at the bedroom window. The wind sucks the curtain out of the window, and it flaps like a dying fish against the side of the house. I don't wanna die without a sound, I think.

"You're up and about," says the man from behind.

I stand quickly.

"Don't be scared. Here."

He hands me something wrapped in a napkin. I unfold it. Cheese. I'm very hungry. I eat it. I sit. The man sits.

"You've quite a taste for cheese," he says.

"I eat all kinds. Dad likes it. Everyone else but us thinks it's gross."

He tells me how in his country they don't eat cheese. He says, When people came to visit from other countries, America, Germany, France, they would say how bad they smelled. *Butterheads,* they called it. He says that when he returned to Japan from school abroad, his father could smell the cheese coming off him. He got a good beating for that.

The man is old, and it's amazing to think that he once had a father. That once he was a boy, like me. That once he was small, like me. Small enough that his father could beat him. Like me.

I tell him Dad's French. Except that also, his mother was Algerian. The man says, Yes, that's just how you look: pretty and copper. I tell him, Dad's just off the boat. I'm done with my cheese. The man reaches into the big pocket of his down vest: more cheese. I take it, eat it. He asks if Dad sometimes feels scared or lonely. No, I tell him. But, I'm thinking, What a weird question. The man says that it can be hard to be away from home. I tell him, Dad *is* home. The man says, Suppose you made this your new home, with me, and I became your new father. Even though I want to stay, I don't like him asking. But, I remember, It's good here. There's lots of cheese. I say, No. I frown. I had meant to say, Yes. Why didn't I? He says, Just suppose. I ask, Why? The man begins to look a little annoyed. For pretend, he says. I want to say, Yes, but I can't. Then I feel it. No. I want to leave, and I just stay quiet, and the man looks angry now because I won't pretend. He's quiet. He tells me that if I stayed I'd soon be happy here. The man smiles, but kind of sad. He nods a little. He tells me, But always a little bit of you would be missing. It's like that for your father, he says.

I wish I had sliced pear for my cheese.

The man talks about there being death in leaving. That everywhere we go takes a bit of us, keeps it, kills it.

I finish my cheese. I tell the man I'm thirsty. I stand.

"I wish," the man says, "that I knew how to ask for more."

I don't know what he means.

"I envy you."

I don't really know what *envy* means, but I sort of do.

We look at each other. Again I say, I'm thirsty.

He nods.

I leave.

♫

The stove top is on with steaming pots, and on the counter is a cutting board and bowls filled with sliced bits of vegetable and meat.

Me and Darla sit watching the man.

"Why're you doing all of this for us, Mister?" I ask.

"It's dinnertime," he says.

"You know what I mean."

He scoops a handful of meat and tosses it into a deep round pan with red circling oil. The man turns.

"I could have left you on the road."

"Yeah, Ewe, stop being such a jerk," Darla says.

"No, no," says the man to Darla. He looks at me. He tells us how he saw us sleeping there. He thought, Should I get them? Should I leave them? He decided to keep driving, but his foot had a mind of its own, and pressed the brake. He thought, What a disturbance they will be.

The man turns for a moment and tosses the pieces of cooking meat around. He adds some sauces that sizzle and fill the kitchen with smells.

"Well?" I ask.

The man turns.

"I guess I needed to be disturbed," he says. "For however long we might be together, I would not be alone."

"You're lonely?" I ask.

"Oh, yes," says the man.

The man smiles and looks at us. His eyes seem to twinkle, but maybe it's only the stove's flames reflected in his eyes, watery from the heat and spice of the cooking. He turns away and doesn't speak again. And we watch him until he's done and he lays out dinner and we eat for a long while in quiet.

"Hey, Mister," I say.

Darla and the man look at me. I glance at Darla, then back to the man.

"We're gonna push off tomorrow," I say.

Darla looks at me. Her mouth opens, but she can't seem to talk.

The man nods. "I will drive you."

"You don't have to."

"No," he says. The man looks at us. He doesn't smile or frown, but his face has an expression, something soft and flat like a face made of cloth, eyes and mouth sown in with thread.

The floor is soft with layers of overlapping carpets and many pillows. In front of the fireplace, the man stretches out a screen so that its four panels make a straight wall. Through the screen the sharp flames soften to a breathing light. The man is a shadow on the other side. He lies down and his shadow vanishes. He holds up a silhouette of a mountain. Then a silhouette puppet of a lady walks across the screen.

"Tomoko lived by a large mountain and she was at the age of marriage. Often she walked alone upon the mountain—"

The silhouette moves up the mountainside.

"And upon this mountain was a relief that turned to a pond after the rains. It was a deep, deep pond."

The man moves the mountain away and replaces it with a pond with swirls of light on top.

"Whenever Tomoko could not be found, Shinji, her father, knew where it was that she would be found."

A man appears. He has a large stomach and mean, sad triangular eyes. The story continues that Shinji has arranged for his daughter to be married and presents her with suitors.

I watch the soft light flicker and I lean against Darla.

But in each suitor the daughter finds a fault. One man is a glutton, and with him she would starve and shrivel and die. A second man has a dark outlook, and with him she would grow pale and shrivel and die. A third man is shallow, and with him she would become parched and shrivel and die. Finally Shinji presents his daughter with a man she falls instantly in love with. With his generosity she could be nourished, with his enjoyment of the light and dark of day and night she could be enlightened, and with his beautiful eyes so deep, she could swim in them and lose herself in him completely.

"The day that her future husband sent the carriages to take

Tomoko to his village, Tomoko was seen climbing up the mountainside. Hours passed, and Shinji went up to retrieve his daughter. He felt a heaviness as he walked, for he realized that never again would he retrieve his daughter from the mountainside."

The man holds up the pond and Tomoko stands beside it. The man holds Shinji a bit farther back so that he is soft.

"And Shinji didn't cry out when Tomoko jumped into the pond to drown herself. He watched the air bubbles until no more came, and he watched the circles that disturbed the pond's surface ease away until the pond was again smooth and tranquil."

The man folds the screen back up. He bows.

"What was that?" Darla asks.

"It was a story."

"But, she loved the guy."

"Yes."

Darla looks at me, then back at the man.

"You're funny, Mister," she says.

"Yes," he says.

Breath against my right ear. Then stillness. Darla nudges me.

"What?" I ask, nudging her back.

We lie in bed. The room is dark.

"Why don't you answer?" she asks.

"What?"

"Were you asleep?"

"No."

She touches the right side of my face.

"Is your—from the accident—your ear, is it bad?"

"Maybe I was asleep," I lie.

"Don't you kind of wish we could stay here?" Darla says. "That's what I asked."

I can't see Darla in the dark of our bedroom, but I can feel her next to me.

"We don't even know his name," I say.

We're quiet. I close my eyes and roll onto my side, facing Darla. I feel myself begin to sink into sleep.

"—didn't call him," I hear.

Feeling comes back to my body. I open my eyes.

"What?"

I can feel Darla's breathing: quick, shallow.

"I never called Joey," she says. "He doesn't know that we're coming."

I sit up quickly.

"I'm sorry," she says. "It's just that I wanted you to come with me."

She puts her hand on me.

"What're we gonna do now?" I ask. "We don't have any-where to go."

I get out of bed.

"Where are you going?" she asks. "Ewe?"

I open the door and close it behind me. The house is dark. Coals in the fireplace seethe quietly, glowing. I watch them for a while. I guess I've always kind of known that she never called Joey; the way she talked whenever he came up: kind of fast, like she hoped to get past it quick, so that I wouldn't ask too many questions, because then, I would have known that she was lying. I guess that's why I never asked her questions. I don't know. It's stupid, I think, doing that. Pretending.

For a while I don't think anything.

But, I came. I didn't know we were going to Daddy Ham's, but I knew she was lying about calling Joey. I was only pre-tending I didn't. I guess I believed about Joey because I wanted to leave. I guess maybe.

Above I hear footsteps. I follow the muffled sound. They

stop, and then there's a single creak of a hinge. Then quiet. I walk to the staircase. There is a small flickering glow of light. I climb the stairs and follow the light, which comes from the third-floor room. I stand by the foldout staircase and listen. There's rustling of fabric. Then quiet. I climb up.

The man kneels on the rug. His body, from his knees up, is perfectly straight and naked. I jerk to a stop. But, he's so still, so quiet, like a tree, that his naked body starts to not seem that weird. It almost looks right that way, and I just watch him. His eyes are closed. His stomach has many smooth short scars. His body is old, thin, and sagging, no hair, except around his penis, where there is a white bush of it. His right thigh has a huge, old scar, and there's a hole in it like muscle has been gouged out.

The man opens his eyes for a moment and looks at me. His eyes are black below his hooded lids, two small caves.

In front of the man is a round candle, which floats in a bowl of water. He closes his eyes and whispers something. In Japanese, I think. He whispers and bows over the candle.

He sits back up. He looks at me.

I stare at his stomach with all the scars. His eyes follow mine, he glances at his stomach, then back at me. We watch each other. I move forward. I reach across the floating candle, touch the little scars. I sit down. I poke at the candle and make it bob. I look at the man. I flick the candle hard. It bangs against the side of the bowl, making a little chime. I stand.

The man suddenly grabs my wrist. "Please," he says. "Please, don't go."

I pull away, back step.

The man hunches forward onto his thighs and cries. When he is done, he rises back up onto his knees. His face is flat.

He tells a story.

He was studying in England when the war broke out. He

had to return home. He was scared. He didn't want to. But, the English wouldn't allow a Japanese man to stay, and his family demanded it. He became a pilot. He had honor. His plane went down. His leg was injured. His radio still worked. He looked at the sky. It was beautiful. He didn't want to fill it with hate and death anymore. He crawled away. He watched his plane burn, and with it, all communication.

They thought him dead. He was from a wealthy family. His picture was in the paper, a hero.

The man smiles and asks if I'm bored. I shake my head, and sit on the floor in front of the man.

He was captured. But he bribed his way out with gold. Gold watch, gold fillings, gold jewelry. He moved over large areas, continents. He was useful. He spoke Cantonese, English, French, German. He worked for his former enemies, the Americans, because he hated the war, and it was the right thing to do. But, all that had been his life, who he was, he had given up. He had no home, his family was slaughtered. America dropped a bomb. He returned to his mother country afterward. He retrieved his family's property, fortune. He had looters shot. He was an American, an American officer. He was a ghost. He was dead.

I look at the man's body, filled with scars. "You've tried to kill yourself?" I ask.

The man nods. "Many times, with that sword," he says, glancing at the sword hanging on the wall.

"My mother did the same thing, but on her wrists," I say. "I found her that way." I look up at the spiral ceiling, lost in shadow. "I don't know why she did it," I say.

Thoughts run through my head, but they're too big, and I don't have the words to fit them inside. I lean close to the man. I kiss him on the cheek. Then, I want to get away from him. I turn.

"Wait." The man walks to a desk across the room, then returns. He holds my watch. He puts it on my wrist.

I look at Mickey's hands. One's on the 1, one's on the 4. 1:20.

"I set it," the man says.

I look at the date. 11 11.

I do the math: twenty days away from home.

"Thanks," I say.

"You left it in the bathroom that first evening," the man says. "I hope it's okay that I fixed it."

"Good night, Mister," I say. I climb down the first staircase and down the second staircase. I feel my way along the hallway to the bedroom door. Darla is breathing evenly and deeply. I get into bed.

I put the watch hard against my left ear. I listen to the *ticktick, ticktick*. Behind it I hear another sound, softer, a *clink* between each *tick*. It sounds like a tiny hammer hammering out each second. I begin to fall into the ticks. The ticks become huge, like the revving of a motor. Like a motor revving on a boat, racing us forward, and I can feel the wind.

ten

The man is up when me and Darla come out of the bedroom. He wraps sandwiches in wax paper. He puts them in a canvas bag.

"Will you help me put the cows out before we go, children?" he asks.

We open the door to the barn and the cows lumber from their pens and wait to be led to the field. The little red cow stays back, standing alone in its open pen, raising its head. Once the other cows are out in the field the little red cow moves to the front of the barn. It takes a single step into the yard, stops, then walks out into the sun, into the yard, swaying its head and slapping its tail, walking down the long driveway.

"She's no longer scared," the man says. The man has to jog to catch up with her. He turns her around and leads her back home.

*   *   *

We load our things into the back of the truck. The man loads in a box. The box has no top or bottom. Inside the box is another box, then another and another, forming a solid cube.

We drive for three hours and the man lets us play with the radio. He asks if we would like lunch. We park beside a windy field. We can see the ocean. There are many people in the windy field, running and pulling on the sky full with plastic kites that ripple and snap as they dip and shoot and circle.

The man places the canvas bag on the bench.

"I was very happy to drive you," says the man. He smiles. "But, I must confess that I was also quite excited at the prospect of testing out the kite I built."

He unwinds the string. Darla holds the first box and the man has me reach in for the smallest box and walk backward. The boxes each have walls of thin paper, some are solid color, others have swirling designs of gold paint, and some are off-white with dried rose petals or blades of grass pressed into the paper. Box after box slides out, each attached to the others with string, forming a line many feet long. People race by us, hooting, their shiny kites rippling loudly. The man runs forward, and the kite rises gently, like a long snake up a hill, and it climbs on the wind until it hangs high in the air, softening the sun through the many colored walls. The man ties the kite to the bench, and it sits in the air, swaying lazy in place above the plastic kites that rattle and dive below. The man takes out a sandwich from the canvas bag, sits up straight, and eats his lunch, not once checking on his kite.

Me and Darla take sandwiches and cans of apple juice and tell the man we're going to the water.

The wind blows. The ocean's green-gray and it curls and crashes onto shore. It feels like a long time since it's been just me and Darla together. I feel almost like I'm seeing her after a long time of missing her. It's exciting like that. It feels good, but I will never say.

"—So big," Darla says, looking out. "Never seen the ocean in person before."

We unwrap our sandwiches and eat.

"Joey's mind is gonna be blown to bits." I laugh. "Probably won't be able to speak for an hour."

Darla looks at me and smiles. She lowers her head, then looks back out to the water.

It takes under an hour to reach Wilmington. Darla finds Joey's letter and tells the man the address. The man looks in a little book and finds where it is. In fifteen minutes we're parked beside a small brown house that sits in front of a backyard of trees.

Darla hugs the man tight.

"Hey, Mister," she asks, "what's your name?"

She releases him. The man smiles, and begins to blink.

"I've not heard anyone say my name in so many years." He's quiet. "It is Shinji."

Darla touches his arm and says, "Thank you, Shinji."

We get out of the car and take our things out of the back. The man holds two packages wrapped in brown paper and hands one to each of us. He stands in front of us, very still.

"Thank you, eternally, children," he says. He bows, then he returns to his truck and he drives away. For a few moments, even when the truck is out of sight around a bend, we can hear the faint creak of its old shocks, until finally it is perfectly quiet.

We walk to the house. No one's home. We sit on the front steps.

Maybe it's a little scary, I think. We're alone again. But, we're together. I look at Darla, just to make sure she's there. Really there. Maybe I was stupid to make us leave. Shinji would have been nice to us. Maybe we should have stayed.

I don't know why. I just couldn't.

We're quiet. The street is quiet. Sometimes I hear Darla inhale, like she's about to speak, but she never does.

Maybe it is a little scary.

I try to think of something to say, but nothing comes to mind. The sun goes bright then dim with the passing clouds. I look at my watch. 2:07.

It becomes solidly overcast.

Darla stands. She walks through the yard, into the trees. We walk for a little while. Behind, I can no longer see the street or houses. Darla stops. She looks at me.

She puts her arms straight up, and looks at the sky.

Suddenly she lets out a short, loud scream. It moves across the empty forest like a puff of smoke. She closes her eyes and screams again, harder and louder. Then again, clutching her arms tight into her body, bending over a little.

She straightens up, and looks at me. She exhales a large breath.

"Now you," she says.

"No."

"Why not?"

" 'Cause."

"Just try."

I look at her and let out a little scream that sounds more like I'm saying the scream.

"Louder," she says.

I shake my head.

She turns her back on me. "I won't look," she says. I wait, looking at her back. I try again, louder, but stop quickly, embarrassed. Darla doesn't move.

There's a smudge of sun behind the clouds. It hurts to look at. I stare until there's a little white blindness in my eyes.

It's a shrill sound at first, then it gets deeper and louder,

like it comes from my stomach, my feet and fingers. I begin
stomping the soft ground with both feet at once. I fall to the
earth, and scream. I roll. I thrash around the fallen twigs,
acorns, and leaves.

I stop. Darla still doesn't move. I stand up. She turns.
Strands of her long hair blow across her face. She tucks them
behind an ear.

We walk back to the house.

We sit silently for a long time.

The sun reappears.

We look at each other, and it's like we both remember at
the same second: we have gifts.

My note says, *May the high waters never rise dangerously.*

The man has taken in the old army pants so that they fit
me, falling below my ankles.

Darla's note says, *Having everything is having nothing. May
you continue to fill eternally.*

She holds the finely detailed shadow puppet of the daughter Tomoko. She holds it up to the sky so that the sun glows
through the cut of her eye.

eleven

Darla's frowning at me. Not at me really, at my hand. She squints, trying to see.

"What?"

We sit on Joey's porch. The sun makes some color in the sky.

Darla scoots over. She grabs my wrist, looks at my watch. "Three-twenty," she says. She looks at me, still holding my wrist. "Thought it was broken."

"Shinji fixed it."

"When?"

I shrug.

"Well, when did he give it to you?"

I snatch my hand back, and look forward, but out of the side of my eye, I still see Darla watching me.

She mumbles something, then scoots far away, moving out of the corner of my eye. Because of my dead right ear, and because there's some wind, I'm not sure of what she says. Something. Either "Shinji's would have been cool," or "Stingy and mean as a mule."

I think about that for a long time, looking out. When I do look back to Darla I know that she'll have a pinched-up bratty face. But, when I look, it's open, like it's hanging there. Like Darla's gone away, and she's left her face, eyes open, mouth parted, just hanging there. It's kind of dead-looking. She blinks sometimes, though. And as I watch, a tear rolls down, from the wind maybe.

A school bus stops down the block. Kids get off, walk up the street. They talk and chew gum and laugh and run, and they all look when they pass us.

It's strange seeing kids again. A whole mess of them. It's been a long time. I want to run out. I want to forget everything, and just run. Run and say stupid stuff. But, it seems odd to do that, like: how do you just do that? Why do you just do that? They're like a pack, like animals I'm watching on a nature show.

I see two girls. They walk slow and talk and nod. They wear pretty dresses and have skinny legs. One girl has lemon-colored hair and is very pretty, the other one, who isn't so pretty, has almost white hair.

They stop in front of a red brick house across the street. They lean forward and kiss each other, one cheek, the other cheek. The almost white head walks away, and the lemon head watches her for a moment, and the way she stands so still and straight in her pretty pink dress and pink sweater she could be on top of a cake. She turns, like a ballerina, and her white shoes clickity-click up the walkway to her house.

I turn to Darla.

"Why don't you marry her?" she says.

"What?"

Darla leans against the porch banister. "Do you see Joey or what?"

I shake my head.

"That's just great," she says very nasty, looking away.

⚬⟋⟍⚬

The street's empty again.

"Maybe he's on a team or something," I say.

Darla rifles through the bags and gets her mangled pack of cigarettes. She puffs smoke. "Cold," she says, like it's my fault.

We're quiet.

The door of the red house opens and Lemonhead walks out. Holding a wicker basket, she takes a seat on a swing-bench on the porch. She lifts the lid of the basket and takes out fabric and thread and needle, and begins sewing.

Darla looks at me watching. She stands, crosses the street. I follow. It's a yellow bathing suit, but more cloth-y than that: like what those running, rolling, hopping girls on the Olympics wear. Across its front are faint white lines: a drawing of a bird flying over a rainbow. Lemonhead sews sequins over the lines.

Darla looks at me and makes a vomit face.

Lemonhead finishes sewing the wing of a bird before she'll look up. First she looks at Darla and her cigarette, then at me. She squints. "You been in an accident?" she asks. "That's a big ugly bruise."

"It looks worse than it is," Darla says.

"And look at the ear," Lemonhead says.

Darla turns my face, looking at my right ear. "It's just swelled is all."

Lemonhead shrugs, goes back to sewing. "You-all the new family moved in next door?"

"We're just visiting," I say, wanting to speak. "You know: Joey."

"They've moved back?" she asks, looking up.

Darla stops puffing her cigarette.

Lemonhead goes on. "Have you—what I mean is, Joey wasn't in school today. He was in Mr. Hart's class with me—"

"Like you know everything," Darla says cutting Lemonhead off.

"Who's ever heard of a little girl smoking?" Lemonhead says.

Darla puts the cigarette between her lips.

"Where's he?" I ask.

Lemonhead smoothes the outfit and begins on the bird's head. "I couldn't say. They just left. In the middle of the night, must have been, because one morning the house was just empty."

Darla pulls on my sleeve. "Come on, Ewe."

I open my mouth to talk.

"All right, fine," she says suddenly, walking away.

Lemonhead neatly folds her fabric, places it back in her basket.

I squint at Lemonhead. "Were you just messing about Joey?"

She looks at me. "Don't you have parents?"

"I got parents."

"What's that accent you have?"

"From New York City," I say. Then, I close my mouth, realizing that I probably shouldn't tell people these sorts of things.

A woman opens the door of Lemonhead's house. "Who's that you're talking to, Virginia?" she says to Lemonhead, looking at me.

"He's from Mr. Hart's class, Mother."

"Tell him it's time to go."

Lemonhead nods. She stands, leans close. She whispers, "You really from New York City?"

I smile.

"You'll come back?" she whispers, but before I can answer she runs inside.

Evening has come. We watch the street turn blue, and we watch the darkness move across the street and up driveways, turning houses to shadow, windows to lit yellow squares. My stomach burns from hunger, my body shivers from cold.

We don't make a sound except for snuffling the dripping snot back up into our noses, and we don't move from Joey's front steps. What are we going to say? Where would we go? Joey's gone. Where is he? When did he go away? Was he gone before we left home? Have we been running to an empty house the whole time? I wish there were a grown-up here. I wish they would drive up, then pick a restaurant for us to eat in. I'd go anywhere, but I'd secretly wish for them to choose pizza. Then why wouldn't I just ask for pizza? I nod to myself. I'd say, Pizza. Then they'd take us for ice cream. No: pie. Pie and a movie. Then, home.

I look at Darla.

"You're the one who made us leave Shinji."

I look away from Darla. I stand. I walk.

Darla calls. "Ewe! . . . Ewe, stop it! . . . Ewe, *you better come back!* . . . Ewe? . . . Come on. . . . All right, fine. . . . Ewe? . . . *I'm sorry.* . . . Ewe! . . . Please . . . *Ewe,* stop it!"

I feel arms around my middle, Darla jumping at me. I fall forward. I'm on my back. Darla's crying. She's hitting me. She's crying and snotty. She's talking, but she doesn't make real words.

She stops hitting me. She looks at me. She stands, she walks back and sits on Joey's front steps.

I lie on the dark lawn. Here I am, I think. Here I am. I breathe deep and don't know what else to think.

Across the street there's a brown shadow behind a white curtain. A hand pulls the curtain aside, and Lemonhead looks out. The curtain falls back.

I look up into the sky and touch the bruised part of my face. It throbs, it's hot to the touch, but it's numb. I pinch at it, hard, until it hurts. I return to the steps, sit next to Darla.

Across the street the door to Lemonhead's house opens. Her shadow moves across the walkway, then turns and walks along the sidewalk. She holds something, a bag maybe. A car comes down the street. I see Lemonhead stop. She watches. The car turns up Joey's driveway.

We sling our bags over our shoulders and dash from the porch, down the street. Lemonhead crosses. We stop.

"Mr. Samuel Haswell," she says, watching him get out of his car. He looks at us, then walks up to the house. "He lives there now. Bachelor it's assumed. He is not very friendly. When I saw you two on his porch, I thought it might explain his off-putting manner: that it was all along a case of loneliness for his family."

"Do you ever shut up?" Darla asks.

"*Darla,*" I say.

We begin walking.

"I'm going into the foliage to pick a variety of autumn leaves," says Lemonhead. "For my wings," she answers as if asked.

We're quiet.

"What?" Darla asks, very annoyed.

Lemonhead explains that she's getting her Girl Scout wings, which has something to do with her having first been a Brownie, which makes no sense to me, but makes me start thinking about brownies. I like them with walnuts, so I don't really hear the rest because my stomach and mouth are going crazy thinking about brownies, and the best corner pieces where the hard bottom curls up the side and you can taste the butter that Mom greases the pan with.

We reach the end of the road and Lemonhead leads us into a thicket of trees. She has a flashlight. She turns it on.

Lemonhead goes on talking. Darla lights a cigarette and we're both quiet. The trail opens to a small clearing. Lemonhead's flashlight moves over a fire pit next to an abandoned car, sunk into the ground.

"Let's rest," Lemonhead says. She begins collecting twigs and leaves and logs and tossing them into the fire pit.

"Older kids, the undesirables from the other side of the forest, come here to light fires. But, no one will come in this season." She turns to Darla. "Match?"

Darla hands her matches.

Lemonhead kneels before the fire pit and a flame moves along the leaves. A small fire catches, then a large fire. She looks at us. "It's warm here," she says.

We're both cold from sitting outside for so many hours. So cold that we've stopped feeling it. I tingle the moment I step near the fire, and it makes me feel how cold I've been. I start to shiver and I look at Darla and she shivers too, but she stares into the fire and tries to hide it. Soon our faces are red and hot and we stop shivering.

"Oh goodness," Lemonhead says holding up her bag. "I forgot to put these in the trash." She looks at us. "They're peanut butter sandwiches. I read for Mrs. Jackson at the senior home on account of her poor eyesight, and I always pack a little treat for her, and I plum forgot about her dentures and the problems peanut butter causes them. And *I* can not *stand* peanut butter, unlike most children, who just love it."

I nod. I love peanut butter.

Lemonhead lifts the bag. "Maybe you two would like these? I'd be grateful to not have to lug it all the way back home to the garbage can."

Darla looks at Lemonhead, then back to the fire.

Lemonhead asks, "Is it very exciting living in New York City?"

Darla looks at me and bugs her eyes out. I bug my eyes back.

"Mother says it's Sodom and Gomorrah." Lemonhead looks at the fire. "But, I had a friend who moved there. She sent me a postcard. It was of Lincoln Center at night, all lit up, and the fountain lit up too. She told me about a ballet she saw there." Lemonhead looks at us. "Have you been to Lincoln Center?"

I haven't, but I wish I had.

Darla looks past me at Lemonhead on the other side and says, "I've been there a bunch when I was little." She looks back into the fire, shifting her weight a little. "It was so beautiful."

Lemonhead looks at her with a small smile, then she looks at the flames. She stands up suddenly. "I really must be going," she says. "Maybe I'll see you two again, unless, of course, your parents return to pick you up. Good night."

I watch her walk off.

She didn't collect a single leaf.

We eat the sandwiches quickly. I bite my fingers once, I'm so excited. The sandwiches make us hungrier. We pull everything out of our bags. We find five dried apricots. We pitch the tent. I can help with it now, and it's not as complicated as it looked when I just watched Darla do it. But we lie outside in the sleeping bag, looking at the stars, the ghostly sweep of the Milky Way.

"I once saw this show on water babies," Darla says. "It took place in Russia, I think, or maybe California. These women gave birth kinda squatting in a little pool. And out popped these gooey babies, their little arms and legs flapping like frogs, swimming. Just like that! 'Cause inside the moms' bellies they were like fish." Darla's quiet, then, "Mom was passed out in her bedroom. I turned off all the lights and watched the show until real late. I felt kinda cheated. I wanted to be a water baby, you know?" Darla looks at me and I nod. "I thought about how I can't swim, but how I was once a water baby 'cause once we were all little fish, but 'cause I was born in the air, I forgot how."

We stare at the stars.

"I swim good," I say. "I had lessons, though," I add so Darla won't feel bad.

"That's just the same," says Darla. "You forgot how to swim 'cause you didn't do it again, after you were born, until you took lessons. Isn't that silly? You learned something you once knew how to do, but had forgotten how to do because you were . . . just sort of living, like normal. Learning to walk and talk, going to school."

That makes my brain feel crazy, and I don't know what to say.

"Ewe?" she says.

"Yeah?"

Darla stares at me, but doesn't say anything. Then she shakes her head. "Nothing," she says. She looks at the sky, and we're quiet for a while.

"We're probably on the news," I say. "That's why that girl keeps hanging around. We're probably on the news and we're probably famous." I laugh a little.

I look at Darla, but she's not listening.

I go quiet. And we both stare into the sky.

twelve

It's beautiful. Silent and pretty, ice like sugar. Fog.

Slowly I wake up. I squint. Early morning sunlight falls through the bare trees, and my left ear is turned to the ground, my deaf ear to the air. Across the ground is a thin layer of frost, and from my mouth, frozen breath.

I hear a crunching in the forest. Footsteps scampering. I sit up. I look around and see nothing. A squirrel, maybe a bird.

Darla's curled in the sleeping bag, only the top of her head poking out, a little circle of pink scalp where the hair parts. I stand, and the coldness hits me. I move around to get warm. I collect wood.

I try to light a fire, but everything is covered with frozen dew. I cup my hands and blow on them. I jog in place.

I think I see something in the corner of my eye. I turn quickly. Only trees.

I wind my watch. 6:32. 11 13.

Crunching again. It slows. It stops. Behind me. I freeze. I turn.

A dog, old and mangy. One of its eyes is missing, covered with an overgrown scar. Its back sags, its body's scabby, its fur's dull. It holds something in its mouth.

I step forward, it runs off.

I go through the bags. I have an idea: find the little portable stove, light it, get warm. I look through one bag, then the other. Everything is on the ground. I look a second time. It is gone, lost. I put everything back into the bags.

"It's so cold." Darla's rocking on her heels, sitting huddled in a ball.

Now that it's deep November: some days winter visits, like it's reminding us that it's coming.

"We don't really have any more cold clothing," I say. I take out some shirts. "Here, though. Let's put these on under our sweaters."

We quickly take off our shirts and sweaters and we're naked on top. I look at Darla. She's like a leaf, skin tight against her bones.

I lean forward, hand her a few shirts.

She makes a face. "Your breath stinks."

We finish dressing. We stomp and hop, the cold still clinging to our now-covered skin.

Darla goes through the bags, twice like me, dumping everything out. She looks up. "Where's my travel purse? With my comb, my toothbrush?"

I shake my head. "We lost the stove too."

Darla looks crushed. I think, probably because of the comb. It was pretty, made of wood, flowers carved in along the handle. She used to just hold it after she was done combing her hair, running her thumb back and forth over the teeth, cleaning away hairs and lint. But, Darla doesn't say anything about it.

I count our money: $176.43. I put $40 in my pocket.

We're awake, we're cold. We walk. Walking feels nice. The forest floor crunches and the sun is bright. I feel tough, me and Darla walking alone, fat with our layers, breathing out white breath.

Darla looks at me. "The cold's made your bruise better," she says. "Your ear looked like a giant apricot before." That makes her laugh and laugh.

We pass the dog. Darla screams, which makes the dog bark, a funny bark like a rooster imitating a toad. At its feet I see what it had been carrying before: a raggy stuffed rabbit doll.

Then I see him: a boy in the distance, hiding behind a tree, watching us.

"I see you," I call.

Darla looks.

The boy ducks his head back behind the tree. He waits a moment, then he steps out. The dog continues to howl. The boy walks over.

"Quiddit, Bernice," he orders.

The dog goes quiet, picks up the rabbit doll, and drops it at the boy's feet.

"Saw ya'll b'fore. Me an' Bernice was practicin'."

The dog wags its lame tail when the boy says her name. And when the boy looks at Darla he looks away quickly, his cheeks and ears going pink.

We walk. The boy's name is James. We come out the other side of the forest. We walk on the street. The houses are smaller than on Lemonhead's side, the lawns, tiny and bald and muddy.

James has to shoo Bernice many times, before she'll go

home. He pleads with her that he'll miss the early bus for the free meal before school.

"Breakfast?" I ask.

Ahead is a huddle of kids.

They look at us funny.

A boy with orange hair and ugly orange freckles asks, "You still out tryin'a teach that ol' bitch to hunt?"

A few boys snicker.

"She's a good one," James says.

"Good t'make-a belt outta all right."

I miss that from The Block: snapping. Snapping on people, being snapped on. *Yer mama's so fat, her ass and stomach live in different zip codes. Well, yer mama's so fat, she asked me to scratch an itch on her back, I had to hail a taxicab.*

The boy looks at me and Darla. "Who y'all," he asks.

Darla moves a little behind me.

I try to think of a good snap. Finally I've got one, *Damn if I played connect the dots with all them nasty freckles on your face, my pen'd run out of ink before I got through,* but the school bus turns the corner.

The kids begin to shuffle.

I look at Darla.

"Oh no, Ewe. I'm not getting on that bus."

"I'm freezing. Aren't you freezing?"

"I'm freezing."

"And they've got *breakfast.* Aren't you starved?"

"But, Ewe . . ."

The bus driver boredly says hello to the group, then he turns to his open window, blowing out smoke from his cigarette.

It's a long ride and that's fine: I don't want to ever get off the bus. I swing my feet and they warm up, and I feel the top of my feet and my toes and the soles of my feet. Who would ever think that I could miss feeling the soles of my feet? But, I start to miss all kinds of stuff I never even thought about before.

James sits across from us. He studies a piece of paper, then looks away, closing his eyes. He starts mumbling. He looks back at the page, and says, *Dang*.

He tries again, mumbling. Then he goes quiet, stuck.

I say:

"And miles to go before I sleep,
And miles to go before I sleep."

Darla looks at me. James looks at his page, then to me.
I like them looking at me.
"That's right," he says.
"You gotta memorize that one for school?" I ask.
"Yup."
"I had to once too."
"Why's he gotta say it twice you figger?" James asks.

When I had to memorize the poem for class, I asked Mom that very thing.

"Some people say it's 'cause he's dying, so it's supposed to sound kind of tired and sad. But, he might just be regular tired and dreamy-like 'cause he's been riding around all day."

James looks at me for a little bit, then a smile moves across his face. "Yup. That sounds pretty good, all right."

The cafeteria is in the basement of the school, just like at P.S. 75. We go on line. They have eggs and sausage patties, or cereal and fruit cups. We get the eggs, then go back on line and get the cereal.

"What do you wanna do now?" Darla asks.

I'm warm. I've taken off my layers except for just a T-shirt.

I shrug.

"There must be something to do in this town."

I look at Darla.

She waits. "What?"

I shake my head. "Nothing."

We walk. The kids file upstairs to class. Class, where I bet they have nice wooden desks, and colored paper cutouts of leaves taped to the windows because it's fall, and turkeys made from the outline of a hand. And in those classrooms kids will get mimeographs with its purple letters that smell like medicine and make you dizzy and your brain white if you sniff too long, which you always do. And you play with all the things in your pencil pouch, your pencils and pens, your erasers, your bubble gum cards of Fonzie or Farrah. And up in one of those classrooms I bet there is a kid like me whose desk is starting to smell rotten, because in the cubbie below the desktop he's been putting the apples from his school lunch since September, except Mom wasn't home making your lunches until October, so Dad had to make them and he always forgot the fruit, so your desk doesn't smell as bad as it could. And all the other things up there. Drawing time and math time. Gym. Sitting in the school library as Mrs. Ronn goes on and on about the Dewy Decibel System, as you hold an encyclopedia below the desk slowly ripping pages out, and the whole time, every minute starting from when you're waiting outside on line to get in at eight-thirty, and before even, on the walk to school, or at home over your cereal, in your bed right after Dad's shaken you awake, and you look at your Peanuts pillowcase where Charlie Brown says, "The problem is that at night I don't want to *go* to bed and in the morning I don't want to *get out* of bed," and you think, like you think every morning when you read the pillowcase, "How true." Even then you count the minutes, then the hours, until three, then the days until Friday, then the months until summer, when you'll finally be free.

Kids bump and nudge past, up the stairs to all of that.

"Ewe?" Darla is annoyed.

"It's so cold out."

"You wanna go to school?!"

Lemonhead and Almost Whitehead walk up the stairs. I smile at Lemonhead, but she's looking directly at Darla, whispering about Darla with Almost Whitehead as they pass. "Would a bath kill her?" "Do you see that hair?" "And those clothes: church charity bin."

I look at Darla, but she's staring at the floor. I have to use the bathroom. She follows. We use the toilets, then meet at the sinks. Darla looks at herself in the mirror. Her eyes sparkle. I look at my fading brown bruise. Over the sink is a dispenser of pink powder soap. I put some on my palm and wet it and put some on my finger. I open Darla's mouth and rub my finger over her teeth.

"Rinse."

I do the same. It's gritty, tastes gross, but after, my teeth are nice and smooth.

I work soap into a lather. I rub it on her face, then mine. Darla smiles a little. There's grubby dirt on our hands, arms, necks, and the water has carved trails through the grubby. Darla cleans her arms, neck. She looks for twigs and leaves in her hair. She wets her hair lightly and combs it long with her fingers.

Walking out, I remember the dry leaves we have to use for wiping, and I run back in and steal a roll of toilet paper.

It's warmer out and we walk into town, stripping one shirt, then another and another, tying them around our waists. Town is the biggest we've been in since New York, but it's still a lot cleaner and quieter than home. As we walk I make a list in my head of things that New York has that Wilmington doesn't.

Drunk bums on Broadway. Glueheads, potheads. Lemon cookies, five cents a piece at the bodega. The big rooster walking around behind the bodega counter. Sal's pizza. The Block.

We walk by a bus depot. I look at the board inside, but we pass before I can see if it says New York. We pass a bookstore and I tell Darla that I want to go in. We walk down the aisles until I find the shelf for poetry.

"Are you looking for something, or are you just looking?" Darla asks.

"I'm looking for something."

A lady with a knapsack walks over and says, "You guys need any help?"

Darla points at me with her thumb and says, "He's looking for something, but he won't say what."

"Quit telling!" I say. I look at the lady. "I'm looking for a book that my mom's got a poem in."

"Your mom's got a poem in a book?" Darla asks.

"Yeah, so?"

"Aren't you two supposed to be in school?" the lady asks.

Darla just looks at the lady.

"We're visiting," I say. "We got vacation where we're from."

"Are you putting me on?" The lady smiles.

We both shake our heads.

"So," says the lady, "what are you looking for?"

I try to remember what Mom called it, then I do. I say, *"Little Nothing Literary Magazine from the Midwest."*

The lady puts her hand to her suddenly smiling mouth. "That's its name you say?" she asks.

"That's what Mom called it."

"Do you remember if that magazine might have had another name other than *Little Nothing Literary Magazine?*" the lady asks.

I nod and close my eyes. I feel a nudge on my side. I know it's Darla and I know what she's going to ask. I keep my eyes closed and say, "I saw it on a piece of paper, this helps me remember."

The black of closed eyes becomes bright: the light through the living room window. I can hear the radio playing in the kitchen. I look up. I'm on the couch, and there's Mom. I want to say hello, but this is remembering, so I can only watch. Mom shows me the piece of paper. On the top is the name. I read it out loud. I open my eyes.

The lady looks at the shelf and takes out a thin book. I look at the contents and find Mom's name. It's a long poem, but I read it.

The lady stands behind me, and Darla stands next to me, and they read the poem too.

"Is that your mom?" the lady asks.

I turn. "Yeah."

Behind my back, I shove the magazine down my pants.

"Is she here with you in town?"

"Nah." I turn to Darla. "I wanna go now," I say.

I walk away. Darla follows. We walk outside. The lady calls from behind.

"It is so beautiful, the poem," she says. She is crying.

I look at her. The tears don't run down her face, they collect on her bottom lids until her eyes look like soft white stones. I don't understand the poem, but it makes me sad. It makes me think, that something beautiful isn't something pretty only, but is something that makes you feel something, like remembering, only not in the past, but like watching a

movie, only more real than that, but not as real as everything
else, but better somehow.

⸎

We buy food with my $40. We buy a box of wooden safety
matches. I find a comb, hand it to Darla. She smiles and puts
her hand on my shoulder for a second. I also buy a map. Darla
looks at it but doesn't say anything.

We go to the forest. We sit in the abandoned car and watch
the cool autumn sun set fiery between the tree branches. We
light a fire, and return to the car.

"I wondered if you two had settled here, or if you had
gone on your mysterious ways." Lemonhead walks out from
the shadows of the trees into the firelight. Her hair is in big
curlers and a plastic cap.

"We don't want you coming around checking on us,"
Darla says.

"You'll have to forgive me about today. But, the truth is:
I'll do it again. I know they say the Lord loves us all equal and
all that, but he doesn't live in Wilmington, North Carolina,
where people get ideas in their heads. My mother says I have a
station, so I don't have a choice." Lemonhead leans against the
car, back to us, and stares into the flames. "I know you-all
don't have any parents around." She turns, smiles. "Don't
worry, I won't tell. But, maybe I'll visit from time to time?"
Lemonhead looks at Darla. "Tell me about the ballet at Lincoln Center." She climbs into the backseat.

Darla makes her lips tight.

Lemonhead slouches back into her seat and pouts. "Most
folks would jump at the chance to be *my* friend."

In the distance, we can hear Lemonhead's mother calling
her. Lemonhead sits up very straight, quickly climbs out of
the car, brushes herself off.

"You-all coming to the pageant this evening?" she asks.

I look at her.

"The Thanksgiving Beauty Pageant?" she says. "The winners get to sit on the Thanksgiving Day parade floats."

I nod. Darla's not listening. She's reclined her seat back flat. She's looking up, since the car has no top, at the dark sky.

No one says anything else, and Lemonhead leaves.

I take out the magazine and read Mom's poem again. Darla is quiet and lets me read it a few times over. I can feel Darla looking at me.

"I like, in the poem, that part, what she says about the day," Darla says.

I look at her.

"Like when we were on the train that night, after Daddy told on us." Darla pauses and kind of smiles, to tell me that she knows now, and that she knows that I knew the whole time, but thanks for not making fun of her about it, and for just being nice and letting her pretend for a while. "And we watched the sun rise. It really *did* seem like something broke, like the sun broke something."

I frown. "That's in the poem?" I ask.

Darla looks at me. "She wrote it about *that* day, didn't she?"

"What day?"

Darla looks at me. She says, "Remember the day we hid in the clothes hamper? When they found us?"

I nod.

"I saw them that day," Darla says. "When your mom reached in and took the clothes off of us. I wouldn't have thought anything if she hadn't had them on *both* wrists." Darla's quiet. "I once saw in a movie where a lady did that to herself in the bathroom. Is that what happened, Ewe? The poem kinda sounds like that."

Inside things float. They fall. They burn. Ash. Cold.

"You wish I didn't know, right?"

I shrug.

"So, it is, huh," Darla asks, "about that day?"

I remember *that day*. *That day* was the first time I saw the poem. I remember that I didn't want to look at Mom, so I looked at her pad. I read the first line, but it didn't mean anything to me. There was blood on the page, and there was blood that ran along the planks of the dock that dripped out of Mom and fell into the water.

"I found her," I say.

Darla looks at me, waiting for me to finish. I don't want to. I look at the sky.

I'm not sad and I don't want to cry. I'm cold, and I say so, and I get out of the car and sit next to the fire. Darla follows, sits beside me. I look at the poem, but I don't read it. I look at its shape, at the two fat stanzas on top and bottom of the skinny middle stanza. I let my eyes blur, and the words turn to soft squiggles. The two fat stanzas look like they're squeezing the skinny middle stanza. It's like the poem says: things happen that make you sad, or feel stupid, but really it's the things that you can't tell are there, like the day, things big and invisible, that make you feel *really* bad.

I throw the book into the fire, with my eyes still blurred. The pages curl up like a mouth opening with many tongues, like it's screaming but can't make a sound, and the tongues curl in and turn black, then gray and thin, and bits of page break apart and float on the heat away into the dark night.

And then we just sit there, watching until the fire dies out.

thirteen

Sitting slumped in the car's backseat, Darla leans her head on my shoulder and stares out ahead. I stare at the sleepy blinking embers of the dead fire. Out of the forest is scampering, then her old, croaking howl. James scolds, *Shut it, Bernice.* As their footsteps near, James whispers to Bernice, asking if she smells us. I look at Darla. We both smile, thinking the same thing, sinking low in the seat, hiding. Their footsteps are right there and I hear James kicking at the dead fire, making the embers seethe angry for a second. James says to Bernice, *They for sure was here.* They're quiet, and then their footsteps continue past. Me and Darla have to bite our cheeks to keep it in. We peek over. In the weak moonlight we see them, through the trees in the distance. We climb out of the car, finally letting out our laughs, then follow, slow to be careful of not making too much sound.

We get to the edge of the forest and see James ahead. We follow, walking for a couple of streets, then cutting left for a few more streets. We come to a big boulevard, busy with shops and traffic. Ahead, a parking lot and a crowd.

A sign outside a community center says: 1977 ThaNksgiv-iNg Miss WilmiNgtoN Beauty PageaNt. At the base of the stairs sits Bernice. Her tail thumps when we say, "Hey, Bernice." We get in free because we're kids. There's a stage with a glittering gold turkey backdrop. The auditorium is filled with people on foldout chairs. It's hard to hear with all the voices, and unless I point my good ear in the right direction, everything is a mishmash of sound like moving water. Up front, near the stage is a foldout table where three old men sit. JUDGES, a sign says.

A little girl stands on the stage. She wears a pink dress with white fringe. She holds the dress out at the bottom and turns in a circle. She walks to the edge of the stage, winks at the judges, then leaves. People in the audience all smile and nod. The emcee says something about that ending the Petite Miss part of the program. Up next the Little Miss segment. Older girls, our age, strut out, hip-hip hip-hip, in bathing suits and makeup.

We walk around the crowd. Bits of conversation flutter past like leaves in the wind. I don't like it: there are too many people, too many sounds for my one ear to figure out. I want to go.

Onstage is a girl with a potbelly, dressed in a sparkly blue bathing suit and a sparkly blue cowboy hat.

Darla walks ahead of me. She talks, but the hum of the room fills my ear.

I nod, say, "Uh-huh."

Darla stops and faces me. Darla laughs, then she looks at me. "Why aren't you saying hello?" She gets closer, touches my silent ear. "Your ear *is* bad, isn't it?"

I slap her hand away.

"Then, don't be rude," she says.

I turn around. James.

"Don'ya think?" he asks me.

I look at Darla. She's laughing and nodding. She says, "Yes."
James likes Darla laughing, his cheeks and ears going hot.
We sit. Sitting feels better. Safe.

Girls strut across the stage, one after the other, waving,
smiling, looking at the judges.

I stare at their faces, but I can't tell a thing from that: they
all look the same. We sit to the side, so we can see the girls
waiting to go, fidgeting behind the curtain. There, their faces
do all sorts of different things. Some look like they're going to
cry or be sick, some are excited, some are kind of snobby,
some look blank, like they've forgotten where they are, like
they're thinking about somewhere else.

Where are you thinking about? I wonder.

I watch as all the different faces behind the curtain come
out onto the stage and, one by one, become the same face.

I look at all the grown-ups. They nod and shake their
heads at the different girls onstage. None of them seems to
notice the girls when they're backstage.

"Gross," I say.

"Shut up," Darla says.

"You don't think?" I ask.

Darla shrugs and looks down, talking into her lap. "Some
of them really *do* look beautiful." She pulls on the sleeve of
her ladybug sweater. The cuff is frayed and dirty. "It's not the
worse thing in the world," she says. She looks at James and
asks, "Do you think?"

"Girls are meant to be prettied up once in a while," he says,
looking at Darla. " 'Course some girls seem prettied up no
matter what they got on." James quickly looks down.

Lemonhead walks out. She wears the yellow outfit. The
sequin bird flying over the sequin rainbow twinkle bright
across her front. Her long blond hair is combed and wavy and

piled on top of her head, with little white flowers woven in. Her face is clean and white with powder, pink on her cheeks and light blue over her eyes, light light pink on her lips. Her pale eyes remind me of Mom, and they sparkle by the stage lights. She starts dancing. She spins across the stage lightly, and arches her arms like thin branches in the wind. She collapses to the floor and balls up, then slowly her body opens like a blooming flower, swaying and opening, and her head rises up like air, like something growing before my eyes.

"You're staring," Darla says.

"No, I'm not!" I say.

"You're in love with her," Darla says.

"I hate her!" I say.

"She can be mean," James says.

We're quiet.

Lemonhead's dance comes to an end. She bows her head to the side and closes her eyes, holding her arms out and crossed. Then she drops her arms and bounces offstage.

"She's beautiful," Darla says.

I look at Darla, but say nothing.

James goes to get us something at the concession stand. He's gone a long time and Darla goes to find him. Older girls with boobs and hips, and longer faces start coming out. I look around at all the people in the audience. I think, grown-ups are all very ugly. Not just that most of them are fat, but also how the men all sit with their arms crossed like they know about everything before it happens, and the way they look off bored, nodding whenever the ladies talk to them. And the ladies with the way they turn their heads up and glance down their noses and tight lips, and whisper.

If some of the guys from The Block were here, we'd have a good time. We'd collect ants and drop them on the grown-ups' shoulders. We'd crawl under their chairs and ball up

paper and light it up. We'd scream, *Fire! Fire! Fire!* We'd hoot
and slap five watching all the fat asses running for the doors.

I make fists, excited.

I wonder what the guys are doing right now. Probably
some Big Kid is messing with them. I laugh just thinking
about it. Probably, they're lined up, shoulder to shoulder,
lying on the ground. I can see it. My face right next to Reid's.
And after his, Max's, Jimmy's, Ron's. And down The Block I
see Fly getting ready to do a long jump over us. He shows off
for the other Big Kids, doing stretches and stuff.

"Reid," I whisper.

"What?"

"Sit up."

"Nah!"

"I'll do it if you do it. Hey, Max."

Max looks over.

"Sit up."

Fly starts running toward us. Other Big Kids hang out, all
cool, laughing bored.

"Shut up, shut up: he's coming, he's coming," Jimmy says.

"Come on," I say. "If we all would just sit up at once—"

Down on the far end of the auditorium, I see Lemonhead.
She leans against the wall in her outfit, watching the older
girls onstage. I walk over.

I wonder who Fly landed on. He always lands on one of us on
purpose so that the other Big Kids can go, *Haw, haw.* And when
they're done laughing, they look away. Sometimes the person
who's landed on starts crying. Then we have to make him feel
tough again. We let him win at handball, or we say we're sick of
our soda and does he want it because we're gonna toss it anyway.

Lemonhead sees me.

"Hi," I say.

She nods, she looks straight ahead.

"Nice dancing," I say.

"I told you before that I couldn't mix with you in public," she says under her breath. She leans against the wall, facing the stage, back to me.

I lean against the wall behind her, my good ear facing her.

I look at Lemonhead's back. Her skinny neck, her thick blond hair. I reach out to touch her, my good ear facing the wall now, the *har-har-humble-hum* of the room bouncing into it. I'm underwater, slow. I watch my hand. I see her body turning toward me. My hands grab her on either side of the stomach. I hear a shrill scream, bouncing off the wall, into my ear. I look up. I see on the stage. A girl, who has stopped her routine, stands looking at us, arms crossed. The judges, the emcee are turned, looking at us. I look at the audience. They look at us too. A woman screams again, running through an aisle toward us. Lemonhead's mother. The sound of her screaming bounces off the wall into my ear. It sounds far away that way. It's funny, because she is very close.

I say, "Darla said your dance was pretty. Good as Lincoln Center, she said."

Lemonhead whispers, "You better get off me."

Her mother's hands, right there. *"Dirty trailer tra—"*

I dodge. It feels good to dodge. I haven't dodged in a long time. I'm great at dodging. Her mother stumbles, slams against the wall. *Ha ha! That's right: Bruiser's a lightnin' fast badass!*

I run quick, dodging through the legs of all the ugly people. I run out the front doors, down the stairs. Laughing still, I turn a corner of hedges. I stop dead in my tracks. Darla and James. She's on tiptoe. They hug tight. They make turning back and forth hugging motions. My throat makes a small gurgle and my stomach feels deep and hollow and cold. Bernice is nearby, lying on her side. She sees me, her tail thumps the ground.

I run.

I run through town, losing my way, running until I find my

way again to the woods, running until I reach the old car, tripping and landing on my stomach. The ground is cold and the
dirt and ash stick to my wet cheeks. I start to scream so loud
that I can't see, and I hit the old car with a long branch until
it's broken away to a nub.

I feel empty and light. I walk over to the pit and start a fire.
I collect branches and make it blaze high. I sit and watch the
flames.

I fall asleep.

I wake suddenly. The fire's low, it's cold. I collect sticks from
under the dark trees. The flames grow high again, it's warm. I
think about Mom. I try to remember. I think I dreamed about
her. I can't remember, but the feeling of her is near me. The
feeling of *that day* is inside me. I remember it and I feel it again
like I did that day. I can smell it: the mossy-ness of early morning lake, the flowery-ness of dew. And the blood. There was a
lot. It smelled too. I don't know how to put it. It smelled like
warmth. Like the smell of skin in a bath. But it also smelled
cold. Warm and cold smelling, like on freezing days when I
make a fist and blow into the middle of the fist, the way it
smells when the cold and warm meet on the skin that way.

I lie back, my good ear facing the crackling flames, looking
up at the branches overhead, lit by the fire.

"Mom, what about me?" I whisper.

I roll onto my side, look into the fire.

"You weren't thinking of me when you did it, Mom."

I sit up, jab at the fire with a stick.

"You tried to leave me."

I let my stick rest: its end catches fire.

"Mom, I don't want to leave Darla."

I bring the burning stick close to my face, until all I see is
flame.

"But, I want to come home."

I whack at the fire. Cinders fly up.

"Mom, is it better now that I'm gone?"

I stop. I listen.

"Mom?"

I whack the fire hard.

"I want to come home now."

I whack.

"But . . ."

Whack.

"It's better without me there."

Whack.

"It's better without me there."

Whack. Whack. Whack. Whack. Whack.

"I don't care."

I'm standing over the fire. I'm winded. I stare at the flames.

"That's not my fault, Mom."

I throw the stick in. I sit back down.

"It's not my fault. I'm coming home."

Darla stands over me, she's panting hard, like she can hardly breathe. We look at each other. She starts crying, just like that.

"I thought you left. I thought you left me."

She stands there with her arms hanging at her sides. She starts to hiccup like a little kid.

"I saw you two," I say.

Her chin quivers. "All those girls up there were so pretty," she says.

"I talked to that girl, the mean one. I told her that she was a good dancer. I made her laugh."

Darla looks at the ground, then sits. "I bet she worked real hard on that dance," she says. She looks at the fire, then at me. "That was real nice of you."

fourteen

Sometimes my silent ear hurts. A pressing pain that turns to a sharp pain like a cold slice of metal slowly slicing through my ear.

I lie very still in the sleeping bag, looking up at the tent wall. Darla's asleep, I'm crying. I want to hide my tears, but I'm scared to turn my head away, because when I move the cold slice of metal shifts, cutting deeper, sinking far into my brain. I make a little sound. *Ooohoo. Ooohoo.* A little whale. *Ooohoo.*

Darla turns. "What's—?" She looks. She sits up.

I can't move. I'm scared of the metal. I look at Darla, crying. I can't hide because of the metal. *Ooohoo. Ooohoo.*

"What the matter?"

The pain eases away suddenly. But, I cry harder.

"I can't hear nothing in my ear. It's broke. Don't laugh. It hurts. I want someone to look at it, I want it to not hurt."

Darla puts her hand on my chest.

"I want someone to look at it."

"Okay, Ewe. We will."

"We'll go home?"

Darla wipes some snot from her nose. She smiles, leans over me, kisses away a tear. She lays beside me, our faces side by side. We look at each other. We move an inch, our lips touch. We kiss. We move apart. We look at each other, our faces so close that we're a little cross-eyed. That's funny. We giggle, quietly at first. Then it's like a wave, and we're tumbling inside it, washed away and out of control, holding our stomachs, crazy with laughter.

I wake up.

Darla turns around. The map is on the ground, open.

"I don't know why I was looking at it," Darla says, "since we'll probably just take a bus or something."

Darla opens the box of an apple pie we bought yesterday. We eat with our fingers.

Darla looks away while we eat. She won't look at me, even when I crane my head forward.

I look at the map. Along the coast of North Carolina is a line of islands. Joey told me about them. The Outer Banks.

"Let's go here first," I say, pointing, leaving a grease stain on the islands.

Darla blinks, looking over at the map. Her lips smile very softly.

After breakfast, I ball up some toilet paper and dip it in a cup filled with puddle water. I hold Darla's face and hands, and rub them clean. Then she does me. We rub damp leaves over our teeth. But, Darla finds a mint in her pocket. She bites it in

half for us. We pack everything up. We walk to town. I
remember the bus station. I looked at the map. We need a bus
to Cedar Island.

We walk for a very long time. We keep a lookout for cops.
Darla wears a pair of her mother's sunglasses, and I wear a
wig as a disguise. Sometimes people pass and look at us and
whisper. We know it's because we're famous, probably on the
news, milk cartons and all, so they recognize us, but since
we're in disguise, it takes them a second to remember where
they know us from until it's too late and we've vanished. I like
imagining their faces when they finally figure it out.

We drop our bags, and sit leaning against the station. The
cool air is nice, but all the sweating and then the cool, we get
the chills, and snot begins. My head feels hot and light.

Darla takes out her cigarettes. There's only one left and it's
broken. She balls up the pack and throws it into the street,
kind of bratty. I go through the bag and take out the pack we
stole from Summer. Darla lights two, hands me one.

"How long you been smoking?" I ask.

Darla looks at me. "Since we came away from home."

"Do you really like them?"

Darla shrugs. "No." She shrugs again.

We're quiet. Our sweat dries and the sun shines and it's a
nice day. Darla says she wants to buy our tickets.

"You better not fool me like last time."

"I just wanna get them."

She returns. "It's not leaving till four-thirty. I had to buy
one child ticket and one adult 'cause the guy in there was giving me a look. We only got ninety-eight bucks left."

We watch the cold morning sun turn bright. Long shadows
cast by low buildings turn short by midday. The quiet street
gets crowded with people at lunchtime, then the street goes
quiet again for another hour or so, and the shadows reappear

on the other side of the street, and they slowly stretch out. And kids fill the streets after school. Then the street goes empty again. The silent shadows grow across the street, up the sides of buildings, and everything is blue shadow, then night creeps low along the gutter.

In all this time I can't think of one thing to do, or one place to visit one last time—write my name on a wall, run down the street screaming, *something*—that would say: this is us, this is who we are, this is what we've done and this is where we've been. Something that would make all of this be remembered by someone except me and Darla. But, we won't say good-bye to Lemonhead or James, and probably one day they'll forget us like sometimes I forget Daddy Ham or Shinji or even Dad or Mom or Daniel or Jordan or The Block. We will forget one another like we all never happened. And Joey. I never found him, but I feel like he's leaving me again. I still remember him real good, but probably someday I won't.

Here I am! I feel angry. Don't forget me: how can you forget me? But, maybe that's how it's supposed to be. If your head was to get cluttered with remembering *everything* it would be like trying to find something in a pigsty bedroom with everything out in tangles on the floor.

Then, I don't know why, I think of Dad. I remember the time he was making the miniature of the summer cottage for Megan. I remember how stupid I was. How I thought it was for us. How I knew who Megan was, but I pretended like she wasn't really real. How I was scared even to say her name like that would've made her more real. I remember how I asked Dad some question I can't remember now, and how he looked at me, a little like he hated me, and he said, "You're a romantic like your mother." I went to the dictionary and looked up *romantic*. It said it meant a lot of things, but I knew Dad meant it in a mean way, so I read the mean definitions, and it said, "without basis in fact; fanciful, fictitious"—which I also had to look up—"Not practical." It took me a long time to make sense of all the words, but after spending an afternoon thinking about it, then I understood. What Dad was saying was that I was like a baby the way I always made up stuff to believe, like believing in Santa Claus, or that thunder was God bowling. But, thunder is thunder, and Santa Claus is Mom and Dad buying me stuff from the What I Want list I write every year.

Looking at the last bit of red sunlight ease away from the building side, I know that Dad would think that I'm being romantic, my wanting to grab hold of something, to not let go, so that forever I'll have a little bit of it. That is *fictitious*. That is *not practical*. All those things we did: they're over and done with. They're gone. They're not here anymore, except in remembering, and remembering is not real like my hand is real, or this bag I lean against is real. I want to pretend. I want to stop everything, and pretend that all this is special. But, what's so special? It's all just like a blackboard, and now I should erase being a runaway and all the stuff before, and put up a new lesson. I'll forget Lemonhead, Joey. One day I will, I know that. And I'll be fine. I won't be sad, because I just won't remember.

I look at Darla.

If she went away would I forget her?

If I went away would she forget me?

Darla looks at me. She leans out and looks through the window of the station at the clock. She sits back. "It's time to go."

I nod.

She looks at me. She hugs me hard. She doesn't let go, she says, "Shut up. It'll be different when we get on the bus. It'll be over. Just shut up."

I hug her back. Hard.

We let go. I smile.

We collect our bags and walk to the waiting bus.

Maybe being romantic is just seeing what is really there. Maybe, to not be romantic means that you're being a baby and pretending you don't see it or feel it, pretending like nothing's a big deal. Maybe it's *not* being romantic that is fictitious, not practical, a lie. All I know is, there *are* some times and some things that are special, Dad, and I can't pretend like you, a not-romantic, that they aren't.

Night is here. I spit on the ground, I lift my bag, I get on the bus.

fifteen

The ferry is real big, filled with cars and people, and we walk on just like that. We hide our stuff, so we don't look like runaways. The air is cold, we walk to the front of the boat. Behind, the lights of land get smaller, and ahead the skinny moon lights the tips of the waves. I hang my head over the railing and watch the fat ferry hull push through the water.

P-shh . . . P-shh . . . P-shh . . .

I close my eyes and sway. My face and body suddenly went very hot and aching while we rode on the bus. The wind and the cool sea air feel good.

Darla leans against me. She says something to me.

I point to my bad ear and shake my head.

She moves to my other side. "Sorry. I said, it's like forever," she says, nodding out into the black water.

It's nice having someone know about my ear.

"Actually, we're only on the sound right now. But, on the other side of the island is forever. The ocean."

"I like pretending I'm a bird flying over the water," she says. Darla climbs up on the crossbeam of the railing and she stands a few feet off the ground. She opens her arms like wings, her legs pressing against the railing. She laughs and flaps her wings.

I slip my fingers through a belt loop of her jeans.

We get cold and the snot and shivering start, so we walk around. We go to the cafeteria and buy hot chocolates. We sit on a bench until we're warm. Darla holds her cup with two hands. There are tiny cracked islands of nail polish left on her fingernails, and underneath them, dirt.

Darla smiles and between sips says, "Good." She has a chocolate mustache, two brown curls on either side of her mouth, and it makes me remember that first night, waiting in the bus station sipping hot chocolate in New York. I can't believe that *that* was me. What did I think about that night? I try hard, but I can't remember: but, it's not just like I've forgotten, it's like it's impossible to remember. Impossible as reading someone else's mind. But, it's my mind, I think, feeling dizzy, feeling crazy.

We walk down metal hallways. We walk between parked cars and trucks. Most cars are empty: people in the cafeteria, on deck watching the water, the night. There's a station wagon. The doors are open. Inside, on the backseat are jumbled blankets, picture books, dolls, pillows, McDonald's wrappers. Darla waits outside. I lie down, cover myself in a blanket. It smells of soap and bologna, spit and sugar. Family trip. I like sleeping on family trips. I like driving when it's night, the soft sound of the wheels whirling outside.

I get out, taking a blanket.

We pass a truck with a logo of a crab on the side. A man

sits in the truck, his head back, mouth open, asleep. The news
is on the radio. A storm is coming, a hurricane from the
Caribbean. They're hoping that the winds out of the west will
take it off course from the eastern coast.

We go back outside, lean against the wall. The island is
getting close, the lights bigger. I can see shapes: houses, a
street, the beach.

"Ewe, we should get into disguise when we get to the
island." Darla tries to smile. "We should get into disguise so
we can have fun, just you and me."

I wrap the stolen blanket around us. It's soft, wool. Our
bodies go warm, our faces, cold. There's a ringing in my head.
A low electrical hum. It presses against the inside of my head.
It makes my good ear hear funny and far away, my mouth
tastes of metal, my eyes see squishy and blurred. I'm sleepy.
Darla nudges me. I look at her. Her face is tired and her nose
is red, flecks of raw skin from wiping wiping wiping the
watery snot onto her crusty sleeve.

"Snot," she says, pointing at my nose.

Right then I feel it drip over my lips, down my chin. I can't
wipe anymore. It stings like the pink spot of a picked scab. I
put my nose on the knee of my jeans, my head under the blanket. I leave it there and let my pants slowly soak up the snot.
It's dark and warm, and it's nice to hear the water through the
blanket, hearing people's voices and footsteps outside. I think
about all the things I miss hearing from inside. Rain, tinny, on
the car roof, driving at night. The wind off the Hudson. Darla
in the cans and string across the courtyard.

The ferry docks. A big sign: CAPE HATTERAS. We walk. We
find the beach. It's very cold. The wind rolls out of the black
Atlantic. We huddle close beneath our sleeping bag and stolen
blanket, pulling our knees to our bodies, so only our faces show.
We rock and giggle, but we don't say anything for a long time.

"You're gonna have to dress like a girl 'cause that's the only kinda costume we got," Darla says.

"Except for your mom's wigs, there isn't anything else, since you wear boys' clothes."

"They're not boys' clothes."

Far, far off is a light in the sky, very soft: a lighthouse.

"Why do people say we look alike?" I ask, turning to Darla.

" 'Cause we got tan skin." Darla shrugs. "People are pretty stupid. When Mom made us first convert, it was weird. People would see us and call names sometimes. I've heard those boys you play with call lots of names."

"I'm part Arab. Jordan calls them sandniggers. Mom's just plain American and Dad's French and Arab."

"Your brother's stupid," Darla says.

I don't want to talk anymore. There's a thick fog, and by it I can see how the wind moves. Darla's talking. I turn my head until my good ear catches the wind, and her voice fades away.

Darla pulls on my shirt. I look at her.

"So, well, all right?" she says.

I nod, since I haven't been listening.

"I got a dress you can wear," Darla says.

"You don't have any dress that I've seen," I say.

Darla frowns. "Like you know everything," she says.

"Well, I haven't *seen* it."

"Well, I haven't *worn* it," she says. She looks out to the ocean and softly says, "There wasn't any occasion to."

sixteen

I know that it's very early from the color of the sky. Like colored chalk, I think. Like the fat pieces of chalk I draw on the sidewalks with, that's what the colors are like. And the soft feel of the air, like the chalk when you draw really fast and it becomes smooth and powdery.

It's still cold, but the wind has gone away. My face is moist with dew. I touch my nose. Dry. Darla is asleep. Something smells bad. Warm and sour. I lean close to Darla's head. I feel heat, and smell the bad smell. I get up and walk to the water. My head feels airy, bouncing on a string, cheeks burning, eyes watery, stinging when I blink, and I keep having to remember: *I'm awake, I'm awake. I'm walking, moving. I'm awake.* I can see the lighthouse far off, white like air against the gray sky. The packed sand by the shore is cold and hard against my bare feet, and they go numb. The water's *shoush shoush* fills my good ear. Everything looks different in this sort of silence.

Things seem far away, and lonely, sort of. I see some birds and I make bickering sounds for them. Large smoky clouds move overhead out from the beginning of the sea, I make a low whistling sound for them.

Ahead a dock. A group of men sitting on beach chairs fishing. I walk under it. It feels good: hidden, listening. I press my fingers against the hard white barnacles like shells on the thick, dark dock pillar that smells of oil and salt.

"Figure these clouds're coming off that hurricane down there?"

"I figure."

"Hasn't been one bite: sure 'cause of the fishes being spooked by it. They can tell those sorts of things, fishes and animals can."

"That why my wife gone running for the hills earlier?"

The men laugh.

They go quiet for a while.

"They say it's gonna be one gale of a storm."

"We always get hit hard."

"When you say she's coming?"

"A day or two if she don't turn out to sea."

"My odds are on it sticking to the coast."

"I figure."

I walk away, returning back along the shore. I feel light, like I'm floating.

I'm air, I think, I'm air.

"Hey, boy," one of the men calls.

I keep walking.

"*Boy!*"

I stop. They're calling me? I think, I'm air: I float. I turn. The men all look at me. I realize that they see me, that I shouldn't let them see me.

"You're up mighty early."

I nod.

One of the men taps his friend on the chest. "Imagine my boy getting up so early on a Saturday morning."

The men all laugh.

My leg is wet. Why is my leg wet? My head floats. I feel my pants. It's warm. I peed on myself. I look back to the men. They're not looking at me anymore. I turn. I walk.

I can see Darla. She's still asleep. But, as I get close I hear her laughing. She lies on her back, staring up at the sky. When I reach her she rolls her eyes over and laughs harder.

"What 'cha laughing at?"

"I don't know."

We look in our bag. We have two chocolate cupcakes left.

We eat. Eating makes me feel better. The morning's turned golden. We pack.

Darla looks at me. "Where's the tent?"

I shrug.

Darla starts looking around. Under things, inside things, places it couldn't possibly fit. She searches crazy, sand flying.

"We musta left it on the boat," I say.

"You were the one carrying it."

Darla looks at me like she wants to kill me. But, she looks pretty, her cheeks very red like two roses.

"Just get your mom to buy you a new one when we get back."

"But, I'm gonna need it when you— It just won't work, is all. We need it now!" Darla pushes me.

I push her back, hard. I didn't mean for it to be so hard, but it feels good. Her feet are in the air, she lands on her back. She rolls onto her stomach.

"What if it rains, huh?" she says into the sand.

She rolls over.

"You got sand on your face," I say.

"You gonna hit me again?"

"You're lying to me," I say, giving her a hand up.

We begin walking.

"You didn't ask me anything. How could I have lied?"

"I don't know. You just did."

We walk for a long time. Thick clouds move across the sky, covering the sun again.

We pass a closed-down gas station. The doors of the garage are covered with graffiti. DO BONGS. MUFF DIVING. KILL DISCO FAGITS. LONG LIVE ROCK.

I walk up to it, past the rusted gas pumps to the side of the garage where there's a pay phone.

I dial *0*. I tell the operator I'd like to make a collect call.

The phone rings.

"Hello?" I hear. The operator talks, then quiet. *"Hello? Hello? Honey?!"* says Mom.

I can't breathe.

"Please say hello. Operator? *Operator, are you still there?"*

Quiet.

"Honey, please—" Mom starts crying.

"Hello?" says Dad.

Why are you home? How can you be home? Why aren't you out looking for me?

A wind blows out of the ocean turning my peed-on pants cold. My head begins to float again. Dad's voice talking: something about them being sick with worry. His voice asks me, where I am. It tells me to go to the police. His voice begs me. I like that. Dad's voice has never begged before. I like that. Beg, I think.

Why aren't you looking for me?

I look at Darla. She sits on the ground, cross-legged. Dad's voice speaks. In the background, Mom's crying.

"I'll be home soon," I say, soft, like my words are made of dry leaves. I hang up. I walk past Darla and stand in the middle of the street. I bend down and grab my legs and squeeze my head tight between my knees, and I stay like that for a long time.

We walk.

We come to a big house. It's brown and faded, abandoned. There's a metal sign nailed onto the side. FOR SALE. Through dirty windows we see a large empty room, through another, a bar and some tipped-over tables and old chairs.

"We can get into disguise in here," Darla says.

We walk around the house to the front entrance. There's a large porch and overhead wooden letters, MOTEL. None of the doors are open. We break a window. It's dusty inside. On the second floor are bedrooms.

"I wanna wash," Darla says.

She leaves and returns with a bar of soap, rust on one side from a metal soap tray. Darla goes first, then me. The water's cold. My skin is dry, scaly. There are lots of white lines from where I've scratched scratched scratched, some places the skin has gone red and raised. I wash all over. I scrub around my toes, my arms, neck. I watch the dirt swirl away in the water. The cold water hurts like fists on my burning body. But, I like the feel of the soap and all the suds. It takes away all the dirt and sweat and snot and dribbled pee and b.m. and twigs and ash and smoke.

It's weird. I can't explain. Suddenly I can't tell if any second before this second was real. I think something, and the second after, I try to remember: did I just think that? Or do I just think I thought that? The dirt runs off me, swirling in the water that twists down the drain. I think of different things that have happened. And for each one, I think, Did that happen? Everything is shifting: all the seconds before this second are washing away. I see them, like flashes, different moments from before. I see them, for real, in the swirling dirt. Like lots of tiny figures swirling in the water. I see faces and places. They come off me. It feels good. I'm not sad. I just sort of watch. Like a dog watching a turtle on its back. Everything goes away. The water takes it all away. No more dirt comes. I am clean. The water runs clear.

I crouch and close my eyes and let the water hit my back. I've gone so cold that I don't feel cold anymore. I feel hot like I'm inside a fire. But then, like how it happens with the feeling of being burned, it goes back to cold. Then, it's neither. My body is fading away. Go away, I think. I feel darkness. I am darkness. I am nothing.

I start jerking around like crazy. It makes me open my eyes. My body's shivering. I can't stop it. I crawl out, and lie on the cold bathroom floor, and I shiver for a very long time. I shiver so hard that I bite my lip and my head rattles against the hard floor. And it only stops when I start sneezing and sneezing and sneezing, and the snot starts running, and that's okay because anything is better than the fever.

"We gotta get into our disguises," Darla says, waiting for me. She hands me white tights, a white turtleneck, a brown corduroy dress with white and pink flowers sewn across the chest.

"No."

"We gotta get in disguise."

I look at her. No one's looking for us, Darla, I think. Don't you know that?

I look at her face: you don't know that. Baby, I think. You don't want to know that. I think of saying it, *No one's looking for us!* But, I don't.

"You promised."

I turn away.

We're going home. They're our homes, Darla, and we're going home. They're *our* homes.

I sit on the bed. For the first time, I put on the pants that Shinji gave me.

Darla looks at me, then she turns. She goes to the bathroom. She has a rusted carving knife. She stands in front of the mirror.

"Where'd you find that knife?"

"Downstairs."

Darla grabs her long hair in bunches and starts cutting. Her face scrunches up, her eyes close tight.

"Why you doing that?"

Her face goes like a fist and I can tell it hurts like crazy.

"We don't have to get in disguise."

Darla pauses, takes a deep breath, like she's about to dive underwater.

"I'm telling you."

She grits her teeth. She has to run the knife back and forth quickly to get through her hair. She drops clumps into the sink. Tears come out of her eyes.

I go to the other room. I walk around the empty motel. Sounds: things moving. *Ghosts,* I think, excited. I walk into a room. A window is broken, bits of paper flutter around. *Wind,* I think.

I return.

Darla's sitting on the bed. Her face is blotchy. She smiles. Her hair is short and choppy. She's in disguise.

seventeen

It's evening, it's growing dark. We walk and walk, but we can't find anywhere to buy food. We come to the lighthouse. It's big and white, and its light shines strong in cones into the rolling fog. We sit, leaning against the base of the lighthouse.

Waves crash against the land, their crests lit by the spinning light.

"I wonder how far out you can see this," Darla says, looking up at the lighthouse.

"Real far," I say.

"Hundreds of miles?" she asks.

I shrug.

"Whatever happened to that photograph of your mom as a little girl?" Darla asks.

"Mona?" I say. "Left her at Ham's."

We're quiet.

Darla's turning her head, slowly from side to side, her

mouth open in an O, imitating the spinning beam of the light-house. "I was just remembering stuff and I hadn't seen it in a long time," she says.

I look at the water. "Remember that time you saw me Uptown in Riverside Park. That first day I saw you again, when you'd just moved back?" I ask.

Darla nods.

"Sometimes I'd take long walks. They were the biggest adventures I'd ever had on my own. But, every time, I'd always get scared. I was scared to be Uptown alone that day." I smile. "I don't know. I don't mind so much going home now. Like that day, when I got home, I felt stupid, a stupid little cry-baby, because I'd been scared. Every time I took a long walk, I'd always run home, scared. But now, I don't feel stupid any-more."

"Did you leave that photo on purpose, or did you forget it?" she asks.

I shrug.

" 'Cause you can't remember, or 'cause you don't wanna tell?"

"It wasn't neither," I say. "I just kinda left it there, but not on purpose or on mistake, kinda like on both."

I look at the water. I look at Darla.

"When you wanna go home?" I ask.

Darla looks at me. She makes her mouth an O again, turn-ing her head out toward the water.

⌒⌒

Near the lighthouse is a campsite. It's empty. We unroll the sleeping bag next to a fire pit. We drape the blanket over two upright sticks for shelter. I think it's a good idea to hide our stuff in case anyone comes along wanting to rip us off. I walk into the trees. I find an old door. I dig a shallow hole with an old oar I find. I stop a lot, tired, dizzy. I look at my watch. I haven't wound it in days. It's stopped. There's no way to find out the right date or time, so I can't set it. And looking at it, it seems like something a little kid would have. Mickey Mouse. His happy, hopeful smile: I can just hear his high voice, *Hi kids!,* telling some story, me sitting at home along with all the Mouseketeers in the TV, like some dumb, little kid. I take it off, throw it into the hole, covering it, along with everything else, under the door.

We find some wood, pile it into the fire pit. But we've lost our matches.

"I had a birthday," I say. "Before. I don't know when exactly. Around Shinji's." I look at Darla. "We're both ten." I smile. "Now you're not older than me."

"Yes, I am."

"But, not as much as before."

"I'm practically eleven. December thirtieth."

"Well, for a little bit then, we're the same age."

"For like a month."

"A month and a half."

Darla looks at me for a little while. She stands, is lost in the shadows. When she returns she has some sticks and sea grass. She takes two sticks and makes them into a cross, tying the sea grass around them so that they'll stay. She pulls at the frayed cuffs of her ladybug sweater. Green and red, white and orange yarn threads unravel. She takes the threads and starts looping them, starting in the middle of the cross, around and out, until there's a colorful diamond, like a cobweb, tied around the cross. She hands it to me.

"Happy birthday," she says. "It's called a God's eye."

I hold it in front of my face. "I'm watching you, Darla," I say in a deep voice. "Ooooooohhhh."

"Shut up."

I put the God's eye in my lap.

"I wanna make one."

Darla ties two sticks into a cross and hands it to me. She pulls some more yarn off her sweater. I weave it around. My head spins. My God's eye is much smaller, but I can't do any more. Everything is fuzzy. I want to topple over.

I stick them standing up in the ground at the head of our sleeping bag.

We crawl into the sleeping bag.

I look at them.

I roll over.

I fall asleep.

I wake up. I look. Darla's eyes are open too. Her face is pale, wet. Old sweat, new sweat, sick breath.

"Fire," I say. "I'm on fire."

Darla nods. "Me," is all she says.

My clothes stick to me. I'm sweating, on fire. I kick my pants off, my shirts, sweater. I'm naked. I sit up, my top cooling in the night air.

"Better?"

I nod.

Darla takes off her clothes and sits up.

I see her ribs. Her nipples are softer-looking than mine. They're funny, like two tiny pink jellyfish. I press one with a finger. *Ding-dong.* My head, the balloon. Burning balloon. Darla runs her finger down my side. I look down. Ribs. My body aches: sitting hurts, moving hurts, breathing hurts, the weight of the sleeping bag on my legs hurts. I look at my nipples. Red leather coins. I press one. *Buzzzz.*

We lie down. We sleep.

I wake. I'm freezing. I put on clothes. Darla shivers in her sleep. There are tiny red veins on her eyelids, white crust around her mouth. I nudge her. She opens her eyes. She looks scared, confused.

"It's cold," I say. "Put on clothes."

She puts on clothes.

She leans over, vomits, and continues to vomit until nothing more comes out, then she just makes vomit sounds for a while. She stands. I stand.

"Water," Darla says. She drags the sleeping bag.

I pluck the God's eyes out of the ground.

We walk.

We come to a dock. The planks are moist and cold. Stars in the sky. Ropes and pulleys on boat masts whistle and clang. We come to the end. A rowboat covered in a blue tarp. Darla pulls the tarp off, accidentally untying the rope that moors it. She ties the rope back. She steps in.

"Don't."

"Yes."

I get in. Lie down. The boat rocks.

Rock, rock. Rock-a-bye-baby . . .

I lay one God's eye on top of me, and one on top of Darla.

We look at the stars. I stare real hard at one, and all the rest begin to vanish.

I'm a single star. I'm falling, falling through space. The boat rocks. Rock-a-bye-baby, on the tree top. . . . Sleep.

⁓

I open my eyes, it's still night. Darla's asleep. It's very dark out. I close my eyes and listen to the ocean. The wind has died down, and the docked boats have become quiet. Only the ocean stirs.

I nudge Darla, but she makes an annoyed sound from her sleep. It's dark out, but I can see her face. It is hot, red, it glows.

I have to pee. I stand up. The boat shifts, and I almost fall over, looking out to the water. I turn to the other side and put my foot out for the dock. Then, I put my foot back into the boat, and stand there for a moment, looking at the land.

Land is dark. Dark as the water and dark as the sky and they seem like one. Land is far away. So far away that the swiping lighthouse beam is small like a fat firefly, and the other lights—houses? streetlights? I can't tell—are far away pinpricks, like a neat line of stars. I can't see where land ends and water begins. I see only darkness. Water and more water.

Endless, slapping, black water on every side, as I slowly turn and complete a full circle.

eighteen

All the splashing from the oars wakes Darla. I forget, almost, that she's there, or I'm here, or the boat is beneath me. I stare straight into all the black. Black water into black land into black sky, and I paddle hard, digging into the water, dragging us toward the small lights.

Darla says, "Ewe." She says, "EweEweEweEweEweEwe." I turn around. She doesn't sit up. She lies there, face turned to the starry sky. I see blurry from all the squinting into all the moving black water and from the fever, and when I turn and look, Darla is a faint thing, like smoke, her body covered by the blue sleeping bag.

"Why're you——" says Darla. Then she inhales quickly. "How far have we drifted?" she asks.

I am far away. I'm high in the sky, looking down. I'm deep inside my head, looking out. My mouth moves. "I'm taking us home. We're very sick. I touched your forehead. It was very hot. Mine too."

Everything trembles now. The stars, Darla, the boat. My
body shakes hard. I try to stand, I want to run. *I'm going home
now, okay?* I slip and fall backward. I land in the boat and hit
my head. I shake on the floor. Darla rises up over me like a
floating thing, her arms go out, the blue sleeping bag drooping
like heavy wings. She rises up high, then swoops over me. Her
faint, pale, smoky face, and then, faint, pale, smoky hands,
shush over me. Trembling, still trembling. Her hands then on
my face. They're warm. My face is numb and thick feeling
and cold like blubber, and her hands burn against it. Her hands
move over my face, over my eyes. Closing my eyes. Shaking
slowly leaves me like I'm a hallway and a crowd is passing
through, down to my feet, then passing away, and I become
still and empty and light.

Blue angel-wing sleeping bag around me. Stars in the sky,
bright and hard like rock candy. Below, water passing crinkling, gently, slipping beneath us, slipping fast like wind
pushes clouds. Darla's hands on my chest, now cold like
sticks covered in ice. Darla's face above me, tight, looking
out.

I say, "Wey me? Whem we?" I think hard. "Where *are*
we?"

Darla has been making soft sounds, talking to herself.
Now, she looks down. She says, "Very far. Far, far away. But,
look, you can still see the lighthouse."

I follow her pointing finger.

Darla's face, floating cold in dark night, turns back and
forth. "We're too far."

Darla looks down. Her face smiles beautiful, like the first
ever thing to be beautiful, the thing that happened first to
make a person think, *Beautiful.* That is Darla's smile.

I fill up on smile, like moonlight, like a waterfall. Darla looks out again. I squint. Darla, stars, black night blur. Soft, like a veil. I close them more. Close them all the way. Dark, but not like night or ocean. Empty dark, shallow dark.

Sleep.

I open my eyes. Darla's sitting, staring out. I sit up next to her.

I tremble once, looking at the cold faraway pinpricks of land light.

"As long as we're in the boat we're okay. As long as we can still see land . . . ," I say. I look at her. "You're my best friend, Darla." I say.

She doesn't say anything for a long time. She doesn't look at me. She says, "Are you just saying that because we're out here?"

I nod, because I know what she means. "Nah," I say. "I mean it for real."

Darla looks at me. She kind of smiles, like she's about to say something, but she stays quiet. The smile stays for a bit, then it just sort of fades away.

The water's now totally still. It's flat and reflects the star-filled sky perfectly, like a black mirror.

"It's like we're floating in the sky," I say. "Look at the stars in the water."

Darla nods. She lies down. I lay next to her.

"Holy shit!" she screams out, echoing over the perfect ocean, laughing. We both scream and scream and scream, and we rock the boat back and forth, and the reflected stars warble in the ripples we make.

We go quiet, and the boat goes still. And all the ruckus and sounds echo away across the endless ocean. The huge quiet that waits like figures in the dark, moves in and surrounds us.

❧

I must have fallen asleep, because I open my eyes and night is gone. My body aches bad, but I don't feel outside it, or deep inside it. I just feel like me. I touch my forehead. It doesn't burn, my fever's broke. Must be from the cold ocean air. Once Jordan had such a big fever, his face was puffy and blistered, that they had to take him to the hospital. The fever stayed high, and they had to break it. They dunked him into an ice bath. He told me after, how much that hurt. I think, that's why I ache: because my fever was broke.

Darla's sitting up, in the middle of the boat, facing the open ocean. She's jammed the God's eyes between the planks of the boat's bow. The endless sky is pale and red on the edges. We're far out, almost far enough out to see over the edge of the world, at the sun down below crawling up the side of the sea.

Darla holds the oars out of the water. She puts one in and gently strokes, turning the boat around toward land, then she slowly starts to paddle through the glassy water. She leans forward and digs the oars deep into the water, and she strokes harder and harder, her body bending forward, and pulling quickly back. She rows and rows, furiously. Then she tips the oars out of the water. The boat glides and slides sideways and we face the open ocean again. Darla looks over her shoulder toward land. She dips the oars into the water and gently strokes, and the boat begins moving toward the red eastern sky. The blinding cap of the sun pokes up over the water, and a long fan-shaped reflection stretches across the ocean toward us like a golden road. Darla continues to move us into the reflection. I look behind and the boat breaks the golden road, a blue wake.

Darla looks at me, sees I'm awake. I take hold of an oar and begin rowing. The boat slowly turns away from the sun, back toward land. Darla rows the other oar harder, turning the boat back out toward open sea.

"Quit it," I say.

I paddle my oar harder, we turn back to land. Darla dips her oar into the water, and the boat turns to the sea.

"That's not funny!"

Darla tilts her oar out of the water.

The sun continues to rise, a blinding thing in the sky.

I row and row and row.

Out in the ocean, we can see every corner of the sky. There's a sound to our left, far away that I'm not sure it's real. I stop paddling and look over. A rumbling. The world is blue, then over the southern edge of water are quick flashes. The bottom of the sky smudges with darkness, like spilt ink soaked into the edge of a page. It takes shape. Clouds, like rolling waves, dark, up out of the sea and into the sky. The clouds rise higher. The rumbling becomes louder. We can see the jagged edges of lightning cutting through the clouds, lighting their dark bellies.

The sky overhead is clear. A light breeze kicks up, and the water begins to ripple. High up in the sky is a plane. It reflects the bright sun across its silver body. I wave.

The boat begins to bob. Darla slips into the sleeping bag. I move to the front of the boat and watch the faraway storm move closer, racing across the sky. Below the clouds the ocean is dark, and as the clouds move nearer to us, I can see the ocean, dimpled by rain, and the land, dark and yellow-gray, bent and whipped. I look at the sun. It's strong, its rays warm on my skin. The boat rocks as the ripples stretch out into swells.

Darla opens her mouth, but closes it without saying anything.

I hold on to the sides of the boat. Above us, thin white and
yellow clouds that whistle high in the sky race ahead of the
main body of the storm, quick like smoke. Behind, the storm
approaches, splashing and thundering, green ocean curling over
white. A heavy wind circles, howling low and deep. Above,
more and more fast clouds collect, and they become thicker and
slower, and the sky quickly covers over with the rolling clouds.
The sun goes dim and cool, but I can see the circle of it. The
rain moves like a curtain stretched across the ocean.

The sun disappears.

The morning goes dark. Rain falls hard, and we are
drenched immediately. I look to the north, at the moving front
of the storm, like the opening of a cave, and the sunny day
beyond it. But, quickly it vanishes, until that last spot of sunny
day is gone and the world is covered in darkness.

The boat's tossed back and forth. We both start screaming.
The storm blows hard, and I can't see or hear. The boat fills
with water.

Darla's still in the sleeping bag and just looks at me.

I paddle hard toward land. The ocean is rough, like the
world itself is being tipped back and forth, from side to side.
Waves crash against us, behind us. I paddle as hard as I can,
watching waves curl behind us, paddling fast up the back of a
wave ahead, resting for a moment as we ride it forward, like a
sled on a hill, paddling hard again to get up the back of the
next wave.

My arms are tired.

Darla's eyes go wide.

I turn.

A wave grows out of the sea like a mountain. I freeze. It

rises higher and higher, building itself from within, water rushing up its middle.

For a moment it seems to stop, to churn in place. From behind smaller waves rush up its back. The mountain wave wobbles. Wind blows, water sprays white. Then it begins to tip, a sharp curl. It makes a deafening, ripping sound.

I close my eyes. I paddle.

Everything goes away. All the thrashing storm sounds, all the lashing and splashing and pelting of the wind and rain and ocean. It all goes away.

The air's turned to water. I float. I look. I see Darla rising out of the boat, weightless, the blue sleeping bag around her legs. I can hear only the warble of water. Overhead a ceiling of the water, like liquid glass, broken by the shower of rain. I see the God's eyes floating, spinning. I reach for one. The churning water suddenly sucks them away. Then I feel myself being pulled up. Quickly.

The terrible sounds suddenly start again. The crashing waves, the crackling thunder, the deep, howling wind.

A wave shoots me high, up into the air. I can see Darla beside me, rising up. The boat springs up below us, and falls back to the water. I stop rising. I fall down. I land hard in the boat, on my back. I see Darla fall. I see Darla vanish into the dark water. I sit up quickly.

Darla is right beside the boat, her face just below the surface. Her face, perfectly clear. Her face, open and shocked. Her face, tight, trembling. I reach to grab her, and she reaches to grab me. The sleeping bag is tangled around her. It fills with water. She is heavy and the ocean pulls her. She looks right into my eyes. She is slipping. She is too heavy, she is being pulled down. She looks at me. Her face, terrified, like a terrified animal.

Then, in a blink, it's all gone.

Her face goes calm, chin turned a little to the side, like she sees something. She looks up, but not at me, at something above me or beside me. Her mouth opens a crack. Bubbles run out. Her eyes become heavy. She closes her mouth. Her body twitches twice, very hard, and she almost gets away. She goes still. Her eyes are calm and pale. She looks at me. Blue dots pop in her brown eyes. She relaxes her hand. She begins to slip through my fingers. I catch her by her wrist. I am screaming and I am crying.

Darla's head sinks down, and her body goes heavy. She is a weight and her body helps the ocean pull. I reach my other hand down, and pull with all my might. The boat tips on its side. The black water pulls at her, the bottom of the ocean pulls at her.

A shadow runs across the water. I look up, and see the wave just as it crashes, sending the boat rushing forward. I feel the cold flesh of Darla's wrist, then I feel the cold water rake through my empty fingers. I fall back hard, and I hear a quick crack as my head slams against the side of the boat.

Overhead I see the mass of clouds, churning and swirling, like muddy whirlpools. I see a light, a pink flare, like a low shooting star, streaking across the sky.

My eyes begin to flutter, black, world, black, world, fluttering like nervous wings, and my head and all of my body feels light, like they aren't here, like they're sheltered from the storm, like I'm being lifted up. The fluttering slows, black . . . world, black . . . world. I feel my body shake. I'm laughing. I'm laughing hard. A storm of laughing. My fluttering eyes slow, then slow some more.

Until finally just . . .

Black.

return

one

I feel for the On Account of Being Deaf list in my back pocket. I unfold it on my lap.

Carrot cubes and peas and pale chicken slide out of my shepherd's pie, across my plate on brown gravy. Mom nudges me. She nods at my little blackboard. She's written on it.

Be encouraging. Smile as you chew your meal.

Dad cooks half the week's dinners now. Megan broke up with him. Jordan told me that on the first day I was back. He wrote on my blackboard, *You know what happened to her?* I didn't know who he was talking about. I stared at him. I didn't know anything, except: there he was, here I was. Home. Everything was silent. Then he wrote, *The bitch dropped him.*

The next day I walked around the apartment. I was still using a walker. I went to Jordan and Daniel's room while they were in school. It was in my head. *Bitch.* Everything was silent, but in my head the word made a sound. A tearing sound. I thought it would make it go away. It made sense when it did it. I wrote the word *Bitch* all over his desk. When he returned from school, he dragged me into his room. His mouth moved. He yelled. I couldn't hear. I watched his mouth. I craned my head until I was right close to his mouth. His yelling made a small wind. Suddenly his mouth closed, and the little wind stopped. He let me go. I looked at him. He moved back a little, then pushed me out the door. I saw his face for a second, before the door slammed closed. It looked like something. A little scared.

Daniel keeps his head down all the time. His hair has grown long and he smells of b.o. and smoke. His eyes watch from behind the hair. Sometimes I want to touch him.

I look at my blackboard.

Be encouraging. Smile as you chew your meal.

Mom sees me looking and smirks.

Dad leans over to see what's written.

I lift the blackboard, tilt it toward him.

Mom tries to take the blackboard back, but Dad's already read it.

I put it down.

Mom stares at me, but I don't look over. Mom looks at Dad, who shakes his head.

I shovel a forkful of shepherd's pie into my mouth.

After, I couldn't remember anything. I'd say, "Tell me, I know it's something bad." I couldn't hear my own voice. Mom would look at me and touch my ear to remind me I was deaf. I'd say, *"Tell me, tell me!"* I'd feel the words coming out of me, the way my chest and neck would squeeze to push out sound. I'd get angry, until finally Mom's mouth would start moving. But not being able to hear her made me crazy, and I didn't know what else to do but to still scream, "Tell me, tell me!" even though it made it worse each time because I couldn't hear. So, eventually Mom wrote the list.

Mom sat for long hours in the hospital room with me. It was a white room with a window that faced a brick wall.

I kept asking until finally, Mom wrote the list.

But, by then I had begun to remember. When I first remembered, it felt near, like it was happening right at that moment. But, after a while of remembering it, I was able to close my eyes and push it away, and I could look at it like it was far away.

I was in the hospital for months, sleeping. Then, I woke up. A half-sleep. Sometimes I'd float to the corner of the ceiling and watch us below. One morning I woke for real. Days went by and I was blank and my body couldn't move right, and I'd look at it laying there shriveled like some creature had sucked all of the liquid out. I began to ask what had happened. And one morning, I woke and I was alone, and I looked around and I knew: I didn't want to talk. I didn't think about it. It was just something I knew.

I've been home three weeks. I can walk on my own now. My weight is almost normal. There aren't any tubes in me. Sometimes I can't smell very good because sometimes I smell the hospital. Sometimes I smell salt and fish, and I can taste it. Sometimes I turn around quickly, sure someone is there and I feel my heart beating and I breathe quickly in, but I can't hear the breathing, so I breathe in again and again until I've breathed so much air that I feel like I'm suffocating.

*   *   *

From the living room window I watch the no. 5 bus cut through the park. I take out the list. I don't know why, but I like reading it.

ON ACCOUNT OF BEING DEAF

1. Brave Boy found lying on the boat. Asleep in the rough waves. Pale and light, a miracle that he floated safely inside the hurricane. Everyone says so: "A Miracle!" Some say, "That child was watched over."
2. Sailboat's sail torn by the razor winds, sent out a distress flare. Coast Guard on way to rescue distressed boat came upon Lost Brave Boy, even though he was out of their course. Coast Guard reported that their radar went down briefly, their course altered by wind and wave, thus finding Lost Brave Boy.
3. Sick Boy goes to hospital.
4. Sick Boy sleeps all the way until mid-January 1978.
5. Heartsick Mama at hospital that first day.
6. Heartsick Mama followed Lost Boy.
7. Lost Boy and Lost Girl (Darla . . .) left clues behind on their trail.

Riverside Park is dark, the trees bare. The lights across the Hudson River in New Jersey are small and cold. I push Darla out of my head every day. Not the remembered Darla, which I can watch when I close my eyes, small and far away. A different Darla. One that I don't know, like if she were still alive, how different she would probably be. That's how it sometimes feels, that she's still alive, running around, being Darla, somewhere else, someplace I don't know about, but who, at night, returns to me and who, in the day, I push away.

Sometimes, in the silence of deafness, thinking becomes

very loud. Sometimes thoughts bounce around. But, sometimes it's just nothing. Lots of nothing.

8. Clues:
   a. First collect call; operator informs us of Virginia whereabouts.
   b. Darla's daddy calls from West Virginia.
   c. Total silence. Lost Boy & Lost Girl flee into the Great Wide Open.
   d. Two letters received. One from Lost Boy, one from Lost Girl. Dated from stay with Darla's daddy, but postmarked days later, northeastern North Carolina. Authorities contacted. Lost Boy and Lost Girl sighted near freight train junction. Objects found in train: toothbrush, comb. Objects found on road, eight miles away: portable stove, transistor radio.

Darla must have sent the letters after Daddy Ham's. I didn't see her do that. Did she want to go home? And what about Mona? Didn't they find her? I left her in Daddy Ham's cubby below the sink. I left the cubby doors open so they'd find her. Is she still there, next to the smelly sponges and soaps and buckets and dark?

   e. *Wilmington Gazette:* see attached article.

Mom has stapled a newspaper clipping to the back of the list.

1977 Miss Wilmington Thanksgiving Pageant
Marked by li'l beauties & li'l scoundrels

The article talks about the pageant's highlights and winners, about a disruption when a "feral boy," which I keep meaning to look up, attacked the "sweet beauty," Miss Virginia St. James, ten years old.

The angel-like Miss St. James was shaken, but not seriously harmed. She informed officials that she had met the boy previously. He hadn't ever offered a name, but Miss St. James had learned from the feral boy that he was a runaway from New York City. It is believed that he is accompanied by a little girl of approximate age.

    f. Second collect call; operator informs us of North Carolina Outer Banks whereabouts.
   9. Heartsick Mama following clues, steps behind. Was on shore when Coast Guard returned with Cold Boy.
10. Found Boy's right ear damaged by unknown blow. Left ear severely infected by water and cold and fever.
11. Operations soon to restore hearing.

I put the list away. Outside, I watch the wind blow through the black park. Watching without sound makes everything look remembered. Everything looks a little slower, a little smaller. Sometimes it almost feels like nothing I'm seeing is happening now, and I wonder if something's happening behind the remembered things I'm seeing.

Darla's mother went crazy. There's a whole story, but I don't know it. Two weeks before I got home she was sent away.
No one's heard from Daddy Ham.

              *   *   *

I take the back cushions off the living room couch. I pull out the sheets and blankets and pillow that I keep under the couch and make my bed.

The first night, I sat and looked out my bedroom window at Darla's room. I tapped on my window for her to come. I picked up a make-believe can and string and said her name. A light went on in her living/dining room. A couple entered through the front door. A woman went to Darla's bedroom and took off her shoes. The bed was too big and it was in the wrong place. Darla's pink record player was gone. The woman turned her head to the doorway and her mouth opened and closed, talking. A man in the living/dining room talked back. The walls were a new color. There were no candles. The woman nodded, then she walked to Darla's window and pulled down the blinds.

Lying in bed, I just wanted to close my eyes to sleep, but I felt something weird. I sat up. I put my pillow to my nose. I smelled the blanket. I got on my knees, smelled the bed. Mom. They all smelled of Mom. Her hair, her breath, her cocoa butter skin cream. I turned on the bedside light. On my white plastic bedside table sat a square box of tissues, a few books. It was clean. Before it had crayon marks, and *Happy Days* stickers on it, a box with stuff in it: sunglasses and sea glass and Wite-Out and colored rocks and a magnifying glass. There was a plant near the window, silk slippers under the bed.

I rolled up a shirt for a pillow and slept on the floor.

The next night I laid a sheet, blanket, and pillow on the living room couch. Mom wrote on my board, *What are you doing?* She wrote, *Sleeping here?* With the inheritance from Granpa, Mom had started renting a small apartment fifteen blocks away on West End, which she uses in the day as a writing studio. She wrote on my board, *Would you like to sleep at the studio?*

I erased Mom's sentence with my hand, and refused to read anymore.

The living room then became my new room.

Dad moved his miniature stuff to my bedroom. He nailed a bedsheet over the living room doorway, which stays tied up in the day.

From bed I look at the glowing sheet-covered doorway. It will go dark sometime after I am asleep. I pretend it's alive. I pretend it's protecting me. I pretend that it will keep them out. But, it doesn't. They come in.

Since I've already missed so much school and haven't gotten my operations yet, I'm not going back until next year. Mom wants to go away and work on her writing. Her friend is lending her a cabin Upstate. Mom says there's a pond and there are trees and mountains.

I close my eyes. I imagine the house, quiet and snow covered. When I dream I can hear. I hear the thin whistling of wind through the pine needles, the soft *poush* of snow clumps slipping from heavy tree limbs. I hear the soft crunch of feet in the snow moving away from me. I follow the sound. I look for footprints in the snow and I'm inside the forest. I smell the pine-spice, and I look at the trees making long black shadows by moonlight. I run. I fall. The snow is freezing and I can't move. I look for a person, even a shadow, but there is nothing there except for the cold white.

⤫

I watch The Block from the window. They're puffy in down jackets and they're small and run through the white park. They would make fun. *Hey deaf boy. Hey deaf boy. What'm I saying? What'm I saying?*

A couple of days ago Dad gave me a paper with a bunch of

names written on it: the guys from The Block. On top, Dad
wrote, *All your friends who have called for you.* Next to that he
put a smiley face, except he did it sort of wrong: the mouth
was too long and didn't curl up enough, so it looked a little
happy, but more, it looked embarrassed, like it had farted and
was trying to play it off like it hadn't. I looked at the sheet,
then left it next to me on the couch. Later, Daniel saw it. On
my blackboard he wrote, *They only called because their mothers
told them they had to.* I read it and looked at him. He looked
off, like he felt bad. He quickly erased that, wrote, *Don't tell
them but i think they are all kind of scared of you.* I looked at
him again. I smiled a little. Maybe he was lying, but it felt
cool, them being scared of me, and for a second everything
felt normal again.

Jordan's tried to get me to talk. He's yelled, "Talk! Talk!"
    He's shaken me, held me upside down, held a pillow over
my face. Once, his eyes got big because after smothering me, I
really couldn't breathe. His mouth moved quick. He held me
tight, rocked me. He rubbed my back and I felt his heart beating fast. Inside I could feel what it was: it was a lever that had
come loose. It was spinning round and round, trying to catch
onto a nub, and until it did, the door that makes the inhale and
exhale couldn't open and close. I could feel the handle spinning, then finally it caught onto the nub. Jordan must have felt
that too. He looked at me, and saw I was breathing again. He
wiped his eyes. They were wet. I touched his eye, where there
was a tear. That changed him back. Suddenly, he picked me up
and dropped me to the floor outside of his room.
    Daniel's never asked me to talk. But he stares a lot. He
squints, he frowns. I think he's trying to talk to me telepathically. Sometimes I want to tell him that telepathic isn't real.
    At night they come in. Separately. I open my eyes, and

they will be there. Daniel touches my face and pokes at me like I'm something strange he has found. When I look at him, he takes his hand back and leaves. Jordan pushes my face down. When I don't do anything, he might give me an Indian burn. Still, I won't do anything, so he just looks at me, straightens my blanket and leaves.

In the days Jordan and Daniel and Dad are at school, so I go with Mom to her studio.

"Hi, little lamb," her lips say. I can read lips when they move slow and say something simple. Sometimes I mess up and mistake words: *dream* for *green, burned* for *bird.*

Mom writes on my blackboard, *How are you?*

She touches my head.

"Soon you'll hear again," her lips say. She looks at me. She writes on my board, *Why won't you talk?*

She wipes her eyes. She quickly erases the last sentence and writes a new one, *People are noticing Mom.*

She holds up a sheet. It's from a magazine.

She writes, *I got accepted again. A big magazine. A national magazine.*

I look at her.

Mom opens a drawer to her desk, takes out a hardcover book. She has painted a swirling sun on it, and the words BRIGHT IDEAS.

"For you," Mom's lips say.

The pages are white and blank. A piece of yarn is glued to the spine of the book, a pencil tied at the end.

Mom looks away. She answers the phone. She nods and smiles. She takes out a date book and writes in it. I walk out the door.

Plowed snow bluffs, dirty where they face the street. I go to the park. Lots of kids, a snow day. I pass the dog run. There is a long skinny dog. He runs in a funny, hopping way, diving headfirst into the snow. I watch his mouth bark. At first, being deaf made the world seem far away, like I was watching out a window. But the longer I'm deaf, the closer the world seems to get, and it's just like it was before only now it's silent.

I miss hearing the wind, my footsteps in the snow, barking dogs.

I walk for a while and watch the park.

What did Darla sound like? I've forgotten her voice, except in dreams. I dream every night. I dream of the weeks I was in the hospital, lying asleep. I sit next to myself watching my sleeping face. I dream of Darla and we talk. But, when I wake up, I can't remember the dream, only that I've had it. Every day I try to remember, and every day is like following footprints, running hard to catch up to the feet, the body that's left them behind, reaching the person, Darla, only when the day comes to an end, and I stop moving and stop thinking, and fall back asleep.

I look up. I'm at The Block. They're playing football across the street on the sloped field. Their faces are pale and winded, their breath is heavy. Max goes out long. The pass wobbles short. He cuts back, his feet slip on the snow, his legs shoot up. He lands on his back. He lies there because it hurts, but also because he's hamming it up. It's funny. I smile. The others pile onto Max. They all slip around, shove snow. They laugh.

They play again. They run and tackle. I feel heat in my body, like I'm playing. I see where I would run if I was playing. One team moves downfield. Fourth and goal. Handoff to Reid. The other team rushes, he cuts left. He's tackled hard from behind. The ball flies from his hands, rolls into the street. Without thinking, I run into the street and retrieve the ball. I'm breathing hard. I run upfield, football tucked, head down.

I feel the cold and I feel the heat. After, we'll all go to Twin Donuts. We'll spin on the slippery, swivel stools and drum our fingers and slap our hands on the greasy counter, waiting impatiently as the Indian owner lines up our cups, pouring in hot chocolate powder and hot water from the big silver urn. And we'll be loud, and we'll be the only ones there except for the lonely old people: hunched lady with a hairy chin, muttering man with a pile of newspapers, cursing bum smoking cigarettes, suddenly laughing, suddenly silent.

I look up, they all stare back like dumb animals. I stop short. Reid moves first. He puts his hand out and I give him the ball.

"Thanks," his lips say. He frowns. His lips move, he says something; I think: "Is it true you're deaf?"

I look at all the other guys. I feel something very small inside me tremble. I see all their mouths opening and closing, and their eyes darting. The trembling thing grows, and I can feel my hands and knees tremble. I open my mouth to talk. Then I close it.

I turn, I run. I run through the snow. I run and I run more until I know that I'm alone again. I stumble, I fall. I feel the shock of snow against my burning face. I curl onto my side.

two

"How do you feel, honey?"

—Mom's voice, weak through one ear. I open my eyes. I'm not asleep. Mom is smiling at me.

I hear the squeaking wheels of a gurney rolling down the hospital hallway. I can hear someone coughing.

"Can you hear?"

I stare at Mom. Her eyes bob over my face. The blue gets darker. She asks again if I can hear.

I nod once.

She holds my face by the cheeks. "Why won't you talk?" Her voice is small. I think she says, "Please," but I can't tell because I can't hear that well, so I just watch her and don't move.

At her studio, Mom has a big phone on her desk, and another in the kitchen. I go to the kitchen. I pick up.

"He's your child as well," I hear Mom say.

Dad quietly says, "He doesn't act that way."

"Stop feeling sorry for yourself."

Dad exhales angry.

"He's back, so—" Dad says.

"What are you saying?"

Quiet.

"Have you already called her?" Mom asks.

Dad waits. "No," he says. "Not yet."

I gently hang up the phone. I walk down the short hallway. Mom's head is in her hand. I open the door quietly. I walk down the stairs, along Riverside Drive.

I open the front door. Down the long dark hallway, past the dining room, in the kitchen music plays. A man with a woman's voice singing in a language that sounds like shushing. Dad passes the kitchen door, singing along, dancing with an invisible partner.

I go to the living room. Dad still has a desk here. There are pads on it and pens and rulers.

I open a pad. Drawings of furniture. Chairs with high backs and skinny legs like deer. In another pad, drawings of a house.

Behind me, arms hug me. I jump, but Dad holds on tight. He touches my ear. "How's it feel?" He lets go. "You'll have your second operation soon. Soon you'll have all your hearing back. Except for the hearing that's been lost forever, of course." He frowns suddenly. "Your mother is very worried. You shouldn't ever just walk out like that." He holds my shoulders. I nod. He smiles.

He goes to the hallway. He picks up the phone. He dials.

"He came here. I don't know." Dad glances at me. "He's fine. It's fine. I'll feed him. Really, it's—" Dad holds the

phone to his chest. "She would like to speak to you," he whispers.

I shake my head.

Dad puts the phone back to his ear. "He's in the bathroom."

Dad returns. He looks at the open pads. "Were you looking
at my drawings?"

I turn to his drawings. I pick up a drawing of a chair. I
like it.

"I'm designing furniture. And actual spaces. You understand? Houses. Buildings. Real houses and buildings, not just
miniatures."

I look at Dad. I don't know why, but I speak. "What were
you singing?" I ask. My voice feels funny. I don't like it.

Dad looks at me. I can see he's trying to be cool, like it's
no big deal that I'm talking. I know it's a big deal. I'm a
romantic.

"It wasn't English," I say.

Dad nods. "French."

"That's what you spoke as a kid?"

"*Oui.*"

"Your mother was Arab. Did she speak Arab?"

"She was Algerian. She spoke French. Everyone spoke
French."

I look at Dad. I look straight at his face, in his eyes. Dad
doesn't have any family like Mom. They live somewhere else.
Africa, maybe. I've never met them, and Dad doesn't really
ever talk about them. But, sometimes I see that he gets letters.
The handwriting's funny, and on the side of the envelope are
two weird words, *PAR AVION*.

I never hear Dad speak French, except when he says our
last name. His voice changes, becomes slippery and low, like
the name's slipping out through his nose. Once he helped me

give it a try. He instructed that the sound should be made between the back and the top of my mouth. When I tried it made me choke.

"Do you miss speaking it?"

Dad tilts his head from side to side, and right before his head stops moving, it sort of nods a little.

"Do you think in French or English?"

"English." Dad smiles. "Except counting. I still can only count in French."

I don't want to talk anymore. I go and turn on the TV.

Dad makes us sloppy joes.

We eat in silence. I wonder where Jordan and Daniel are, but I don't ask.

"Good?" he asks.

I look at him.

"Not talking again?" Dad waits, then raises his eyebrows. We eat.

"You've missed a lot of school this year," he says. "I called up the principal and he's willing to test you at the end of the year. If you do well you can go ahead a grade next year instead of repeating one."

Dad waits for me to look up from my food.

"I've worked out a schedule. Math, English, science, history— They don't call it history anymore do they? *Social Studies* . . . I will make out lessons for you."

Dad goes to the kitchen and comes back with a chocolate cake. He cuts us both a piece.

"You're going away with your mother Upstate," Dad says. "I'll give you lessons enough for the duration of that trip. You can call me anytime. If you need help, I mean. Okay?"

We eat the cake. Dad puts the dishes in the sink.

"I have something to discuss with you," he says.

My insides go tight.

It's like he can tell. He says, "You're not in trouble."

I follow him to the living room. Dad goes to his desk. He sits next to me with a folder.

"You missed Christmas," he says. "It was very naughty what you did. Really, I shouldn't reward such behavior. But, that doesn't seem fair: your brothers receiving gifts, and you not."

He opens the folder. "I found this." He hands it to me.

It's my Christmas What I Want wish list. I wrote it after the summer when the new Sears catalog came.

"Is there something from the list you want?"

I hand the list back.

"It's only fair that you receive your Christmas gifts." Dad's quiet. "What I mean is: I would really like to get you something." He smiles but also his angry vein rises and falls, rises and falls.

I watch it. I wonder what would happen if I pressed my thumb against it very hard, and just left it there. Would it wriggle around, choking? Would it eventually go still?

"What are the new people like?" I ask. "In Darla's apartment."

"Oh," Dad says. He moves a little away. "Do you want to say something about your friend? It's okay if you do. You're upset?"

"I just wanna know about the new people."

"I guess you've got your mother for that."

"You won't talk about it with me?"

Dad's quiet. "You *would* talk to me about it?"

I shrug.

"A couple. Young. I haven't met them," Dad says.

"I want a tent."

"You wouldn't go away without telling anyone would you?"

"A tent."

✑

In the day, when Jordan and Daniel are at school I can go to their room and listen to records. And after school I can put my head out the window and hear the guys from The Block cursing and hooting and laughing. And I can hear wind, and watch TV, and listen to the hot radiator hiss steam. When I step along where the dirty linoleum bubbles in the outer hallways of Mom's studio's building, I can hear the dried glue crackle. And in courtyards I can hear: voices, running faucets, coughing, spitting, frying, TVs, radios, cooing pigeons on sills. I can hear the small pouring, sandy sound when I scrap at the crumbling cement between bricks. Garbage trucks: I can hear their huge crunching gears, snapping and chewing trash, driving away, dripping out a greenish, scummy liquid that mixes with the rainbow swirls of oil in the gutter, which are silent. I can hear the quick, shimmering sound of the street cleaner, two giant, spinning mop-heads in front. After, I find the metal bristles of their mop-heads that have fallen off. Holding it over a garbage can, I can hear it *sthwapping* on metal garbage cans. I can listen to the different sounds: shallow, deep, depending on where I *sthwap* it. I can hear the cranky old coot screaming at me to stop making that racket. Ear over an open sewer drain. First silent, then a faraway echo: *ommm.*

✑

They must have been talking for a while because I was dreaming that I was sitting with Darla. We followed a sound and dug the sandy bottom of a little green pond. Two clams, each with a set of eyes on top. A blue set, a brown set. The shells opened and closed like mouths. I turned to Darla, but she was gone, footprints in the white snowy ground. I looked back. The brown-eyed clam said, "It's three in the morning." The blue-eyed clam said, "Are you going to ground me, *Daddy?*"

The doorway is lit. Mom and Dad's shadows. The sheet flutters from the open window. Mom and Dad, like reflections on rippled water.

I get up and lie on the floor and close my eyes.

Dad tells Mom that she has to start acting like a mother. Dad doesn't know that it's not a good thing, being a mother. *You a dumb mother,* we say. *Damn that test was a mother!* Sometimes we add the *fucker* part. *You one spastic motherfucker.* Once a bunch of us sat in a circle playing a game: we'd go around and say what kind of motherfucker the person to our right was. When the line got to Daniel, he said, *Actually, all our fathers are the motherfuckers. Think about it.* We all went quiet, kind of shocked as we thought about it, and realized that Daniel was right. Dads *are* all motherfuckers.

Mom says that she and Mrs. Babcock were just blowing off a little steam.

Then, they really start going at it.

I wonder why they can't seem to remember that I can hear again.

I stand.

I touch the sheet. I run my finger over their shadow faces.

Dad stops talking, and it's quiet.

Mom talks very softly. She says, *When I come back, I'm moving into the studio.* Dad's quiet, then he says, *That's it? You want a divorce?* Mom says soft, *I don't want it.*

I stick my head out the window. I stay there until I begin to fall asleep. I miss sleeping with a numb face. I pull my head back. The doorway is dark. I walk down the hallway. I open Jordan and Daniel's door. I look at them sleeping in the moonlight. I close the door. I stand in front of Mom and Dad's room. The door is open a crack. I hear sounds, hurt sounds like they're lifting something heavy. I poke my head in. The

moonlight is white across their bed. White across Dad's naked
back, and white across his naked behind between Mom's open
legs. It's white across her jiggling breasts, and the moonlight
shines white on her face wet with tears. Dad's top is propped
up on his arms, and he goes back and forth. Mom wraps her
arms around him and pulls him down. They move back and
forth. Mom puts her mouth to Dad's ear and she whispers, "I
love you, I love you, I love you."

⌒〇

I found out an hour ago that Dad's seeing Megan again.

It's Thursday late afternoon. Outside, it's dark. I'm in the
studio like usual, except I'm alone since Mom stormed out. I'm
in the kitchen making cinnamon toast for Daniel. Daniel's in
the middle of playing ring-a-levio with the guys. He told me
he got bored and cold just hiding, and he noticed that he was
right here, so he came over.

I hand Daniel the toast. We walk into the studio. Occasionally we hear the guys outside, their faraway calls. *Ring-a-levio,
1-2-3, 1-2-3, 1-2-3.* I carry in an A&P paper bag. I kneel and
start putting the broken pieces of a lamp into it.

Daniel takes a bite of his toast, frowning at the broken
lamp.

"You do that?" he asks.

I clean carefully, starting with the bigger chunks.

Daniel walks to the window and looks out.

"She did it?" Daniel asks.

I look under the chair, under the table for pieces.

Mom was at her desk and I was on the floor doing my math
assignment. The phone rang and Mom answered it.

Mom's phone is a big office phone that used to belong to
Granpa. On it is a button that puts it on speakerphone like the
businessmen on TV have, which is what Mom did.

Megan was in the middle of a sentence, something about wanting to be up front, not wanting to live with open secrets anymore. Mom asked Megan how old she was. Twenty-seven. Megan said she was calling to offer a truck for her trip. Mom asked Megan how she could possibly know about the trip. Mom's voice went low. *Does he know you're calling?* she asked. Megan was quiet, then she said, *Oh God. You don't know that we're, he and I, are . . . ? I thought he told you.*

Daniel puts his face near mine. He squints like he's looking for something on my face. He says, "So, right? Mom broke the lamp, right?"

I just look at Daniel and blink.

Mom yelled for a while, then she asked Megan if she wanted to talk to her youngest. Megan went quiet. Mom told Megan that she had her on speakerphone. Her youngest had heard it all. Mom dragged me over. She squeezed my arm and told me to say hello to Dad's girlfriend.

All the big chunks are collected. I use the whisk and dustpan for the rest.

"Did she find out?" Daniel asks. He lies on his back and stares at the ceiling. He does that a lot.

I watch him.

Sometimes, I hear Daniel. Sometimes when he's alone in his room he makes sounds. He sings, laughs, talks in funny voices.

"How'd she find out?" he asks. He starts to laugh. "Crazy shit, man. Wooo! Messy, messy."

I walk to the kitchen.

Mom hung up. She leaned over her pad and went back to writing. The phone rang. Mom picked it up, hung it up. This happened three more times. Then she just let it ring and ring and ring. The bulb in her lamp died right then. The phone still ringing. Mom went to unscrew the bulb before letting it cool.

She jerked her hand back and screamed, *"You son of a bitch!"* Then she batted the lamp to the floor.

Daniel turns on the faucet over the plate. He makes up a song.

"Father dear,
you need a mop for the mess yer makin'.
Mother I hear,
yer learnin' how to start takin'."

He sings in a Bob Dylan voice. I can remember back to when I wouldn't have known that. But, now I know. I know what a Bob Dylan voice is.

Daniel puts on his jacket. He opens the front door. He touches my shoulder. I don't move. He hugs me tight. He squeezes. I think he says, "Oh," but I can't tell because his mouth is next to my deaf ear. He lets go, and turns away, his back to me, jabbing the elevator button five times quickly.

I'm alone again. There's no TV, no radio. Outside the window is a street, another building. I sit at Mom's desk. I look through her drawers. I find two daily planners. 1977. 1978. I open 1977.

09.18 Returned home. Sewn up. Hospital stench like metal shit.
10.02 Poems sent to:
10.25 Kids called.
11.01 Phineas called. Kids there.
11.02 WVA-Phineas. Found picture of me as little girl (1946?)—kids gone.
11.03 Returned home.
11.10 *New Yorker* called!!!
11.13 Police, Wilm NC. Reports: disturb beaut pag. Fits discrpt.

11.14 Received letter, dated, 10-31 (???) Evidence found at train yard, roadside.

11.15 Eds. NYer called, revisions suggested: v.smart, v.thoughtful.

11.16 Coast Guard. Plane to NC. MY BOY! MY BOY!

11.20 Buy turkey.

11.24 Mother arrives for visit.

11.26 Thanksgiving. *Should have revisions done by this date.*

12.17 ~~Haven't written in WEEKS!!! Nothing! Am I horrible?! I am! I'm just trying to pretend everything's normal! I need this! I need it to stay alive! I'd give anything for you! Why won't you wake up? Are you punishing me? I'd give away the NYer. This is not a diary!!!~~

I close my eyes and breathe long and deep. There's an exercise woman on TV in the morning. She does stretches in front of a felt sunrise, and she says, *Breathe in long and deep . . . mmm . . . exhale: ahhhh . . . Doesn't that just mellow any freak-outs within? Mmm, ahhh. Let the breath push out the freak-out.* I breathe: long and deep, long and deep.

I think of tearing up the daily planner, then I think, no, I will toss out Mom's notebooks. I get to the window with them, then I stop. I put the notebooks back. I sit down. I flip through her 1978 planner. I see that she has written things in that haven't happened yet: our birthdays, when she should start Christmas shopping, when she should buy the Thanksgiving turkey. I look back at the 1977 planner. *11.20 Buy turkey.* Then I look: *09.18 Sewn up, 10.02 Poems sent.* It wasn't just with me; she did it with herself: pretending with poems that everything was okay.

I hear Mom at the front door. I run to the kitchen. It's dark, and I watch her silhouette enter, slowly close the door. Her head is down, her hair hanging like a flag on a windless day. She just stands in the hallway with her head like that. Finally she looks up, calls for me. I lie on the floor. I breathe long and deep. It begins to work: *mellow the freak-out within.* It makes me sleepy, dreamy. I remember my old bed, I would write stuff under the mattress. If I did something wrong, I wrote it. If I hated something, I wrote it.

I can see the bed frame and I read: *I hate you all. Fuk you fuk you.* I remember: that was true, I had really meant it. But, I wrote it so that it would stop being true. So, I gave my bed the *fuk you* feeling, then I wouldn't have to have it. But, even though I didn't want it, I guess maybe I needed to save the feeling also, to remember that I had it.

Mom stands over me. She crouches, scoops me up in her arms, rocks me.

Maybe that's the way it is for Mom too. Probably, it's all true, what she wrote in her planner. So, I guess, in a way, Mom is the daily planner. But, also I know, more than that, this is true: Mom is Mom.

three

It's been days since Mom broke the lamp. I keep waiting for something to happen. It's morning, they're both up. I go into their bedroom, feel their bed. It's warm. I feel my old bed, warm, so I know they're sleeping in different rooms.

I go to the dining room, pull out a chair, facing it to the kitchen, which, in the morning, fills with sun. Mom, still in a nightgown, is pouring coffee. Dad, dressed, waits behind her.

She looks at him, sees the mug in his hand. "Oh. Coffee?" she says.

Dad nods. "Oh, sorry. Yes. Please."

These days, they both say, *Oh,* a lot, like everything's a surprise. Not a big surprise, but smaller, like if you were sitting in a field staring off at nothing, then in the corner of your eye you suddenly saw an animal, a squirrel or rabbit. That quiet surprise. *Oh: hello.* Like that.

Mom pours Dad's coffee. Then, they stand there, a little

frozen, looking at each other. Mom turns, places the pot back into the maker.

With her back to Dad she says, mumbling like she's talking to herself, "Oh, yes: I have to remember to order the mattress finally. For the studio."

"Oh," Dad says. "Mmm-hmm." His body jerks a little, like he's going to move closer to Mom. "So, I guess—" His eyes roll down, peer into his coffee. "So. We're really doing this?" he asks, looking back up.

Mom waits, then turns back around. "Ready for tonight?" she asks, putting on a smile.

"Isn't it stupid: I'm *nervous,*" Dad says suddenly. He goes quickly silent, then he says, slower, in his regular voice, "It's just friends, colleagues—"

I cock my head. I'm not even hiding. I'm just sitting here, watching them. They don't notice. They blink a lot in the bright room. They look clean in the white, morning light. Like on TV, eyes blinking open, waking out of death, walking into the calling, blinding light of heaven.

After a long silence Dad says, "So, you're definitely— Today, I mean: you're sure about the mattress, the style, the size. Or—"

Why does Dad care so much about Mom's new bed? It's not like he's going to sleep in it, I think.

Mom just looks at Dad, except with more blinking.

"Yes, I guess it's all been settled," he says, frowning into his coffee again.

Mom touches Dad's cheek. He raises his head. They look at each other, then Mom leans forward. She kisses him. They look like they're in slow motion, like they're floating, almost. It makes a small, hidden sound when their lips part. Mom wipes her eyes.

"I think I've decided," she says, "definitely, I've decided on the type of mattress."

Suddenly they both bust open laughing, like that's the fun-
niest thing.

Then they go quiet again. They both glance down, at different places.

"This is fucking hell, huh?" Mom says.

"Maybe we can—"

But, Mom just looks at Dad, and he goes silent, then he
nods.

"Thank you for coming tonight," Dad says.

Mom's about to say something, but suddenly, and finally,
they see me.

"Oh."

"Oh."

I just look at them, and they look at me. They both have
small smiles that sit on their faces like toy cars with missing
wheels; smiles lopsided like that, broken like that.

⁓

After dinner we all go over. It's in the basement of the Columbia library. At the front entrance is a sign. Below Dad's name
it says: LIVING SIMPLY: RECENT STUDIES. The room is filled
with adults talking and drinking, some strolling around looking at Dad's drawings on the walls. A man quiets everyone
and gives a little speech. He says Dad's designs are clean, simple, uncluttered. Except for some words I don't know, I mostly
get what the man's saying. It's true, I think. The faces of
Dad's houses are plain: blank walls, except for a line here or
there, a window; the rooms are clean and tidy. Just the way
Dad likes things. But, they're good, I think: not an angry Dad
sort of clean, but a nice clean, a quiet clean.

Across the room, I see her slip in, hide behind a group of
people. The pretty lady. Megan.

I walk up to Mom and Dad. Dad looks at me.

"What do you think?" he asks.

I look across the room at Megan, and keep looking until Mom and Dad look. But they don't look at each other, they both look at me. Mom glances at Dad, then she puts her hand, which is hot and a little moist, on my head.

"I should take him home," Mom says.

"I don't think I can just leave," Dad says.

"No, of course not."

"Where's Jordan?" Dad says looking around. "Jordan could take him home."

"*Stop it,*" Mom says softly, closing her eyes. She looks at Dad. "Anyway, the mattress is coming first thing, so I have to be at the studio early. I should get to bed at a reasonable hour."

Dad leans forward, whispers, "I asked her not to come tonight." He glances at Megan quickly, then back. "I know that you and I— But, still, it didn't seem appropriate."

"I'm going. I think I have to go," Mom says.

"I'm very cross with her," Dad says to himself. Then to Mom he says, "Maybe I should leave with you."

"*No.*" Mom says. Then she smiles quickly. "So, okay. I'm going." Mom looks at me. "Say good-bye to your father."

But, before I can, Mom takes me by the hand. She walks me through the crowd. I turn once, and look at Dad standing alone. I wave to him, and right as Mom takes us through the door, I see Dad smile, and I see his hand rising up, but before he can return my wave, we are past the doorway, moving down an empty hallway.

four

Dad buzzes on the intercom from the lobby. Our bags are in a line next to the door. Mom tells me to go down and begin loading. Dad's outside, stomping his feet to get warm next to a truck.

I walk up to it. Touch it. It's red and big and old. The color's gone brownish. Daniel sits on the passenger side. We look at each other and bunch up our lips: a hello.

"Megan's parents have a farm," Dad says. "Not a working farm." Dad laughs. "I hope this heap will make it," he says.

Daniel gets out and sits on our building's marble entrance steps.

Mom comes down. She climbs into the truck.

"This is a wonderful old truck," she calls.

Dad smiles. Dad loads the bags.

"Come here," he says to me. He hands me a bag. "The tent," he says. "Merry Christmas."

I look at it.

"I'll pack it in the truck," he says.

Mom slams the truck door and walks over to us.

"Where's Jordan?" she asks.

Dad looks at the ground. "He had to go to the library."

"Didn't he come with you to get the truck?"

Dad nods.

Mom looks at Dad. "Okay. Well. I guess that's it," she says.

Mom hugs Daniel.

"Tell Jordan that I missed him," she says.

We get into the truck.

Dad leans into the truck. "Got your studies?" he asks me. He blinks. It's very sunny. His fingers are wrapped through the open window. His face moves, like he wants to say something, like he's going to lean across me to give Mom a kiss. I know he won't, but it's just like that, if that was something they still did.

Mom puts the truck into gear and we drive off.

We go down Riverside Drive. The street is slushy. I see Jordan sitting on a bench with a girl. He has his arm around her. She has one leg over his lap. I see his breath. He looks right at me. I look over at Mom. She doesn't see.

We drive up the Henry Hudson Parkway. Mom unfolds a map on her lap. She tries to read while she keeps an eye on the road.

I pick up the map.

She reaches for it. "Maps are very difficult to read," she says.

I hold the map tight. Mom pulls. I don't let go. Mom looks at me. She lets go. I find the routes.

The city sinks away. The sky opens up. Trees and low houses and long colorless fields. I watch the signs. When I have to, I lift the map and poke at it for Mom to look. In a couple of hours we rise up the side of a mountain. The roads and trees are hardened with frozen snow. We pass through a small town. Right outside

of it, we stop. Our cabin is cold as outside. We unload. Mom fills
the woodstove. We turn on electric heaters with glowing orange
coils and the house warms up, but never enough that I can wear
anything less than long johns, socks, and a union shirt. I like the
cold. I spend a long time playing with the cold on the window
above my bed. I like how the window frosts on the inside, and
waking up, I press my thumb into the frost until a print melts
through, and rays of sun fall on my rag-quilt blanket. I stick
pennies against the window and they stay up until the day gets
later and the sun hotter, and the frost beads up and the pennies
fall to the sill, leaving penny-ghosts in the glass. And late at
night, when the moon and stars are out my window, I listen to
the wind blow through the trees and across the meadow up to
my window, which is loose and rattles. When it's freezing *freezing* cold out, I breathe over and over onto the window and the
window catches my breath in a soft frozen circle.

   Each morning Mom gets up before me, but she's quiet. When
I wake the fire is lit again. Sometimes when I wake and see the
fire in the woodstove I think that I'm at Daddy Ham's and I roll
over to see if Darla's still asleep. When I see that she's not there,
I look toward the kitchen for her, except we have a porch where
Daddy Ham had a kitchen, and then I remember everything.

   Mom writes at a desk below a window, or she writes
wrapped in a blanket on the porch overlooking the sloping
meadow and frozen pond. When she writes, she curls her body
over the pad like she's about to dive in, and her eyes change
expressions like they're watching things horrible or beautiful
or happy or sad.

   I try to write in my BRIGHT IDEAS book, but it's hard. I try
to sit like Mom. I frown and squint and bug my eyes out, but
nothing happens.

   One day I call home. I want to hear their voices. They will
know it's me when they hear silence.

A woman answers. Megan. She says hello a couple of times. Then she's quiet. She knows it's me.

"I'm really sorry. I was expecting a call. I would never just pick up your phone."

I see Mom through the window in the shed.

"I was expecting your father to call. See, I just came over to pick him up, but he forgot something back at the university, so he had me wait here. I was waiting for his call."

I wonder how long she'll talk for.

"I'm afraid your brothers aren't here either."

We're quiet.

"Is your mother's work coming along? It's a big change for you, living in the country."

I look out the window. The shed door is still open, the light still on.

I close my eyes. I can hear Megan's breathing.

"You miss your family," Megan says.

I can hear her spit.

"You miss your friends."

I open my eyes.

"I'll stay right here."

I stay silent for a little while.

I look up. Mom stands there.

Megan says, "What is it?"

I hold the phone out and Mom takes it. She says, "Yes," and "Oh, dear," and, "Of course," then she hangs up.

I look at Mom.

"It's okay, honey. I'm not mad." Mom smiles. She holds my face and looks at my eyes. She says, "Were you crying? Did you cry to Megan? Do you want to talk? Do you want to cry for me, honey?"

I'm hungry. I get some crackers from the cupboard.

*   *   *

We walk through the meadow to the edge of the forest. We hike the moist mountain covered in leaves and pine needles and patches of snow. We hear birds, pass soft fallen trees covered with sprigs of moss, fans of fungus. We climb for a long time. We reach the top. We have lunch.

"See?" Mom says.

Far down I see a moving gray line of water. I look up at Mom. Her hair, pulled back into a ponytail, whips in the wind.

"Know what that is?" she asks. She answers, "The Hudson River."

I look back at it.

"It travels down, past your father and brothers, past your friends. And it continues on to the ocean."

Mom walks closer to the edge.

"Water connects everything," she says. "It carries things to the farthest edges of the world." Mom frowns. "I bet if you could send a wish down to the Hudson, it could take the message to whomever you liked. Darla even." Mom turns and looks at me.

Mom sits down. She pats the ground. I sit beside her. Mom collects some very thin branches and some leaves and some grass. First she makes a cross with two of the thin twigs and ties them together with the grass. Then she covers that with leaves, and secures the leaves with another twig.

I feel my mouth smile.

"What, honey?"

I look at Mom and I feel the smile go away. Watching Mom makes me remember, that night when Darla showed me how to make a cross covered with a diamond of colored thread. I forget its name. I think maybe it was something Jewish. I'll look it up when I get home. Darla would like that. I feel it. That day. I can feel just how I felt that day, and for a second it's like Darla's back. Then all at once it goes away.

Mom looks at me. She wants to shake me, but she doesn't.

I copy Mom. I make a twig plane. Mom stands up, and so do I.

"If you ever want to send out a special message, you come up here, think real hard what it is you want to say, and—" Mom closes her eyes, then throws the plane, opening up her eyes.

I look at her.

"Go, honey!" she says.

Do I have a special message? I throw the plane.

The planes fly, one ahead of the other, rising and flying over the bumps of wind.

"And the plane will catch the thought and carry it down to the river. Then the river will carry it to wherever it needs to go," Mom says.

The planes rise up over the fingers of the bare trees and they glide straight, I'm sure, to the river.

As we go down the mountain, the slanted shadows of the trees fade when the sky abruptly turns gray. A moist breeze blows and suddenly, falling snow. Flakes big and light as goose down. We reach the bottom and cross the acres of open meadow. The snow falls heavily and collects to below my calves. Reaching the house, Mom falls backward. She flaps her arms and legs. A snow angel. She laughs. Her cheeks are pink. She moves, makes another. She laughs and laughs. I touch the snow with my hand. Mom's on her third angel. I watch Mom. I lie on my back. I feel the cold rising up through my clothes. The snow is soft. I watch the flakes appear out of the shimmering gray-white sky. I close my eyes. Mom hoots and laughs. It makes me smile. My legs and arms slowly move, flapping out like an angel's.

five

After dinner, I fill page after page in my book. The words just appear.

My pencil tip wears down.

Mom's outside.

I go to her desk for a sharpener. Then I see her. I pick her up.

Mona.

Mom walks in. She looks at me.

"I thought it was supposed to be our secret . . . You're mad."

I am mad. Why?

The frame has been polished.

I hand her back to Mom.

"Don't you want it back?"

I go to bed.

Mom loads the stove with wood to last the night. She reads

a book in the large stuffed chair in the corner of the cabin. Curled on my side, I look out my window. I watch the snow that continues to fall. The snow angels are almost fully filled in. I want to see them vanish completely, but before they do, I fall asleep.

⌒⌒♭

I sit up quickly. Something wakes me. A sound? A nudging? I look around. Thin rectangles of firelight through the wood-stove grate quiver across the floor. I step out of bed.

Outside, the sky is filled with stars. The snow is smooth in swells and bluffs. Wind blows out of the shadowed forest, across the open meadow. Snow-dust whips and curls. A sound. The wind? Far away, if at all. I pass the snow angels. They're covered whole, but I can see the ghosts of them. I think of Dad. Once he told me a funny thing about houses. He said houses have memories. He said that if you moved a staircase, you could always see an impression of where it once stood. He said that if you walked quickly past you might see it in the corner of your eye, or if you stood and were very still and made your eyes loose, a faint shadow of it suddenly might appear.

I've reached the dark forest. I hear it below the deep wind. *Ooo* . . . Like a voice, a singing voice. *Ooo, wee* . . .

I look into the trees, at the overlapping shadows woven by moonlight.

"Come out," I say.

I wait. Everything goes still. I can hear perfectly, and see perfectly, and I can feel every part of me. Perfectly.

There is a ruckus, a wind. Snow-dust blows thick, and suddenly she appears out of the swirling white.

She is bright, brighter than the moon, and she is pale, paler than the snow. The skin below her eyes is thin, papery, her lips and fingers, bluish. Her hair is long again and it blows in slow

motion like hair in water. She wears her green, flower corduroys and her ladybug sweater.

"Hey, Ewe."

I feel my body shake, icicle water suddenly in my veins.
Darla touches me, and I go still, warm.

"I dream about you every night," I say.

"I know," she says.

"Did it hurt?" I ask.

"At first it hurt like everything, like every kind of hurt all
at once. Then that went away, and it was something real real
nice," she says.

"How come I didn't also—"

"—'Cause, you didn't."

We're quiet.

"You gotta go?"

Darla nods. Tears appear on her face. They shine like
glass, and float down her pale cheeks, fading away then.

"Where are you walking to?" she asks. She looks at the forest, then back at me.

"I don't know. I was following a sound."

"Go back now."

"You too. You come back now."

"Don't be a jerk."

"I wanna go."

Darla smiles. "Nah," she says. She moves close and wraps
her hands around me and holds me. I'm warm with light.

"Good-bye, Ewe," she whispers soft. She kisses me on the
temple. I feel a quick burn, then the light is gone. The night is
pitch dark. No moon, no stars. Dark, and falling snow. I'm
shaking very hard. I'm freezing. Ice inside my feet and ice
inside my hands and stomach. Ice around my heart. I look to
the sky. I can tell: I am freezing to death.

"I don't want to die," I whisper.

I look across the black meadow. Suddenly, a small shaking light appears in the distance. Darkness closes in around my eyes. The light flashes across my face. I fall. My head knocks hard against the ground. My eyes flutter. The light gets closer. Everything goes black.

⁓❦⁓

I open my eyes. Bright, bright white winter morning sun across the floor. I see Mom. Her face is heavy, her hair messy. Her arms are crossed, holding herself. An old man stands with her. She nods to something he says.

I don't know why, but I just want to again. And I know that once I do, I always will.

"Mom?"

Mom turns. At first she can't move. Then she runs over.

"Say something," she says. "Say something else."

"Something else."

Mom laughs. She makes a funny coughing sound because her laughing's turned into crying.

The old man walks over. "How you feeling, young fella?"

It's hard to speak because Mom is all over me. "Fine."

"You gave us quite a scare," he says. He tells me that he's a doctor, and that I sleepwalked in the middle of the night, and nearly froze to death, and by the luck of God, Mom woke up and found me. "A mother's instincts: a miraculous thing." The doctor laughs.

I tell him that I didn't sleepwalk. I tell him that I went out by the light of the moon, and— But, he stops me.

"There you go," he says. "Proof that it was a dream. The moon didn't show itself once last night. It's been snowing solid, take a look."

I look out the window. The snow is high. A bluff presses blue against the bottom of my window.

I frown. I turn away. I want them to go. The doctor leans over me.

"What's this?" he says, brushing aside my hair.

Mom leans over and touches my temple lightly.

"What?" I ask.

"A bruise of some sort," the doctor says to Mom. They discuss the possible causes. When I passed out, they say, I must have fallen on a rock or a frozen pinecone.

"Let me see," I say.

Mom brings over a hand mirror.

I look. It is very faint, pale purple. I smile. It is a circular shape, but not a perfect circle, more like a soft oval. It's a little warm. Yes, it could be a rock or a frozen pinecone, I think, turning my head to look at it closer—I feel them, and they feel good. They come, suddenly in a gush. Tears—but to me, it looks much more like the shape that lips might make kissing good-bye.

six

Really, the smell of coffee kind of woke me up a while ago, but it's the ringing phone that makes me open my eyes for real. I hang my head over the edge of the loft Dad built for me in the tiny hallway between the kitchen and the studio's main room. Below, Mom jogs past with a spilling mug of coffee for the ringing phone.

I climb down. The studio smells of smoke and alcohol and left-out, hardened fondue. Mom smiles at me. I open the window for air. I get a trash bag from the kitchen and empty ashtrays, tossing out bottles, paper plates. I pick up a half-smoked cigarette and a half-drunk glass and pretend to smoke and drink. I talk and laugh silently like one of Mom's friends. I roll my eyes.

Mom hasn't written in the weeks since we've been home. She goes out a lot now. She has gatherings in the studio.

I put the fondue pot and forks in the sink. Propped on the counter is a cardboard poster.

THIS IS NOT HERE
A collective of painters poets musicians thespians
protesters and hope-setters from New York City

Below is a building that turns into a tree reaching for the sun.

That's what they were gathering about last night: their
group, This Is Not Here. They're going to go around for a
month to different colleges and put on shows, do dances, readings, sing songs.

Mom's laughing on the phone when I return. I fill a second
bag. I find my conch lying on its side. Someone's used it as an
ashtray. I dump out a few butts, and wipe away the ground-in
ash using my thumb and spit. I take it and put it back on my loft.

The doctor gave it to me after my second operation to fix
my still deaf right ear. The conch is cut in half so I can see the
spiral inside. The doctor explained that when we hear the
ocean in a shell what we're actually hearing is the echo of air
as it's squeezed through the spiral. He said that if the spiral
was broken anywhere, the echo would end, and the sound
would go silent. He said my ear was like that. Afterward my
ear rang and I wobbled when I walked so I stayed in bed in
Mom's studio for three weeks. The shell's glued to a wooden
base that says: *My Shell's Been Fixed and I Can Hear the Ocean
Again.*

I showed it to Allen Topaz last night. Mom's always asking
what I think about him. *Don't you think he's nice?* Mom asks.
She tells me he's a drummer. She thinks that I'd like him. So, I
was just trying to be nice. He said, *Uh-huh,* kind of nodded as I
explained the shell. He said, *Wow, heavy,* then handed it back.

Mom gets off the phone.

"The place looks super," Mom says.

Mom says words like that now. *Super. Cool. Crazy. Wild.* At
first it sounded weird, kind of gross. Now it's just Mom.

I dress. I sling a packed knapsack over my shoulders, I pick up the trash bags, open the front door.

"I'm going."

"Where?" Mom's face is puffy. She holds her mug with two hands.

"Dad's."

Mom's quiet. "Can you walk okay? Your ear feels better?"

"Yeah."

We're quiet.

"When will you be home? Will you be back for lunch?"

"My friend Cormac's parents are divorced. He spends the weekends with his dad and the rest with his mother. I figure that's how it works." I turn so Mom will see that I've packed a bag of clothes for the weekend.

"We just thought, your father and I . . . ," Mom says.

I wait for more, but Mom just nods.

"Have you called over? I'll call over," she says. She moves toward the phone. She stops. "We're not actually divorced, you know."

"When are you going?" I point at the stack of This Is Not Here posters on the hallway floor.

Mom smiles, steps forward. "Aren't you excited?"

I frown.

Mom sighs, annoyed. "Well, you're coming of course. When did you start hating me so much? Your father's in the middle of midterms, your brothers too." Mom smiles. "It'll be crazy and wild." She crouches down. She looks me right in the eye. She whispers very, very quiet. "I'm scared out of my wits too. Please come?" Mom closes her eyes. Her head tilts forward, leans against my chest. "Please be excited to come with me, honey."

Mom still calls me honey. I stare at her. I swing open the door. I go down the hallway and jam the trash into the garbage chute. I press the elevator button.

Mom's suddenly running down the hallway.

"Honey! Honey!"

She grabs me.

"Where are you going?"

"Dad's."

Her eyes are wide, her skin pale. Her hands let me go. She blinks.

"Really? Really, *really?* You promise?"

I wonder why she's acting like a crazy lady.

"Yeah."

The elevator comes.

Outside I walk up the street. I understand then. She wondered if I was running away. That makes me laugh, that I can scare her. *Boo!* I say, laughing some more.

I walk.

Then I wonder. If she's so fucking scared, why'd she let me go?

⁓◦

It's mid-April.

The cement base of the fence along the park has cracks from the winter cold. Inside them, moss grows. Hippies sit on a stoop, one plays the guitar. A porter hoses down a sidewalk. I pass Marty, a man with a wooly beard, who Dad calls *that bleeding-heart jackass*. He tells me to boycott American-raised chicken. Boys in Puerto Rico have grown breasts from the hormones we use, he tells me. He's always telling us to boycott something: grapes, textiles, the MTA.

The trees and bushes have ball-shaped buds, like swarms of tiny pale green insects.

I reach the Firemen's Monument.

Three Big Kids lean against it. Fly, Gary, Jermaine. The turntable's hooked up. They bop their heads to music.

"Bruiser," says Gary. "Back from the dead."

Jermaine, who's always cool and silent, bops his head hello to me.

"You got alotta beatings owed you," says Fly.

I nod.

Down the block. Reid, Saul, Max, and Jimmy play Chinese handball against a building. I lean into a telephone booth and watch through the wavy plastic window, through the gaps of the graffiti letters. Freedom. Patch 147. Zephyr. Revolt. Cast. Chaos.

I still haven't talked to them yet. I've watched them a lot. From the living room window, from down the block, hiding behind a mailbox, high in a tree. I've wanted to go up to them, but I never can. Whenever I get close my heart starts racing.

I've imagined walking up to them like it's no big deal. I've practiced. *Hi. Yo. S'up, bro. What's up? Hey. Ay. What's hap'nin'?* I've gotten close a bunch of times, but every time my heart starts beating and I start to shake, and every time I turn back and run.

I step out of the booth. I walk.

They all look up, frozen. The ball bounces out into the street. I shove my hands into my pockets, not sure where to look.

The blind of the window above where they're playing is suddenly drawn up. A woman scowling. "You shits get the hell outta here!"

Everyone jumps back. I look at the guys. I look back at the woman.

"Shut up, Fat Lady," I say, our nickname for her.

The guys look at me and smile.

"I'll crack your ass, you little shit!" she says.

I look at the guys. We start laughing. It's the best when Fat Lady gets all in a huff. We love making her get in a huff.

We start singing, *"Fat Lady, Fat Lady."*

"You little hoodlums. You little shits," she says.

The "Fat Lady" song is really going.

Fat Lady's face jiggles with anger. She threatens, like always, to call the cops. We just sing over her. Her blind drops. We're all laughing so hard we're spitting and coughing. I go to the window. It's open behind the blind. I put my ear close. I hear her. There's a lot of snot, it sounds like. That happens when you're crying like crazy. I bet she's crying so hard that she can't see.

I turn back to the guys. I start laughing and hooting again. We calm down.

Jimmy's losing the game. He has seven.

Reid's serving. He looks at me. He says, "You got seven."

I walk to the end. Reid serves. We all grunt and play and try to crush like I've never been gone.

Daniel shows up after the game. He walks with a blond boy his age. Saul and Max meet Daniel and the blond boy midway.

"Who's that?" I ask.

"Johnny Powers," Reid says.

"That's really his name?" I ask.

Reid nods.

Saul and Max and Daniel and Johnny Powers talk in the middle of the block. They lean in, then scurry down into the park.

"Where they going?" I ask.

Reid and Jimmy give each other a look.

"*Cheee-baahhh . . . ,*" Reid says. "It's cheeba all the time since Johnny Powers came around. He goes to school with Max." Reid sneers. "It's so stupid. In the middle of a game, they all suddenly just walk off and get stoned."

"Yeah," I say.

"Like you know," says Reid.

I look at him. "My brothers've been smoking since last summer. There was this house. The McCourts'. A whole mess of Big Kids hung out all day getting wasted."

"Which Big Kids?" Jimmy asks.

Reid looks away, like he's not listening. He picks at pieces of glass stuck in old black gum on the sidewalk. He tosses them into the street.

"Which Big Kids?" Jimmy asks again.

I turn to Jimmy. "Not our Big Kids," I say. "The Big Kids from Massachusetts."

Jimmy looks at me, kind of cross-eyed, like it doesn't make sense. Other Big Kids?

"Any little kids?" Reid asks looking at me sideways, acting bored.

"One." I think of stopping there, but I don't. "A kid named Joey. He was cool." I shrug. "But, he moved. He was kind of a chump about it. He didn't even say anything. He just split."

"Lookit baby," says Jimmy pointing at me. "Lookit him pouting!"

The older boys have scaled a tree. Each perched on a different branch. They pass a joint. Puffs of smoke rise like dandelion heads through the leaves.

"North Carolina," I say. "He moved to North Carolina." Reid watches me.

"That's where I went," I say.

"We heard," Reid says. "We're supposed to be nice to you. All the mothers keep saying when we see you to be nice."

"Don't do that," I say.

"Yeah, I know." Reid punches me in the arm. He smirks. "I know."

We're quiet.

"What's it like," Jimmy asks, "seeing someone die?"

I look at Jimmy.

"I don't know," I say. I know what it's like. I can think of it and I know what it's like, but I don't know how to say it. I shake my head.

"Why'd you do it?" Reid asks.

"I just sort of did. Darla, she's the girl—"

They nod.

"She came over real late one night, asked if I wanted to."

"A girl made you do it?"

I'm quiet. I think about it. I nod. "I guess, yeah."

We're quiet for a while.

They tell me about something called Laser Rock at the Natural History Planetarium. It's cool, they say. You go and they play Pink Floyd and Earth, Wind and Fire and Edgar Winters's "Frankenstein," and there are these laser beams that do all sorts of crazy patterns and things on the ceiling. It's crazy, they say. It's super bad. They say that they'll show me.

We're quiet.

I look at them.

"Wanna hear more?"

It feels like a thing inside me, something caught in my throat that I want to get out. It makes me remember how once I saw a magician. He pulled a scarf out of his mouth. But, the scarf was tied to another scarf, and he began to frown. Then another and another and another. And the more he pulled out, the more there seemed to be. His eyes got wide and surprised and scared, like he couldn't believe that all this time there had been all these scarves caught inside him, and now that he started, he had no choice except to continue pulling them out until there were no more.

Reid slides down so that he's lying flat on the ground. Then, Jimmy copies Reid. They look at me. Then, I slide down. We lie side by side. Clouds pass, making the building look like it's falling forward.

I start talking. I start from the beginning. I tell everything.

seven

I ride the elevator up with Daniel. We watch the rising, glowing numbers.

"I took your room," he says.

He unlocks the front door.

"It's mine," I say.

We go inside. No lights are on. It's dark.

"You don't use it."

"It's mine."

Daniel walks away. I walk into the kitchen. The clock says
6:05, five minutes after dinnertime. Dad isn't home. I touch the
oven. Cold. I sit in the dark at my seat at the dining table. I look
at Jordan's seat and Daniel's. I look at the head of the table that
is Dad's, and the head that is Mom's. Used to be Mom's. I run
my hand over the table. Once we all sat at the table, now we
don't. Now Mom never touches the table. Now I'll touch it only
on the weekends. Now, Megan probably touches it sometimes.

I stand quickly. I want to turn on a light. I pass the window. I stop. Through the courtyard, I see my bedroom. I frown. All that time I was watching them from my bedroom, all that time that I thought I was invisible, they could have seen me. I feel stupid for never realizing that. I wonder if they ever even watched for me.

I see Daniel painting. He shakes his long hair out of his eyes. I walk through the apartment to my room. Daniel has music on. Hot Tuna, the band's name, *Double Dose*, the album's title. The man's voice is slow like mud. The music is thick, faraway sounding.

Hey, we got a long way to go,
so keep on lovin' and make it slow . . .

There are paints and records and clothes on the floor. The room stinks of teenager. Body, smoke, closed windows, drawn blinds.

"Where's Dad?" I ask.

Daniel keeps painting. He shrugs. He's painting on a large piece of cardboard taller than me, wide as my arms out like wings.

"Hey, that's me," I say.

He paints from a photograph taped to his palette: me and Daniel on a roof. It was taken before we went to Massachusetts. I remember: I was happy that day. School had been out for two days, and that afternoon I had gotten a new T-shirt with an iron-on of a guy doing a wheelie on a dirt bike. Mom had just bought a new Instamatic camera and that's why she took the photograph of us, to test it out. I remember that neither of us would smile, so Mom started making silly baby sounds, to get us to laugh. I remember thinking, as I watched her, that it was the first time she had been silly in a long time.

I stand behind Daniel and look at the painting closely. Our bodies are barely there. A pink swoop for a shoulder, a purple line for our sides. It's the grayish purpley blue air, which he's painted in, that gives our bodies shape. I move closer, and my face breaks apart. Pinks and greens and whites, dashes that magically become me from far away. I look a little happy, a little stupid, looking off to the side. Daniel looks right ahead. His head is down and forward. Shadowy green and black and red are dark around his creepy, raccoon eyes. His painted lips pull back, like a wound spring, like they're getting ready to do something. Smirk, talk, sneer, holler, moan. But, no, that's just his lips showing what he wishes he could do. I know if I could see the moment after the moment frozen in the painting I would see Daniel letting his hair fall forward, pretending that we're all not here.

"Daniel, do I got any talent?"

Daniel picks up a pipe and walks to the window, opening it. He lights it, inhales, coughs sweet spicy smoke. He sits on the radiator. He looks out. Darla's window is dark. I look away, sit on the floor.

"People like you," he says.

"That's a talent?"

He shrugs. He stands in front of his painting, his back to me.

"Where's Dad? When're we gonna have dinner?"

Daniel reaches and turns Hot Tuna up very loud.

Dad gets home at 7:26. He turns on the TV, says, "Damn," when he sees that the news is over. He turns off the TV. We sit for dinner.

"Dinner's not at six anymore?" I ask.

"Dinner's at six," he says.

"It's seven-thirty."

"Yes. I got tied up."

We eat, I look at everyone.

"Why were you late?"

"You can't ask him that," Jordan says.

I look at Jordan. He sits in Mom's seat now.

"Things got busy," Dad says.

"What things?" I ask.

"Jordan's right. You can't ask me all these things."

"I called your office."

"You did?"

"No."

Dad looks at me. "I was there."

I tap the teeth of my fork against my plate over and over.

"Stop that," Dad says.

I look at him. I stop.

I lie in the living room. I can't sleep. I walk to the bathroom, but I don't have to pee. I sit on the toilet in the dark. I knock on Jordan's door. He opens the door.

"Can I sit in here? I won't say anything."

Jordan looks at me, turns, returns to his desk.

I sit on Daniel's bed. I watch Jordan do his homework for a while.

"He was with her," I say. "That's why he was late."

Jordan looks at me. "Maybe." Then, "Yeah." He nods a little.

"You ever ask him about her?"

"No."

"You've met her?"

"Yes."

"How's she?"

"I don't know. Fine, I guess."

"She stays here?"

Jordan breathes out. "I'm doing my work."

I'm quiet.

Jordan says, "He sneaks her in, then sneaks her out early in the morning. He thinks he's slick. But I found a box of tampons in the little bathroom behind the toilet."

He goes back to his work.

I listen to the quiet of his pen on the paper, the turning pages of his textbook. It makes me sleepy. I'm suddenly very, very sleepy.

"Hey," he says.

I sit up quickly.

"You can crash on Daniel's bed if you want."

I don't say anything. I nod. I get under the covers, turn away on my side. I hear Jordan's pen start to write again. I listen to it. It's a small, soft sound. I fall asleep.

eight

We go down to the lower level of the park because of flickering lights. It's night. Crazy people and homeless drug addicts and muggers fill the lower level at night. But, I make Jimmy and Reid go down anyway. I tell them it'll be fine. They tell me to shut up, that they're not scared.

"I'm gonna be gone a month," I say. "This thing my mom's doing."

We walk down the marble stairs. We reach the gravel walkway, and it's pitch dark.

"You'll be back after?" Reid asks.

We pass a streetlamp, greenish light because it's been covered in spray paint. We pass back into the dark. We cut over to the grass.

"Yeah," I say. "I'll be back after."

"Okay, look. It's nothing," Jimmy says. "Let's go back."

We reach the light. It's a slaughtered chicken surrounded

by two circles. The first, a bed of clipped flowers, the second, a ring of candles. Its neck has been cut, and its dead
black eyes reflect the cold flames, and its belly has been
slashed, a wave of red blood over its white body. A still
black circle of blood empties around its body, reflecting the
sharp, twitching candle flames with small halos in the deep
red. A few flowers pop up and float as the pool of blood
eases out.

"Aw, that's nasty," Reid says, turning away.

"Voodoo," Jimmy says, quietly. "Come on. It's voodoo."

"Dead chicken," I say.

I touch it with my foot.

It rolls onto its side. The blood's thick because of the night
air. It sticks to the feathers like syrup. Its neck bends, the head
folds under the body. The underneath of the beak is soft,
fleshy. I never knew that.

Dead chicken.

"Can we go now?" Jimmy asks, his head going back and
forth, searching the dark.

I think of making fun of him, but for some reason, I don't.

"Just a dead ol' chicken," I say.

We begin back.

"What'd you think it was gonna be?" Reid asks.

"Yeah, idiot," Jimmy says, walking a step ahead of us.

I shrug. "I just had to see."

⌒

Monday morning, I pack my knapsack to return to Mom's.
Outside it's quiet, everyone's at school. I walk along the sidewalk for a bit. It's weird, like a secret: I'd always wondered
what the day did while we were all stuck in school. I stop,
close my eyes and breathe in. I don't know why: it just feels
good to do. I go into the park. The park feels lonely, like it's

waiting for something to happen. On the lower walkway I see an old man walking very, very slowly.

I look up at the tree. I climb. I can't believe it: it's still here. After all that time. The black cat's bones are gray and thin. I put it on my lap. I think of Darla, sitting here with me that night. I run my hand along where she sat. I think, Right here at this very spot, Darla once sat. Is a bit of her still touching it? Has she left a bit of herself behind?

I climb down.

No, I think. Things are here and then they're gone.

I lay the skeleton on the ground near a bush.

I look at the field. I've run back and forth over it so many times, hollering my head off, I've probably touched every inch. I listen: I don't hear me. I touch the grass: I don't feel me.

I look at my chest. I touch it: Yes, there. I am there. I feel that.

I close my eyes. I smile. I remember her real good. The way she looked, the way she sounded, the way she was.

I look at the cat's skull, its empty eye sockets, its front fangs. I can't believe that once it was alive. I touch the skeleton: it is dead. The cat is gone.

I find a broken bottle. I use it to dig a hole. I lay in the black cat's bones.

I know it's dead, and it's silly to do, but it feels good to do. I open my bag, take out a T-shirt. I lay it over the bones like a blanket.

"Good night."

I fill the hole. I spike the broken bottle in the ground. A gravestone.

I stand, go home.

nine

Mom cuts her long, long hair short and neat. This Is Not Here drive south in a caravan. Me and Mom drive in Megan's parents' truck. We stop at colleges. They give readings and display paintings and sing songs and put on shows. A crowd of students always forms. Some students watch for a while, then get bored. Some laugh, making fun. Others frown like they're thinking hard, and they nod. Some clap, say, "All right." Some walk by, look over but don't stop. Sometimes campus security kicks us off.

A lot, I get bored and angry that no one's my age. Mom makes me hang around nearby. When I tell her that I can take care of myself, she says she's not going to have me wandering around some strange place all by myself. Sometimes I watch Mom do readings, and I whisper mean things. Sometimes I do walk away. After the second time of going off, then returning and walking up to Mom, and having her just put a finger to her mouth to tell me to be quiet because someone from This Is

Not Here was putting on a show, I stop worrying, and just start going off. Mostly, I find a hidden place, under a desk in an empty classroom, next to a big tree on the greens. I ball up and rock and imagine I'm somewhere else. That the guys are with me. That I'm big and I can say, no.

No.

Dad sends mail general post. He sends a matchbox car once, and once he sends a box of candy with a note that says, "Your mother was never fun when it came to food."

When it's nice out we sleep in tents at camping grounds. Allen Topaz opens the side door of his van and plays music and we cook food. Other times we stay in motels. I sleep in a room with Mom. I wake up sometimes and Mom isn't there. She comes back before the sun rises, and she smells like smoke and funny sweat: salty like a used Band-Aid, sweet like over-ripe peaches. She always sighs for a little while, but by the time the sun cracks at dawn she's asleep, and sometimes she's smiling.

In North Carolina This Is Not Here packs up its cars and trucks for a long weekend to "wrap up and wind down" before we head back home. People study maps for places where we could do that. They ask locals for suggestions. I say, Outer Banks. No one listens.

"Outer Banks, Mom. Let's go to the Outer Banks."

"Absolutely not," she says fast and sharp as a clap.

"But, I wanna go."

"*No.*"

I walk up to her. "Outer Banks."

Mom tries to smile, but I can see it's fake. She looks at her map. "Let's find somewhere good to go." She looks at me. She nods. "Okay?"

"I wanna go to the Outer Banks," I mumble.

"Enough!" she suddenly yells.

Mom puts her hand to her mouth. She breathes in and out.

She takes my shoulders, crouches. She smiles. "Please, let's just find another, nice place." She blinks. "You're not going back there."

"Hey, you guys wanna give the group your vote?" Allen Topaz says, walking up to us. He wears tight, diarrhea brown leather pants and a handlebar mustache. He smokes and plays African drums.

"Outer Banks," I say, looking Mom in the eye.

Allen Topaz looks at me. He goes, *Yeehaa*. Mom quickly wipes her eyes, stands. Other members of This Is Not Here wander over because of the ruckus. *Outer Banks*. The words ripple from person to person. They start nodding.

"Perfect idea, little man," Allen Topaz says.

Suddenly I feel bad for the fact that whenever I walk past Allen Topaz, I mumble, *Asshole*. Also, for all the lunch meat I've shoved under the carpet lining the walls of his van.

On the map I point to the Outer Bank island I want to go to.

Mom says, "No, I think this one." Her voice is tight, but only I can tell.

We both look at Allen Topaz.

"Actually, little man, I've gotta side with your mother on this one. If you're going to the Outer Banks, there's really no choice." He looks at Mom, touches her nose with his finger. "My vote's on your island, beautiful."

Mom smiles, giggles a little.

I look away.

"Of course," Allen Topaz says to me, "instead of driving the mainland to our ferry, we could go the scenic route: drive through your island to get to our island, so at least you'll get to see yours through the window."

Allen Topaz puts a vote to the other members of the group. They calculate the time and cost of driving through my island, taking an extra ferry, finally agreeing that it's fine.

I walk away.

I climb into the truck. A package from Dad is sitting on the dashboard. The manila envelope is open, but none of the letters or bills inside are. I flip through them. There's one for me. I mumble, "Gee, thanks, Mom. Jerk."

Surprises indeed come in all sorts of funny ways. It's a surprise even to me to find myself writing to you. I heard the awful news about you & Darla. Remember God loves children & the unfortunate the most.

I don't know what to say & have put off saying anything for months. I just had to get in touch. Watching that on television about you two I think my heart broke in two. Will you write back? I send my most solemn consolation to you. I can't hardly imagine your grief if I find my own self barely able to think or walk from sorrow. I'm sure you've got so many wonderful people to talk to but I haven't any & I wondered could we talk? Please write.

Yours very truly and with deepest regret,
Virginia St. James

There's a photo of Lemonhead on a Thanksgiving Day float in a shiny, puffy pink dress, like a fairy, holding flowers and waving.

I put the letter and picture back inside. I won't cry. I look at the envelope. I think how funny it is that the letter started off in North Carolina, went all the way to New York and then came all the way back to just a few miles from where it first left. It's funny. I think, I'd forgotten all about Lemonhead. I think how weird it is that I can forget people just like that. Funny and weird, I think.

I cry.

*   *   *

We drive for a long time.

I open my eyes, having fallen asleep at some point. The sun is just starting to set. My hand hurts. I look. I've dug my fingernails into the skin of my palm. There are four slits like smiling red mouths. I open my hand and the mouths open.

"Have we taken the ferry?" I ask.

Mom doesn't answer for a minute. She looks straight ahead as she drives. "The first one, yes," she says. "We're almost there. The port for the second."

I can hear a quick flood of gas, but we're locked in a caravan, so Mom has to quickly slow the truck.

We drive for a while. Silently. I watch out my window.

We pass the abandoned gas station. Ahead, I see the lighthouse.

"Please?" I ask. "Just for a second. Can we stop? Just for a second. Please?"

"We'll lose the others."

"I've looked at the map. We can't get lost. It's just one road, straight."

"We're almost at the next ferry. We'll be stopping soon."

I make a face, and that's enough for Mom. She pulls the truck over to the road's shoulder.

The lighthouse is right there.

We're at the end of the caravan. The rest drive ahead.

"Fine . . . We'll sit here for a minute." She leans her head back and closes her eyes, her hands still gripping the steering wheel.

I look at Mom. I open the door and run.

Mom calls, orders me to stop. I hear her door creak open. I run harder. Far off I see the gray haze of ocean.

I hear footsteps behind, Mom getting close. I'm breathing hard. I'm running fast as I can. I feel the wind and it makes tears come from the corners of my eyes so everything goes blurry. I feel Mom's hand on my shoulder. Without looking I slap at her

behind my back. I close my eyes and make my face tight. I try to
move my feet faster. I'm up a slope and I look and see the curling
white waves, small in the distance, crashing on shore. Mom slides
her hands around my front, and pulls me to her. We fall over.

We're on the ground, on our sides. Mom holds me tight
from behind. We both breathe hard, trying to get our breaths.
I feel Mom's inflating and deflating stomach on my back, her
breath in my ear. I close my eyes and lie motionless. Then I
try to thrash free.

"No," she says, tightening the wrap of her arms.

I go still and we lie this way for a while. My side is cold,
lying on the damp evening grass. My face burns like it always
does after I run. Like a fever. A good fever. An alive fever.

"You have to let me go," I say, thrashing again.

Mom's arms unlock. She rolls onto her back.

"Do you think this is easy for me?" she asks.

I stand up.

"I don't care."

I look at Mom. I turn. I walk. Mom doesn't follow at first,
then she's walking beside me. I lead us silently to the campsite.
It's evening and a few tents are up.

I walk into the forest until I find the hiding spot. I lift the
door I used to cover the hole where we ditched our things.
Mom sits on an old tree trunk, watches me. I pull out the duffel bags and slowly go through our things: clothes, books, a
little money, the broken Mickey Mouse watch.

I sit on the ground, rub the dirt off its face. I look at Mom.
I hold it up. I watch Mom to see if she remembers the night
she gave it to me. Her eyebrows and lips move a little, but I
can't tell what she's thinking. Maybe she remembers, maybe
not. I don't care. A nice I-don't-care, like she's thinking one
thing and I'm thinking another thing, and that's fine. I toss the
watch back in the bag.

I find the shadow puppet Shinji gave Darla. I lay it on the ground. I find Darla's Bob Dylan shirt. I inhale. I hold it flat against my front, show Mom.

"It was Darla's. She made it," I say. I smooth it across my front. There are dried orange drippings on it, stains from the oranges we ate when we took the train. I run my finger over them. I can almost hear her whispering to herself, the way she did that day, *"Oh shoot . . . ,"* her lip and chin shiny with orange pulp. I put the shirt on over my long-sleeve, and rub my hand over my chest.

I put everything back into the hole. I kneel over it. I throw clumps of cool dirt on top.

"Honey—" Mom begins, but she goes quiet when I shake my head.

I put the door back over our old stuff, buried.

I walk away, carrying the shadow puppet. I give my free hand to Mom and we walk through the campsite, past small fires, now lit in the pits beside tents. We walk through a long field that ends at high bluffs that we slide down, to the beach. I take my hand back and run, my feet twisting in the sand, until I reach the crashing water. Mom runs behind. I hold the shadow puppet out and look at it. Mom stands next to me. I look at her.

"She liked this thing a lot. She was real proud that he gave it to her," I say. "She's probably sad she lost it."

I throw the puppet up, and the wind carries it out into the water. It floats on the surface until a wave crashes down and it's gone. For a moment she comes back up, Tomoko, the drowned daughter, popping in the air, then she is gone, again, for good.

I walk up the beach. I sit against the bluff. I watch the water. The sun sets behind us, sending out long blue shadows of the bluff grass. To the left is the lighthouse.

"God, you've been through a lot," Mom says.

Mom touches my cheek, my shoulder, lets her hand fall

away, puts it to her mouth. Her mouth stays a little open. Her bottom lip trembles. She puts her lips together, tight. She tries to smile a little. Her eyes sparkle. She wipes them. Then she breathes out. A little like a laugh. A little like a push of air squeezed out by a stomach about to vomit.

"I can't imagine what you think," she says.

I watch.

"I don't want Dad's name."

Mom waits.

"I don't hate Dad. I just don't want his name."

"Do you want my last name, from before I was married?"

I watch the water crashing and receding, crashing and receding. I look at Mom.

"No," I say. "I don't want your name. And I don't want my first name."

"I chose your first name," she says.

Mom looks at me. She hugs me. She lets go.

I think of what a good name might be, and I look out into the water. A light fog turned pink by the setting sun rolls in from the ocean. A foghorn starts, low. In my head I hear giggling. Darla's. And in the wind, and through the bluff grass, and in the shushing of the salt foaming in the crashing waves, I hear her too. I hear her say, "Hey, Ewe. Hey, Ewe."

I say, "Ewe, Ewe, Ewe . . ." I look at Mom.

"You . . . ?" she says. She thinks. "Eu*gene?*" she asks.

"Eugene." I nod.

"What'll your last name be?"

I don't know. I think for a while. Bruiser. *Brooo* . . . Breuster? Brooder? No, I think, no last name: it just doesn't work.

Behind is a soft flapping sound. *Woo-pa, woo-pa* . . . Up over the bluff, mammoth butterfly kites rise up on the golden sunlight. They rise in the sky. Tens of them.

I'm sure it is him. Shinji. I run up the steep bluff on all fours. I reach the top. I open my mouth.

I close my mouth. Mom stands beside me. We walk to the van.

⁓❧⁓

This Is Not Here are parked in the field. Music plays.

The kites are tied to stakes in the ground. Grills are smoking, food cooking.

Allen Topaz meets us and hands Mom a beer.

I watch how Mom smiles at him. Her eyes bright. For a second she forgets about me when she looks at Allen Topaz with bright eyes. I remember her before. I remember her standing in hallways waiting for the loud sounds to go quiet before stepping forward. Her locked in rooms for hours. Her looking at us like she was looking out the window. She doesn't do those things anymore, and I hate her for it, a little bit.

But, also, I'm a little bit glad for it too.

Mom remembers me again, and she looks back at me.

Allen Topaz says, "We stopped and noticed you weren't there. We turned back and found your truck on the side of the road. Anyway, we've missed the last ferry. But, look," he says, stretching his arms out over the field. "What a great dance floor, plus," Allen Topaz points, "there's a campground right there." He nudges his chin at me. "Guess you got your wish, little man."

"Whose kites?" I ask.

"Mine," says Allen Topaz. "Like them?"

"You make them?" I ask.

"Bought them."

"They're cool."

Allen Topaz smiles, but I look at Mom.

She looks at me.

I step away. I smile so that she knows it's fine. I turn and leave them alone.

Mom takes my hands and she spins me. We dance. We dance and all of This Is Not Here dance. Mom lets go, and I spin on my own. I look up at the kites hovering overhead. The sky is dark. I hop and spin. I look out to the ocean. Night rolls across it. Stars appear. I spin and spin. I close my eyes as I spin and I can feel how the world also spins. And I spin with it. I spin fast and crazy. And I wonder, if I spin enough will I suddenly be spinning against the spinning of the world? And if I spin against the spinning of the world long enough will something break? Will I break whatever it is that holds me to the ground? Will I be let go? Tossed into the sky? Let alone to float alone, deep into space? I spin harder and faster. I spin one way, then the other. Which way will break it? How fast do I need to go to break it?

I spin until I can't spin anymore. I stop spinning. I wobble and feel a little sick. But, I can still feel it under my feet: the ground. I'm too dizzy. I can't stand. I fall. I fall to the ground fast like it's pulling me close, like it's holding me tight, like it won't let go. I lie on my side. Everything shifts and swirls. I've spun far away. I see This Is Not Here, dark shadows bobbing and shimmying next to the low orange coals of the blue smoking grills. I look and see the dark, crashing ocean. I wait until I feel still again. I stand. Then I run. I run hard. I see it and I want it. I want to get close to it. I reach it. I jump right into it. The churning spinning crashing thrashing salty sweaty love of it.

This is me, I think.

This is me in it.

about the author

Ian Chorão lives in New York City with his wife, Sylvia Sichel, and their son, Malcolm. This is his first novel.